"Grossman and Fuller deliver gritty insider detail in their thriller RED Hotel, *bringing fact and fiction together in an explosive mix. With pacing that would leave Olympian Usain Bolt breathless,* RED Hotel *is a must-read for international travelers and anyone seeking to understand the new Russia."*

K. J. HOWE
BEST-SELLING AUTHOR, *THE FREEDOM BROKER*
EXECUTIVE DIRECTOR, THRILLERFEST

"Baldacci, Brown, and Cussler: make room for Grossman and Fuller, and check into RED Hotel*! It's the year's most eye-opening international thriller with a true wake-up call for everyone who travels anywhere. Page by page, the exciting plot delivers an inside-out view of the moving parts that make up the ever-changing geopolitical map. My advice—read* RED Hotel *now!"*

ROGER DOW
PRESIDENT AND CEO, US TRAVEL ASSOCIATION

*"*RED Hotel *is a cutting edge story about very real targets all around us. A real world drama that doesn't just suggest what might happen, but is telling us what is beginning to happen right now! A must read!"*

PETER GREENBERG
CBS NEWS TRAVEL EDITOR

PRAISE FOR OTHER BOOKS BY THESE AUTHORS

THE EXECUTIVE SERIES BY GARY GROSSMAN

"Executive Actions—*a masterpiece of suspense.*"

MICHAEL PALMER, *NEW YORK TIMES* BEST-SELLING AUTHOR

"Executive Treason—*a virtuoso tale.*"

DALE BROWN, *NEW YORK TIMES* BEST-SELLING AUTHOR

"Executive Command—*so real it's scary!*"

LARRY BOND, *NEW YORK TIMES* BEST-SELLING AUTHOR

"Executive Force—*as harrowing as it is entertaining!*"

JOSEPH FINDER, *NEW YORK TIMES* BEST-SELLING AUTHOR

OLD EARTH BY GARY GROSSMAN

"*The perfect thriller!*"

STEVE BERRY, *NEW YORK TIMES* BEST-SELLING AUTHOR

"…The Da Vinci Code *on steroids!*"

DWIGHT ZIMMERMAN, *NEW YORK TIMES* BEST-SELLING AUTHOR

YOU CAN'T LEAD WITH YOUR FEET ON THE DESK BY ED FULLER

"Read Ed's book before you take another plane on a foreign business trip. It will change the way you behave."

GEOFFREY KENT, FOUNDER AND EXECUTIVE CHAIRMAN, ABERCROMBIE & KENT

"Fuller brings experience, intelligence, and heart to building relationships."

MICHAEL V. DRAKE, CHANCELLOR, OHIO STATE UNIVERSITY

"Ed's book will give you a competitive edge whether it's Denver, Dubai, or Düsseldorf."

JEAN-CLAUDE BAUMGARTEN, PRESIDENT, WORLD TRAVEL & TOURISM COUNCIL

RED
HOTEL

GARY GROSSMAN

ED FULLER

BEAUFORT
BOOKS

Library of Congress Cataloging-in-Publication Data
Names: Grossman, Gary H., author. | Fuller, Edwin D., 1945- author.
Title: Red hotel / by Gary Grossman, Ed Fuller.
Description: First edition. | New York, NY : Beaufort Books, [2019]
Identifiers: LCCN 2018045182| ISBN 9780825308901 (hardcover : alk. paper) |
ISBN 9780825308017 (Ebook)
Subjects: | GSAFD: Suspense fiction.
Classification: LCC PS3607.R667 R43 2019 | DDC 813/.6--dc23
LC record available at https://lccn.loc.gov/2018045182

For inquiries about volume orders, please contact:

Beaufort Books
27 West 20th Street, Suite 1102
New York, NY 10011
sales@beaufortbooks.com

Published in the United States by Beaufort Books
www.beaufortbooks.com

Distributed by Midpoint Trade Books
www.midpointtrade.com

Printed in the United States of America

Book designed by Mark Karis

To Michela Fuller, my wonderful wife,
Scott Dimond, Elizabeth, Alex, and our granddaughter Cameron Allphin.

ED

For Bruce Coons,
Lifelong friend, superb advisor, dedicated patriot.
Thank you, through all the years!

GARY

GLOBAL NEWS

WAVE OF TERROR

MUMBAI, INDIA

2008

Indian forces battled terrorist gunmen to free hostages at two luxury hotels that left dozens dead and potentially hundreds injured…

BOLD ATTACK AT MAJOR HOTELS

JAKARTA, INDONESIA

2009

Separate bombs tore through the Ritz-Carlton and JW Marriott hotels, minutes apart. Authorities say they were placed by guests…

BEACH RESORT HOTEL TARGETED

SOUSSE, TUNISIA

2015

Gunman disguised as a vacationer attacked the Mediterranean Imperial Hotel killing at least 38…

EXPLOSIVE-PACKED CAR AND A GUNMEN STORM HOTEL

NORTHERN SINAI PENINSULA

2015

Militants attacked the Swiss Inn Resort in El Arish with explosives and gunfire killing at least seven including a judge…

RUSSIA REHEARSES INVASION OF SCANDINAVIA

2015

33,000 Russian troops carried out a mock invasion of Norway and Sweden, rehearsing a takeover of territory in the Baltic Sea...

PUTIN REBUILDING SOVIET-ERA RUSSIA

2014

Vladimir Putin believes it is his mission to restore the Soviet system, the country of his childhood where the Kremlin's power is unchecked...

RUSSIA CLAIMS IT COULD TAKE MAJOR EUROPEAN CAPITALS IN TWO DAYS

2014

Putin reportedly claimed it would take merely two days for Russian troops to sweep into Riga, Latvia; Vilnius, Lithuania; Warsaw, Poland; Bucharest, Romania; and Kiev, Ukraine...

WHAT'S RUSSIA'S NEXT TARGET?

2015

In an ever-uneasy relationship with neighboring Baltic States, home to large ethnically Russian minorities and former Soviet satellite nations, the Kremlin has indicated there is potential for aggression against Estonia, Latvia, and Lithuania to defend Russians in those nations...

US SUPPORT FOR NATO REMAINS IN QUESTION

2018

Ongoing provocative White House statements about the NATO alliance continue to shake the confidence of America's European partners, increasing concerns that the US could abandon NATO's central tenant of collective defense.

PRINCIPAL CHARACTERS

WASHINGTON, DC
Dan Reilly
Senior Vice President,
International Kensington
Royal Hotel Corporation

Brenda Sheldon
Secretary

Alexander Crowe
President, United States

Moakley Davidson
US Senator

Pierce Kimball
National Security Advisor

Carl Erwin
Former CIA Director

BD Coons
US Army General

Jay Reardon
Former FBI Operative

Donald Klugo
Private Security Consultant

Robert Heath
CIA Officer

Gerald Watts
CIA Director

Veronica Severi
CIA Psychologist

General Jeffrey Jones
Chairman of the Joint Chiefs

CHICAGO, IL
Edward Jefferson Shaw
President/Founder
Kensington Royal Hotel
Corporation

BRUSSELS, BELGIUM
Liam Schorel
General Manager,
Kensington Diplomat Hotel

Johanna Ketz
Florist Shop Owner

Lou Tiano
Kensington Royal Hotel
Corporation COO

June Wilson
Public Relations Executive

Spike Boyce
IT Executive

Alan Cannon
VP Global, Safety and
Security

Chris Collins
Senior Vice President, Legal
Kensington Royal Hotel
Corporation

Pat Brodowski
Kensington Royal Hotel
Corporation CFO

TOKYO, JAPAN
Genji Takahiro
Japanese Agent

MOSCOW, RUSSIA
Nikolai Gorshkov
President, Russian Federation

Andre Miklos
An Operative

Victor Markovich
Mayor

Yakov Lukin
Minister of Defense

Nicolai Federov
Director, FBS, Russian
Intelligence

Major General Valery
Borodin
Chief of the General Staff

General Gennady Titov
Deputy Minister of Defense

LONDON, ENGLAND
Marnie Babbitt
Barclays Bank Vice President,
Finance

CAMBRIDGE, MA
Colonel William E.
Harrison
History Professor

PROLOGUE

The man held court in an abandoned warehouse. He paced the cement floor while gauging the resolve of his associates, all personally chosen for the job, all veterans of other assignments. He saw no fear, no hesitation.

One more review. A final assurance that they had everything down.

Satisfied, he released them. Alone, he removed the visuals he'd tacked to the wall: the maps, the photographs, and the timeline. Holding the last enlargement, a photo of a downtown hotel, he let his mind wander to the exquisite details investigators would soon find and bag there. They were the things that never made newspaper or TV news accounts, the minutia cut from the page in editing for space and time. Watches stopped at the same minute. Scattered strands of pearls. High-heeled shoes, none to be worn again. Cell phones fused into plastic and metal blobs. Melted glasses frames. Teddy bears separated forever from their young owners' grasps. Grotesque, ashen shadows on the pavement that marked where the dead had fallen.

Then he pictured the brooms and shovels, the street cleaners and tractors that would eventually return the gruesome kill zone to respectability. Life would go on. But before that, to the man—the leader, the assassin— it would be his work of art.

WASHINGTON, DC
CAPITOL HILL
KENNEDY CAUCUS ROOM
FOURTEEN HOURS BEHIND TOKYO TIME

"No, Senator." Dan Reilly had practiced his tone in front of his hotel bathroom mirror before testifying. He wanted to strike a confident tone, neither friendly nor combative. Strictly professional. But this was the eighth time he had answered "no" to Montana Senator Moakley Davidson in less than five minutes.

So far, Reilly's appearance before the Senate Appropriations Subcommittee on State, Foreign Operations, and Related Programs was going as well as could be expected. Ultimately, he didn't want to create negative headlines for himself or the company. He had a message, and he wanted to deliver it with the right tone and leave quickly.

The Senate committee shared jurisdiction over appropriations with a subcommittee on the House side. An appropriation was exactly what Dan Reilly sought. He represented an American business with global interests—the Kensington Royal Hotel Corporation, with 1,100 owned or managed properties in 98 countries, and another 855 franchises.

Clearly, the Montana senator was trying to push Reilly's buttons, hoping to provoke an outburst. But Davidson didn't know Dan Reilly. He would have been well served to do some research on the witness.

TOKYO

The uniformed driver and two members of his team, all Japanese nationals, huddled in a garage near Harajuku Station on the outskirts of Tokyo. One man, also uniformed, would ride in the truck and serve as the driver's backup. The other would drive a block ahead of the rental car, relaying any traffic issues. Their delivery was that important.

Three other team members had already completed their assignments and left the area.

The driver ended his phone call. He checked his watch. It was time.

WASHINGTON, DC

Though out of the army for seven years, Daniel Reilly maintained a regular exercise routine. He consistently weighed in at 183 and could still pass for someone in his early 30s. But Reilly was actually 42, six-foot tall, with wavy black hair and bright white teeth. Anyone watching him on C-SPAN would see a handsome and confident man who didn't wear a wedding ring. Reilly was single again. Gratefully single.

Reilly, Senior Vice President of International for Kensington Royal, dressed for the cameras in a slim blue suit, a white shirt, and a conservative Countess Mara blue and gold tie. The tie especially popped and emphasized his commanding physical presence. Most of all, Reilly understood the rules of engagement perfectly: when to listen, and equally important, what to say and how to say it.

Corporate savvy came from an undergraduate degree at Boston University and a master's degree in business at Harvard. He credited greater life experience to his two tours of duty in Afghanistan, where he earned his captain's bars and learned to distinguish friends from adversaries. His tact and skill at negotiation came from a Foreign Service stint in the State Department after the army. Each served him well today.

"Mr. Reilly," Senator Moakley Davidson continued, "If you're looking for a blank check courtesy of American taxpayers to—"

Reilly interrupted with another "no." This one more curt than his previous.

As the chairman ranted on without really getting to a direct question, Reilly took in the historic Capitol Hill environs. Corinthian pillars framed the hearing room, which looked virtually the same today as it did in 1910 when it was called the Harkness Caucus Room. Today it was the Kennedy Caucus Room, in honor of brothers John Kennedy, Robert Kennedy, and Edward Kennedy.

The walls didn't have to talk, Reilly thought, considering the archived history. The records from the caucus room were dynamic and momentous, including Attorney Joseph Welch's critical rebuttal to Senator Joseph McCarthy, "Have you no sense of decency, sir?" during the Army–McCarthy hearings and Senator Howard Baker repeatedly pressing the Watergate conspirators in his disarming Southern drawl, "What did the president know and when did he know it?"

Green felt covered the senators' table just as it did during the hearings that brought Richard Nixon down. This was also the caucus room where Oliver North testified in the Iran-Contra hearings; testimony that resulted in charges and convictions.

Dan Reilly sensed the touchpoints with American history in this austere and almost humbling setting.

"Mr. Reilly, let me tell you something . . ."

Moakley Davidson was chair of the subcommittee and was damned if he wasn't going to score something from what he considered a senseless session. He looked up from his notes, now certain he had a *gotcha* question that would earn airtime beyond the live streaming C-SPAN cameras.

"You want the American people to provide a slush fund for your company. Well, sir, it's not going to happen."

Dan Reilly heard the sound bite and the way Davidson phrased it. *That's all you have?* he thought, although he didn't say it.

"No, sir, assuming that's a question," he replied.

Davidson raised his voice and narrowed his eyes. "No? You're employed by a private corporation at a high executive level, yet you've come to this committee with the intention of having Congress open the people's checkbook."

Another non-question.

"With all due respect, Senator, I accepted an invitation to speak on behalf of American citizens who travel abroad—Americans who want to know that the United States government is willing to help protect its citizens on foreign soil."

Davidson seized the moment. The graying congressman, a rancher who had struck it rich when oil was discovered on his property, did not take well to being lectured. He bore down harder on the hotel executive.

"Mr. Reilly, my constituents did not send me to Washington

fourteen years ago as their representative in the House and now the Senate to spend money on American tourists traveling on their own dime to Europe, Asia, or wherever their fancy takes them. Not now, not ever."

Reilly responded in a measured voice. "Senator Davidson, every day Americans travel the globe for pleasure, but so do our nation's businessmen and women. They work hard to bring new revenue into the US, brokering commercial deals and spreading goodwill. But when the hotels they stay in are attacked by terrorists, attacked in many cases because they house American visitors, it must be seen as an attack against America. That, sir, is the only reason I agreed to appear before this committee. To help protect American citizens and their interests abroad."

"That's not how I see it, Mr. Reilly. Not at all."

Again, not a question. Reilly remained quiet, waiting for one. But the chairman shook his head.

"I see that my initial round is up, and I must relinquish my time to the senator from Massachusetts. Rest assured, however, I am not finished with you."

Davidson leaned back in his seat and acceded to Massachusetts Democratic Senator Peggy McNamara.

"Mr. Reilly, thank you for joining us today," the 58-year-old former judge politely stated.

"You're quite welcome, Senator."

"Following up on the chairman's line of questioning," which she really wasn't, "you recognize that the US cannot provide real protection for American citizens traveling abroad."

"I do. That would be impossible."

"Then what are you proposing?"

A real question.

"Terrorism is our new reality. Radical terrorism is responsible for virtually all of the attacks against hotels, most of which are owned or managed by American companies. We considered ourselves lucky in the 1970s when the Irish Republican Army phoned pre-attack warnings.

Those days are over. Modern terrorists aren't polite or politic. Their goal is to kill as many innocent people as possible. Unannounced and dramatically. Terrorism is no longer just a political threat. It's a corporate business threat as well. For us to prepare for this, we have to be armed. Armed with information," Reilly affirmed. "Armed with timely, credible intelligence."

"At what cost, Mr. Reilly?"

"Well, information gathering and sharing has a price tag, but so does the failure to spend."

Moakley Davidson intentionally ignored Reilly's testimony; he was texting and answering emails. Reilly noted the purposeful snub, so he focused on each of the other committee members.

"Senator, members of the committee, there have been terrorist attacks against hotels virtually every year since 9/11. Thousands dead. Tourists and first responders. Children. Christians, Jews, and Muslims. The bombs have not discriminated."

Reilly punctuated his answer with a long silence. He took a sip of water from the glass on the table and breathed deeply. "Nearly half of these terrorist attacks used VBIEDs—Vehicle Born Improvised Explosive Devices. Kensington Royal is examining ways to increase our security perimeters to help guard against such attacks. But that has not thwarted VBIEDs from getting up to barriers at hotels and restaurants or suicide bombers and gunmen checking in at the front desk or sitting down for one last meal. Allow me to show you what I mean."

Reilly signaled a technician to play a video. The members of the panel and observers in the hearing room turned to the nearest of four monitors. Reilly began narrating.

"July, 2009, Jakarta, Indonesia . . ."

TOKYO

The FedEx truck rolled out of the garage. The backup driver closed and locked the door, then hopped in. They slowly drove through Shibuya, one of the twenty-three city wards of Tokyo, passing the upscale department stores and boutique fashion shops that were still open, the bustling nightclubs with locals and visitors in the queue, and expensive restaurants where rich young couples spilled out onto the sidewalk.

As the delivery truck passed the Shibuya train station entrance, the driver checked his watch. *On schedule.*

They drove by the new Shibuya Hikarie shopping and office complex. A taxi pulled in front of them, nearly sideswiping the left front bumper. The backup man swore, but the driver remained cool.

The crowd on the street paid no attention to the white FedEx truck with its distinctive purple and red letters that formed an arrow between the "E" and "X." Indeed it was one of the world's most iconic logos, eclipsed in recent years only by Apple, Nike, and Coca-Cola. To the discerning eye, the arrow would appear slightly off, but from a distance it was good enough for tonight's run.

WASHINGTON, DC

"To most people it was a day like any other," Reilly said as the video played. "Nothing out of the ordinary. You'll see people mingling and a hotel guest casually walking through the lobby—likely a businessman on his way to his room expecting to rest after a long day of traveling."

The guest was seen walking from left to right across the screen. The footage switched from one camera angle to another. At thirty-six seconds into the real-time playback, the man reached the elevator bank.

"Watch," Reilly said. At that instant, an explosion, without the benefit of sound, sent smoke and debris hurtling into the lobby. "A suicide bomber in the restaurant detonated his bomb. The man you were watching died instantly. Died from just being there. He was not alone."

Reilly let the statement sink in and the footage unfold.

After a pause, he continued. "Five minutes later, a second suicide bomber set off another bomb in an adjacent hotel. In all, sixty people were injured and nine died. Both properties were American luxury hotels. They were American, Senator. The JW Marriott and the Ritz-Carlton. The bombs were constructed in an independent flower shop in the Marriott. The two bombers, guests in the hotels, picked them up and walked into the Ritz restaurant and the Marriott conference room. It was as simple and as horrifying as that."

"American deaths?" Senator McNamara somberly asked.

"Does it matter?" Reilly replied.

The senator lowered her eyes.

"Three Australians, two Dutch tourists, one New Zealander, and three Indonesians, including the two terrorists," Reilly explained.

"So, no Americans," Davidson said, smugly reentering the conversation.

"No Americans, but the bomb at the JW Marriott detonated during a meeting of AmCham Indonesia, a branch of the United States Chamber of Commerce in Jakarta. The president of the organization was hosting a breakfast meeting of prominent CEOs in Jakarta's business community."

Reilly added one other comment for good measure—his *gotcha*. "The AmCham president *is* an American, Senator Davidson. Would you count that as an attempted assassination?"

Two other members of the subcommittee were making notes as he spoke.

"One additional thing," Reilly said as the footage rolled. "Jakarta police found a third bomb in room 1808 of the JW Marriott. It had been programmed to explode just prior to the restaurant bomb. You want to know the purpose?"

Even Moakley Davidson was engaged.

"To create panic. To drive more guests into the larger kill zone: the lobby. It's right out of a terrorist manual. Fortunately that bomb did not go off."

"Why this target, Mr. Reilly?" Senator McNamara asked.

"American hotels. American interests. Because Americans were there. We just got lucky, if you want to call it that."

TOYKO

The FedEx truck cautiously continued along Tokyo's streets, sticking to the speed limit. Other vehicles steered around them. Police ignored them. Pedestrians waiting at crosswalks were too busy on their cellphones to take any notice.

WASHINGTON, DC

"I have more video, which I'll send to each of your offices," Reilly said. "But you don't have to wait. It's been on YouTube for years. Just Google it."

He motioned for an aide to bring up an easel and stand. It had ten stacked poster boards with grid lines indicating years, hotels, locations, tactics, casualties, and perpetrators.

"In the interest of time, I won't review everything. But we do have hard copies covering key points."

An assistant distributed bound PowerPoint decks bearing the KR logo.

Davidson tried to insinuate himself into the moment. "If this is intended to—"

"Excuse me, Mr. Chairman, but the witness is mine right now," Senator McNamara proclaimed.

He gave a brusque, inaudible reply and waved her on.

"Please continue, Mr. Reilly," she stated. "The floor is yours."

"Thank you." Reilly stood next to the easel and began. "March 27, 2002. The Park Hotel in Netanya, Israel. A suicide bomber detonated an explosive device in the hotel's dining room. May 8, same year. A Pakistani bus outside the Sheraton in Karachi exploded. October 7, 2004, the Hilton in Taba, Egypt. A suicide bomber drove a car into the lobby. The bomb exploded and 33 people were killed, another 150 injured."

Reilly ran through fourteen other bombings covering Indonesia, Kenya, Iraq, Egypt, Thailand, Pakistan, Jordan, Nigeria, Afghanistan, and Thailand. Many bore the names of America hoteliers.

"They don't necessarily always make the front page. If they do, it's only for a day or two, and with few details. But for us, they are front of mind for a long, long time," Reilly added.

Moakley Davidson paged through the handout. Reilly was convinced he wasn't reading a word of it. Montana was a world away from all of the locales mentioned. He wondered if it would take a direct hit in Billings to make a difference.

TOKYO

The driver stuck to the speed limit, braked for people crossing the street, and came to full stops at the lights. He passed a Shinwa Bank branch, a cluster of seedy "love" hotels not listed by Michelin, and then rows of pubs, karaoke clubs, and restaurants that came alive after dark. He made a final turn onto Dogenzaka. Five blocks from the destination, he dropped off his backup driver, who would have served as a translator if stopped. He checked his watch again. 10:58 p.m. 2258 hours. Two minutes before his special delivery.

WASHINGTON, DC

Davidson noted McNamara's time was up. The chairman turned to the Alabama senator, Bill Cole, who would pick up Moakley Davidson's line of questioning.

"Thank you, Mr. Chairman." The 58-year-old senator, serving his first term, got right to his first question. "Mr. Reilly, can you walk us through why you think hotels are so vulnerable?"

Reilly viewed it as a completely naïve question.

"I will, Senator Cole. While we're in the hospitality business, we are equally in the anti-terrorism business. Hotels are ideal targets. They have fixed locations, limited security perimeters, and most of all they're full of potential victims in an environment that's meant to be friendly and welcoming. Increasingly, we are in the crosshairs of terrorists' sights. We present soft targets, and to my point, timely intelligence can put us in a better position to detect and deflect."

Cole was prepared to rebut his testimony. He shuffled through some paperwork until he produced a document. He held it up for Reilly to see.

"Mr. Reilly, do you recognize this?"

Reilly nodded. "Based on the logo, from this distance, it appears to be a State Department document. I'd like to examine it, however."

Cole gave it to a staffer who walked it over to Reilly.

"And?"

"It is an official State Department travel advisory."

"So you are familiar with this," Cole stated.

"Perhaps not this exact one, but yes, these types of advisories."

"Will you read the highlighted portion, Mr. Reilly?"

Reilly scanned the advisory.

"I'm sorry. Aloud, if you will," the Alabama senator insisted.

Reilly cleared his throat and read the copy.

In recent years, terrorists have targeted police stations and officers. Currently, travel by US government personnel to central areas is restricted to mission-essential travel that is approved in advance by the embassy security office. Whether at work, pursuing daily activities, or traveling, Americans are advised to be aware of their personal safety and security at all times. Extremists may target both official and private establishments, including bars, nightclubs, shopping areas, restaurants, places of worship, and hotels.

"And hotels," Cole repeated.

"Yes, Senator."

"The advisory, issued by the State Department, was for Indonesia. Would you say it is representative of travel warnings issued for other nations?"

"Yes, sir, it is representative," Reilly responded.

"And you have access to advisories of this nature?" Cole asked.

"Yes, I do. Our corporate VP of Global Safety and Security routinely disseminates them, but they are also online."

The freshman senator removed his glasses and glared at Reilly. "Then what else can you possibly need?"

TOKYO

Takayuki Nikaido was already an hour into his dreaded overnight shift. This was his fourth week of all-nighters; his fourth week away from his family. The 63-year-old hotel security officer was not happy with the schedule, but with only a few more years until retirement, he quietly and obediently accepted the shift assignments.

Nikaido scanned four computer screens stacked in two rows. They displayed constantly changing closed-circuit TV images captured by 420 cameras in virtually every corner and corridor of the opulent Kensington Royal Hotel in the heart of Tokyo. They cycled every two seconds except when a camera caught movement in its field of view.

Movements covered on camera included what happened in the halls throughout the twenty-one-story luxury hotel: guests arriving and leaving, couples kissing, kids running, hotel staff going to and from rooms. Other cameras caught, but did not record, empty elevators. Stairways were also covered as well as lobbies, escalators, restaurants, kitchens, storage rooms, doors leading to bathrooms, and subterranean service areas such as the electrical power plant for the hotel and the roof. Exterior cameras, the few there were, focused on the front and back of the opulent hotel.

Videos and still frames were archived for just thirty days on a hard drive in the security office. Another computer hosted a duplicate record, but there was no cloud backup.

Nikaido shared the security office with two younger officers who were playing a game to pass the time. Daichi Eto and Fumio Imamura watched couples on the hotel cameras. They called their game "Hooker, Girlfriend, or Wife." Ten points for hookers, five for girlfriends, two for wives. Eto and Imamura would make a guess as the couples walked through the lobby. Sometimes it would be instantly apparent. Other times, less so, and more fun.

Wives were usually easy to spot, particularly if they were Japanese guests. If older, they generally walked behind their husbands. If younger and less traditional, they walked side-by-side. Girlfriends walked arm-in-arm, looking up and around, talking endlessly. Hookers also walked close to their escorts, but neither spoke nor looked anywhere but straight ahead. Often the security officers playing the game recognized the hired women. At other times, their purposeful mannerisms gave them away. And when it came to hookers, the action often started in the elevator or even in the stairwell. Eto was particularly good at guessing how long an escort would stay with their companion. It went anywhere from thirty minutes to the whole night, depending upon the client's appetite and budget.

Actually, most of the camera images pulsed too quickly to be reliably screened for true security purposes. They were intended as a record for examination against insurance claims after a theft or to settle a hotel/guest dispute. So the team principally made routine log notations, spoke with roving security personnel, occasionally answered a medical call, and played Hooker, Girlfriend, or Wife. Nikaido didn't take part in the game, but he allowed his junior officers their fun. It helped pass the time. Meanwhile, he did keep an eye on the monitors. Reception was checking in a flight crew from American Airlines. Late night conventioneers from the US joined friends at the lobby bar, and an older man and a younger woman entered.

He heard Eto's guess. "Hooker!" He was right.

Nikaido laughed at the repartee and casually focused on the street-facing cameras at the main entrance. They flared with the headlights of passing cars and one larger vehicle, a FedEx truck that was coming to a stop.

WASHINGTON, DC

"Senator Cole, we need deeper intelligence," Reilly proclaimed. "We need a greater level of cooperation from America's investigatory agencies, a pipeline to specific information that will help us deny terrorists access. Public warnings are helpful, but we need to know what's not publicly published."

"Will the senator from Alabama yield," Chairman Davidson interrupted.

"Of course," Cole agreed.

"Mister Reilly . . ." He drew out the last name for emphasis. "What about our oil interests abroad? Corporations of all stripes? Do you recommend that we open our intelligence files to every business and protect every square inch the way we do our embassies and outposts?" The senator smiled as he considered his next thought. "As if we've done a good job at that!"

"Sir, I'm sorry, you're asking exactly what?" Reilly said, reframing the interrogative.

"You heard me. But I'll put it more simply. Do you believe the CIA should be making its files available to your company and every business? Because if you do—"

"Mr. Chairman," Reilly interjected, fixing his eyes on Davidson with no intention of giving any ground to the arrogant senator, "an attack on an American hotel in Mali or Jakarta impacts confidence in Paris and New York. When it comes to targets, there's no *us and them.*

It can happen anywhere—from the world's capitals to America's smallest cities and towns. While hotel chains can and must take steps to protect their clientele, we do not run a global intelligence service. The United States does."

TOKYO

At this time of night? Nikaido thought. *Odd.*

He typed a command on his computer that brought the front portico camera full screen. The FedEx truck slowed down, swung into the valet parking area, and came to a full stop short of the entrance. Its headlights were on high beam and remained that way. The brilliance flared the camera lenses trained on the area and blinded anyone approaching the truck.

Nikaido tapped the officer to his right. "Daichi, look at this."

"What?"

"The truck."

"Damn driver has his brights on," the younger man said. "Hard to see. FedEx?"

"Yes, and he can't make a delivery in front, or at this hour," Nikaido added. "He needs to go to the service entrance. Call down there and get him out."

"Too late," Eto said. "The driver's getting out."

WASHINGTON, DC

"We're not the CIA or Homeland Security, Mr. Reilly," Moakley Davidson chided.

"I know you're not," Reilly shot back. "But this committee represents the interests of Americans and their safety is in your best interest, just as it is in ours. We have to find ways to work together."

TOKYO

The FedEx driver turned his back to the hotel entrance, ignoring the valet's shouts. Rather than taking out a package for delivery, he continued to walk away.

Takayuki Nikaido grew more concerned when the driver failed to stop and even crossed the street. In just a few steps he would be out of camera range.

"This isn't right," Nikaido declared, his heart racing. "This isn't right," he repeated.

Nikaido quickly stood. He grabbed his only weapon, a baton, and tore out of the security station, through the lobby, and toward the portico.

Eto followed a few steps behind while radioing a warning. Imamura, confused, didn't know what to do. He watched his colleagues run off, briefly taking his attention away from the monitors. Distracted, he missed seeing two men hurriedly leave through the hotel's rear entrance.

WASHINGTON, DC

"Hotels invest a great deal of money to install protective techniques. But we are not in the intelligence business," Reilly testified. "Our computers aren't tied into the nation's security databases. We are response driven. As I've said, general information is no longer enough. Mr. Chairman, members of the committee, planning for emergencies requires communication, collaboration, and control. Don't you think it's time?"

TOKYO

Takayuki Nikaido covered the distance from the front door to the truck in just eight seconds. His eyes darted between the truck and the driver, who was already well across the street. Nikaido looked inside the truck. No keys. No way to push it out of the way.

"Clear the area!" he screamed. "Now!"

WASHINGTON, DC

"Terrorism is a tool of religious fundamentalists, lone wolves, individuals determined to make a statement, and nations intent on nation-building," Dan Reilly said. "Left wing, right wing. Separatists, environmentalists, fundamentalists, nationalists. It's a political tool." He lowered his voice. "A deadly political tool."

TOKYO

The driver, now more than a block away, faced the hotel. He watched a security officer frantically bark orders. None that would make a difference. He actually wished he could be closer to gaze into his eyes and to see that special moment between life and death. It always fascinated him. One moment alive. Existing. The next, nothing and nothingness. But what of the in-between. The space between the two. The instant. The nanosecond. Is there a recognition? A feeling? What could it possibly be? As an assassin, it had long been an area of personal research.

WASHINGTON, DC

Reilly leaned toward the microphone to continue, but commotion outside the hearing room drew his attention. The disturbance quickly evolved into shouting, and a sergeant at arms was dispatched to the hall.

Everyone turned in their seats as a man rushed in. He bumped into the security detail, but powered past.

"I've got to get through." Spotting Reilly, he called out to him. Then he saw the cameras.

Reilly recognized the intruder, who was a young executive on his staff.

Reilly stood. "It's okay. He's with me."

The officer released him.

"Excuse me a moment, Mr. Chairman. If you'll please."

Davidson was annoyed, yet no more than he projected during his questioning. "Mr. Reilly, this better be important."

"I'm sorry, sir. Just a moment."

The executive, now fully aware the TV cameras were following him, nervously stepped forward.

"Quickly!" Moakley Davidson demanded.

The gallery buzzed with curiosity as the man slid next to Reilly, cupped his hand over the microphone and whispered into his boss's ear.

Davidson cleared his voice; another audible display of his displeasure.

Reilly stuck a finger in the air indicating he needed a moment. He nodded twice as his aide briefed him. The conversation concluded with Reilly letting out a long breath.

"I'm sorry," he stated, focusing again on the arrogant chairman. "We've just gotten terrible news."

Simultaneously, three committee members felt cell phones vibrate in their jacket pockets. Even Moakley Davidson's phone pulsated. He fumbled trying to retrieve a text.

Reilly raised his voice. "You'll have to excuse me. Our hotel in Tokyo, the Envoy Diplomat, has been bombed."

Without asking permission, Daniel J. Reilly gathered his papers and abruptly left.

More cell phones vibrated and rang at different pitches throughout the gallery. For the first time during the day, Senator Moakley Davidson was utterly speechless.

TOKYO

There was nothing left of the FedEx truck—1,500 pounds of explosives had decimated the area and anyone within 50 feet. The portico had collapsed. Shrapnel shot through the lobby at more than 400 feet per second, decapitating people in the bar, ripping through bodies all the way to the elevators. But it was only the beginning.

Sixty seconds later, as people rushed out, three other bombs detonated. Fireballs shot up through the elevator banks. Debris poured through the hallways. The eighth floor swimming pool collapsed, flooding the floors below with 97,500 gallons of water. Eighty-one people died in the first few minutes. The fate of another 125 would not be known for hours.

Emergency vehicles screamed toward ground zero. Rubberneckers seeing an opportunity to shoot viral video ran to the smoldering scene. But most people, fearing another bomb, pushed and shoved their way toward safety. In all the tumult, no one took any notice of a tall European man strolling by quite casually. Not the first responders or the police. Not the gawkers or the survivors. No one focused on the man with a blue shirt tucked under his arm and a very satisfied smile on his face.

PART ONE

FLASH POINT

1

POTSDAM, THE GERMAN DEMOCRATIC REPUBLIC

DECEMBER 1989

"Fool!" Nikolai Gorshkov slammed the telephone headset down with such brute force it cracked in two and sent plastic shards upward, grazing his face. "A fucking functionary!" the 37-year old, thin, blond KGB lieutenant colonel shouted. "Can't be bothered. You have your orders," he said, "so carry them out!"

His aide, a younger lieutenant, was busy fulfilling those orders. But he nodded in complete agreement. Andre Miklos knew well enough not to interrupt his superior when he was on a rant. He motioned to other KGB agents who were in earshot not to say anything either.

"Popov. Stanislav Popov," Gorshkov whispered the name he had just scribbled on a sheet of paper. "Never forget that name, Andre. Never."

"Yes, sir!" said Miklos.

The senior officer—a spy whose cover was as a translator—now crumpled the sheet and tossed it into the wood-burning stove with the other secret documents the members of the Potsdam KGB office were destroying.

Stanislav Popov. Stanislav Popov. Miklos mouthed the words as he fed more files into the stove.

"He'll pay, Andre. Stanislav Popov will pay," Gorshkov said under his breath. "He'll pay dearly for abandoning us."

The smell of scorched papers made the men cough as they worked on the top floor of the block-wide, three-story KGB headquarters in Potsdam, which was known as KGB Town. Together they were destroying four years' worth of work; a comprehensive operation titled "Luch."

The documents chronicled East Germans they'd tricked, coerced, and recruited—journalists, professors, scientists, and technicians who had plausible reason to travel abroad and steal Western technology and NATO secrets. There were boxes filled with personal files, surveillance reports, arrest orders, interrogation transcripts, and records of Westerners entrapped by the KGB, all destined for the burn. Those were the most important secrets to destroy. Going up in smoke, a cruel picture of human rights violations by Moscow, by the KGB, and by the men covering their tracks.

"Luch" was a daring KGB operation designed to secure badly needed Western know-how and intellectual property, executed out of the Potsdam office. Even the senior officer had to admit the Soviet Bloc was depressingly behind the US and Europe. There was no more visible evidence than the fact that agents and politicians preferred to work on the West's Commodore PCs rather than their own inferior, Russian-built computers.

Now, each page they tossed into the stove represented painstaking work and the infrastructure that had supported it, all to benefit Russia, to rescue Russia. And now Russia was not there for them.

"Disorganization! Idiots!" the senior officer murmured. "All of our time wasted."

He blamed Mikhail Gorbachev's directives. He blamed the decades of incompetence.

The lieutenant colonel went for another document box, this one near the window. Before lifting it, he split the dusty louvered shades to peer outside. Anti-Russian and anti-German Democratic Republic crowds milled about, more today than the day before, and getting angrier by the hour. Students in particular had been feeling more empowered over the past two months—but they were not alone. Protesters who wanted the Soviets out included the elderly who had suffered since the end of World War II and women whose husbands and sons had been rounded up by the GDR's dreaded Ministry of State security, the Stasi, never to be seen again.

The end had been coming for two months, since November 9. That's when an East German government spokesman bungled an announcement. He misstated that the frontiers were to be opened immediately. Hearing the news, thousands of East Berliners rushed the heavily armed border crossings demanding to be let through. Throngs overwhelmed the beleaguered guards who waited for orders to come down. *Shoot or don't shoot?* Those orders never came. By morning, the Berlin Wall, the very symbol of Soviet tyranny, had been breached and with it, Communist domination over East Berlin and throughout East Germany crumbled.

Now it was Potsdam's turn to feel the change sweeping across Germany. The KGB mandate to the staff in the massive Potsdam office: *Destroy everything.*

Across the street from the KGB outpost was one of Potsdam's main Stasi headquarters. The KGB case officer relied on Stasi contacts to obtain personal favors, including a very basic one—a telephone in his flat to run operatives outside of typical work hours and also cultivate and manipulate political relationships. The telephone provided that access. But he now feared that Stasi records on his calls could expose him. The smoke coming from the Stasi building chimneys gave him little consolation. *So much to cover up,* he thought. *And no help from Moscow.*

Even though Potsdam was the GDR's ninth-largest city, Moscow viewed it as an important post because it housed a KGB prison used to interrogate and execute Western spies and Soviet soldiers arrested for desertion, mutiny, and anti-Soviet activity. Shortly after the fall of the Berlin Wall, the lieutenant colonel asked for assistance and protection from the Kremlin, but none came. Then he demanded it from the military, and finally from his venerated KGB superiors. *Destroy everything* was the only response. And so, abandoned, they continued to follow their orders.

Gorshkov closed the shade, but not before a rock came hurtling through the window. It barely missed him. His neck veins tightened, his cheeks turned bloodred, and his eyes flared with hatred. But the hatred wasn't directed at the German protester. It was reserved for Stanislav Popov, the last in a long line of bureaucrats to deny his request. The hatred extended as a proxy for all of the Popovs in the chain of command.

"Sir!" Miklos shouted.

"I'm all right."

He felt the winter cold that flowed through the window and now stoked the fire. But burning hotter was the flame inside the KGB agent. He told his aide, "Stanislav Popov and everyone like him will pay, Andre. With their power, their money, and their lives."

It was a proclamation born from betrayal. It might take years, even decades, but KGB agent Nikolai Gorshkov vowed to collect on the political debts.

2

PRESENT DAY

Once Reilly left the Senate hearing room, he phoned Alan Cannon, a friend, confidant, and, more importantly, the Kensington Royal Vice President of Global Safety and Security.

"What do we have?" Reilly asked.

"Mostly what CNN's been reporting. Sketchy, but the uploaded cell phone video looks really bad."

Reilly double-timed down the marble staircase through the Russell Senate Office Building, out onto Constitution Avenue, and into a waiting town car.

"Any word from our people?" he asked Cannon.

"No." Cannon paused and lowered his voice. "We're trying everyone. Circuits are busy."

"Damn it," Reilly said. "Hold for a sec, Brenda's calling in from Chicago."

"Hi," he said to his assistant, Brenda Sheldon.

"See my text?" she began. "There's been—"

"I know. Haven't read anything yet, but I'm on with Cannon, getting up to speed. I'll need—"

"Flights. Our travel agent is already working on it. I'll send you the options."

"Hitting the office here first, but see what's available to Chicago this afternoon."

Reilly ended the call with Sheldon and returned to Alan Cannon.

"Okay, from the top," Reilly instructed as the car made its way toward the KR Washington offices on K Street.

"Whole front is blown out," Cannon reported. "Truck bomb. Other detonations inside. Still burning. Damage extends well into the lobby. Same in the back of the house. I'm watching a live helicopter feed on CNN. Can't tell much more. Fire trucks have arrived, but you know the procedure. Another bomb could be set to explode to knock out the first responders. An anchor is trying his best to describe the footage, but they need a translator for the Japanese coverage. But there's no question. It's ours."

"Any contact with the GM or security?" Reilly asked.

"Just their voice mail. Nobody's picking up," Cannon replied.

"What about Matsuhito at the KR Suites across town?"

"Good idea."

"Have him go over and keep him on the phone the whole time. In the meantime, I'll call Chicago and get our crisis team together. Should be back at the office in ten."

*　*　*

Reilly's call to Kensington Royal headquarters triggered the assembly of the crisis team. It included senior management, heads of legal, public relations, and HR, and alerts to all the regional executives. This was practiced procedure that now seemed lacking in an actual attack.

The ten minutes back to the office Reilly estimated turned into twenty-five. DC traffic was snarled by a presidential motorcade. He phoned Brenda Sheldon.

"I've cleared everything on your calendar and confirmed you out of Reagan on a 2:20 p.m.," she said. "PR is dodging calls from the news. They want to send crews over to your office in DC or here."

"Absolutely not."

"That's what June said, too, but you might see cameras here anyway."

June Wilson, Kensington Royal's public relations veep, would manage them. Reilly had more important worries.

For the rest of the ride, he ran through the crisis agenda. Foremost on his mind: the lives of his staff and guests.

* * *

Reilly raced into the office building that KR shared with Washington lobbyists, lawyers, marketing and PR agencies, and a Korean broadcaster. He waved at security, used his ID card to activate the elevator, and rose to the 18th floor.

Kensington Royal's DC operation covered half the floor, housing twelve full-time staffers and offices for Reilly and Cannon. Everyone was huddled in the conference room watching a fifty-inch TV screen.

Cannon spotted Reilly as he walked in. He looked the part of a security officer: rugged, square jaw, piercing eyes. The 47-year-old Cannon kept his brown hair, graying only slightly at the temples, short, military-length. He hadn't changed it in decades.

"Did you reach . . . ?"

Cannon lowered his eyes. They were not so piercing now.

Reilly stopped. There was word, and he could tell it wasn't good.

"Fujimori," Cannon sighed. "Fujimori and three young people at reception. Gone."

"Oh my God," Reilly said. He'd hired Niko Fujimori as general manager knowing that the hotel would be best served culturally with a Japanese national in the front office.

"We lost others, too, Dan. A valet, two members of the security team, and more staff inside. All told, I don't know yet. It's terrible."

Dan Reilly hugged Cannon, pausing for a moment to allow himself to feel the weight of what had happened. Then he pulled himself together.

"All right," Reilly said. "Let's get to work."

The Tokyo bombing on top of the Congressional hearings reminded him he wasn't just in the global hotel trade. He was in the anti-terrorism business.

* * *

Dan Reilly had two offices—one in Washington and one in Chicago—but he generally worked out of DC. His trusted executive assistant was in Chicago, but actually everywhere, at least on a virtual basis.

"You're going to have to hurry to catch your plane," Brenda said on the phone. "Out the door in five."

"Car?"

"Downstairs, waiting. Let me know how long you want to be here. I'll start booking Tokyo flights."

"Thanks, Brenda. We'll all meet tonight. I'd say late morning out to Tokyo."

"Japan Airlines and American have 1:00 p.m. flights. United a little earlier at 11:00 and 12:30."

"The earlier the better."

"Want me to coordinate with Mr. Cannon's flight?"

"If possible. But he may need to deal with other security issues."

"What do you want to do with your calls?" she asked.

"Email the list. Anything pressing?"

Reilly could hear her fingers fly over the computer keys.

"The Moscow acquisition. The mayor wants to see you when you're there."

"I bet he does," Reilly said sarcastically. "Put that on hold."

She read his tone loud and clear.

"What else?" he asked.

"Mr. Shaw wants to talk about Tehran."

"Hold that, too. Other problems?"

"Nothing that can't wait."

"Fine. Keep everyone calm. Especially the press," Reilly added. "I'll call again after I get through security."

"Fly safely. You'll make things good," she said.

Good was no longer going to be good enough, he thought.

3

TOKYO, JAPAN

Dan Reilly's cab drove up as close to the hotel as possible, which wasn't very close. Yellow police tape cordoned off the area from several blocks away. Permission to enter required proper identification and a friend in high places. Reilly had both. He was met at a security checkpoint by the US Ambassador to Japan, Ruben Norte. Reilly instantly recognized him from the luxury hotel's grand opening two years earlier. He stood a good foot taller than most of the people who surrounded him and had a commanding boardroom presence. Norte intended the post, a political gift from the White House, to be the last chapter of his career.

"Mr. Ambassador!" Reilly said warmly. "Thank you for meeting me."

After a quick handshake and a flash of his ID to first a Tokyo policeman and then a government security officer, Reilly was allowed inside the perimeter.

"What's the status?" Reilly asked.

"Two more died in the last hour. So many in critical condition. Missing limbs, eyes. It's awful. They're in seven hospitals across the city. Now, everyone's worried about another attack." The ambassador paused. "And I thought this was going to be a cushy outpost."

"They don't exist anymore, Mr. Ambassador."

"Ruben. It's Ruben. It was Ruben in Detroit when everyone thought the American auto industry would tank. It's Ruben here."

"Thank you, sir."

"Let's walk," he said.

Fifty yards ahead, there was utter devastation. Reilly gaped in horror as he took it in. It was far worse than it appeared on pictures sent to his cell phone and the footage on the news.

The columns holding up the portico were gone along with the portico. Rubble covered indistinguishable burned-out car chassis, some containing bodies draped in sheets. The medical, security, and fire personnel all wore surgical white masks over their noses and mouths.

All the glass was blown out of the lobby and as far as Reilly could see, many of the floors. The lobby smoldered. Water draining from the hotel flowed with a darkish red hue. Reilly knew why.

"It could be another day until everyone is accounted for," Norte said somberly. "Dogs are still finding survivors, and . . ." The ambassador didn't complete the sentence.

At that moment, Reilly saw Kensington Royal's VP of legal, Chris Collins, and waved. Collins had been closing a deal in Beijing and was able to beat his colleague to Japan. The company lawyer was talking to a Japanese man with a lanyard ID draped around his neck. Reilly presumed he was a police detective.

Collins had a surgical face mask tucked under his chin, ready for use. He wore a blue Brooks Brothers shirt, and a conservative black and blue print tie, which was loosened at the collar.

"Dan," he simply said in greeting. Reilly noted that Collins' shoes were soaking wet.

"Chris, thanks for getting here so fast."

The lawyer acknowledged the comment with a sad nod.

Reilly introduced Collins to Ambassador Norte. In turn, Collins introduced his companion.

"Dan, Mr. Ambassador, this is Superintendent General Ginshiro Yamato of Keishichō."

Reilly recognized the name. He was far more than just an officer.

Yamato was the ranking head of the police force of one of the world's largest cities: the Tokyo Metropolitan Police Department, with more than 43,000 strong. He was a slight man, around fifty, with wire-framed glasses, a dark suit, and a blue tie. He could have passed for any Japanese businessman except for his eyes. They communicated indisputable authority that gave him an overwhelming, commanding presence.

"Thank you for your assistance, Superintendent General," Reilly offered, shaking his hand solemnly.

At this point, Reilly noticed that Yamato was accompanied by his own bodyguards. One approached and whispered something in Yamato's ear. The superintendent general quickly excused himself. Ambassador Norte also stepped back to talk to an aide. This gave Reilly time to confer with Collins.

"How are you holding up?"

"Terribly, but probably better than the corporation."

It was a predictable statement coming from legal.

Reilly's cell phone rang. He noted the caller ID and said, "Brenda," to Collins before answering the call.

"Hi. What's up?"

"We're getting calls from press around the world," she explained. "June wants to issue a more detailed press release. And a quote." She paused. "From you."

"Jesus. I just got here. Tell her I'll email something in a few hours."

"Sooner. The boss is on her. They want attributable quotes, but cleared through legal first."

"Well, I'm right here with Chris. We'll work up something."

"She wanted something 'encouraging,'" Brenda added. "Her word, not mine."

Reilly looked around. There was nothing "encouraging" in view. Debris everywhere. Dank, smoke-filled air. Haunting outlines of charred bodies on the street. Women's shoes, ruined jewelry, stopped watches, fused glasses, and the saddest thing of all, a blood-soaked teddy bear.

"I have to call you back," Reilly said. He hung up, not even considering what hour of the day she was working or whether she'd gone to sleep.

Reilly checked his 1940s Gruen watch and did the math in his head. He quickly texted a thank-you and that he'd have something for her soon, and then she should go home. Next he returned to Collins.

"What are you hearing?" he asked.

"GMs in Singapore, Delhi, Seoul. They're worried. All saying the same thing."

"Of course, they're talking to one another. Email . . . no, call them. Schedule times for me after 9 p.m. Tokyo time. Thirty minutes each. And tell them to start checking IDs at the door and post additional security."

Reilly was beginning to formulate a plan. *Singapore, Delhi, and Seoul were worried,* he thought. *If they were, others would be, too.* And for that matter, so was he.

"Anyone taking credit?" Reilly asked.

"Don't know. That's a question for the ambassador or the police."

Reilly walked toward Ambassador Norte. He stepped over and around debris, all personal affects with no person to claim them. The dank odor was now getting to him. He separated the smells: smoke, burning embers, plastic, gas, oil, and . . . human flesh. It was an all too familiar odor—the scent of battlefields.

He asked Norte the same question he had posed to Collins.

"Surprisingly no one yet," the ambassador answered. "Some light chatter on the internet. Nothing credible. I'm in touch with the State Department. They either don't have anything or they're not sharing it. I understand police are checking for any evidence in the FedEx truck. Prints, anything left behind. But there's not much left to examine."

"And our people, Chris?"

"Still accounting for everyone. Our nighttime security head was the first to react. He ran right out to stop the bomb. Caught the blast full force. We lost him and others."

"I want his name. I want everyone's name and numbers so I can talk to their families."

"Be careful what you say," the lawyer warned.

"Jesus, Chris! Just give me the names."

Reilly tried to comprehend the true extent of the devastation. He pointed out a section midway up the structure, thinking no one in the immediate area could have survived.

Norte filled in the details. "The bomb just below the swimming pool followed the first by about a minute. Timed just as people began rushing out of their rooms. Cruel beyond belief. It brought the pool cascading down. We're still accounting for guests who were blown out or drowned. The fire department said that the water did help contain the fire damage—not a great consolation."

"It must have been someone in the hotel," Reilly bluntly said.

"What?" Collins asked.

"Someone who stayed in the hotel surely did his homework and knew the vulnerable spots," Reilly continued. "The computer records . . ."

"It'll have to come from IT. From our corporate reservations," Collins said. "All the house computers were destroyed."

Reilly walked forward into the lobby. More destruction. Again, worse than he had imagined. Support beams were exposed where walls had been. Elevator banks destroyed. Blood and body parts splattered everywhere. He hadn't witnessed anything like this since Afghanistan.

"I'll bet more devices were timed to go off downstairs and in the back when people were escaping," Reilly said. He wasn't asking. He was reciting from the terrorist textbook.

"That's correct, Mr. Reilly," Superintendent General Yamato said, overhearing him. "One in the elevator shaft to drive people to the stairwells. Another in the northeast stairwell—maybe more."

"Damn them to hell," Reilly exclaimed through a heavy cough. "Got another mask?"

Norte stepped across the rubble and retrieved one from a doctor. "Here, but they don't recommend going in further."

Reilly put on the mask and ignored the warning. As he stepped over the downed beams and cement blocks strewn throughout the lobby—or what was left of it—he took in the electrical and chemical fumes and the smell of burnt flesh. More memories.

Everything that could burn burned. Everything that could break broke. Two minutes were enough.

Outside he had more questions. "What do you think? At least five devices?"

"That's our current count," Yamato said. "We're still looking for more that didn't go off, or were timed to detonate late."

"And I think it would be accurate to assume that if the driver of the truck walked away, this wasn't a suicide bombing," Reilly added.

Yamato closed his eyes and nodded. "That's a fair assumption."

"Wouldn't that rule out some of the usual suspects? Al Qaeda? The Taliban? ISIS?"

"That's largely beyond my scope," Yamato said. "But yes, some of these groups like to walk away these days. Remember Paris. Not everyone was there to meet Allah in the moment."

Reilly sighed. Tactics were changing, but hotels remained a soft target with high propaganda value. But that value was only good if a group cashed in on the media coverage, and so far no one had. After twenty-four hours, that seemed highly unusual. It was a thought he kept to himself.

"Anything available to screen from the security cameras or cell phone video?"

"I asked," Collins said. "The security hard drive was destroyed. The hotel doesn't back up to the cloud."

"A second drive?"

"In the lower security office, right next to the loading docks where another bomb exploded. Gone."

"We've got a lot to rethink," Reilly said, putting his hand on Collins' shoulder. "Starting now."

He thanked the Tokyo police chief and exited the building with Collins and the ambassador.

Outside Reilly stepped back and looked up and down the street. "Ambassador—" He stopped to correct himself. "Ruben, what about local area surveillance cams—ATMs, traffic CCTVs?"

"That's a question for the National Police Agency or Naichō, Japan's Intelligence and Research Office. They're the equivalent of our CIA. They're taking the lead. But you'll see a whole other team working in the shadows. They're from The Tokyo Metropolitan Police Department Public Security Bureau. T.M.P.D.P.S.B., the agency responsible for the country's public security. It's unlikely we'll get anything directly from them. Naichō and the National Police Agency will be your best contacts."

"Even more than the Metropolitan Police and Yamato?"

"If it involves foreign influence, yes," the ambassador replied.

"Estimates on the amount of explosives?"

"Wouldn't know and wouldn't know how to measure it. You?"

"Somewhat." Reilly's service as a US Army intelligence officer required weeks of training in explosives. Some of that knowledge showed up in the deck he had prepared for the Senate subcommittee. Now that presentation and testimony seemed light-years away.

Sudden shouts in Japanese from a policeman interrupted his thoughts.

Reilly didn't understand the order, but he certainly read the hand gestures. He grabbed the ambassador's arm.

"Away from the building! Fast!"

Chris Collins got the picture, too. They ran across the street and added even more distance between them and the hotel. Two bomb-sniffing dogs rushed past with their handlers while five men in protective outerwear entered the destroyed lobby.

Reilly saw what he recognized as a black SWAT command center truck the size of a semi on their side of the street. "Wait here," he said.

He went to the truck's center side door and flashed his ID to an officer. Fortunately the Tokyo policeman spoke English and got clearance over his radio to let him enter.

Inside, Reilly introduced himself to the commanding officer. He was told to stand in the back row facing a series of monitors, each fed by remote wireless cameras. He counted eight views. On the main line monitor were images from a roving robot camera that rolled toward an indistinguishable area.

"Where's it going?" Reilly asked the officer.

"The heating plant. The dogs found another device."

A technician in the first row switched another view to the main screen. It showed a POV helmet cam from a member of the bomb squad who slowly crawled forward along the wet floor around the back of a boiler until he came within a foot of a package about the size of a shoe box.

Reilly watched as the bomb squad officer slowly examined the package from the outside. He was careful not to touch it. He heard the man's heavy breathing through the wireless feed.

The officer standing with him translated a portion of the running dialogue.

"From the size of the box and the proximity to the heating plant, he believes the bomb is C-4. Probably under five pounds. He's described the box as wet with the smell that damp cardboard gives off. It's possible that the timer shorted or burned out due to the runoff from the pool."

The bomb squad officer backed away as slowly and as carefully as he had entered.

"He's calling for the robot to X-ray the package. This will take some time. Now everyone has been ordered out of the building," the officer explained.

Fifty-five minutes later, the X-ray had been read. Experts determined that water had indeed short-circuited the device. The bomb squad members retrieved the package. Next it would be up to one or more of the investigatory agencies to look for identifiable markings, fingerprints, or other ways to trace its origin.

Reilly thanked the officer, a captain with the National Police Agency. They exchanged cards, and Reilly asked if he could be kept informed.

The captain simply said, "To the best of my ability."

It was more than he had gotten the day before from Senator Moakley Davidson halfway around the world.

SINGAPORE

The team converged onto Marina Bay in Singapore via circuitous routes. None of them were traveling the same way. Their flights took them from Tokyo to Yokohama, Nagoya, Kyoto, and Osaka, then on to intermediate airports in Malaysia, Thailand, and Hong Kong before arriving at the Conrad Centennial Singapore Hotel.

They traveled under the same passports they used to enter Japan. Now those identities would disappear forever. They would assume other names and wait in different parts of the world for their next orders. They worked for only one man—the driver of the FedEx truck.

That man now stood before them in a fourteenth-floor suite at the hotel in the heart of Singapore's most famous shopping district, where they were conducting a prearranged debriefing. The four men knew to be punctual and obedient. The commander demanded both, and more: silence, loyalty, and their individual special skills in constructing and delivering lethal weapons.

But now it was time to evaluate the operation and trigger their hefty payments. Though he knew each of their names, they didn't know his. He always referred to them by number.

"One?" he asked in English.

"Detonation on time with maximum blast field."

Two spoke less eagerly when prompted. "The device in the heating plant failed to detonate. I assure you, it was wired correctly, sir. I believe humidity or water may have affected the electronics. I'll do my own testing."

The driver glared at Two. "That means the police have the bomb."

"Yes, sir. But rest assured, there are no fingerprints and none of the wiring and components will be traceable."

"Except the box." He bore down on Two. "Are you positive there were no identifying markings?"

Two paused before speaking as authoritatively as possible. "Positive," he replied.

The driver read the expression. Even though he believed the man hadn't fucked up, his hesitation told him he'd make a change in his team. A permanent change.

The other members reviewed their assignments and discussed their exfiltration. No one had been stopped or questioned.

"Well then, it is time for a toast. After that, you will be on your own," he announced.

He went to the refrigerator, removed a bottle of vodka, and poured five glasses. "To success and good health!" he proposed.

"To our success," everyone repeated.

Feeling the pressure on him was over, Two blurted a loyal *"Za ná-shoo dróo-zhboo"*—*To our friendship*. Something he wouldn't be enjoying for very long.

TOKYO

Reilly ignored Collins' objections over what to tell the grieving Japanese families. The last to visit were the widow and two teenage children of the security officer.

"Mrs. Nikaido," he respectfully began through his interpreter, "please accept my heartfelt condolences. Your husband placed his duties above himself with true honor."

Reilly waited for the translator to finish. He'd already told the young woman to convey the tone precisely as he delivered it. Sincerely and compassionately.

"I met Mr. Nikaido only once and have a clear picture of him. He was dedicated to his job, but told me he was looking forward to retirement. It was coming soon."

After the translation he got to the hardest part and went well beyond the lawyer's admonition.

"Mrs. Nikaido, there is an insurance plan that will take care of your family," Reilly said. "I also pledge to see your children through college. Their tuition and expenses will be covered. Mr. Nikaido gave his life. It is the least I can do."

"Mr. Reilly, my husband also spoke well of you," the 54-year-old woman respectfully replied with her eyes lowered. The translator conveyed her sentiment. "'A good man,' he said. I accept your offer in his name."

"Thank you, Mrs. Nikaido," Reilly replied after the translator had finished.

Now she lifted her head and stared directly at Reilly. It was as if a completely different woman had appeared.

"But there is one thing more," she now said in perfect English.

Reilly tilted his head.

"Ah, you are surprised?" she asked.

"I'm surprised by your English."

"Mr. Reilly, I am not the simple accepting wife. And by coming here, you are more than I would have expected."

As he looked at her, he saw something more powerful than the sadness he heard.

"Therefore you can do more," she continued.

"What?" Reilly asked.

"Find the people who killed my husband. Find them and make them pay."

The look was unmistakable. Hatred.

* * *

Reilly set up temporary headquarters at the Dai-ichi Hotel Annex, a comfortable local business hotel. Joining him for meetings were his colleagues Chris Collins and Alan Cannon. The head of security had arrived on the morning flight.

"Dan, Chris. What's the latest?" Cannon said as soon as he stepped inside the suite. He didn't use the word *count*, but that's what he meant.

"Three more souls overnight," Reilly replied. "Naichō took over. They pulled the computers from the two security offices. They're working on recovering data, if possible, from the hard drives now."

"I've got a contact inside. I'll call," Cannon said. "What else?"

"Take a breath, Alan. How about some coffee and a muffin?" Collins offered.

"Sure. I guess I came in like a bat out of hell."

"Rolling thunder. Sit down, we'll walk you through what we have."

As they sat around a low coffee table, Reilly and Collins reviewed the information they'd culled.

"We have the names of everyone who was checked in at the time of the attack," Reilly began.

"What about people who left up to seventy-two hours before?" Cannon asked.

"Working on them."

"Good. I'd recommend even earlier. If there was a surveillance run, it might even go back two or three weeks."

"I'll let Chicago know," Collins replied.

"And then I'll start running all the names through HSI," Cannon said, referring to Homeland Security Investigations. "I'll also hit up the bureau. I'm sure Naichō will be doing the same. They'll cross-check with Interpol and all of their sources. What else?"

"We're looking at the conventions and VIPs in the hotel," said Reilly.

"Any likely targets?"

Reilly intoned a *no*. "A Rolex watch club convention, mostly Texas buyers. A Hollywood production company on a film survey. A doctor's convention. Some Romanian folk singer and his entourage. Nothing relatable. Could have the same kind of mix at any major hotel in the city."

"Details on the explosives?" Cannon asked.

"It's only an estimate, but something like 1,300 to 1,600 pounds in the truck, which they just determined was painted to look like a FedEx delivery vehicle. Don't know much about the bombs inside."

"American casualties?"

"Serious injuries, no deaths," said Reilly.

"But the issue of hotel liability can impact the entire Kensington chain of hotels," Collins added. "It's our image."

"Any lapses in security?" Cannon asked.

"The obvious," Reilly sighed. "I think we were very vulnerable. I tap-danced around it at the hearing, but Alan, we've got serious problems.

Not just here."

"That's only for this room, Dan," Collins interrupted. "Never ever admit—"

"Chris, enough! This is the first we've been hit, but not the first time for the industry. It's time for serious and fast improvements."

"You know what I mean," Collins warned.

"I do. But we're reactive, limited, and only equipped to patch up afterwards. That can't cut it anymore."

"Agreed," Cannon said. "What are you thinking?"

"We start by addressing our weaknesses," Reilly replied.

"Starting where?"

"Here." Reilly took a deep breath. "Here and everywhere."

He pulled a list that he'd drawn up earlier from his sport coat. "There were no barriers and limited street surveillance," Reilly said. "Also, the plant facilities were accessible to guests, and there were inadequate locks. Hell, we might as well have given them an engraved invitation."

"Jesus Christ," Collins said. He was beginning to get a true sense of the bigger problem.

"What's scarier," Reilly continued, "is that Tokyo isn't the only place we're negligent."

"Another word, Dan," the attorney stated.

"Careless."

"Try loose."

"Okay, loose. And as I said, not just here in Tokyo. I had Brenda poll other regional presidents." He bit his lower lip. "We've got big holes in our security."

"Better surveillance would have been easy to add," Collins complained. "Wouldn't have taken much."

Cannon now studied Reilly's list. "You're absolutely right. We've had upgrades, but not enough. We haven't turned it into a global initiative."

"None of us have, Alan," Reilly agreed. "So we get to it now. Any news from your security contacts?"

"Well, coming from a geopolitical perspective, this doesn't have any apparent signatures."

"How can you tell?" Collins asked.

"Fundamentalist terrorists are getting more coordinated, but want publicity," Cannon explained. "They market terror. It elevates them. Gets them followers and cash."

"So what are you saying?" Collins asked. "No one's come out publicly yet?"

"Nope."

"To my thinking, that rules out ISIS or radical Islamists."

"Just like that?" the lawyer countered.

"Just like that. But if you'd prefer, put them lower on the list."

Reilly had the next question. "Who's higher?"

"I have no idea."

* * *

Four days later, Alan Cannon's words still swirled around Reilly's head. *I have no idea.* The response stayed with him through his stay in Tokyo. Now it kept him awake on his return to Chicago.

I have no idea. If the usual suspects weren't responsible, then who? he wondered.

Reilly knew that Cannon would surely work his sources, inside and out, but he decided to tap one of his own as well.

During his career, Dan Reilly had spent a significant amount of time flying around the world to Kensington's properties, meeting with general managers, nurturing relationships, and developing prospects, negotiating, and launching new opportunities. Long ago he adopted author John le Carré's philosophy, "A desk is a dangerous place from which to view the world."

He was reaching the seven million mark as a frequent flier, which kept him frequently away, and a very poor partner. His marriage to Pam, the human resources director for a Washington law firm, lasted less time than their courting. Four years of excitement, meeting in international capitals, three years of waiting for him to come home from his travels, and eighteen months since with off and on regrets.

Though he had been a failure in marriage, Dan Reilly was successful in business, a likely candidate for president stripes at some corporation. He believed in working foreign relationships as much as company friendships, understanding and showing respect for local traditions and customs, and keeping a dynamic list of go-to people on speed dial.

Due back in Congress in a few weeks for a second Senate Committee appearance, he vowed to testify about the borderless business world he inhabited, where successful deals were made as often over the dinner table as in the boardroom. He reinforced it among staffers at meetings by awarding them crisp twenty-dollar bills every time they used the word *global*. One day he had to call a time-out because it was costing so much.

Today he oversaw properties in every continent except Antarctica. And in every business encounter, he tried to keep in mind the other person's interests and needs. Most of all, Dan Reilly was a big believer in ditching the desk.

All of this had worked up until now. But on the flight back to the states, he thought he fully comprehended the paradigm shift that was taking place in his world, the global change that faced him.

Yes, global, he thought as he took out a twenty from his wallet. *Soft targets made hard news.*

4

CHICAGO, IL

Dan Reilly had a large, northeastern corner suite in the twenty-one-story Kensington Royal building. He had a great view of Lake Michigan from one window and downtown Chicago from the other. Overall, he felt that the structure was conservative but striking—a combination of glass and cement, with the glass artistically reflecting the lake and the cement imbuing the headquarters with gravitas.

His office on the nineteenth floor reminded him he still had room to grow in the company. As open as upper management was, he still needed an appointment for the twentieth and twenty-first floors. That was about the only indication of command structure at KR.

With the title Senior VP of International he worked with the team, but reported to Edward Shaw, the corporation's venerable founder and partner. Considering there was no president of International, that title and commensurate salary were available unless he seriously fucked things up. He thought this was one of those times where he very well could. More important than the job, the cost of failure might mean more lives.

Returning to his office, he was instantly welcomed by Brenda.

"Glad to see you," she said warmly.

"Good to be back. It was—"

"You don't have to say. Just relax. I'll get you coffee and fill you in."

Reilly went to his desk, sat down, and swirled in his chair. Sailboats dotted the lake, tacking into the offshore wind. Water-skiers jumped the two-foot waves. It was a world apart from what he'd seen in Tokyo.

"Here you go," Brenda said. She handed him his black Colombian coffee and sat across from him, putting her notes on his desk.

Brenda Sheldon had worked with Reilly from his first day. She was as loyal as the day was long. And, given his travel and the time zone differences, her days as his executive assistant were *very* long.

She was married to a Chicago cop who Reilly figured was either extremely understanding or loved night shifts himself. Though not required, Brenda always wore a dress, usually blue or teal. The color accentuated her dyed red hair and light complexion. She was in her mid-fifties, the mother of twin girls just out of college, and as much a rock at home as she was for Reilly.

Brenda was due for a vacation in August, but she had already warned her husband that it might have to be postponed. The one-word explanation sufficed: "Tokyo."

"So who's knocking on the door today?" Reilly asked.

"Mr. Shaw. Twenty-one in fifteen," she stated. That meant the twenty-first floor in fifteen minutes.

"Good. Thanks for scheduling me so fast."

"Of course. Also, June has TV requests. She's willing to grant you a few no's, but she wants a yes or two as a follow-up to your quote."

Reilly had released a quote vetted by Chris Collins' legal department. It was less than he wanted to say and more than Collins preferred. He spoke about the company's commitment to helping the families of the victims through the crisis, including transportation and accommodations, financial aid to those in need, and the promise to work with law enforcement authorities in Japan.

Reilly looked at the list.

"No, no, no, no, no, and no," he said.

"You're doing CNN," Brenda said. "That's not negotiable. June already figured you'd pass on the others."

"Oh my God, what can they be thinking?" He read the list aloud. "Discovery Channel's *10 Most Dangerous Places to Visit*, History Channel's *Hidden Hotel Secrets*, and Travel Channel's *Hotel Horror Stories*! There's really a show called *Hotel Horror Stories*? Do these people have any idea what just transpired?" Reilly asked rhetorically.

"Reality TV," she responded.

"Reality?" he scoffed. "Give me a break!"

Brenda reviewed four other press requests, each earning an immediate no.

"You look beat," she said, maneuvering away from the business at hand.

"Just down," Reilly replied. "It was a draining trip."

Brenda knew enough not to try to console Reilly.

"Do you think you'll get to the bottom of this?" she asked.

"Hope so." He stopped and rethought his answer. "Hell, to be honest, I don't know. We're targets, but we're not players. Somehow we have to up our game."

"What can I do to help?" Brenda asked, thoughtful as ever.

"Keep my calendar clear and stay by your phone. I'm mulling something, but it's going to take a lot of coordination and money."

"I expect the coordination will come from you," she said. "And the money?"

Reilly sipped his coffee, stood, and pointed to the ceiling.

"Like you said, twenty-one in fifteen. Now ten. It's time to hit the bank."

* * *

Reilly bounded up the stairs to Edward Shaw's executive floor—two flights in twenty seconds. He opened the glass door to the president's suite and was greeted by Nancy Barney, Shaw's longtime secretary. She was efficient, proper, and always wearing bright colors to match her mood. Her gray hair was by choice, but her smooth, youthful skin belied her age.

"Dan!" she exclaimed. "Welcome back." She saw the same tiredness that Brenda had, but didn't comment.

"Thanks, Nance. How's everything?"

"As good as can be expected."

"You've got that right. Is Edward ready?"

First name basis was acceptable to Shaw. In fact, preferred. But depending upon the news or the sense of urgency, Reilly defaulted to "sir."

"Yes, he's expecting you. Give me a sec."

She hit the intercom button on her phone and spoke into her headset. A moment later she cleared him to enter.

Edward Jefferson Shaw was standing with his hand out for Reilly. He was two inches shy of six feet, wearing a black sweater-vest and white shirt with a red tie and black slacks. He had a full head of hair and a robust, open face. Though he was as shrewd as any CEO, he also retained the business ethic that was the foundation of Kensington Royal. *Everything mattered and everyone mattered.* It fit the company decades ago when he had ten employees and one food delivery truck in downtown Chicago. It defined the corporation as a Fortune 500 business today.

Shaw had long ago given Reilly virtual carte blanche, recognizing that he couldn't keep his international executive grounded. He had hired Dan Reilly from the ranks of the State Department, where he had worked after he retired from the army. Shaw needed an executive with a global view. What Reilly didn't know about the hospitality industry he'd learn, and what he understood about the world was exactly what Kensington Royal needed to expand.

"Edward, good to see you."

"Likewise, my boy." Edward Shaw was twenty-five years older so Reilly didn't mind the term. It was another endearing part of his boss's personality.

"Let's go over to the couch. Have you had coffee yet?" Shaw asked.

"Just a quick sip. I could use more."

Shaw laughed. "I'm sure you could." He poured a cup from a silver pot in the seating area. "Here you go."

Once they were sitting, Reilly brought Shaw up to date as best he could. So far no organization had claimed responsibility for the attack. A few people were able to leave the hospital. Another died. In short, nothing he hadn't heard from Alan Cannon.

"I know you want to stay connected to this tragedy," Shaw began, "but you'll have to move on, my boy. There's a lot of work that—"

Reilly rarely interrupted his boss, but now he interjected, "Sir—"

"Dan," Shaw stopped him. "It'll help take your mind off the tragedy. Alan can stay with the investigation. Lord knows Chris will keep legal buttoned down. Right now I need you elsewhere."

This wasn't what Reilly wanted to hear. He closed his eyes for two seconds to clear his thoughts and took a deep breath, deciding what to say.

But before he could, Shaw continued. "There are three immediate challenges. Opening up discussions with Tehran and Russia, and tracking that damned hurricane. Have you heard?"

Reilly hadn't, so Shaw explained, finishing with, "So that's where you need to focus."

"Of course, I'll work on those areas," Reilly began. "But I can't let Tokyo go."

"Not completely," Shaw conceded. "I wouldn't ask you to do that. I want you to oversee the rebuilding."

"It's beyond rebuilding. It's rethinking our whole approach to security. We were an open, easy, vulnerable target. There were lapses. Ones we can learn from."

"We're not a security organization, Dan. You said as much in Washington."

"Sir, we need to take the long view. If you'll allow me an extended metaphor?"

"Do I have a choice?"

"Well, I'd prefer you not put it that way," Reilly said.

"Go on. You've had a hard time. The pulpit is yours."

"The best example I can think of is Henry Ford. His road to the top began when he doubled his workers' pay to $5.00 a day so they'd be able to afford the product they were manufacturing. At that same time he trimmed the cost of his Motel T from $850 to $290. Win-win for his assembly-line workers and the nation's economy. As a result, the Model Ts rolled off the lots—fifteen million of them. But something else happened. Something we can't let happen to us."

"What was that?" Shaw asked.

"Hubris. Ford started pontificating on things he knew nothing about. History. Politics. Right down to the customers' tastes. He dismissed the notion that people might want a Model T in a color other than the black he manufactured."

"Are you suggesting hubris in this office, Daniel?"

"I'm saying we can't afford to let it happen. Look, there's a lesson here. What Ford wouldn't consider, Chevrolet did. And in addition to color, they made accommodations for customers who were short on cash. Enter the General Motors Acceptance Corporation. They facilitated loans by becoming the bank."

"And?" Shaw pressed.

"And Henry Ford's salespeople tried to alert him to GM's practices and the threat to their business. One chief executive, a member of the inner circle and extended Ford family, was so concerned he cautioned Ford in a letter. Ford responded by firing him. Model T sales subsequently tanked. Hubris, sir. Henry Ford failed to be open to changes he didn't understand, to listen to views other than his own. We can't afford to make mistakes like that."

Holding Shaw's attention, Reilly doubled down. "Sir, you know as well as I do that according to market research, customer safety is number one."

"Yes, the corporation—"

"Beyond the corporation, it has to be number one in our minds, too. As responsible people."

"You better not be suggesting that I don't care!"

"Of course not. But if we don't visibly act now in the interest of safety and security, if we don't seize this moment, from a business standpoint we risk losing our position of leadership and devaluing our brand. But an even greater risk? This could very well happen again, and we have to work toward preventing it through every means we can. People put their trust in us. Let me help."

The company founder settled back into his dark brown Westminster leather chair without speaking. He folded his hands. This was his thinking time.

Reilly eased back in the couch to wait.

After thirty seconds, Shaw huskily cleared his voice and said, "Go on." It was neither an affirmation nor a dismissal, but a sign that he was forming a position.

"My testimony to the Senate was to officially get what we're only hearing very unofficially. And because of our limited information, we have little to act on. But we're not alone. Virtually the entire industry suffers from the same problem. *We* have to change our approach."

"And do what?" This was Shaw at his sharpest.

"Research, prepare, and implement."

"Implement what?"

"I'll be able to tell you that after our research," Reilly promised. "But a way to protect our properties."

"This isn't what we do."

"No?" Reilly now risked arguing with his boss. "You've seen what's happened at Middle Eastern and African sea resorts. After attacks they've had to slash their prices. But who wants to go get shot up even at bargain prices? Terrorists are trying to kill Germans in bikinis. They want to destabilize the economy and make people lose faith in the government. Kill tourism and you give birth to radical ideologies."

"Cannon says that may not be the case in Tokyo."

"But it could be in many other cities. And if we build in Tehran . . ." Reilly trailed off, allowing the implication to speak for itself.

Shaw rose and walked over to the large window behind his desk. He looked out onto Lake Michigan as Reilly had earlier. Answers always seemed to be out the window.

"And this plan of yours?"

"Not formed yet, but yes, a security plan," Reilly said.

"This security plan will be a game changer for us. You might be putting a big fat target on the front of every one of our properties."

"Or preventing them from actually becoming a target if we look harder to penetrate."

Shaw turned back to the room. His voice was serious and steady when he said, "So when do we do whatever this is that you want to do?"

"Now. Today."

"Chris will balk."

"I'll handle him."

"No, you'll include him. And Alan will have to be involved."

"Absolutely. Alan's essential."

"If I agree, what do you need to get started?"

Reilly smiled. "Money. A lot of money."

MOSCOW

Sergei Kozlov loosened his tie, opened his collar, and removed his suit coat, draping it over his arm. It was unseasonably warm and humid for Moscow, and the air-conditioning in the Kremlin couldn't keep up with the need.

Kozlov wished he had time to stop at home and shower before seeing his mistress. It had been a long, hot day of conferences for the outspoken minister of commerce. Positions to defend, reports to make, critics to crush . . . But his urge to fuck was greater than his desire to refresh, so he told his driver waiting at the ministry carport to head directly to Ivana's apartment.

The Russian bureaucrat relaxed into the backseat of the sleek black ZiL limousine dispatched from the Kremlin fleet. It wasn't his usual car. When Kozlov asked about the change, the chauffeur explained that he had been assigned a different vehicle for the afternoon, a more comfortable upgrade to try out. The limo had a Rolls-Royce-inspired design with a unique swept-back look, one of the new generation of ZiLs that Nikolai Gorshkov had ordered into service.

The minister relaxed for the first time in hours. Much of the day's sessions had focused on Belarus's trade dispute with Russia. Kozlov was the face of the Russian trade position and Gorshkov's designated attack dog against the Belarusian president, a rogue dictator in his own right. Trade agreements were at the root of the dispute, which grew with every report in *Izvestia,* on the Russian side, and the *Belarus News,* which obediently covered the Belarusian despot. It had been a tense day with terse threats and counter threats that were leaked to Russia's press before the meeting had concluded.

Sergei Kozlov was the perfect front man, brusque and crude, a bully on a bully's team. He was careful never to challenge Gorshkov directly, but at the same time, he never wanted to appear weak in the eyes of the president. So he used his bluster when and where it was needed and according to his instructions.

Soon he would be in his lover's arms. He drifted into a light haze, fantasizing about the ways she would please him as they drove onto the Khoroshevsky Bridge over the Moskva River Shortcut. Lost in anticipation and at ease in the new limo, Kozlov didn't hear the sound of an SUV downshifting next to them. He also didn't hear his driver curse as the vehicle began to crowd them. But he did hear the car horn.

"What's up?" he complained.

His driver took one hand off the steering wheel and pointed to the car on their left. Kozlov looked over just as the darkened right rear window of the SUV rolled down and a man wearing a ski mask raised a Saiga-12 shotgun. Before Kozlov could comprehend what was happening, the assassin fired. Kozlov was the first to die. Then the driver. Neither had time to question why the car they were assigned that day didn't have bulletproof glass.

CHICAGO

"Bullshit!" Chris Collins exclaimed.

Livid at Reilly's proposal, the Kensington Royal attorney jumped to his feet. "It's not our job. Show me where our business plan says we're in the anti-terrorism profession! Jesus, Dan, I know you like being in the field, but who appointed you field general?"

This was the meeting Shaw had instructed Reilly to call. Reilly, Cannon, and Collins were in neutral territory—one of the smaller conference rooms on the sixteenth floor of the KR building. Reilly sat at the table, remaining perfectly calm. Alan Cannon did the same. It would take composed, thoughtful discussion, and both men knew Collins would quiet down and ultimately listen to reason. Ultimately, but not yet.

"It's not like that, Chris. So take a breath." Reilly wished he hadn't added the last comment.

"You take a breath!" Collins retorted. "You know how many lawsuits I'll probably have on my desk after Tokyo? Any idea how deep into international law I'll be diving? The cost of outside counsel, depositions, settlements? And now you want to make us more of a target?"

"We're already a target, Chris. Tokyo proves that. So I'm proposing we make it harder for anyone to consider us a good one."

"What, with mercenaries and AK-47s? Paramilitary forces? That'll be just great for the stock." Collins was agitated now, and had begun sweating. He rolled his chair under one of the AC vents. It served to cool off his rant.

"Look, soon we'll be the largest hotel chain going, right?" Reilly asked.

"And?" was all that Collins offered to the known fact.

"Well, that makes us a leader. Leaders lead. And we are going to take the lead on this." It was a declarative statement.

"You're right about one thing," Reilly added. "It's not in our business plan, but going forward it must be a key part of our business strategy. We can do it quietly and internally and hopefully not draw a lot of attention in the process."

The back-and-forth moved into Alan Cannon's expertise and responsibility. "Actually, we do want some public attention," the head of security stated. "Some defensive measures should be visible to the people who count."

"And who's that?" Collins asked.

"The bad guys."

OUTSIDE OF MOSCOW

Acting on an anonymous tip, Moscow police and the FSB tracked down the SUV to Shchyolkovo, twenty kilometers north of Moscow. Minutes later they narrowed the search to a block of brownstones. Years earlier it had been home to a conclave of Belarusians, a key element that led authorities to believe that Belarus operatives could be behind Kozlov's assassination an hour earlier. If so, Gorshkov would certainly put the blame squarely in the hands of the Belarusian president.

The FSB searched buildings one by one as police closed off the area. They moved quickly, focusing on one residence mid-block. Seemingly out of nowhere, twenty heavily armed Spetsnaz officers, each with Izhmash AN-94 assault rifles, tore out of black SUVs and hit the building. Firing at a rate of up to six hundred rounds per minute, they secured the first floor killing two, rushed the second floor taking out three, and then took out four more on the top floor.

The assault was perfectly executed in under ninety seconds. There were no survivors.

Within minutes, Russian media had details on the mission, which was considered completely successful by all counts. The stories were accompanied by commentary on the worsening relationship between Russia and Belarus. The killing of the minister of commerce was seen as a provocation that might require a response.

The long game, not mentioned in the discussion, was the fact that Belarus was on the western border of Russia and a gateway to its other former Soviet satellite nations. It was one of many countries that Gorshkov wanted fully back under Russia's thumb and well outside NATO's grasp.

CHICAGO

"Okay, so what do you propose?" Collins asked.

"A phased plan," Reilly explained. "First, we set up a committee of experts. They listen to our concerns, identify the major challenges, and together—and I said together—we come up with a prioritized program."

"It'll cost," barked the lawyer.

"I've got the seed money covered."

"From your budget?" Cannon asked. "I sure don't have it in mine."

Reilly pointed a finger upwards.

"Shaw approved this?" Collins asked incredulously.

"I wouldn't be talking to you now if he hadn't."

"I hope you know you're a real shit," Collins said finally, laughing.

Reilly took it as a compliment and laughed as well. "Been one for years. But I promised Shaw I wouldn't move forward without you both onboard."

"Kiss ass," Collins said.

"Consensus builder," Reilly replied.

"Well, I'm in," Alan Cannon said. "I have some ideas for potential committee members. It may take time to coordinate schedules, but we can do it."

"I've got a few suggestions, too," Reilly replied. However, he still needed one more member of the management to agree. He opened his hands wide, encouraging a decision from Chris Collins.

The head of legal sat down, grabbed a yellow pad from the center of the conference table, and simply said, "Let's get to work."

Reilly was more than ready. "Thank you," he said, pulling multiple copies of a report from his briefcase. "We can start with some basic research courtesy of the State Department. It's worth looking at. Nothing classified, but eye-opening."

He distributed the printouts.

"Every day, the State Department evaluates threats to US interests around the world."

"Heard your testimony," Collins said.

"Yes, but that barely scratched the surface. They cover Asia, the Middle East, Africa, Europe, South America, Mexico, and here at home. I suppose they also track Antarctica, but there's nothing to report from down there. But I've dug a little deeper. I've got a white paper on the kinds of threats terrorists could unleash on an American city, well beyond a lone wolf with a gun, which we've seen far too many times."

Reilly prompted them to turn to page seven.

"Holy shit," Chris Collins exclaimed while reading ahead. "Everything from a ten-kiloton nuclear device to an aerosol anthrax attack. Jesus! All of this is possible?"

"Possible enough for us to get smarter," Reilly said. "Keep reading."

The study chronicled widespread casualties caused by a pandemic influenza attack, a chlorine tank explosion, and the release of chemical and biological nerve agents, with deaths in the hundreds of thousands.

To Reilly's point of view, there was little Kensington Royal could do to prevent such a massive attack. But they could do more to defend against a bold, hyperlocal, scalable attack on a hotel.

He found support for his plan deeper in the State Department report: Scenario 12.

"This is what we have to protect against. Terrorists hit a property with LVBs, large vehicle bombs. In addition, they have time-delayed IEDs, improvised explosive devices, set to go off in the escape routes. Sound familiar?"

"Completely," Collins admitted.

"It's all here, perfectly describing the attack in Tokyo. The first detonation is designed to create fire, smoke, and havoc. The building might be structurally damaged, but people survive and flow into the common areas and exits. Then the next wave is timed for when the first responders arrive."

"So what can we do?" Chris Collins asked.

"Whatever we need to do. Sophisticated crisis forecasting, management and staff retraining, and on a physical basis, heighted surveillance measures and the installation of defensive parameters. Altogether, it means we're going to rewrite our security plan starting today!"

5

NOVOSIBIRSK, RUSSIAN FEDERATION

1994

After the fall of the Berlin Wall and the collapse of Communist rule in the German Democratic Republic, Nikolai Gorshkov publicly resigned from the KGB. Publicly, but not officially. Soon after, he was recalled to Russia and assigned to Novosibirsk, the third largest city in Russia and the most populated city in the Asian region of Russia. He moved his wife and two children in with his parents and accepted a post in Novosibirsk State University's sociology department. At least this was his latest cover story. He reported to the university vice rector and also to Moscow, recruiting moles and spying on students. In his own words he was "a KGB officer under the roof." The university post also allowed him to study his internal enemies' weaknesses and test his political future. It paid off.

A year later, he left the KGB to work with Russia's new wave of democratic reformers. This brought him closer to the power base in the waning years of the Soviet government. He accepted a new job, Deputy Mayor of Novosibirsk, serving in the administration of the first openly elected mayor in the city.

During his term, Gorshkov intervened for the mayor with political rivals in the legislature. Through his efforts, he earned more political currency in the reconstructed Russia.

He cashed some in after the dissolution of the Soviet Union on December 26, 1991. Gorshkov headed a committee to bring new businesses to Novosibirsk. Situated in south central Russia on the banks of the Ob River, near the Novosibirsk Hydro Power Plant, he saw opportunity to attract, spend, and make money. Accordingly, Nikolai Gorshkov worked all sides of his deals for years.

By 1994 he had accumulated immense wealth and power. This allowed him to have a public persona, but he also continued to lurk in the shadows. That's where he always chose to meet and conspire with his former KGB lieutenant, Andre Miklos.

The five years since Miklos had worked under Gorshkov in Potsdam had hardened the young man. He had been assigned "liquid affairs" by the KGB and its short-lived successor the Federal Counterintelligence Service, FSK. His specific duties, keyed to his unique skills and training, included abductions and assassinations, all under the directive to clean up squishy internal loose ends.

Gorshkov and Miklos now met on one of those loose ends, though not for the state. They discussed a personal mission.

"Do you foresee any difficulty?" Gorshkov asked in the basement of a warehouse outside of the city.

Through his contacts, Gorshkov had access to such places; secure and guarded. But still, he never met his protégé twice in the same place, and never with anyone else around.

"None," Miklos responded. "It will be a terrible accident. But in those last moments he will recognize me and think of you before he dies. He'll remember Potsdam. But he won't have time to apologize to his wife and family. No time even for a last prayer. Only a terrified instant for guilt and regret. I'll see it on his face."

Neither man mentioned the name. It had been ingrained in their minds for five years: *Stanislav Popov*.

6

TOKYO, JAPAN

PRESENT DAY

A week after meeting in Chicago, Alan Cannon returned to Tokyo on the invitation from his Naichō contact, Genji Takahiro.

From the airport, Cannon proceeded directly to Naichō headquarters on the sixth floor of the cabinet office building. The intelligence agency, Japan's equivalent of America's CIA, was still smarting from ongoing political scrutiny.

In January 2008 a Naichō official had been accused of spying for the Russians. Though the Kremlin denied the charge, Genji Takahiro and others who had public faces took great care with what they said.

Takahiro wore a light grey suit that hung loosely to cover the handgun on his belt. He delivered his greeting warmly, but with little inflection. The 52-year-old agent offered to unofficially cooperate with Cannon. However, because of the 2008 scandal, Cannon figured he'd get some information, but not everything. *Still,* he thought, *Takahiro had invited him.*

"I have something for you to see," Takahiro said. "Come with me."

This was already more than Cannon expected.

Takahiro walked the American to a standalone computer in a small room. Cannon observed that the desktop was not tied into Naichō's mainframe. This would prevent anyone who used it from "inadvertently" uploading any content or downloading any viruses.

"Everything you need to see is on this USB drive," Takahiro said. "Please sit."

Takahiro leaned over and inserted the thumb drive. The contents were password protected, requiring Japanese characters to open. He typed them in, then pointed to a freeze-frame now on the screen.

"We've reviewed more than fifty CCTV cameras in the surrounding streets. They include cameras from the Metro police, businesses, ATMs, and others." He didn't explain what *others* meant. "We put the footage together into a video, which I have for you to watch."

"What will be I looking for?"

"The same thing that prompted my call to you."

"Mr. Takahiro," Alan Cannon began, "we're both busy and considering the urgency—"

"Please. I need your opinion."

"On what?"

Takahiro struggled for the English word. "A . . . hunch."

There were roughly twenty minutes of city surveillance footage on the thumb drive. Cannon gave it one full screening, starting, stopping, and logging each shot on paper with the visible running time code and a description. This pass took sixty minutes. When he finished, he looked at his list and rated the shots: wide, medium, close; sharp to blurry; bright to dark. Overall, Cannon recognized that Takahiro wanted him to get familiar with the geography and the character of the streets immediately after the attack.

Cannon turned around to speak to Takahiro, but he was gone. So instead he addressed himself to the computer screen. "All right. Talk to me." He began a second pass, this time watching more closely and disregarding shots that, to his mind, revealed nothing. He also looked for people who appeared in multiple camera views. This took another forty-five minutes.

Cannon stood up and stretched. Takahiro had returned with a cup of coffee.

"I thought you might need this," he said.

Cannon looked at the cup. The hot liquid was light brown. Takahiro then handed him precisely one sugar.

"Thank you. You know what I like."

"Of course. We're in the intelligence business."

It was both humorous and a reminder that Naichō had eyes and ears around the world.

"Any opinions?" Takahiro asked.

"Not yet. Still due diligence."

Cannon got back to screening. The third pass was more strategic. He found the computer icon for the snipping tool function and made some still frames, which he saved on the desktop. After finishing this process he examined key frames, deleting all but three: one wide from a street corner Metropolitan Police camera, another from an Instagram posting by someone running away from the scene, and a third from a street-facing store security camera. They all covered the same area at one minute and forty-three seconds following the first blast.

What was most noteworthy, seen through his own well-trained eyes, was that everyone was running away as quickly as possible. Everyone but one man.

7

"Where are we today?" Reilly asked. He had tasked Brenda Sheldon with scheduling the experts they had chosen for the new Kensington Royal defense committee.

"Like herding cats," she explained. "We had solid dates on the calendar at the end of the month. Okay for you, Alan and Chris, and almost everyone else locked. But in the last three hours it's fallen apart."

"Ask different candidates then. I don't want time to get away from us without getting together," Reilly replied.

"I don't think we have to start from scratch. Maybe some encouragement from you," Brenda proposed. "You're persuasive. Turn up the juice."

"You're right. Line 'em up."

"Will do. In the meantime, you're going to want call Raul Bustamante. He's nervous about the hurricane."

"I've been following it. Looks bad."

Brenda knew Reilly well enough to be prepared. "Your travel suitcase is in your closet complete with a charged sat phone. A new tube of toothpaste, too."

"Always one step ahead."

"It keeps my kids clothed and well fed."

"Then get me Bustamante and book me a flight."

"Oh, that's already done. You're out at four this afternoon, connecting in Mexico City, and I have a private jet as a backup in Mexico in case the Delta flight is canceled."

Reilly looked at his watch and calculated he only had two hours to make calls from his office. He could do more on the ride to O'Hare.

Brenda had Raul Bustamante on the phone from Mazatlán by the time Reilly reached his desk.

The call with the Kensington Royal hotel general manager confirmed the danger and underscored the need for Reilly to make the flight. Mazatlán was an important property. But more to the point, there were more than 150 American guests who had probably never endured a Category 4 or 5 hurricane.

Reilly made four more calls to the counterterrorism experts they'd identified as consultants. Two fell out completely and needed to be replaced. Another good prospect, an independent international security agent, a mercenary, wanted more money and was using the calendar as a bargaining chip. He solved the problem with the mercenary the fastest way possible—with more money.

"Okay, I'm out of here, Brenda," he said, suitcase in hand and a leather backpack over his shoulder. "Car?"

"Downstairs waiting," she said. "With a turkey sandwich."

"Thank you. I love you."

"Sure you do," Brenda said jokingly. "Just be careful."

8

THE ITALIAN ALPS

1994

Stanislav Popov and his wife had intended it as their last big drive before the twins, Nadia and Elina, left for school. In three weeks the girls were to begin international studies at Lomonosov Moscow State University. With this road trip, they could check off their thirteenth annual thrilling mountain ride, one for each year since the children were four. The girls had wonderful memories of these summer vacations, with photo albums chronicling every one.

They got an early start as planned—early enough to avoid the traffic and enjoy the hairpin turns along Torri di Fraele Pass, a full 1,941 meters (or 6,368 feet) above sea level.

The fully paved road began a few kilometers west of Bormio, Italy, led up from Premadio, and progressed through two tunnels carved into the edge of the Italian Alps, along a river, and past a dam. All beautiful.

At its highest point, one could stop to take photographs of the Towers of Fraele, two Roman stone outposts constructed in 1391 to guard a frontier pass. It was the site of a 1635 battle where two thousand warriors were killed. Seventy years ago the structure had served as a World War II communication base. The vista also took in the majestic mountains of Lombardy, Fraise Lake, and snowcapped peaks stretching in every direction. But most people braved the 25.9 kilometer drive to experience the thrill of driving one of Europe's most dangerous roads.

The family reached the summit at 8:15 a.m. They took pictures and picnicked on bruschetta, mascarpone, and pears bought that morning in Bormio. After one last family photograph, it was time to head down—a little faster and a little more confidently—along Torri di Fraele Pass and its eighteen hairpin turns.

In most places the road was barely wider than a single car. Guardrails periodically appeared, particularly at the switchbacks, but they were only two feet high and really there to show where the road stopped and open air began. Bicycles and impatient drivers made it even more dangerous. One of the latter was on the family's tail now.

Stanislav Popov saw the Nuova BMW X1 catch up to them. He noted that it accelerated to within two car lengths—two car lengths too close. It hung close for two kilometers, and then, when the road widened, began to pass. But instead of completing the maneuver, the driver stayed parallel.

Stanislav stuck his left hand out the window and waved the driver ahead. There was room to pass. But the BMW stayed with him. Stanislav honked and motioned again. The driver held his position. Stanislav slowed down, and the BMW did the same.

Stanislav swore. His wife gripped his thigh and his daughter Elina in the seat behind him raised her camera.

Ahead, the next critical turn. Stanislav Popov honked hard again, yelling *"Spostare stronzo!"* in acceptable Italian. "Move asshole!" Then he took his eyes off the road, and in that single moment he saw a cruel smile on the driver's face. A familiar face? His mind raced. *KGB? Yes. Moscow? No. Where?* All this in two seconds. Then a memory. *Germany. German Democratic Republic. Potsdam.* Gorshkov's man.

Stanislav didn't hear his wife's scream or feel her fingernails digging into his leg. He didn't hear his daughter Nadia's cries or the clicking of Elina's camera. And he didn't have room to maneuver his rented Fiat when the larger, heavier BMW nudged his car to the right.

There was no shoulder to pull off onto. No room to stop before the turn ahead. No time to do anything other than to tell his family he was sorry.

Elina Popov was still taking pictures on her Minolta when the car launched from Torri di Fraele Pass at the 1,550 meter mark.

9

BEIJING, CHINA

PRESENT DAY

The Russian delegation was in its third day of meetings hosted by the Shanghai Cooperation Organization. At the top of the agenda was reinforcing Russia's intentions to support the partner trade nations, comprised of China, Russia, Kazakhstan, Kyrgyzstan, and Tajikistan. The group was formed to mediate border disputes, but more recently sought to fight ethnic and religious insurgents.

Anton Nechayev, the minister of energy for Russia, represented Moscow's interests. Across the bargaining table, the Chinese delegation was led by Minister of the National Energy Administration (NEA) Lee Kang. Nechayev maintained an air of bravado and urgency in the official sessions. He carried the same impolitic tone later through dinner conversations at Da Dong, one of Beijing's famed five-star restaurants. For Russia, it was all business, all the time.

Nechayev was in his forties and in some ways resembled a fast-talking Wall Street broker. His job: sell his plan to improve Russia's oil relationships with China beyond the current 2030 agreement. He promised increased oil trade, favorable co-ventures, and border security in return for China renewing its loan agreements to Moscow.

The notion of border security made Lee Kang especially curious.

"Do we not have such an accord in place?" the 63-year-old Kang asked, leaning back in his chair at the restaurant. His body language said *convince me*.

Nechayev knew Kang was much more than just a trade envoy and quite capable of ending the discussion at any moment.

China and Russia already had a twenty-year agreement signed in 2001, the Treaty of Good-Neighborliness and Friendly Cooperation. The relationship had been reinforced when the Chinese president made a state visit to Moscow.

"Our agreements recognize and honor our shared border," Nechayev acknowledged. He slid his plate of Peking duck to the side and leaned in to his companion. It was a very Russian, un-Chinese move. But Nechayev wanted his message to be completely understood.

"You have growing territorial issues with Japan," he continued, referring to the island-building China was aggressively pursuing in the disputed China Sea. These were important transportation routes through which 39 percent of Chinese non-Russian oil imports passed.

"Yes," Kang replied quietly.

"We have concern on our Western frontier," Nechayev said.

"Nations friendly to the Russian Federation?"

"Beyond those borders," Nechayev whispered.

The two men sat eye to eye. Kang, schooled in international affairs with a degree in Russian history, grasped Nechayev's intent. There was much more at stake. He heard exactly what was left unsaid. The issue was NATO. It had been years since the two nations operated under the post-World War II Sino-Soviet mutual defense agreements—agreements that contributed to the West's fear of Communism. It was time to renew.

"I understand," Kang replied.

"Then I trust you will bring the initiative to your president, a good friend of the Russian Federation," Minister Nechayev implored.

"I will."

"Well then, let us toast," said a pleased Nechayev, raising his glass of

Chateau Hansen, a more than passable Chinese red blend.

"To our mutual benefit," the Russian proposed.

"Our mutual benefit," Kang echoed.

As they sipped and smiled, the Chinese minister considered the ultimate implications of the pact, if formalized. *This went well beyond oil and trade. If, for some reason, Russia's Western oil markets were shut off, the ever-expanding Chinese need could prevent economic disaster in the Russian Federation.* But, he reasoned, Gorshkov wants more: *A backdoor national security pact with China to make NATO rethink its posture.*

Kang lowered the glass, and in time-honored Chinese tradition, he decided to negotiate further.

"China is already your nation's top trade partner," he began. "We certainly would invite more. But, unless I'm misinformed, 80 percent of your oil exports and 70 percent of your gas exports go to European market nations. Can your output support more?"

This frustrated the Russian, who thought they had concluded their business. He put down his glass.

"The Ministry of Energy wishes to reduce our dependence on the EU market," he explained. "The bilateral economic cooperation that led to the Eastern Siberia–Pacific Ocean oil pipeline affords the opportunity for expansion. And if we are to build on the pact with the construction of a gas pipeline as well, we will provide for a more secure China, which is now the world's biggest energy consumer."

Kang smiled. *Russia was protecting its own interests, with oil merely being a part of it.*

"If you were to give an identity to such a relationship, what would you call it, Mr. Nechayev?"

"For the sake of discussion?"

"For the sake of discussion."

"We would consider it a strengthening of our Treaty of Good-Neighborliness and Friendly Cooperation." *How did they ever come up with that name,* Anton Nechayev wondered to himself. It almost made him laugh. "But perhaps we term it a mutual economic *defense* rider."

Lee Kang nodded. "An interesting choice of words. But let us be clear, you are actually speaking about an economic mutual *offense* agreement."

Nechayev smiled. "A fine point for our superiors to discuss."

"I will speak with the president."

"As I will mine."

10

MAZATLÁN, MEXICO

Hurricane Gracie had been building intensity in the Pacific for twelve days, fueled by warm El Niño waters. Now it was on a collision course with Mazatlán and promising even more destructive power than previously forecast. Winds were predicted to hit 170 mph at landfall, making it the worst storm to bear down on the resort city in decades.

Dan Reilly's commercial flight landed under darkening skies. It was the last scheduled flight in and would be the last going out.

The air was heavy with rising humidity. Deplaning, Reilly removed his jacket and rolled up his shirtsleeves. The air was stifling, and he perspired all through customs.

"Señor Reilly!" The shout came from hotel driver Miguel Rivera. "Mr. Reilly!"

Reilly gave the familiar driver a quick hug. "Good to see you again, my friend. How is your family?" He didn't remember their names, but recalled that Rivera and his wife had three young children.

"They're good, but afraid."

"As soon as you drop me off, go get them. They'll be better off in the hotel ballroom than at your home."

"*Gracias*, Señor Reilly. Thank you, I will."

"How many hours do we have until it hits?"

"Six, maybe seven. The forecasts are bad," Rivera said.

"Six hours. God."

From the car it took Reilly three attempts to connect with the Kensington Royal Resort general manager. When he did, he got an update on the race to board up the windows and the status of other emergency measures.

"Any change on the direction?"

"None. We're right in Gracie's path. Winds picking up within the hour," Raul Bustamante said in a booming voice. "Full impact around 3:00 a.m., maybe earlier."

"Your staff may be at risk if they remain in their homes." Reilly knew the area's lower income residential construction was generally cheap if new, and flimsy if old. "Tell them—"

"I've already begun to get the word out. They're welcome to stay at the hotel."

"Good. How many guests still on the property?" Reilly asked.

"One hundred and twenty-six. Those who could left on fights earlier today. Most couldn't book seats. Believe me, we tried."

"Move everyone to the ballroom. Nowhere higher than the second floor."

Reilly heard Bustamante pass along the order, or what he assumed to be the order, in Spanish.

The general manager then went through the basics: fresh water, food supplies, ice, flashlights, first aid kits, communications, and emergency power. Bustamante was in the midst of explaining how much backup power they had when the phone went dead.

"Damn!" Reilly said. He wanted to make sure doctors were also called to stay in the hotel.

"Try mine." Rivera gave Reilly his cell, but that didn't work either. The winds were kicking up and a tower had likely toppled. It was going to make the job of getting employees to safety harder. It also prevented Reilly from getting a call from Alan Cannon in Tokyo. An important call.

When Reilly arrived at the hotel, a tall, distinguished man wearing a classic blue blazer, grey slacks, white shirt, and a solid blue silk tie stepped forward to greet him. It was Raul Bustamante.

"Glad you made it," the general manager warmly proclaimed. "Wish you didn't have to."

"I'll drink to that just as soon as we can," Reilly replied. They shook hands and Bustamante led him inside.

"You can change in the office. We've put a mattress on the floor for you, but I have a feeling no one's going to get any sleep tonight."

He was right. The rain was beginning to pelt the oceanside resort, slicing west, whipped up by the oncoming winds. Within an hour they were in the middle of a full-fledged storm, with winds rising up to 50 and 60 mph. But worse lay ahead.

Maintenance personnel handed out walkie-talkies, the only means of communication beyond shouting. Outside, staff worked in pairs with ropes tied between them. An hour later, winds clocked at 90 mph. Another hour after that, 120. Plywood covering the windows rattled enough to break the glass inside. Guest and employee family members moved further toward the inner walls. Children cried.

Thirty minutes later the electricity went out. Emergency generators kicked in, but they only provided limited light and no air-conditioning.

Forty-five minutes later, landfall—dead-on.

The howl alone was frightening, but the building itself seemed to shiver and rock with fear. Inside, hundreds of people huddled together. Many prayed.

Deep green lightning hit so close that everyone could feel the energy. The thunder was deafening. They heard cars propelled by the wind crash into the hotel and telephone poles snap. Tin roofs from blocks away hurtled toward their sanctuary, adding to the cacophony.

Even Reilly wondered how truly hurricane-proof the Kensington Royal Resort was. He had experienced hurricanes before, but never like this. He tried to picture what he would discover when he stepped outside as he helped console the children.

Suddenly the wind and rain stopped. Cheers broke out in the

ballroom. Cries of joy. But Raul Bustamante warned them that it was only a temporary reprieve. The eye wall had just passed. Calm might only last thirty minutes.

Many wanted to use the bathrooms. Bustamante had a maintenance supervisor check to see if the water still worked. It did. He allowed people to leave, but with the urging that they should return to the ballroom immediately.

Reilly, Bustamante, and his senior staff ventured outside to evaluate the damage. Moonlight made it easier to see. Shingles were ripped off the roof. The pool was strewn with branches, fish, and anything that hadn't been tied down in the beachside restaurant.

The street leading to the resort resembled a war zone. Flipped cars, fallen trees, downed power lines, and dislodged hunks of cement. The worst was the flooding. The hotel entrance was surrounded by sandbags, but water had seeped through. Soon it would be in the lobby and flow into the ballroom. The general manager called for his staff to shore up the barrier. The wind would shift in a few minutes and drive the water right in.

While they rushed to build a higher barricade, Reilly slogged through one hundred yards of knee-deep water, calling out for anyone who might need help. There were no answering calls. Further away from the property he feared there'd be multiple deaths. It was inevitable, given the way many people lived.

The sky began to darken again. Reilly felt the wind build up from the backside of the hurricane. He picked up his pace, shocked at how fast the storm had intensified again. Less than twenty-five minutes. Blinding horizontal rain fell so hard it hurt. Reilly ran.

The second wave was far more severe than the first. It lasted three exhausting hours, as the storm slowly moved over the land.

After it had passed, Reilly reemerged, shining a high-powered flash-light around the property. The hotel had withstood the storm, but it would take millions, multiple millions of dollars to bring it back online. More importantly, however, everyone under his care had survived.

"Oh my God," Bustamante exclaimed as he joined Reilly. "I've never seen anything this horrible."

"We will rebuild, Raul. And tell your staff that their jobs will be guaranteed. They'll receive full salary during reconstruction." This was just the first of his promises. Next he had to insure the hotel guests would get safe passage home.

* * *

"Hello, Brenda. It's Dan. Can you hear me?"

He had tried calling for hours, but the satellite signal constantly failed. The phone finally connected after the skies began to clear.

"Noisy, but working. I've been so worried. We've been following the news. It sounds terrible."

"A lot of cleanup and rebuilding for us. A lot worse for the locals. Here's the immediate problem: No commercial flights in or out for at least a day. But we have more than a hundred guests to get back to the states. I'll need a 727 or 737 in here as soon as possible. Can you connect me with transportation?"

"Sure. I'll put you on hold."

Ten minutes later Brenda returned to the call.

"No go, Dan."

"What do you mean?"

"Travel couldn't handle it without authorization from legal. The office had to locate and consult with Mr. Collins." She paused.

"And he wouldn't approve?"

"Liability issues. He said just hang tough."

"I've got guests stranded! Some of them are elderly and a few could use medical attention. We've been through a very scary night."

"Maybe if you talk to him," Brenda suggested.

"Better than that, I've got my corporate card. Connect me with the private fleet you use."

A minute later Reilly was talking with a representative who, after also putting him on hold, turned down the request as politely as possible.

"I'm sorry, Mr. Reilly, I simply can't fulfill your request. Your corporation has a high credit limit, but this is out of the ordinary."

"So is a Category 5 hurricane!"

"We have planes available out of Miami, but we'll need to set up a higher line and that will take time."

"What kind of money are we talking about?"

"Depending on your dates . . ."

"Immediately after General Rafael Buelna Airport opens up down here."

Reilly heard typing.

"That's $152,609 round trip, based on twenty-four hours. But again, I can't authorize it without an invoice number faxed to us."

"I'll give you an invoice number." He could make one up. "But a fax? Hell, nobody uses faxes anymore."

"We do."

"Then I'll give you my American Express Corporate Card."

"That might work," the representative said.

Reilly read the account number and waited.

A minute later the fleet sales office manager said, "I'm afraid not, Mr. Reilly."

"Why?"

"The expense is well over the credit limit. Now if you have that invoice number and a fax?"

"I'm in Mexico. We've just been hit by the worst hurricane in forty years, and I have no fax! I'm trying to get people out!"

"Mr. Reilly, I wish I could help, but I can't."

Reilly took a second to compose himself. "Yes, I understand. You said $152,609?"

"Yes, but that's just an estimate. It could go higher if . . ."

"And less if we get out quicker. Please stay put. I'll call you back." He quickly told Brenda, who was still on the phone bridge, not to hang up. "Plan C," he said.

"Which is?" Brenda asked.

"Call Sam Wheeler at AMEX. His private number is in the system. If the president of American Express International won't approve the expense, it'll cost them millions when I cancel their agreement with our hotels."

Brenda knew he'd do it, too. So did Wheeler, minutes later when he heard Reilly's threat.

"That critical, Dan?" the AMEX executive asked.

"Absolutely. I promised I'd get them out, and now you can become a hero and part of the rescue, or the villain and see a huge chunk of business disappear. Want me to do the math for you?"

"No! Just tell me what you need."

Reilly did.

"That's highly—"

"Highly necessary, Sam. I'll wait while you do it."

Twenty minutes later, Dan Reilly had his 737-800 ready to depart Miami as soon as the private airline could get cleared to land in Mazatlán.

When he finished, Brenda remembered something else. "Alan Cannon's been trying to reach you. He says it's very important."

* * *

Reilly tried to reach his colleague, but couldn't. A call back to Brenda revealed that Cannon was in the air, apparently without internet service. That made Reilly anxious, but there was work to oversee in Mazatlán and a new complication. His driver warned against going into town to pick up supplies.

"Señor Reilly, it's not safe. The gangs are moving in quickly, breaking into stores, taking everything they can. A few have tried to stop them, but they've been shot at." He suddenly looked especially worried. "And I've heard they're heading this way."

"The police?"

"It's Mexico. There's only so much that they'll do."

Reilly contemplated the alternatives if trouble reached the resort.

"Miguel, how good is our security team?"

"Like I said, it's Mexico," said Rivera with a helpless shrug.

That meant they'd step aside if looters came.

Reilly shook his head. "Mexico. Afghanistan."

"What?" the driver asked.

"Nothing. Just people are the same everywhere." He paused as an idea formed. "Feel like earning yourself a nice bonus payment?"

"Yes." Rivera smiled. Money always talked.

"Then come with me."

Five minutes later, Reilly briefed his general manager on the situation and simply asked, "So Raul, how much cash is in house?"

Bustamante was stunned by the question and the implication. "You're not thinking . . ."

"Not only thinking, doing. Miguel will drive me into town and I'll come to a financial solution with the cartel boss."

"You hope."

"Okay, I hope. The terms will be cash for staying away. Leave the resort untouched, guarantee safe passage in and out of the city for supplies, and insure our people get to the airport safely. They'll be richer for the efforts. So again, Raul, how much do you have locked up? Whatever it is, it'll be less than settling lawsuits if we can't protect our clientele."

"I don't know. Maybe 180,000 pesos. About 10,000 dollars US. And another $5,000 in just American currency."

Reilly didn't volunteer his experience in Afghanistan in such matters with local insurgents, but he did explain that an early bribe could take kidnapping or worse off the table.

"Miguel, now it's your turn. Will you drive me into the city and get me in front of someone who holds the power and can control his men?"

"Yes, Mr. Reilly."

"Good." And to the general manager he added, "Miguel earns a thousand US dollars for driving me, and another grand if I strike the deal."

Surprise and concern were clear on Bustamante's face. The general manager had only recently transferred from a Kensington Royal hotel in Madrid and had never encountered issues like this.

"Chicago will reimburse you," Reilly said. "I promise."

"I'm not worried about your word. It's your safety."

* * *

Dan Reilly worried about his own safety more than Bustamante would ever know. He was the only son in a family that had wanted more children. But this hope was lost when his father's jeep drove over a landmine in Vietnam, and he was killed instantly. His mother never remarried. She brought Daniel up on her husband's pension and death benefits and her own salary as a 911 call center operator in South Boston.

Elizabeth Reilly frequently worked night shifts, so Daniel often spent evenings on his own when he was in high school. He could have taken the fork in the road that would have kept him in Southie. But his mother always told him to aspire to more.

More in the 1980s meant getting into Boston Latin, making it on time to math and science tutors in Back Bay, and never, ever getting into trouble that ended up with a call to 911.

She enrolled him in *Taekwondo* classes in Cambridge, a high school computer workshop at MIT, and a life-changing summer program with the Police Academy. Through the program, he was introduced to how departmental branches worked at the Boston Police Department. He toured the Ballistics Unit, the Police Academy, the shooting range, the heralded mounted unit, the juvenile division, the harbor patrol, and of course police headquarters and the 911 hub.

He kept with the program for three years. It got him into a dedicated fitness routine, on track with leadership and mentoring responsibilities to younger kids, and ultimately a path to walk in his father's shoes.

The police work earned him glowing letters of recommendation from the Boston chief of police. They went to the admissions department and the presidents of NYU, Yale, Boston University, Boston College, and Tufts. But because of his commitment to help his mother, Reilly ruled out leaving Boston for college.

He chose Boston University, enrolling in the undergraduate business program with a minor in criminal justice, and got a full ride. For living expenses, he took a part-time job as a uniformed Pinkerton security officer at the Prudential Center.

One late night during his senior year, he walked smack dab into a robbery at the mall. Reilly was lucky he didn't get shot, but a blow to his head took him down. Another security officer called 911. His mother was on duty—little surprise that the Boston Police and an ambulance arrived in record time.

Reilly's description resulted in arrests and his testimony put three perpetrators away for years. He lost two weeks at school, which gave him time to think about his future. The memory of his father loomed in his mind. At graduation he decided what he wanted to do. Enlist.

The army reviewed his background and fast-tracked Reilly into the twelve-week OCS, Officer Candidate School, in Fort Benning, Georgia. From there, he went to an Arizona outpost fifteen miles north of the Mexican border. It was a special facility, the home of the US Army Intelligence Center and the US Army Network Enterprise Technology Command (NETCOM). Fort Huachuca would be his home for four months. From there he went into the Defense Language Institute at the Presidio in Monterey, California, for intensive studies in Farsi and Russian. Nine months later, with a basic command of the languages, the army awarded his studies with a ticket on a Boeing C-17 Globemaster III to Afghanistan.

Very few people knew what he did there or the connections he made.

11

MAZATLÁN, MEXICO

FOLLOWING THE HURRICANE

Rivera drove Reilly through the town in the highest clearance truck on the property. Even with the 11.2 inches the Ford 150 Raptor provided, most flooded streets couldn't be navigated. Those that could were riddled with heaps of floating trash including household items, roofs, broken poles, and sewage. Worse were the bodies.

Looters were at work, with no police in sight.

"Most people are smart enough to stay out of the gang's way," Rivera said. "Once the gangs are through, the stores belong to everyday thieves and rioters. It's better than Christmas morning for them."

In desperate situations, which this was, everyone except the mourners could be a threat. That's why Reilly sought to make an unlawful deal with people who held power. It's what he'd done with tribes in Afghanistan.

It took more than ninety minutes and a circuitous route to get to their destination. Six men armed with semiautomatics, from original Russian to Chinese and American variants, stopped them at the bottom of a long driveway leading to a huge white villa. They leveled their weapons at the truck.

One of the men stepped forward and ordered Rivera and Reilly to get out, come to the front of the truck, and kneel on the soggy ground.

"*¿Quién eres? ¿Qué quieres?* Who are you? What do you want?"

Rivera explained that he was accompanying an American hotel executive who wanted to make an offer.

The lead guard laughed. "*¿Una oferta? Si tienes algo que queramos, la tomaremos!* An offer? If you have something we want, we'll take it!" He laughed again. "*¡Dámelo!* Give it to me!"

"*¡No!*" The reply to the demand was Reilly's. "*Sólo será negociar con Señor Santiago.*"

This earned Reilly a rifle butt slam to his back.

"Señor Santiago," he repeated.

Just as he was about to get another punishing blow, a voice boomed over a speaker.

"*Ya no más. Lleve al americano.*"

The guard who had been speaking motioned with his AK-47 for Reilly to stand.

"I'll be back," Reilly told Rivera.

Rivera, still on his knees replied, "I sure hope so."

With that, the man urged Reilly forward. Halfway up the driveway littered with debris, Reilly looked back. Rivera had been allowed to sit up and smoke. Reilly smiled inwardly. *He knew how to get here, and he seemed familiar with the cartel.* When he considered it, it wasn't really surprising.

Dan Reilly was ushered into the first floor of the magnificent estate. He heard the hum of generators that powered light and electricity. He was grateful for the air conditioning and utterly surprised when a valet offered him a bottle of Evian.

He had waited no more than a minute when a thin, handsome man close to his own age sauntered down a grand staircase. He wore a red and blue pinstriped shirt, tan pants, and a blue blazer. Not the wardrobe Reilly would expect from anyone after a devastating hurricane, let alone the region's drug cartel kingpin.

"Señor, you put me at a disadvantage. Though you likely know my name, I do not know yours," the Mexican said in flawless English.

"Daniel Reilly. I work for the Kensington Royal Resort. I flew in just before the storm hit."

"You picked a bad day to visit Mazatlán, Señor Reilly."

"I needed to come to help, Señor Santiago. It's my job."

"Your job surely did not include taking the chance to visit me."

"No it didn't, but it was necessary."

"Very brave—possibly stupid."

"I've been accused of both," Reilly replied.

"Then let me talk to the brave man, not the stupid one. Why are you here?"

Reilly paused to study his adversary. He was intelligent and charismatic, with dark eyes that glistened. But Reilly didn't doubt for an instant that Santiago was as ruthless as he was suave.

"To propose a deal," Reilly said directly. "Less a matter of money than of principal."

"A deal with little money is not a good place to start," the cartel kingpin stated.

His eyes grew colder. Reilly focused on them. "Perhaps there is more at stake."

"And what would that be?" Santiago asked.

"A mutual interest in the economy of the community."

Santiago's expression warmed. "A most interesting choice of words, my friend. Let us take this to the library." He gestured toward a door to their left. But before entering, Santiago stood inches away from him and asked, "What is that you want to negotiate."

"Protection."

12

TWO DAYS LATER

"Collins is livid," said Edward Shaw. "You put the company on extremely shaky legal ground. The Mazatlán mayor has threatened to file a complaint with the State Department over your deal with Santiago!"

Shaw read from a list atop a file folder that he held. He paced in front of his nineteenth century oak desk. Dan Reilly sat with his arms folded and legs crossed, ready for more. More came.

"You authorized nearly $15,000."

"By the time I was through, closer to $25,000," Reilly said.

"Okay, $25,000 in payoffs and payouts that will need a whole new line item. You damn well better hope the IRS doesn't question it! On top of that, you coerced an American Express president and made unauthorized personal promises to hotel guests regarding their safe passage. And you guaranteed hotel employees full pay while the resort is closed! I have finance calculating the cost of that pledge. As I understand it from Raul Bustamante, all of this was within a few hours."

"About twenty, sir," Reilly responded. The rant took Reilly back to a dressing down in Kabul from a commanding officer.

Shaw took the files and tossed them in his wastebasket. He offered a half laugh. "Bustamante also said you alone are responsible for getting our guests out safely, quickly, and without complaint. That you demonstrated real courage meeting directly with the region's most dangerous and powerful man. That you instilled loyalty in the staff by taking in our employees' family members during the most destructive hurricane they've ever experienced."

Reilly reported back with the same good nature, "Yes, sir."

"And in doing so you've given Kensington Royal a positive marketing story to help balance Tokyo."

"That's out of my area, Edward."

"Sometimes I wonder what isn't out of your area. You continue to surprise me, son." Shaw struck his hand out. "And thank you!"

"It's what I do, sir."

Reilly had never revealed everything on his resume, and he wouldn't now. But Shaw's comment implied a certain suspicion.

"Oh, and for the record," Shaw added, "any releases that are going out, you acted with authority and under my direction. Got that?"

"Cover fire?"

"More to the point, I'll take the credit."

"Better for both of us," Reilly replied, understanding the reverse would have been the case if his decisions had gone to hell in a handbasket.

"Okay then, on to new business."

"Before you jump into that, Alan may have a lead," Reilly said. "His plane back had equipment problems and was redirected to Kuala Lumpur. He connected on his stopover, and he's finally getting out today. But based on what he told me, we'll want to run it by some of our DC contacts."

Shaw didn't ask who. Between Alan Cannon's FBI years and Reilly's term with the State Department, he considered them well placed.

"One more thing, sir," Reilly added. "We've also nailed down our consultants and we're on the calendar for our first session. Collins is on board, too."

"Good, but you still have to smooth Chris's ruffled feathers."

"No problem," he lied. It would take some effort.

"Money okay? You have your agenda?" Shaw asked.

"Sort of yes on both. A few requested higher fees. I need them. So I said yes."

"Of course you did," Shaw laughed. "And the agenda?"

"Working on it, including a way for us to evaluate a range of threats and trigger procedures. We would have been better prepared in both Tokyo and Mazatlán, which are on opposite ends of the threat spectrum, if we had an overarching plan."

"How far along are you?"

"Early on. I've been working on some possibilities. We really need input from the committee though."

"As far as I'm concerned, this is your ship to sail," said Shaw. "In the meantime, you're going on another trip this week."

"Where?"

"Tehran."

* * *

Reilly returned to his office with a quick question for his assistant. "Anyone speaking to us in travel after my end run?"

Brenda Sheldon laughed. "It'll take some smoothing. No worries. From the online release PR sent through, it looks like Mr. Shaw managed the whole thing."

"Didn't he?" Reilly joked.

"Aren't you upset?" she asked.

"Not at all. Plus it takes the heat off so we can get some big things done. Hope you're ready."

"Always am."

"Good. Then let's schedule a meeting with Collins today. If it's better, I can go to him. Then Alan Cannon when he's back in. And early dinner reservations tomorrow in DC at the Old Ebbitt Grill."

"For?"

"For two. I'll take care of the invite."

"Oh?" she said coyly.

"No *oh*. Strictly business."

"Any name?"

"Mine."

"I meant the other name," she quipped.

"I'll have to try to remember someday."

Maybe what I can't get with Congress's permission, I can get on my own, he thought.

Brenda got the message. "Okay. I'll book the flight. Back in the morning?"

"Just the first leg. Tomorrow an overnight from Dulles to Tehran. And a hotel. Keep the return open."

"Busy boy," Brenda said.

"And it's going to get a whole lot busier."

* * *

Reilly let Chris Collins vent. He got an earful of corporate law, a lecture on federal statutes that strictly prohibit conducting business with known drug dealers, and a primer on SEC regulations.

"You exposed this corporation to huge liabilities and potential prosecution," said Collins. "It's my job to protect us. But I can't do that if you're working against our best interests. Maybe the man upstairs is with you *this* time."

"He is," Reilly retorted.

"This time," Collins underscored. "But even Shaw has to answer to a board."

Reilly hadn't considered that fact. There were *others.*

Collins continued for another two minutes. He didn't invite a rebuttal, but Reilly had one. He delivered it calmly.

"Chris, I'm sorry for the distress. The problems. But here's what I need. Find me the legal wiggle room, the workarounds, and the shortcuts you're willing to live with. We'll be better if we can react as a team in a crisis."

This was the same conversation he once had with a general in

Afghanistan—a general who failed to understand there were missions beyond the stated mission, responsibilities for real-time decisions that couldn't be calculated in advance.

Collins sighed deeply. "I won't sweep things under the rug."

"I'm not asking you to. Just work with me. Help me."

"No end runs?" Collins asked.

"I'll try," Reilly said.

"No secrets . . ." Collins paused before adding, "unless I tell you I don't want to know."

Dan Reilly maintained a serious expression while smiling inwardly. "Sure."

* * *

Alan Cannon finally landed that evening. He passed on having dinner with Reilly—sitting down at the computer with the thumb drive was his only priority. Sandwiches from a commissary machine would do just fine.

The Kensington Royal security chief explained to Reilly the process the Japanese intelligence officer had put him through. "I'll spare you the time and effort," Cannon said. "But I'm glad I did it myself. It made me examine the video closely, which validated Genji Takahiro's judgment."

"So let's see," Reilly replied.

Cannon had a copy of the file. He skipped through the footage until he got to a view from a closed-circuit police camera on the side of a building. Dust, likely from the blast, covered the black housing. It made the wide-angle image blurry.

"Hard to see, but it's still important. I'll come back to it."

Next he jumped to a second angle from an internal store security camera that faced outward. It showed a crystal clear shot because pressure from the explosion had blown out the window.

"Now watch," Cannon instructed. "Normal speed first."

Reilly saw people running left to right, others walking quickly.

"They're getting away from the hotel as fast as they can. See, some are bleeding. They were hit by shrapnel and flying shards of glass."

"Got it."

A mother carried a small child. An elderly man limped past the camera, his leg bleeding. A motorcyclist pushed his inoperable bike through the street. A group of teenage girls ran by.

"I don't . . ." Reilly began.

"Keep watching."

A man comforted a woman. His jacket wrapped over her shoulders. A young man tried to make a call. Everyone moved quickly, appearing no more than three seconds in the camera's view.

Then another man walked into frame. Walked.

"That guy?"

"Exactly," Cannon said.

"Everyone else is in a mad rush. He's just walking away from a catastrophic event. Would you be walking?"

"No way!" Reilly exclaimed.

A moment later he was out of frame. There was another wide view from an additional police surveillance camera which gave more perspective on how casually he walked.

"Maybe he was injured," Reilly noted.

"Naichō distributed still frames to all the hospitals. No one saw him."

"So you have a closer shot?"

"Not another, but enhanced. Take a look at the store camera slower, blown up, and effected."

In slow motion, Reilly could actually see the subject bring his head forward after looking backwards in the direction of the devastation. Then, an unmistakable sly smile appeared on his face. Cannon froze the image.

"Jesus!" Reilly exclaimed. "The guy's gloating."

"Would you say victim or perpetrator?"

"Perpetrator," Reilly answered.

"My thoughts exactly. Takahiro's running the picture by his contacts. I've sent it to the bureau. We need to tap into every global facial recognition database."

"Absolutely."

"From the wide shot we can even calculate the pace everyone is moving. Makes a strong case that the laggard could be one of the culprits. And with that smile, he had no intention to commit suicide. If we ever recover video off the hotel hard drive we should have positive proof."

Reilly watched the footage again. He felt the man walked with authority and pride. He tapped the face on the screen. "Any guesses as to his nationality?"

"From a profiling point of view . . . ?"

"Yes," Reilly replied.

"Only an opinion, but this guy's not Middle Eastern."

"Which means?"

"Not one of the usual suspects."

Reilly stared longer and harder at the computer. "Can you make me a copy, I want to share this with a friend tomorrow."

"Who?"

"An old army buddy. A guy I was going to see anyway. Now I have even more reason."

Cannon looked at Reilly with a slightly askew eye. He pulled another USB drive from his jacket pocket.

"You can trust him?"

"Yes," Reilly replied.

"Then take it."

Reilly thanked Cannon and dialed Brenda.

"Change of plans, Brenda. Earlier flight to DC in the morning and cancel Old Ebbitt Grill. I'll see my friend at his office."

13

WASHINGTON, DC

Early the next morning a driver dressed in black waited for Reilly at baggage claim at Reagan National Airport. Reilly saw his name on an iPad display and raised his hand. The driver walked forward.

"Mr. Reilly?"

"Yes."

"Daniel Reilly?"

"Yes."

"I'll need to see identification. Your photo ID, please," the driver stated.

Reilly complied. Given where he was going, this was not unexpected.

After checking and returning Reilly's driver's license and Kensington Royal identification card, the driver simply said, "This way, sir."

The morning air was already oppressively thick with Washington summer humidity. Reilly was glad that the town car was close, and the air conditioning was pumping out cool air by the time the vehicle exited the lot onto Aviation Circle.

Before merging onto George Washington Memorial Parkway, the driver asked if Reilly wanted to leave his bags at a hotel.

"No, thank you." He didn't bother explaining that he'd be flying out later that day from Dulles.

Reilly fell into a deep sleep for the rest of the twenty-five-minute trip in morning traffic. It helped make up for all the travel he had been doing lately and the resulting lack of sleep.

He awoke as the car turned onto the Virginia State Road 123, drove about a half a mile, and then made a left at a restricted street. Two short left turns later and they came to a gate that required the driver's ID card and personal code and Reilly's identification. Ahead was a second gate with a traffic light. If it turned red, cars had to stop and await further clearance. If, for any reason, they kept going without permission, a steel barrier would automatically deploy from the roadbed.

The driver got a green light and proceeded the rest of the way to the George Bush Center for Intelligence in McLean, Virginia. The CIA headquarters.

* * *

Reilly left his suitcase in the town car. As the driver opened the door and led him to the entrance, Reilly took in his surroundings. There were two main office buildings: OHB, the Original Headquarters Building constructed in the early 1960s, and NHB, the New Headquarters Building completed in the late 1980s. Also on the campus was an auditorium known as "The Bubble," and another structure, a small modern house, which was a day care center where children were known by numbers.

Reilly walked past officers in black uniforms inside the austere white Alabama marble lobby of the new building. There were armed with M4 carbines, which were shorter versions of the M16A2 assault rifle. He was familiar with the weapon, though he hadn't kept up with its use on the firing range.

Reilly took in the symbolic artwork, the inspirational messages, and most of all the staid statue of "Wild Bill" Donovan, head of the OSS, the predecessor to the Central Intelligence Agency.

The driver, without a doubt a gun-carrying agent himself, escorted Reilly to the main security post. Once again, he produced his license and office ID. But now Reilly also had to state his business.

"I have an appointment with Robert Heath," he told an officer at the desk. No use of the word *meeting*. No purpose stated. All polite, but to the point.

"Social security number, Mr. Reilly?"

Reilly recited the nine-digit number.

The guard typed his name and the number into the computer. A moment later, the guard said, "Please take a step back to the line on the floor and look at the lens."

A camera was positioned on the lobby shelf. Reilly posed for a headshot that was quickly printed onto an ID card with a big "V" and the declaration "Visitor Escort Required."

He inserted it in a plastic sleeve and presented it to Reilly adding, "Please wear this at all times."

"Thank you."

"You're good to go, Mr. Reilly. Welcome to the CIA. Agent Heath is expecting you."

An officer stepped forward to accompany Reilly to the elevator and on the ride up. Robert Heath was waiting for him on the second floor with a hearty handshake.

"Bob, great to see you!" Reilly said, grasping his outstretched hand.

"Likewise," the CIA operative said with a smile. "How have you been?"

"Busy. Really busy," Reilly replied.

"I'd guess so." Heath knew full well what Reilly had been dealing with. "Sorry about Tokyo."

"Thanks."

As Heath led Reilly to his office, Reilly noticed that his old friend had gone completely bald and gained some weight. Not completely surprising considering he walked with a pronounced limp now and likely was no longer able to run marathons, let alone do field assignments.

Heath was two years younger than Reilly. They'd met on a mission out of Kabul; Reilly, the army officer, Heath the CIA's regional eyes and ears. Heath owed Reilly his life.

While on a patrol to root out a Taliban leader, their convoy lead driver had spotted a young boy writhing in pain by the side of the road. The Humvee pulled over. The rest of the caravan slowed. Two infantrymen, their Colt M16s in hand, exited the vehicle to secure the area. They scanned the terrain, concerned about nearby rocks, but saw no threats. They signaled the driver and captain, who got out to assist. It was to be their last act of kindness. The boy held a detonator wired to a backpack bomb. Then he pressed the button. The blast took out the vehicle and instantly killed the four men at ground zero along with two more in the first Humvee.

The three Commando Select armored vehicles, distinguishable by their V-shaped hulls and ceramic painting, were forced to stop suddenly behind the Humvee. With nowhere to maneuver they began to back up. But not fast enough. They were ambushed by the enemy, hiding behind a stretch of boulders.

The Americans returned fire from their Browning .50 caliber M2 machine guns and Mk 19 automatic grenade launchers. But almost instantly bombs buried in the road went off, propelling two of the vehicles, each with a squad of four soldiers and two special observers, ten feet into the air. Heath and Reilly were the two observers.

Survivors struggled to get out from the heavily reinforced but now upended Commando Selects. Four were cut down the moment they stepped out to take up defensive positions. Three others died inside. Heath took a bullet in the leg as he cleared the door. Reilly caught him as he fell backwards. As the remaining standing Select vehicles continued to answer the enemy's barrage, Reilly went for the door on the opposite side, dragged Heath out, and found cover in a gully.

With no view of the battle, Reilly pulled Heath twenty-five yards farther away where they found refuge between two boulders. Reilly kept pressure on Heath's leg and waited.

Eventually the shooting stopped. Seconds later they heard joyful screams and the sound of automatic guns shot into the air. The Taliban had won.

That day Dan Reilly had saved Robert Heath's life and kept him alive until four hours later when a pair of army Sikorsky UH-60 Black Hawk helicopters flew over the kill zone and spotted them.

That was Heath's last assignment in Afghanistan. Reilly stayed on another four months investigating a lead indicating that command had ignored verifiable intelligence of an imminent attack—intelligence that could have prevented the massacre. He brought it to senior officers who denied the claim. Reilly followed the trail of evidence higher, all the way to a field general. When he tried to make a case for the cover-up in the field, he was reassigned to Washington.

Back in the states, Reilly continued to pursue the case that had cost the lives of nineteen men. A year into it, he learned that the one-star general in question had quietly retired and evidence of the attack had been expunged.

Reilly resigned. Thanks to a friend, he took a job with the State Department. That friend was Bob Heath. It was the beginning of Reilly's career in international affairs—a career where Heath and Reilly never lost touch.

* * *

"Okay to pop a thumb drive into your computer?" Reilly asked once they were seated in Heath's office.

"Not really." Heath said. "More broadly, not at all."

The CIA might not be as susceptible to computer viruses as most government agencies, but it was still at risk.

"Yours?"

"No. From Naichō."

"Love them like a brother." Heath laughed. "By the way, I don't trust my brother."

"Any alternative?" Reilly asked.

"We have an off-the-grid PC down the hall. Requires separate login that changes every day. I'll get it."

While Heath went to get the computer, Reilly looked out the

windows onto the campus. People were coming and going. Agents known and unknown carrying America's secrets and the world's problems on their shoulders. Spies with secret identities and those who decoded transmissions. Operatives who survived war zones—some who one day might not return.

Dan Reilly didn't doubt they accepted the risks. If they died in the line of service, their names would be etched without fanfare into the OHB lobby wall. The list was growing, although their deaths usually weren't reported. In contrast, those who had died in Reilly's international hotel made news, if only for a short time.

Chris Collins was right about one thing, he thought. *We do have liability.* But Reilly defined liability as an obligation, a responsibility to the people who put trust in the company.

In the spy trade, the CIA was also referred as "the Company." Now Reilly saw the parallels and the overlaps of the two. Both served people. Both needed timely, accurate, and actionable information.

The room felt cold. Reilly shivered, but it wasn't the air conditioning.

14

ALONG THE OB RIVER VALLEY

RUSSIAN FEDERATION

1996

Construction on Nikolai Gorshkov's dacha was complete. It resembled an old villa he rented outside of Potsdam, but built better, like the new Russia, and it came with security, both inside and out—also like the new Russia.

The dacha was located in a picture-perfect river valley ninety minutes north of Novosibirsk. Gorshkov and a group of seven friends, principally businessmen from the city, became a virtual fraternity, carpooling weekends to his dacha.

They spent much of the time contemplating the seismic changes in post-Soviet Russia and what they would mean for them. Over their vodka-fueled discussions they replayed Gorbachev's political blunders, the rise of Western greed and crime in the Russian Federation, and what they'd do if they were running the country.

It was generally the idle talk of eight drunken men, except for Gorshkov. He only considered that *if* temporary. He framed everything with historical perspective, arguing how vulnerable their new Russia was without its expanded borders.

Gorshkov routinely ended these gatherings, mostly filled with rhetorical boasts, with a toast to better times. This weekend, he forgot the toast. He was anxious to excuse his guests and get onto real business. Andre Miklos was waiting in another room.

"I'm sorry it took so long," said Gorshkov after his guests had left. Normally he was not one to apologize, but he had a special relationship with Miklos. "Any difficulty getting past the security gate?"

"None," Miklos replied.

That was both good and bad, Gorshkov thought.

Miklos snickered. "I know that look. Don't worry. I'm better than your guards. They never knew I was there. They won't know when I leave either."

"Well, apparently I need to make improvements with my staff," Gorshkov laughed. "But we have work to do."

They talked again about the failures in Potsdam, how far out and removed they felt, how Moscow had turned a blind eye toward them when rioters threatened. And as always they resolved to never let that happen again.

"I have something important to tell you, Andre."

"Yes?"

"I'm leaving Novosibirsk. I've been called to Moscow. It'll be a new beginning. On the inside."

"FSB?" Miklos asked.

"Better," he responded. "A new job. In the Kremlin. Amassing intelligence on the bastards who are still ruining Russia. You will have a new job, too." He smiled with great satisfaction. "With real growth potential."

15

LANGLEY, VA

CENTRAL INTELLIGENCE AGENCY

PRESENT DAY

Heath finished watching the video on Reilly's USB drive. He leaned back and drew a large breath that filled his checks.

"Dan, you understand no one has formally asked us to get involved."

"I'm asking."

"And if I say yes?" Heath replied.

"Then we help each other. Advance word, warnings. Information we can use. Like I testified."

"Intelligence."

"Well yes," Reilly said. "Intelligence. Nothing really sensitive—"

"Advance word and warnings are sensitive. And they come with a price," Heath stated without a hint of humor.

Now Reilly hesitated.

"Information costs, even among friends," the CIA operative continued. "But we could make this work. You're in a perfect job. You travel, you meet business people of all stripes, including government officials, and you're willing to mix it up with the cartel."

"You know about that?"

"Yes. Nice job, by the way."

Reilly merely smirked.

"In truth, brother, you've got a great cover."

"Wait," Reilly exclaimed. "This is further than where I was going. I liked it when our relationship meant we had occasional meals, talked about old times, and you simply gave me a heads-up when it counted . . ." He trailed off.

"So we add another dimension. We share," Heath stated. "You and me. Like you say, when it counts."

"You want me to be a source?"

"There are other terms."

Reilly knew them, but he didn't say them aloud. Not yet.

"Informally," Heath said, using the word of the day.

Dan Reilly pushed his chair away from the computer and leaned into Heath.

"You want *me* to work for the CIA. To gather intelligence for you. You realize the risk to my job?"

"Yes, and the benefit to it as well. You said so yourself at the hearing. You've asked for access to real intel. Well, I'm going to do better than that. It'll help as you put together your own advisory committee to reassess your company's vulnerabilities."

"Jesus, is there anything you don't know?"

"Yes. A lot. That's why we need you."

Reilly sat quietly.

"Look Dan, it's not as if you haven't been preparing for this. The army assignment, the State Department posts."

"And if it's so apparent to you, won't the guys on the other team make the same assumption?"

"They might. But so far you've had access to everyone you've ever needed to meet."

Reilly leaned back. He was thinking. Heath gave him the time.

"If I do this, and I'm saying *if* . . ."

"Yes."

"I just report."

"Yes."

"No sneaking around bushes."

"Just information."

"No leaks."

"None. You'll be considered a friend of the agency, which you already are. Call it a salaried friend."

"Right," Reilly declared. "*Informally*."

They shook hands on it, with Reilly more tentative than excited.

Turning back to business at hand, Reilly and Heath discussed how they would identify the man in the video.

Heath explained that they'd run the face through the CIA's comprehensive facial recognition programs first. He also asked for the names of all the Tokyo hotel guests and their passports going back one month.

"The Japanese already have that. Not a problem."

"And background checks on your employees."

"Harder, but not impossible," Reilly answered.

"House cameras."

"No hard drives survived. No cloud backup. That's part of my problem. Internal security." Reilly reflected on the destruction. "The bombs were smartly placed."

"An inside job?" Heath asked.

"Possibly. Or someone with a high degree of sophistication and training, and an exit strategy."

"But for what purpose?"

"Don't know," Reilly replied.

"Let's move this along to some people who might have some insight."

Heath bought a half hour and called in Company experts to meet with Reilly.

Their new relationship was moving fast.

* * *

"Dan, this is Roosevelt Dubois and Veronica Severi. Both on the counterterrorism desk with close counterparts at DHS. Rosie and Veronica, this is Dan Reilly a personal friend. He should be considered a friend of the Company."

Friend had its own meaning, Reilly thought as he shook hands with both agents.

"Dan is VP of International at Kensington Royal Hotels. You know about the attack on their Tokyo property. Suffice it to say, he's not a newcomer to intelligence, so don't treat him like one."

"Okay," Dubois said.

"Right," added Severi. "Nice to meet you.

Severi was in her early fifties. She wore her brown hair in a bob with bangs skimming the top of her glasses. She was thin, attractive, and dressed smartly in a blue pantsuit with flat shoes. Reilly noted that she had a wedding ring, but Dubois did not.

Reilly surmised that Roosevelt Dubois had more than desk duty. He was big and tough. Reilly pegged him at 6'3", mid to late forties.

"So, here's what we have," Heath said. He introduced the footage, and to save time, told them what to watch for. After three passes at varying speeds, Heath froze the headshot, grabbed the image with his snipping tool, and enlarged the frame.

"Ever see this guy?"

"New to me," Dubois said.

"Same," Severi added.

"Any first blush reactions?" Reilly questioned.

"Self-assured," Severi began. "His pace. Not the gait of someone fleeing. His expression, too. Not someone who intended to commit suicide—then or ever."

Reilly was impressed. "Nationality?"

"More Rosie's area. I come at it from the psych side."

"Psych?" Reilly asked.

"I do more than just confirm identity," Severi explained. "I look for motivation, which computer models can't predict."

"How?"

"Well, Mr. Reilly, there's so much in a face and body language.

There are signals and markers that suggest what may be going on inside like issues with women, antiestablishment tendencies, radical views. Tattoos can reveal a subtle story," Severi continued. "I also look for nervous tics that would make an individual stand out in public, inflated egos, visions of grandeur . . . Tips are everywhere to read."

"You can figure all of that from one photo?" Reilly asked.

"Not completely, but often it's in the eyes. They can tell so much. Take you for example."

"I think that's good enough, Veronica," Bob Heath interjected.

Of course she was already forming an opinion, Reilly thought. "No, please go on," he said. "I'd like to hear what you think."

Severi looked at Heath, who shrugged.

"Well, you are self-assured, authoritative, and a man of action," she began.

Reilly glanced at Heath who opened his arms with the kind of gesture that said, "See."

While she spoke, Agent Dubois started the video again and grabbed still frames of various other people. He began to line them up against the shot of the man in question.

Severi continued. "You're not married, but you were until fairly recently. The ring finger is still filling in a tan line where the ring was. It also says you're so busy you haven't been on a vacation for quite some time. The way you sit, mostly squared off and straight, suggests that you recognize leadership hierarchy. That comes from military experience. Given your age I'd venture you served in the Middle East or Afghanistan. Likely both. But you don't appear to have the eyes of a killer."

Heath broke in. "I think Mr. Reilly got more than he expected, Veronica."

"You'd be great working for a dating service," Reilly commented, quickly getting off the subject.

"Maybe when I retire," she replied in good humor.

"Okay, so you mentioned the guy in the video," Reilly said, getting back to the suspect, "I've nicknamed him Smug. It seemed to fit his expression."

"Very astute," Severi said.

"Do you have any other immediate reactions to what you see?" Reilly asked.

"Yes. Tight body. Physically fit. Military or paramilitary trained. No facials scars that I can see. That makes him doubly dangerous. Someone who can do maximum damage, strike first, and get away unharmed. He definitely didn't plan on dying that day. He's a man to steer clear of or," she paused and looked at Heath, "take out."

"Okay, everyone," Roosevelt Dubois said. "I put these images together. What do you see?"

They turned their attention to the computer screen where Dubois positioned Smug above six screen grabs of six other people from the footage.

"Beyond the difference in their desire to get out of the area fast?" Heath asked.

"But what's in the images?" Dubois prompted.

Reilly, who'd spent the most time with the video and had been on the ground twenty-four hours after the attack, studied the still frames. He put himself back into the aftermath with its lingering smell of explosives, the stench of human remains, the sight of burned toys, fused jewelry, fire-tinged papers, and utter devastation.

"His back," Reilly observed. He pointed to Smug.

"Yes," Agent Dubois said. "What about his back?"

"Smug has more residue on him than anyone else. That puts him closer to the initial blast. Plus," his finger moved up to the suspect's neck, "the back of his neck is slightly discolored. A burn?"

Severi raised her eyebrow. "What did you say you do?"

"I didn't really. But I'm in the hospitality business."

"Hmm," she intoned, looking back and forth between Reilly and Heath.

Reilly smiled. "We always look at people. You know, size them up. I meet a lot. So back to *Smug*. Any other ideas?" Reilly inquired.

"Let's rule out obvious points," Dubois stated. "He's not Japanese, so it's not a homegrown attack. Not Hispanic or Middle Eastern either."

"I'd say European," Reilly noted.

"More specifically Polish, Russian, Ukrainian, or maybe Romanian," Dubois concluded. "Lots of possibilities. Yes, for my money, your Mr. Smug is from somewhere within that region."

"Russian maybe . . ." Reilly mused, looking at the photo intently.

16

Before he left CIA headquarters Reilly made a request that added to Severi and Dubois' curiosity about Reilly's true career pedigree.

"I think it's best I drive back into DC or Arlington. Spend some time walking around, then take a cab to the airport. A CIA car to Dulles, and then a plane on to Tehran makes me feel a little exposed."

"Tehran?" Dubois asked.

"Meetings on a possible new hotel property. My job to evaluate."

Dubois agreed. "It'd be better not to pull up in a Company car or with a recognizable driver."

* * *

Two hours into Qatar Airways' overnight flight to Tehran, Reilly sat upright in his private first-class seat compartment. He opened his computer to reexamine the archived booking records from Tokyo's Kensington Royal, covering the day of the attack and a month prior. There were two thousand names. He focused on European travelers. That narrowed the list significantly, but it was still far too long a list to reveal anything without more resources. He'd given the same file to Heath, part of his new "job," for CIA evaluation.

Not yet tired, he signaled a flight attendant for dinner. He started with the "classic Arabic meze"—a combination of hummus, tabouleh, and muhammara served with Arabic bread. The attendant offered him a newspaper, and he chose the *London Guardian*.

For his main dish, Reilly had the thyme roasted chicken breast served with gnocchi and seared tomatoes. To accompany the meal he selected the Errazuriz Don Maximiano Founder's Reserve, a luscious Chilean cabernet blend. It was during his second glass, after his dinner had been removed, that a story in the British paper caught his eye. "Memorial Concert to Honor Celebrated Romanian Singer Kretsky." *Kretsky,* he thought. *The name.*

He began reading. The connection was spelled right out in the article.

> Janusz Kretsky, noted Latvian composer and singer who died in the deadly terrorist attack at a Tokyo hotel, will be honored in a Bucharest concert this Saturday.
>
> Kretsky achieved international fame producing and recording soundtracks for underground Romanian films. He was heralded in socialist circles and compared to France's Jacques Brel.
>
> Kretsky was an unabashed supporter of Russian citizens living in Romania, Poland, and the Baltic states, and an outspoken critic of NATO expansion. Earlier this year, Poland's annual rock festival in Oświęcim canceled Kretsky's scheduled performance. Organizers condemned comments the artist made that urged the West to give up its paranoia and twenty-first-century imperialism, while ignoring Russia's own incursions in Ukraine and Crimea.
>
> The 39-year-old artist had become a hero to Russian-speaking separatists residing in the former Eastern Bloc countries that now are democratic NATO members.

The story continued, covering Kretsky's lyrics and career, and included photographs at a sold-out Moscow concert.

Reilly tore out the *Guardian* article, folded it, and tucked in his pocket. He wasn't sure why he did it. Maybe it would be one of those things he passed onto Bob Heath.

17

For Veronica Severi, 11:00 p.m. could still be the middle of the workday when she threw herself into a challenge.

No matches, none, nada, she said to herself. The man whom the hotel executive had named Smug was either a newcomer to the scene or a highly experienced operator working well under the radar. She was inclined to believe he was the latter, and a most deadly one at that.

Severi was an expert in the CIA-developed facial recognition technology (FRT), which was later also adopted by the FBI and the Immigration and Naturalization Service. There were experts in each agency, but Veronica Severi was everyone's role model. She was renowned, as Reilly experienced, because she didn't completely rely on a run of algorithms. Severi believed that it still took the subjective human mind to evaluate collateral information. Her rule was, "When technology is augmented by experience, probability will increase."

Again she looked at the key frame, the "probe image," from the thumb drive Reilly had provided. *Looked at* didn't begin to describe it. She talked to it.

"Come on," she said aloud to the picture. "Tell me something."

Smug simply looked smug.

She enhanced the image in Photoshop, removing most of the noise and sharpening the facial features. So far no match with any other photograph in the database.

"Who are you? Why were you in Tokyo? Where do you work?" she asked the image on the computer screen.

The trouble with FRT was that it could only find a 100 percent biometric match if a matching photo was in the database. But performance not only depended on the depth of the archive and the quality of the original image, but the image clarity of all possible matches. In other words, the odds were stacked against a fast, reliable search if the subject was off the grid.

Reliability was also contingent on other factors: relatable environments in source and matching photographs, the age of the photos, optical focal length, and effective pattern recognition based on distinct facial features.

"Okay," she said to herself. "You won't talk? Then let's play chess. Time to figure you out."

Severi flipped a page on her notepad and started writing down her observational estimates.

Height: 6'–6'2" based on the car behind subject.

Weight: 180-200.

Eyes: dark, hazel or green. Cold.

Hair: brown, black eyebrows—possible dye job.

Scars or other distinguishable features: none.

Now how old are you? she wondered. He looked young. Twenty-five?

Severi studied the probe image again. "No, you made yourself look younger, didn't you?" she whispered.

She studied the photograph more. Then it came to her. His fitness level. He clearly worked out daily. *You're older than you appear,* she reflected, *a boss who still likes to get into the field. That's why you're smiling. You're self-satisfied.* Severi congratulated Reilly. He'd named him accurately. *Smug.*

The agency's database went back decades, but was richer with more recent photographs.

Severi realized she needed to run a more comprehensive search dating back to when Smug was in his twenties. For that, she'd need to photographically de-age him.

She brought the image into another program, hit a few keystrokes, and watched the hour glass rotate. Soon she had Smug at 20, 25, and 30.

Severi now ran the younger renderings through the database with search parameters from twenty years to ten years ago. Since the hunt would take hours, at 2:00 a.m. she finally called it a night.

18

TEHRAN, IRAN

ESPINAS PALACE HOTEL

From the moment Reilly deboarded the plane he felt eyes on him. In addition to some not-so secret police assigned to shadow him, Iranian soldiers kept Reilly in full view. What they saw in person, the airport security cameras also recorded. But it was when he approached customs where Reilly, fresh from a visit to the CIA, felt things could really go bad.

As he presented his documents, the veteran agent glared at him, tempting Reilly to act out of the ordinary. His look telegraphed his distrust. Inwardly Reilly worried that if there were anything that could get him arrested, this man would find it, and if not, he would invent it.

"State your business," the customs agent barked in heavily accented English. To make his point further understood, he pushed his jacket aside so Reilly would see his Glock.

"I am a hotel executive. We are exploring the possibility of opening a property in Tehran." For good measure he decided to add, "The meeting was called by the minister of economic development. I am here at his invitation."

If this meant anything to the officer, he dismissed it. He held on to Reilly's passport. "Do you have a letter to confirm your meeting?" he asked.

Damn, Reilly thought. He didn't. But he should have. More importantly now, the question was bait. Reilly resisted taking it.

"No, sir."

"And I am to merely believe you?"

Reilly smiled. "Sir, you may call the minister's office if there's any question."

"There is a question, and I'm asking it. Why have you really come to the Islamic Republic of Iran?" The customs officer signaled two Iranian soldiers to step forward.

Reilly paused before answering. This gave him a moment to calmly phrase his response and not give the guards any reason to react. "Of course, you must understand that such matters are confidential. Again, if you have concerns, you may make a call. I can provide you with the number."

Reilly knew the guard had it. He also knew that the Iran Customs Administration was actually part of the Ministry of Economic Development and Finance. *So why the hassle? Did they suspect a CIA connection?*

"Mr. Reilly, I think you're hiding something. I'm known for never being wrong."

"Sir, I'm vice president of International at Kensington Royal Hotels. As I stated, I arrived in your country at the behest of your government with the intent to establish a business relationship. This will be our first meeting."

Reilly decided he needed to show more resolve. Carefully. Smartly. Enough time had passed for any red flags to hit the custom agent's computer. He bet none had.

"I'd hate to report that Iran is unfriendly to the tourist trade. Now if you don't have any other questions, I would like to have my passport back."

He casually glanced over his shoulder, aware that a long line had queued behind him with impatient, exhausted travelers now likely worried they were in store for the same thing.

"I have a meeting I must get to."

The customs agent cleared his throat, realizing intimidation was no longer working. He moved on to a series of standard questions. Reilly affirmed he was not transporting alcohol or narcotic drugs; gambling tools, weapons, or explosives; magazines, publications, or films that violated the religious or national dignity of Iran; or cash beyond the legal allotment.

The agent stared at Reilly long and hard one last time. Reilly stood confidently under his gaze. Finally the customs officer indignantly stamped his passport and returned it with his visa.

"The Islamic Republic of Iran welcomes you," he coldly stated.

"Thank you," Reilly said, with the same insincerity.

Reilly took the waiting town car to his hotel, convinced he had been tested. But for what? *As a businessman or a spy?*

* * *

"Mr. Reilly. *As-salāmu 'alaykum.* Peace be upon you," Hosni Samir Madani offered in greeting thirty-five minutes later.

Samir Madani was the trade envoy assigned to Reilly. He was a heavyset, middle-aged man with a closely cropped beard. He wore a conservative light brown suit with a white shirt buttoned to the collar. All things considered, Reilly pegged him as former military.

"So honored to meet you," he added.

"*As-salaam 'alaykum,*" Reilly replied. "Thank you. I share the honor."

The two men shook hands in the lobby of the Espinas Palace Hotel, a lavish new 28-story, five-star hotel in the Sa'adat Abad neighborhood in northwestern Tehran. The hotel was built on 15,000 square meters of desert, set against the Alborz Mountains. It looked like it could have been transported directly from another reclaimed desert—the Las Vegas Strip.

With Iran's goal of adding 125 hotels and increasing visitors to twenty million by 2025, the Espinas Palace was a great advertisement for the tourism industry.

Reilly admired the work. The sparkling golden rotunda with carved reliefs celebrating heroic Persian battles. The highly polished marble floor had statuary reminiscent of the Gate of All Nations at the ceremonial capital, Persepolis. The magnificent chandelier suspended from the center illuminated a fresh flower setting so large that the scent had wafted his way the moment he entered the hotel.

If this was intended as a way to set the bar high, it worked. The Espinas Palace was absolutely palatial. *Hard to top*, he thought. If Kensington Royal came to Tehran to manage one of the new hotels, they'd be judged against the Espinas Palace Hotel.

"I trust your transit was good?" Samir Madani asked.

Reilly had no doubt that the head of the Iran-Foreign Joint Venture Association, an agency under Economic Development, had been briefed on how difficult its officer had actually made his entry.

"Oh, just fine," he said cavalierly. "Everyone doing his job."

Samir Madani voiced an almost inaudible, "Hmmm." "Well, I'm sure you're anxious to check in. Let us meet for dinner. Say 17:00? I will have a driver waiting for you in the lobby."

"That will be fine."

"Should you feel up for exploring, we are quite near the Carpet Museum and our heralded National Museum of Iran. Both are worth a visit."

Reilly thought that might be a good idea. He could also determine if Samir Madani had anyone following him.

"But let's get you checked in. Then the rest of the afternoon is yours."

When he reached his room on the twenty-third floor, it was apparent that his host had provided far more than the usual business room. Looking out, he had an expansive city view. Inside, it certainly fit every description and then some for an executive suite. On the ceiling were arrows indicating the proper direction to face Mecca for prayer. This wasn't new to Reilly, but he'd never seen it so artfully painted, even in Kensington Royal's hotels in the Middle East.

Most of all he was interested in surveillance apparatus. As an industry insider, he started with the fundamental knowledge that every hotel is a pre-equipped, functional laboratory for gathering information on clients. It began when check-in slid a credit card, or earlier if the reservation was guaranteed online. Further intelligence then came from phone numbers dialed on house phones and websites visited if logged in through the hotel Wi-Fi. And then there were the pay-per-view movies to consider. Even though a film title would not appear on the final bill, the hotel management could find out what had been watched and who had watched it.

Rarely was the data viewed or mined. But a business executive, diplomat, or world leader staying internationally had to take care. Information could be passed along, sold, or stolen for the purpose of compromising talks or discrediting characters.

Now in Tehran, Reilly was also concerned about more active devices that might be employed in his suite. He casually walked around looking for cameras, which likely covered the living room, bedroom, bathroom, and possibly the closets.

He didn't detect any, but that didn't mean they weren't behind the mirrors, which seemed to be strategically placed to reflect every quadrant. As for microphones, they could be in the lamps, phones, and even more discreetly in the bed. *Pillow talk.*

This definitely wasn't a secure place to have confidential calls. His training in the service told him that despite the thaw in US–Iranian relations, he shouldn't consider anywhere he went private.

Reilly opted to stay in and rest for three hours. Later, waking to his own cell phone alarm, he showered, dressed in a light green linen suit, and took the elevator down for his ride. As promised, a driver was waiting, his government Mercedes running and cool. Reilly was grateful. It was 122 degrees outside.

They drove into the heart of the city. This was Reilly's first trip to Iran. It was every bit the metropolitan hub, built up with Middle Eastern character. Towering new glass and cement office buildings cast shadows across century-old souks. Traffic flowed along six-lane downtown streets, in and around dedicated bus lanes, and through the

Grand Bazaar and the Tajrish Bazaar. Iran was definitely making itself a more welcoming destination.

The car pulled up in front of Alborz. The driver explained that it was one of Tehran's oldest and most famous traditional Persian restaurants. "The filet kabab is the best you'll ever have. But pace yourself. It's all wonderful." It was their only conversation since Reilly got into the car.

Reilly entered the restaurant and was led to an elegant table with gold utensils and gold-rimmed glasses atop a black silk tablecloth. Hosni Samir Madani rose from his seat to welcome him.

"You rested well, I hope?" he said shaking Reilly's hand again.

The question immediately confirmed Reilly's suspicion. His activities *were* being monitored.

"Oh yes. I travel a great deal. Jet lag doesn't hit me as long as I get a power nap in."

"Then you are a better traveler than I, my friend," Samir Madani replied. "Now we eat, get to know one another better, and talk just a modicum of business. We'll leave more for the morning meeting."

The driver had been right. The meal didn't disappoint, and the filet kabab was particularly wonderful.

Reilly tried to keep the dinner conversation light and intentionally vague. He talked about his passion for skiing, the type of thrillers he liked to read on his Kindle, and how he was married to his cell phone and no longer to his wife.

Samir Madani laughed at the last comment. "Yes, business travel, the great . . . what is your expression? Home-wrecker?"

"Yes, you never know where it can lead," Reilly said obliquely. He'd seen how his host subtly probed for details to everything. But Reilly had mastered the ability to be completely conversational and yet say nothing substantive at the same time.

Moving the subject away from the personal, he made an observation. "On the drive in I saw construction everywhere. I'm sure you're proud of where Tehran is headed," Reilly said. He intentionally stopped short of adding *since most sanctions eased.*

"I am. We've built more hotels in the last year than the total number in the last century. Our tourism industry provides the lens through which the international community will see the new Iran. I'm sure you're aware of Accor's growth."

"Yes, Europe's largest hotel group. Two four-star hotels already here."

"And more coming. The same with Rotana, which was the first hotel management company to announce its expansion plans. Four hotels, and still counting. Of course the arrival of more trusted American hotel corporations will truly signal that Iran is open for business. And to get tourists and businesses to our country, we're ordering hundreds of new passenger planes that we couldn't purchase until recently."

Even the Iranian avoided the word *sanctions*. It was still too charged a word.

"There's so much to see, Mr. Reilly, to celebrate, to explore. And tourism will turn Iran's economy around. We're building for a tsunami of tourists in the coming years. We have the most breathtaking Islamic architecture. You've had a taste of our sensational food. Our beaches are beautiful, and we even have skiing for you. Try Dizin. It has twenty ski lifts and has already been recognized by the International Ski Federation."

"I'll put it on the list."

"And we certainly hope the esteemed Kensington Royal will join in the development, for your benefit and ours. We'll talk more about it tomorrow when I unveil an investment package that you should find most attractive."

19

"Bob, can you come down?" Veronica Severi asked over the phone. "Sooner the better. Now's the best."

"Give me twenty, twenty-five minutes," Heath replied. "Have to see the director."

"You might want to stop by here first."

"Really?"

"Really," the facial recognition technician replied.

Heath called CIA Director Gerald Watts' office and bought himself an hour. He made it to Severi's computer station in ten minutes.

"Okay, Veronica, you got me at 'really.' What do you have?"

"This." She clicked on the enhanced probe photo of Smug. It was sharper than the original.

"Much clearer. Good job," he said, hoping this wasn't the only reason she'd asked him to delay his meeting.

"I ran it against everything in the database. I got a possible match with, of all people, the deputy director of transportation and public works in Santa Rosa, California. Similar features, but it seemed way off base. I downloaded other photographs of the guy and was able to confirm the false positive."

"Okay, so no go, and . . ."

"And a few more false positives easily confirmed with reanalysis and a few phone calls."

"So nothing," Heath concluded.

"Not until I gave it more thought. I knocked some years off the subject, narrowed the search parameters to relative years, and tied into some off-site archives."

"Tied in?" Heath asked. "Is that a euphemism for hacked?"

"Let's just stay with tied in."

"Tied in, then," Heath replied.

"My target field was the late 1980s to 2005—about a fifteen year spread to allow for five different age regression likenesses."

She clicked on the desktop. Five younger versions of the original image opened. "I ran these against our archives, but again nothing credible. Then the outside databases. ICON gave me a hit through the German paper *Hamburger Abendblatt.*"

By ICON Veronica meant the International Coalition of Newspapers, an aggregate of hundreds of publications old and new.

She brought a new JPEG up of a grainy news photo, which she lined up next to one of the younger computer depictions of the subject. There were definite similarities. Heath could see it in the eyes and cheekbones. Maybe the chin. A furry winter hat obscured the hairline.

Severi worked toward creating a more direct matchup. She cut out the hat on the archived picture and pasted it on top of the regressed image.

"Could be," Heath proclaimed. "But forget my eye. What's the computer probability?"

"It's 85 percent." She showed him the actual computer mapping on the eyes, nose, and mouth. "I'd sure like to back it up with another photo."

Heath was about to congratulate Severi when he stopped. "Was there a cutline description assigned to the archived photo?"

Severi smiled. "Yes. This is why I wanted you to check it out before you went upstairs."

She opened the source file and expanded the view to make the original newspaper clipping easier to read. But Heath couldn't read it. It was in German.

"I assume you've translated," he said.

"Of course." She brought the content up.

Heath read quickly once and then again. "Holy shit!" he exclaimed. "Print that for me."

"Already have," she said, handing him a sealed legal envelope.

20

TEHRAN, IRAN

Back at the hotel, Reilly decided to relax in the lounge and order a cup of sharbat, a cool, sweet Iranian drink. He was one of about a dozen visitors. Sizing up the room, he determined that two men were government moles. A loud French-speaking group of four were there for business. There were two couples. He listened to hear what languages they were speaking. One was German, the other Russian. Sitting alone at a small table was a very well put together woman reading London's *Financial Times*.

While he was deciding where to sit, his cell phone vibrated. Alan Cannon.

"Hi Alan, what's up?" Reilly said, backing out of the lounge.

"Working on Tokyo," the KR head of security said, choosing to be careful on an open line.

"Good to hear," Reilly replied. "Anything?"

"Yes and no. I got a feeling something's half a bubble off plumb."

This gave Reilly pause. "Oh?"

"Just a feeling." Cannon had effectively communicated what he wanted to tell Reilly.

Reilly replied, while working through *something's half a bubble off plumb*. The meaning of the expression came to him.

"Well, that's got to keep you up," Reilly replied, staying vague. He saw no eyes on him, but he couldn't know if there were any ears listening. There was definitely something cryptic in what Cannon had to say.

"It does. When will you be back?" Cannon inquired.

"Tomorrow's really my first business discussion. Then back on the plane the next morning. I have a stopover in London. How about we talk then?"

"Good."

They wrapped up with small talk and said goodbye, and Reilly returned to the lounge, continuing to think about the phrase Cannon had dropped. *Half a bubble off plumb.*

Nothing had changed inside the lounge. The men Reilly potentially ID'd as SAVAK, Iran's secret police, hadn't followed him. The French businessmen and the Russian and German couples remained ensconced in conversation. The woman reading the business pages still sat alone. He decided to change that.

"Market okay?" he asked, walking over to her corner table.

She looked up from the *Financial Times* and smiled. "Nothing seismic on the London Exchange," she replied. Her brown eyes sparkled in a way that brightened her entire face, which was appropriately framed by a blue hijab. Her clipped British accent and playful inflection seemed all the more welcoming.

"It all depends who you're following," she added. "I'd say you'd be interested in the New York Exchange and Kensington Royal stock."

Now he was surprised. "You have me at a disadvantage," Reilly said.

"Quite so." She laughed. "We're actually friends on LinkedIn, though we've never met."

"We are?"

"We are. Apparently I use it more effectively than you do, Mr. Reilly."

"Still at a disadvantage."

"Marnie Babbitt," she said. "Barclays London. And no doubt, we're both in Tehran for pretty much the same reason. New business."

"You're very, very good, Ms. Babbitt," he said.

"So I'm told."

Dan Reilly wondered if she meant her reply as a deliberate double entendre. He wondered enough to ask if he could sit down.

"Please," Babbitt said warmly.

Reilly saw a truly self-assured businesswoman who fully understood how to present herself in a Muslim country. Her ankle length dress covered everything and revealed nothing. Her makeup was understated and her jewelry worn as accents, not for show. He figured she was 35 or 36. No wedding ring. His interest was piqued by this intriguing woman, but he was also on his guard.

"Barclays. I haven't done any business with your bank," he commented.

"Not yet, but there's no time like the present, Mr. Reilly."

"We'll have to see," he returned.

Over the first cup of sharbat, he learned that she was an Oxford business grad who had come up through the ranks with jobs at Booz Allen Hamilton, Deloitte, and Citigold International before joining Barclays.

"Glad to see Barclays back in Iran," he offered. This was a pointed comment to show what he knew.

"And it's my job to make it right this time."

They were both talking about how Barclays had been fined $298 million in 2010 for violating sanctions against Iran, Libya, Sudan, Burma, and Cuba. The ruling came down to the banking institution for defying the Trading with the Enemy Act and the International Emergency Economic Powers Act. Now, however, the British bank was legally free to conduct business in Iran. And apparently Marnie Babbitt was a door opener.

"So, Mr. Reilly," she said, finishing her drink, "perhaps we can do some business together."

Reilly had been thinking the same thing. *Depending on the incentives that Samir Madani had in mind, Barclays financing could be key.* He'd keep an open mind.

"Well, you never know," he replied.

"Are you committed to opening here?"

This was a question he'd deflect. *Too probing*, he thought.

"Can't say." *And won't.* "But with the changes happening, we can't ignore it. Iran is pouring a ton of money into tourism."

"For the long haul, too," she offered with a roguish smile. "We really could work well together."

"You can tell that over one drink?"

"Oh yes, and you should see how much better I'd get to know you in a country that serves martinis."

"Well, Ms. Babbitt, I suppose we'll have to find out," he said willingly. Reilly liked the dance. But so far she was leading.

"I've done my homework on you, Mr. Reilly," she added.

"Oh?"

He assumed a *go ahead, tell me* posture.

"You're not one to walk away from trouble. You get involved. You're decisive. People are already talking about Mazatlán."

"Oh?" But he really thought, *Oh shit.* "Nothing to talk about," he added humbly.

"Okay, you're also modest. I like that. You have the reputation for being willing to make decisions—hard ones—without hesitating. Decisions that others would avoid. You act like a leader, and you sound like one, too. I saw clips of you on CNN. You gave it to those senators straight. That's high on my list, too."

"Thank you, but I think you've got me confused with somebody else."

"And that leads me to another thing."

"Uh-oh," he joked, feeling all the more uncomfortable with her reading. Between Marnie Babbitt and Veronica Severi's appraisals, his life apparently was an open book.

"You put your ego aside."

"Oh that," Reilly sighed with relief. "Yeah, it's probably cost me some bonuses."

"See, right there. You're a damned good manager. But I sense—"

Reilly quickly interrupted to go on offense. "My turn. Let me give Marnie Babbitt a read. You're a good poker player who can out-psyche a business opponent with flattery. It works for you."

"You think I'm trying to do that?" She stiffened.

"Up to a point. You may have passed it."

"Got me on one."

"You also take your work seriously. I'll bet you've risen in your career because you've argued against bad deals as much as you've made good ones happen. Maybe too loudly sometimes, which cost you promotions. That's why you've worked for five corporations in, I'd say, less than fourteen years."

"Okay, that's two right," she said uncomfortably.

Now Reilly relied on what he did know about Barclays' recent business. "You said no to a new Dublin hotel. Yes on a position with Hilton in Amsterdam. You walked away from Prague. I can only speculate. The company rightly prohibits bribes."

"Mr. Reilly, I think that's good enough," she interrupted, sounding vulnerable herself now.

"And if I have my information right, you're recommending against an oil play in Beijing that will probably get you in Dutch with both the Chinese and the Russians."

"Really, enough, Mr. Reilly, especially since most of this isn't even in the papers," Babbitt insisted.

"Right," Reilly laughed. He was pleased with the way he had maneuvered the dance by taking the lead. "I think it's safe to say we're both pretty good at what we do and we should find reasons other than business to keep talking."

She smiled and asked, "Did they give you one of the suites?"

This threw him off his game. "That's fast. We've jumped to the bedroom?"

"Ah, Mr. Reilly, behave. I was only wondering if they've rolled out the red carpet as much for you."

"Yes. Very nicely," he said trying recover from his inappropriate remark. "It's the most palatial suite I've been in, and I've been in a lot."

"However good yours is, they have better. Like the top-floor suite where President Gorshkov stayed."

"Oh," Reilly said. "I'm sure we could ask to see it."

"I tried," she said with a slightly exasperated note in her voice. "No luck. They explained they're making upgrades based on client requests."

"Not good enough for Gorshkov?"

"Even richer billionaires. And he stayed before they officially opened. The hotel was the main residence for the Russian delegation when they were here for the Gas Exporting Countries Forum. Apparently Gorshkov's visit forced them to get it in shape early."

Reilly didn't say it, but he believed the rush was either to put in surveillance devices, or at the risk of being discovered, to take them out.

"You never know," is all he said. He wondered if she was savvy enough to share the same thought.

21

MOSCOW, RUSSIAN FEDERATION

1999

Nikolai Gorshkov curried favor with Boris Yelstin. It paid off when the president first reinstated Gorshkov's authority as a spy making him a *silovik* again, a security official; a man with power—deadly power. As a senior officer in the Federal Security Service he compiled files on corrupt energy oligarchs who desperately tried to pay him off rather than face exposure. It only worked one way. To Gorshkov's benefit. And in less than a year Gorshkov used the intelligence and finances to eliminate obstacles and craft his next move upward. Yeltsin brought his disciple into the Kremlin, making Gorshkov a deputy prime minister.

Now, Gorshkov's goals were personal and patriotic. Personally, he sought to multiply his holdings and strengthen his political hand, while his nationalistic desire was for Russia never to return to a period of paralysis. He vowed to restore Russia's position in Europe and the world. He had no loyalty to any specific ideology or form of top-down governance, so long as *he* would eventually be at the top.

Gorshkov worked hard from within to rebuild Russia, first by helping end the financial influence of the oligarchs. His tactics were well within his experience. Threats and murder. First consolidating control over the energy sector. Next other businesses. The banks, the media, and transportation.

Inevitably, and through shrewd, never reported manipulating, Nikolai Gorshkov advanced again, this time to first deputy prime minister. After obediently serving two subsequent regimes, Gorshkov was elected president.

As his first act he invited Russia's few remaining private corporate titans to the Kremlin. He gave them 48 hours to divest 50 percent of their holdings to the government and to stay out of politics for *life*. Life was the operative word. Those who heeded his warning would be left to enjoy their riches. Those who didn't? Gorshkov didn't have to complete the thought. The businessmen and women had heard rumors about Gorshkov's "problem solver" who was particularly adept at dispatching permanent punishment. They didn't know his name, but he had all of theirs.

The rumors were basically true. Gorshkov's assassin worked around the globe. He was secretly funded by Gorshkov and with no limit to the number of false identities and poisons at his disposal. He was a chameleon and an assassin who had long eclipsed Carlos the Jackal, for years the world's most notorious terrorist.

Andre Miklos was a consummate professional: ever-devoted to Nikolai Gorshkov and always ready to complete a mission for his old comrade.

"You never rest, Andre," Gorshkov jokingly said when they met after his most recent assignment. Miklos had gassed a corrupt oil magnate—a fitting tribute, even according to Western headlines. "You need a vacation. How about the Amalfi Coast? Lose yourself in some hot, rich, frustrated married woman who's looking to get fucked."

Miklos smiled. It was a very good idea. The timing worked. First a stop in Ukraine, then onto Italy. He spoke more than acceptable Italian, and he would use an Austrian ID.

"I will."

"Good. And while you're there you can take care of a problem."

Miklos smiled. "Oh?"

"A journalist. Anna Petrovich. She's been digging back into an old story for a Romanian newspaper and has an American book contract in place. We'll deal with the paper second. But first, see to it that she makes *other* kinds of news."

He didn't go into any further detail—he didn't have to. Miklos was familiar with the newspaper and how critical it was of Gorshkov.

"Anna," Gorshkov said sweetly, "will be vacationing in Ravello."

"A lovely place."

"By the way," Gorshkov chuckled, "she's very attractive and holidaying away from her husband." He handed Miklos a file. "There's more in here about her *personal* predilections."

Andre Miklos grinned as he read the FSB report. *Definitely pleasure before business*, he thought.

22

The second day of Reilly's visit to Tehran began with a late morning tour of the new Economic Development Building in downtown Tehran. The ultramodern structure, designed with a Gehry flair, was a statement about Iran's future. Samir Madani's mission was to reinforce the point that the government was backing up its commitment to tourism with vision and money. Beyond the walk-through, there was no other propagandizing. However, Reilly got a reminder of the kind of country, and likely the nature of the business, he would be involved in if they came to terms.

"I understand you met Ms. Babbitt last night."

Reilly raised an eyebrow.

"Oh nothing so sinister, Mr. Reilly," the government official said conversationally. "Actually we shared a delightful breakfast this morning. We talked about a variety of options, including a joint venture between Barclays and Kensington Royal, with a twenty-five-year managing contract. So, rest assured, you are in a new Iran."

"Thank you. Perhaps there will be an opportunity. I look forward to meeting with Ms. Babbitt again myself."

Adjourning to a conference room, Samir Madani brought in his development team. They had a colorful PowerPoint presentation, a backup deck, Excel spreadsheets, details on available land, and renderings based on KR designs in other major capitals.

The underwriting was more than Reilly expected, but it didn't guarantee anything. After all, this was the Middle East, where negotiations really began after contracts were signed. So he nodded and studied the financials without giving an indication of his position, even when pressed.

Lunch was served in the conference room. The afternoon session commenced with Madani in full sales mode.

"Mr. Reilly, I invite you to talk to anyone you'd like. You'll find our people literate, well-informed, and technically savvy. We are a large market. The largest in the Middle East, in fact, with 80 million hungry for foreign trade and travel."

"Europe sees the potential," he continued. "Yet the United States business community remains slow to recognize the positive. Sadly, you'll pay the price for waiting from the sidelines. Our initiatives with EU nations grow every week."

The Iranian leaned closer. "May I speak from the heart, Mr. Reilly?"

"Please." Reilly couldn't wait to see where this would go.

"Millions of Iranians dream of America. They crave American consumer goods. Our own trade ministers quietly acknowledge that it's the place Iranians most identify with."

"Remarkable," Reilly said.

"The US should view the Islamic Republic of Iran as a willing partner from which to launch business throughout the whole region. We are big, and we are safe, without terrorism."

"Ah, Mr. Madani, let's stay on that topic," Reilly replied. "Undoubtedly you've seen the news from Tokyo. Our hotel was attacked by as of yet unidentified terrorists."

"Yes, I'm sorry. I should have extended my sincere sympathy. An oversight with no excuse."

"Thank you," Reilly responded, equally politely. "But to my point, we have a close working relationship with the Japanese government, Tokyo police, and their intelligence agencies. In turn, they share information with Interpol and the FBI." Reilly intentionally avoided mentioning the CIA.

"Excuse me for a moment," said Samir Madani, addressing the others in the room. Reilly understood he was dismissing them. This interpretation was confirmed when everyone left with polite nods.

"I'm sorry, Mr. Reilly. Please continue," he implored.

"Thank you. It's really this simple. For us to feel secure in your country, we would need prior assurance and preestablished crisis plans, with 24-7 contacts and the promise of complete and full cooperation at the highest level."

Samir Madani listened. It was much more than he thought he'd have to deal with or report on. "This may be beyond what other hotel franchises have required," Madani pointed out.

"With all due respect, sir, if Kensington Royal comes to Tehran in any capacity we will need assurances. We will accept an Iranian national as general manager, but security will be under KR control."

"We would have issues with foreign or private armed guards. I'm sure you can understand the problems that would pose for my government."

Reilly thought that for a man who couldn't speak with authority on the subject, Samir Madani was doing just fine.

"I do," Reilly acknowledged. "If we construct a secure property and we have a completely open relationship, our in-house team can work with yours. I suspect, however, that such a relationship will be a challenge for your leadership and that could stymie your department's best intentions."

The Iranian stood up and walked around the room once. He remained standing directly opposite Reilly.

"No doubt your experience in Japan has shaped your opinion."

"Sir, this is fact. And yes, Tokyo, has made a difference for us. But it has done the same for others in Mumbai, Jakarta, Bamako, Sousse, and Burkina Faso. The list goes on. The news is not good for tourism.

The news would be far worse if an attack occurs in Tehran and we end up being unable to work together."

Now it was Dan Reilly's turn to stand.

"As Tehran becomes more of an international destination," he continued, "American properties, French and German properties, even your own hotels and resorts might become targets of foreign terrorists or homegrown cells. To put it bluntly, like it or not, we are in the anti-terrorism business now. You have to determine if your nation's tourism industry realizes that as well."

"My friend," Madani said, "let us bring the proposals to each of our respective superiors and keep our discussions open and friendly."

The Iranian straightened his jacket and walked around the table to Reilly with his hand extended.

"Agreed," Reilly said, shaking on it. "We will consider this our beginning." Reilly, however, believed it was over. He had asked for too much.

23

At the same time Reilly was conducting his meeting in Tehran, an elderly traveler was waiting patiently at the check-in line at a hotel in Kiev. He wore a velvet hat, wire-framed glasses, and a frumpy jacket, and didn't appear to be in a rush. He was virtually invisible in the business hotel lobby; just another weary traveler who wanted to call it a night.

The queue took ten minutes. The clerk at reception apologized to the man for the wait.

"Not a problem," he said in halting Ukrainian, handing over his German passport and credit card.

"Just one night, Mr. Richter?" the clerk asked in German.

"Ah yes, thank you," Karl Richter replied. "Your German is appreciated. Yes, one night, perhaps two, if business requires."

"Certainly. Just let us know tomorrow before 13:00."

The rest of the process continued without additional conversation, which the German preferred. When he was given his electronic room key he replied, "Thank you," in forced Ukrainian to be polite.

The man would only be remembered as elderly and pleasant—never as a suspect. That man's real name was Andre Miklos, and now he had work to do.

In his room he removed his laptop, went through three levels of security, and reviewed the target report assembled by his operatives. He'd conduct his own survey in the morning when the hotel would be busiest with checkouts. But on first blush, the plan looked good from the placement of devices to the execution.

The Klovska Classic Hotel in downtown Kiev was a strategic target in a larger strategic mission. Outwardly, the hotel retained its nineteenth century charm, but it had twenty-first century upgrades, a four-star standing, and enthusiastic ratings on Yelp. Visiting government delegations often chose the Klovska Classic for its convenience, services, and charm. Andre Miklos selected it because of a scheduled visiting delegation.

He went to sleep that night wondering if the room he was in would still be there in a few days.

24

"Half a bubble off plumb?" Reilly asked two days later from United Global First Lounge in Heathrow where he had phoned Alan Cannon.

"Just a feeling," Cannon replied. "Glad you got the gist."

To understand the phrase, Reilly relied on the construction. It referred to a leveling device used to exact a midway point perfectly aligned horizontally or vertically. Half a bubble indicated that something was a touch off, not quite right. Or for that matter, wrong.

"About?"

"I think the FBI is stonewalling. I've got the feeling that they found something and they're not letting on."

"Explain," Reilly requested. He was feeling uncomfortable considering he was also working an inside track with the CIA and they were likely talking with the FBI. *Cross purposes*, he wondered.

"Crickets. Nothing. I can't get my fucking calls returned from my old office."

"It's just been a few days," Reilly offered.

"Yes, but no calls returned? To me? Feels like they got a match and they don't want to talk about it."

"Give it a little more time. You don't want to burn your bridges."

"I won't. But the hairs on the back of my neck are prickly. Feels like this whole thing has been kicked up to a higher level."

Reilly consoled his KR colleague, but couldn't explain why he might not be hearing from the FBI. For the first time, he felt like he was in the middle and . . . a liar.

"Maybe I can suss some things out. Give me a few days," Reilly proposed.

After his call with Cannon, Reilly phoned Brenda Sheldon. She had some changes to his schedule. The Senate subcommittee had moved up his second appearance. They wanted him in four days.

Damn, he thought.

"Email me the latest stats, Brenda. Hopefully the Wi-Fi will be working on the plane and I can give this some more thought." He wanted to hit the senators harder this time.

25

"Mr. Reilly, let's begin where we left off."

"Thank you, Mr. Chairman," said Reilly, detecting a more forthcoming tone from Senator Moakley Davidson.

"Is everything okay after your Tokyo attack?"

Okay? Reilly thought? *How can it be okay? Dozens dead. Others who will suffer for the rest of their lives.*

"I beg your pardon, Senator?"

"Are things returning to normal?" Davidson continued.

"Am I still under oath? Is this part of the testimony? Are you seriously asking if everything is okay?"

"Well, yes," Moakley said, not realizing how foolish he sounded.

"Then, Mr. Chairman, I'll answer it this way. Things are not okay. We are living with a *new normal*. On average somewhere in the world a hotel is attacked every 14 days. On average, 7.54 people are killed in each attack, 6.96 are injured. That is the new normal. Kensington Royal felt it two weeks ago. So, no, everything is not okay, Senator Davidson."

The senator glared at Reilly and leaned into the microphone, but an aide had the good sense to pull him away and whisper something in his ear.

"To most, these attacks may seem irrational," Reilly continued. "A waste of human life. Death with no reason. But there's always a reason, whether or not the perpetrators are making a political statement, creating fear, or instilling distrust. And there's a reason, whether they've planned on an escape route or are hell-bent on dying in the process."

Davidson wanted to cut in, but he recognized it would appear impertinent, something he didn't want to show on Fox News, let alone MSNBC.

"Violent terrorist attacks test governments and security personnel. Examples? Look at the way al Qaeda changed the way we fly after 9/11. Now ISIS has changed *where* we're willing to travel and if it's even safe to conduct business in risky zones."

The chairman found a way in. "Mr. Reilly, I merely asked a question about the attack on your company's property as a courtesy. You're giving this committee a lecture."

"Not the committee, sir. You. With all due respect, I'm answering your question. It will never be normal there again. It will never be normal in any resort, café, theater, county office building, or government embassy. Not abroad or in the United States.

"The new normal? After the ISIS attack that brought down the Russian charter plane resulting in 224 lives, Egypt hired a London consulting agency to review security procedures at Sharm El Sheikh International Airport. Couple that with the attack at a Red Sea resort where vacationing tourists were stabbed by two militants. Egypt's tourism minister pledged millions for bomb-sniffing dogs, body scanners, and other counter measures.

"No longer can people go somewhere and simply relax. While tourists are the visible target, terrorists actually seek to foment instability, to shake faith in a government's ability to protect people, to bring down a sector of the economy that relies on outside dollars, and to create the vacuum for a new order to rush in."

"I understand your point, Mr. Reilly," Davidson replied.

Doubtful, Reilly thought.

"Then tell me, could the attack in Tokyo have been prevented?" Davidson asked politely.

Finally, a substantive question.

"We could have stood a chance with better intelligence. More training for our people to distinguish anyone on a reconnaissance run from everyday guests. Access to intelligence databases at check-in. Admittedly, it's a big step forward. But airlines, for instance, have such access, including real-time updates on threats. How can we, in a parallel business, possibly defend against the most dangerous terrorist groups in the world without assurances that intelligence will be made available to us as well?"

"Are you suggesting that information was withheld?"

"How could I possibly know, Senator? What kind of investigations can a hotel chain run on the Islamic State, Taliban, Jabhat al-Nusra, al-Shabaab, and the other fifty-eight terrorist organizations known to be operating in the world today?"

"Make this as clear as a bell for me. You have no access to information today?"

Reilly was under oath, so he'd have to talk around the question. "As I've previously testified, Kensington Royal has some information. Open State Department warnings and security advisories we subscribe to through private agencies. In addition we employ former intelligence officers now working for major consulting firms. By and large they're aggregators compiling, publishing, and distributing information. We need to be higher up in the food chain. We need timely, specific, and credible intelligence."

"Confidential intelligence flowing into your corporate hands, Mr. Reilly?"

"I prefer to describe it as advance word to help us save lives, Senator."

***

CIA HEADQUARTERS

"A couple of birdies told me you caused quite a stir in town yesterday."

Reilly laughed at Bob Heath's comment. "Guess I did."

"Pretty ballsy, Reilly."

"Well, Davidson pissed me off."

"Apparently. I got a call from the director asking about our relationship."

"What did you say?" Reilly asked.

"Enough. No more. That we have a mutual desire to share information."

"Then how about sharing," Reilly suggested.

"Working on it."

"Well then, here's a question. What came up when you ran the photo? Who the hell is Smug? And have you been talking to the FBI? Because they've stopped talking to our head of security."

Heath hesitated. "Let's just say it's all flowing through the system."

"Bob . . ." Reilly read Heath's pause as a red flag.

"What?"

"Cut the bullshit. You got a match."

"I didn't say that."

"You sure as hell did. 'Still in the system.' I wasn't born yesterday. I can read you better than anyone."

"Nothing really verifiable," Heath acknowledged.

"But you got a hit," Reilly shot back.

"Nothing verifiable," he repeated. "That's all I can say."

"Suddenly I'm a clearance problem?" Reilly thought for a moment. "Or try this on for size. You're working with the FBI on what you found. Either you, or they, or you both have confirmed something."

"Don't jump to conclusions."

"And like I said, don't bullshit me, Bob. Alan Cannon got shut down at the bureau and I'll bet you a lobster dinner that you're doing the same with me right now."

"Look, it's complicated. I can't say."

"Jesus, Bob. It's me. I brought you the damned video."

"We would have seen it eventually. Your buddy gave it to the FBI."

"Thank you for the confirmation that you're talking with them."

"We're talking," Heath replied uncomfortably.

"So, Jesus Christ! Just tell me."

"Look, I can't, Danny." Heath only used *Danny* when he was feeling contrite with his old friend. "My hands are tied. At least for now. We have to kick this upstairs."

"The director?" Reilly asked sharply.

"Up, upstairs."

"How high?"

"Up, up, upstairs."

Reilly got the message loud and clear. The White House.

26

MOSCOW, RUSSIAN FEDERATION

APRIL 9, 2015

It had been a good day for Boris Litvenko. The retired Russian colonel and head of the reformist party "Russia One" had just won approval from the Justice Ministry to participate in the December parliamentary elections.

Litvenko had enemies, but Liberal Russia had supporters because of his credibility as an anti-war leader. His stock had risen when he served as vice chair of the Kusinitz Commission, which was established outside of the Kremlin to investigate the inciting incidences that led to Russia's advance on Crimea. Even though his work was shut down, Litvenko kept the issue alive, forming a committee of human rights advocates, most of whom were openly anti-Gorshkov.

The wide-eyed, wild-haired reformer was on a mission. But so was the man who was waiting for him near the entrance of his Moscow apartment.

Litvenko stepped out of his car, straightened his grey weave sports coat, and wished his driver a good night. The 52-year-old politician smiled, feeling good about the news coverage he had been getting lately in the West. It had been a good day.

The stranger approached from behind. Litvenko didn't hear him as he raised his Makarov pistol equipped with a silencer and shot Litvenko three times in the back.

Litvenko's short-sleeve blue shirt turned beet red as he collapsed to the pavement, never to rise again. The assassin ran away.

Later, the press would report that Litvenko was the eleventh member of the Russian parliament killed in less than a decade. Andre Miklos had not kept count himself. But Nikolai Gorshkov, rising in Kremlin hierarchy, had.

27

WASHINGTON, DC

PRESENT DAY

Gerald Watts briefed the president. The lanky new CIA director never minced words. He spoke unemotionally and without shading that required any interpretation. Everything he brought to the White House was declarative and important.

"Are you sure?" the president asked after hearing Watts' presentation.

Alexander Crowe, former NASA Space Shuttle astronaut-turned-senator and now first-term US president, was also known for getting right to the point. He'd seen attempts to destabilize the government from outside and within, and encountered people who wanted to take him down and take him out. So when his CIA director came to him with a problem, he listened.

"Facial recognition is a reliable tool made more reliable when working with picture-perfect images," Watts replied.

President Crowe was aware of the breakthroughs with facial recognition technology. Though not so easily admissible in court, he knew his intelligence agencies relied heavily on it from ports of entry to closed circuit cameras peering down on major city streets. Watts gestured to four photographs he had brought that were now on the Oval Office coffee table.

"I can't describe any of these as anywhere near perfect," Watts continued. "They're out of focus, shot from a distance, or copies that are generations down from the original. We've sharpened and enhanced them. When the software sees enough signatures, identifiable markers—eyes, cheekbone structure, one ear lower than the other, teeth—well, then it gives us a probability decision."

"100 percent?" the redheaded 51-year-old president asked.

"Well below that, but a probability worth considering."

"Can we get any other backup?"

This is when the CIA director revealed another detail.

"The FBI came up with the same possibility at their Quantico facility—independently, and using the same original photograph. More important to me, my chief analyst stands by the assessment."

The president leaned back in his wooden captain's chair, left behind by his predecessor. It had belonged to Admiral Halsey long before that. "Any thoughts on the motive?" he asked.

"None, Mr. President, only speculation." Watts explained the possibilities that they had come up with so far. "That said, we don't know who he is or his motivation."

"So at this point we have an offshore attack, no known purpose, and no Americans killed."

"But an American-managed hotel. An American corporation."

"Yes, Gerald, but in Japan. Not here. Given the speculation and the lack of any evidence, I don't see any immediate threat to the United States. There's nothing that is . . ." the president leaned forward and continued, "formally actionable."

The CIA director left with an oblique order: Nothing formally actionable. *Formally.*

* * *

A week later, the select committee members filed into KR's Washington conference room on K Street. They were prompt and ready to work. These were serious men and women, experts in their fields, thought leaders, and influencers who worked in the private sector and often in the shadows.

Alan Cannon accompanied them from the lobby, and Dan Reilly greeted each at the door. One by one they took designated seats behind name cards around the large oval walnut table.

"Welcome everyone," said Reilly, taking a seat near the middle of the table, not the very end. This removed any sense of hierarchy, while giving him a clear view of the invitees.

"Many of you already know the man to my right, our head of global security, Alan Cannon."

Cannon nodded hello again.

"Next to Alan, Kensington Royal COO, Lou Tiano."

Tiano, 55, was a career employee who had helped Edward Shaw grow the company over the decades. He had a warm smile and an open face that often masked the shrewd corporate acumen beneath. Tiano wore a classic light blue Brooks Brothers suit with a white shirt, a gold tie, and expensive Italian shoes. He was the most put-together man in the room.

Reilly continued the introductions. Sitting next to Tiano was the company's CFO, Pat Brodowski. Tall, blonde, and shrewd, she had been recruited from Citibank to bolster the company's financial department. A year into the job she was promoted to chief financial officer. It was no surprise Reilly seated her within whisper distance of Tiano.

"Now to my left, our head of legal, Chris Collins." Ever the lawyer, Collins' yellow pad was already filled with questions.

"Chris is here to keep us honest," Reilly said, realizing that honesty wasn't necessarily first and foremost on the invitees' minds. They were primarily in the intelligence, security, and safety businesses, after all.

Beside Chris was KR's lead corporate public relations officer, June Wilson. Next, the company's IT chief, Spike Boyce. The youthful, blond, and casually dressed Boyce tipped his pencil as a salute to the committee.

Directly opposite him was former CIA Director Carl Erwin, a veteran

Navy SEAL. Now retired at 67, Erwin was a go-to high-level security consultant, and arguably one of the most experienced in the world. To his left was retired army general BD Coons, and to his right, former assistant FBI director Jay Reardon. Reardon, ten years younger than Erwin, had collaborated with the CIA chief on many investigations. His specialty was terrorism. That gave him a key seat at Kensington Royal's table.

One more over was the mystery man in the room. The scarred and barrel-chested Donald Klugo was president and CEO of GSI, a company that operated out of Jordan. Global Security Initiatives provided guns for hire, a mercenary force with boots able to quickly hit the ground once flown into danger zones on their two Airbus Beluga Super Transporters. Klugo had worked with each of the invitees, but there was no official records of any of his missions.

Each of the invited experts would earn $50,000 for the first two-day session and one-day follow up.

Now Alan Cannon took over.

"Here's the schedule. We work from now until 10:00 a.m. We'll take a ten-minute break, then back with a working lunch brought in at 12:30. Another break at 2:00 p.m., and we'll wrap at seven. Help yourself anytime to coffee and pastries on the sideboard. Of course there will be no audio or video recording. No attribution. Accordingly, we encourage brutally honest thinking to make this company more responsible and more capable of handling today's threats against our industry."

"Brutally honest?" BD Coons immediately interrupted.

"Yes, General."

"You should have had this meeting ten years ago. Anything you implement now will be catch-up."

Cannon was about to respond, but Reilly cut him off.

"I'll take it, Alan," he said. "You're right, General. But I'm committed to making changes starting now."

The general looked at the other KR executives. "You said 'I'm committed,' Mr. Reilly. Unless everyone is committed, this will be a royal waste of time and effort." His sarcastic use of the company name was not missed. Coons stared at each of the executives, testing them. Lastly he settled on Tiano.

The COO returned the look. "General Coons, this has the endorsement of the president of the corporation," said Tiano.

"Not good enough," Coons argued. "I don't see him here. So don't waste my time or the time of my colleagues. As far as I'm concerned, any one of you on the business side can sink it. If Ms. Brodowski is not on board, money won't be there. Mr. Collins needs to embrace the legal risks and look the other way if there's something he doesn't want to see. Ms. Wilson will have to carefully control outbound messaging, while Mr. Boyce surely will have to rebuild his IT network. So with all due respect to your venerated president, I ask again, is *everyone* committed?"

He gave each of the company's power holders another deep stare.

Brodowski nodded. Wilson reported in with a clear, "Yes." Boyce gave a thumbs-up. Realizing that was too casual, he added a strong verbal, "Yes, sir."

Only KR's attorney held back.

"Mr. Collins?" General Coons said in an accusatory tone. "Are you with the rest?"

Collins skimmed his notes, all prepared in advance to bring the session into line with his legal concerns. He nervously cleared his voice.

"Mr. Collins?" Coons demanded.

Chris Collins looked at his pad one more time. Taking a deep breath, he turned it over and met Coons' eye.

"Yes. Yes, I'm onboard."

"Good," Coons said. "Then I'm here to work with you."

Dan Reilly was grateful that Coons had put the entire group to the test. As only an outsider could, the two-star cut through the crap. He imagined how Coons had done the same thing in the field, the Pentagon, and in the White House.

The general smiled. "I believe you were speaking, Mr. Reilly?"

"Thank you," said Reilly. He then began explaining the immediate goal. "*We*," Reilly emphasized, "must develop practical procedures to assess threats. We have to establish relationships, whether open or covert, with American and global intelligence networks to access and act upon information. And by acting, we become proactive, a global leader in our industry, and a company that has entered the fight against terrorism. With that, I open the floor."

"Mind if I start with a little history?" former CIA director Carl Erwin asked.

Reilly encouraged him to continue.

"The first hotel bombing in modern history was carried out in 1946 at the King David Hotel in Jerusalem. The terrorists, assuming you accept the term in this case, were an underground militant Jewish organization. The hotel served as headquarters for the British authority ruling over Palestine, the Secretariat of the Government of Palestine, and the British Forces in Palestine and Transjordan. The bomb took out much of the southern wing of the hotel, the quadrant that housed intelligence records. This suggests it could have been an inside job— an Israeli spy within the British and Palestinian administration. It is something for you to consider in your own properties. Can you trust your own people? But back to that July 22 attack—91 people died. It became a model for strikes to come. The lessons since tell the same story. Hotels represent the countries where they're headquartered and, by association, often that government. They are soft targets, difficult to protect, relatively porous, and easy to penetrate. You have a constant flow of people rarely identified by security, and in our realm, they offer a clear field."

These were the cold hard facts made all the more real because the danger had come home.

"So, the question is, what can be done to affect the terrorist attack cycle? An inevitability today."

"Attack cycle?" COO Lou Tiano asked.

"I'll take that," former FBI agent Jay Reardon said. "It's a systemized plan. The steps terrorists take. But first, let me make this clear. You are not the police. You are not the military. I'm pleased to see Don Klugo here for the sake of discussion, but you do not have a paramilitary force. You are plainly and simply the target. You have to learn what to look for, and then get professionals in to help."

Tiano had a KR embossed pen in hand ready to write on his notepad.

"In order, here's the attack cycle: target selection, strategic planning, final preparation and staging, the actual attack, exfiltration if the intent is not suicide, and media exploitation."

Collins was writing now, too. "Can you go slower?"

"Yes," Reardon said. "Number one. Selection of the target. Is the target symbolic? Will it create impactful media attention? Can it cause maximum physical damage and loss of life? Will it be successful? Drilling down deeper, any attacking forces will conduct surveillance on multiple hotels, maybe as many as ten to twelve in an area. They collect basic intel and prepare target folders. We call it the CARVER matrix. CARVER for Criticality, Accessibility, Recuperability, Vulnerability, Effect, and Recognizability. OSS agents in World War II came up with the acronym for the French underground to ID possible targets, and it became a mainstay for US Special Forces in Vietnam. Through the process, the most vulnerable building in the target zone becomes the best target."

"Can't it be turned on itself for defense?" Reilly asked. "To think like a terrorist and therefore foil a threat?"

"Absolutely. They surveil for visible security, locations of closed-circuit cameras, retractable steel bollards and cement barriers, metal detectors, and dogs. You should be making sure you have some or all in place. Take ease and opportunity off the table and you'll save lives."

Reardon stood up and walked over to the coffee urn. He continued to talk as he poured out a cup and returned to his seat.

"So a terrorist puts together his target folder. Now based on this field intelligence, a final target is selected out of the alternatives. Then comes the planning component—the how and when. They practice offsite and conduct trial runs and asset deployment. This is when an attacking force gets their equipment inside or near the target.

"Given this clear, predictable, and absolutely required template, counterterrorism forces look for the same things, but with the goal of tightening the gaps and vulnerabilities. Our job is to *disrupt and deny*. Make the target unattractive. To put it more simply, visible defenses should make it *not* worth the effort. That's the best way to take a location off the target list."

"Jay, can you explain the steps to accomplish that?" Cannon requested. He was on a first name basis with the retired FBI agent from their days together at the bureau. "And let's drill down into what we can do."

"It comes down to distinct interdiction points. First and foremost, deter through highly obvious security measures: guards, cameras, patrols, and barriers. Second, train staff. You know the phrase, 'If you see something, say something.' You'd be surprised, but you can even turn the cleaning staff into unofficial operatives. If they see maps in hotel rooms with detailed markings that appear outside the ordinary tourist notations, speak up. If they find more than a typical amount of 9-volt batteries or battery packages, speak up. If they notice remote-control devices, speak up. If someone asks them about routine shift time changes for hotel staff or security, speak up. If they notice guests taking multiple selfies or pictures of the hotel that include closed-circuit camera placement, for God's sake, tell security. And in case they don't move on it, get to the general manager or whoever will get the blame if they ignore the obvious."

"Wait a second," Chris Collins said. "Doesn't this border on profiling? I can see lawsuits in the making here. Turning housekeepers into spies?"

"Since you invoked spies, Mr. Collins, I'll take this one," Carl Erwin volunteered. "This is not about profiling. It's about being vigilant. I take it your concern is religious or racial profiling?"

"Well, yes."

"That is generally an American domestic issue. Many hotels that have been attacked have been in Muslim-majority nations. There, Caucasians stand out. So no, this is not a matter of profiling. And more to the point, you are facing a far bigger problem than a lawsuit from a guest who may be questioned."

Collins took in a deep breath. Reilly patted him on the arm and felt that his colleague was beginning to get it.

Donald Klugo leaned into the conversation for the first time. He instantly commanded attention with his deep voice and staccato delivery.

"I guess you invited me because you want my opinion." It wasn't a question and Klugo didn't stop. "Well, unlike the men to my left, all government guys, I'm the one they quietly call when a job has to get done that they can't do. I run a private international security firm with a fancy name that Googles easily. But the truth is, I'm a mercenary, running a mercenary squad that can deploy anywhere in the world. Not to beat around the bush—we kill people."

For his next comment he focused on the KR lawyer. "Too indelicate, Collins?"

Collins offered a hand, palms up. A sign of acquiescence.

"We worry about the bad guys, not the law," Klugo continued. "Because in some places, there is no law, only chaos. Trust me, I've researched your international properties: Jerusalem, Cairo, Beirut, Mumbai, New Delhi, Jakarta, Seoul, Cartagena, Mexico City, Amsterdam, Berlin, Prague, London, Paris, and a whole helluva lot more. You're going to need me on speed dial unless you come out of this meeting smarter than when you walked in."

"Mr. Klugo, we're only smart enough to call this committee together," Reilly said. "Please continue." However at that moment, Chris Collins' phone rang. Klugo gave him a dirty look.

"Look, you're paying for my time, so don't waste it. Turn off your fucking phones and pay attention," Klugo demanded.

Everyone on the KR team complied.

"Let me make it simpler for you," the mercenary proposed. "Four Ds: Detect, Deject, Delay, Defend. If you learn these rules, you'll have a better chance of saving lives and property.

"D1. *Detect.* This builds on what you've already heard. Do you have the eyes and ears to detect surveillance? A new street vendor? Someone who's sitting at a park bench across the street for an inordinate amount of time? People claiming they got lost in your subterranean levels where you house your electrical? Too many questions about the hotel being asked? You train your people to recognize behavior out of the ordinary, you reduce the odds of being targeted.

"D2. *Deject.* Deject the bastards. You already heard it. Deject them with permanent barriers outside the hotel that prevent trucks from stopping too close. Deject with bollards that can be deployed quickly from under the road. Test these regularly. Word will spread that you have active defenses on your perimeter.

"The more exposed you are, the more visible you want your defenses. You're not reinventing the wheel. We're used to this at airport security points. Nothing new. Bag searches. Metal detectors. Visible security. Electronic Trace Detectors. X-ray machines. Swab analyzers that read explosive residue. Hell, they're all there. So when threats are evident, you step up. And of course get some fucking bomb-sniffing dogs. They're better than humans at this."

The litany silenced the room. Satisfied he'd made his point, Donald Klugo continued, "Next, D3. *Delay.* Delay and you make an attack harder to execute. Plain and simple. Terrorists don't want problems, especially the ones who are determined to live another day. So anything that can delay a mission jeopardizes that mission."

The mercenary waited for his KR students to catch up. "Now for D4. *Defend.* Are your security personnel armed?"

"No," Alan Cannon replied.

"Then make arrangements to change that."

"That's a serious liability problem," Collins said, addressing the issue. "The hotel is responsible if a bystander gets shot by an employee. There's less exposure if police are assigned to the hotel. We've done that."

"Well then, here's your problem," said Klugo. "Depending upon what country you're in, you can't always trust the local police. So at least up your perimeter patrols to occur hourly or, better yet, even more frequently and not on a regular schedule. And make sure the people you have on security are fully caffeinated. If a suspicious vehicle approaches, security can engage a hydraulic bollard and block the suspect. If they're asleep, you're dead. And increase those visible defenses I gave you!"

The conversation that followed, smarter and more focused because of the preliminaries, took them to their morning break. Reilly and Cannon caucused in the men's room.

"Well worth the effort," Cannon said.

"Only because it's coming from people other than us," Reilly countered.

"That's what consultants are for," the security chief laughed. "But these guys are the real deal. It's an episode of *Scared Straight!*"

Reilly agreed. They needed experts to come in. Cannon's FBI experience could only go so far with the KR management. And Reilly couldn't talk about everything and everyone he knew, especially now. He felt the best possible outcome would be a critical baseline understanding on which they could build an action plan. He was already thinking what that might look like. But they still hadn't talked about motives and motivation. Reilly raised the point when they were back in the session.

"The right question to ask," former CIA director Erwin noted. "A terrorist act is almost always some form of political act. That doesn't mean a government has to be behind it, but the act itself is planned and committed with the avowed goal to cause a political effect. Are you familiar with the Prussian officer Carl von Clausewitz?"

Only Donald Klugo nodded.

"Clausewitz was a solider in the Napoleonic Wars. After Napoleon defeated Prussia in 1806 at the Battle of Jena–Auerstedt, Clausewitz worked on rebuilding his country's army. He wrote what would ultimately become one of the world's greatest works on warfare strategy, *Vom Kriege*, translated as *On War*. He focused on the relationship between war and foreign policy. Clausewitz saw war as a continuation of policy, arguing that war is not merely a political act, but a political instrument. No matter what the exigencies of a particular war might be, he contended that 'the political view is the object.' Keep that in mind. It is the ultimate truth of the people behind the terrorist."

The conference room shades were drawn, and KR management had told their staffs they were not to be interrupted. But there was a knock at the door, and Brenda Sheldon slowly opened it.

Reilly had flown in his assistant to help in the DC office during the meetings and his Congressional appearance. Before the critical security meeting, he had told her who was worthy of an interruption. Anyone not mentioned could wait. This had to be one of the few sanctioned people.

She made an embarrassed face and quietly apologized. "Sorry." She gestured to Reilly with her index finger to come out.

He pushed away from the table. "I'll be right back. Please keep going." He intentionally did not meet any of his committee members' eyes.

Once outside and away from the door Brenda started. "I know, no interruptions, but I tried to text you."

"We turned off our phones," Reilly explained. "What's up?"

"You told me to let you know if I got a call from a *Jack Ryan.*"

"Right. Any message?"

"No. I said you were in an all-day meeting."

Reilly wondered what it could be. Jack Ryan was a fun code name he'd given Bob Heath in honor of novelist Tom Clancy's CIA hero. Since Heath had never phoned his office before, this had to be important.

He turned on his cell. He saw that he had missed a call. The call came with no caller ID.

"Okay, thanks Brenda."

She hung close to him, hoping for an explanation. "Anything you want me to do?"

"No, thanks."

Reilly ducked into an empty office and dialed a number by heart.

"Thanks for calling back," Heath answered. "We should meet."

"Oh?"

"Yeah, I owe you a lobster. How about the usual spot? Tonight?"

* * *

Dan Reilly bypassed the waiting line at Old Ebbitt Grill. Robert Heath had beaten him there and scored a secluded corner table in the back room.

Old in the restaurant's name wasn't just a marketing moniker. Old Ebbitt Grill was the capital's oldest watering hole, dating back to 1856. As a saloon in the early years, presidents Ulysses S. Grant, Andrew Johnson, Grover Cleveland, Theodore Roosevelt, and Warren Harding bellied up to the bar. Before he was president, William McKinley was said to be a resident when the establishment also had rooms.

With all its history the Old Ebbitt Grill still fell on hard times. It was sold in the early 1970s for just over $11,000, and in 1983 moved to its present 15th Street location, a beaux arts building that had been a former theater.

Today the plays staged in the restaurant were all high dramas, cast with dialogue from political actors like Reilly and Heath. They took place over scrumptious meals set amidst priceless antiques, Washington memorabilia, gas chandeliers, English lace curtains, and a mural depiction of a Mathew Brady photograph of Grant.

Reilly sat down ready to get right into it, but a waiter interrupted. He had an order of steamed mussels in a white wine tomato broth and grilled flatbread with ricotta cheese, roasted butternut squash, arugula, and crispy prosciutto coated with a balsamic reduction.

"No need to look at the menu," Heath said. "The lobsters are next."

As much as Reilly wanted to discuss business, Heath delayed it. "Tell me how your first session went today."

Reilly explained the progress and his belief that they'd turned a real corner with the company's lawyer.

"No mention of . . ."

"No, of course not," Reilly answered.

"Good. Keep it that way. For your own good."

The warning carried a great deal of meaning. Most of all trust and the potential lack of it.

"Talk to me if anyone raises any questions," Heath added.

"I will."

They chatted about old times for fifteen minutes until Reilly brought the conversation back around. "You ever going to tell me why the hell it was so urgent we get together tonight?"

Heath smiled. "Enough foreplay?"

"Definitely."

"Okay." He lowered his voice. "I'll start with unconfirmed, uncertain, and an under 50 percent reliability factor."

"You wouldn't be speaking to me with that kind of percentage," Reilly maintained. "Try again. What do you have? You damn well know that Cannon's already being stonewalled by the bureau. So don't you hold out on me."

"Okay, okay," said Heath, acknowledging the point. "One step at a time though. Your Mr. Smug is not al Qaeda or ISIS."

"No shit, Sherlock," Reilly stated, not trying to be funny. "Remember, I brought you the damned video. Tell me something I don't know."

"Dribs and drabs," the CIA officer said.

Reilly saw more dinner coming, and the two steaming lobsters put the conversation on hold.

They ate their meal and, thirty minutes later after their table was cleared and coffee had been served, Heath returned to business. "Let me tell you a story," he said.

"Fact or fiction?"

"Let's just call it a story."

"Okay."

"Nine, nine, ninety-nine."

"What?" Reilly asked.

"September 9, 1999. Three hundred people died in a terrible apartment bombing in Moscow. Chechen rebels were blamed. Boris Yeltsin launched an attack against Chechnya."

"I remember. Bloody. Awful."

"Yes, it was. But do you remember anything about the investigation?" Heath asked.

"As you said, Chechen rebels."

"I said they were blamed. I didn't say they were responsible. Months after the September 11 attacks we knew a great deal about the terrorists—their identities, their nationalities. In Russia, little was reported other than that Chechens did it."

"Propaganda. The Kremlin controlling the press?" Reilly queried.

"More."

Engrossed with what was obviously the preamble, Reilly gestured for Heath to continue.

"It was 1999. The year's important. Boris Yeltsin was president. He and his family were facing charges that they'd squirreled away a fortune in secret bank accounts—money linked to illegal transactions with a Swiss construction company. He was also an alcoholic and sick beyond anything the public heard. A political movement called Unity was building, building quickly enough that he could lose the parliamentary and presidential elections scheduled for the end of the year. And here's where it really gets interesting."

"Oh, it's already interesting."

"Yeltsin had a plan, taking a page out of Stalin's playbook from the 1930s. It required buy in from the FSB, sing-along from the press, and a white hat hero on a rearing steed. He also counted on the Russian people rising up against an identifiable threat. To the point, he conspired to destabilize the newly re-formed government, declare a state of emergency, and potentially cancel the elections. How?" Heath asked rhetorically. "Create an act of terrorism against Russia, instill fear, and then solve it, thereby shifting attention away from his personal political problems."

"A false flag," Reilly added. "Like conspiracy theorists applied to 9/11."

"Ridiculously in our case. Not so in Moscow. State journalists helped seed anxiety, warning that Moscow would be targeted by terrorists. That began midsummer. It was followed by increased press reports on Chechen separatists building strength, a clear threat to Moscow's dominion over the Russian republic."

"All calculated."

"Remember, I said it was a story." The CIA agent smirked.

"You also mentioned a white hat," Reilly reminded him.

"Getting to that right now. Yeltsin had people in the wings, including high-ranking members of the FSB. You know a key player."

"Hardly a white hat," Reilly commented. "Putin and now Gorshkov."

"Correct, and fiercely loyal. Able to bury Yeltsin's scandals and attack some of his most vocal and visible political opponents and their wives."

Heath slowly sipped his coffee, drawing out his narrative.

"Step-by-step intimidation," he continued. "Calculated and orchestrated."

Another sip.

"But to truly galvanize the hearts and minds of the Russian people, to stimulate nationalistic fervor, something dramatic was needed. Where the earlier propagandizing about Chechen rebels had fallen short of arousing Russian spirit, an attack on the homeland could."

Dan Reilly completed the sentence. "Bombings."

The restaurant had all but cleared out by this time. Heath continued, more animated now.

"Precisely. After the bombings, three in all, in three different cities, the Kremlin linked the terrorists to Osama bin Laden. They were said to have trained in Chechnya. A few weeks later, another bomb was discovered in Ryazan, about one hundred miles southeast of Moscow. The next day retaliations against Chechnya.

"However, the bomb found in Ryazan was linked to the FSB, which the intelligence service later explained was part of a 'training exercise' containing nothing more dangerous than sugar. Was the FSB caught in the act? It didn't really matter. The war was on, and Yeltsin had the support of the country."

"Some of the timeline is coming back to me," Reilly said. "But how much of this is confirmed?"

Heath laughed. "Considering we never had a chat with Yeltsin over shots of vodka, who's to say?"

"How about you?"

"I suppose it makes for a good political story. But there's more."

Reilly asked whether or not they needed to leave the restaurant. The CIA agent told him not to worry. "Taken care of."

"Spoken like a true *Company* man."

"In 2000, trials began. Five suspects were charged with preparing the explosives. They went to prison for life, and the evidence was never made public. A second trial two years later found two other defendants guilty of terrorism. Their case was also sealed. Now for the fun stuff," Heath continued.

"Fun? Can't wait," Reilly responded.

"When it came to the Moscow bombing, we know that none of the accused were in the city at the time of the explosion, moreover, they weren't ethnic Chechen. In time, many presumed to be on the inside of the plot disappeared or conveniently and publicly died. A key player, an FSB officer we believe may have actually carried out the bombings, was killed in a car accident. A commission was established to examine the facts. One commissioner was shot in Moscow. The others took great care in what they brought up. But it didn't end there. A journalist, Anna Petrovich, who had long covered the story and was rumored to have new sources, died suddenly while on vacation in Southern Italy. The earmarks of another FSB murder."

"With Gorshkov's fingerprints," Reilly noted.

"Worth considering."

It was nearly midnight now. The check had long ago been paid, and Heath wound down leaving an open question. Reilly went for it.

"What does this all mean?" Reilly asked.

"What does *what* mean?"

"The story, damn it!"

"To the point, we have something of a match on the photograph," said Heath.

"You know who he is!" Reilly exclaimed.

"No. We don't."

"Then?" Reilly was confused.

"We don't know *who* he is, but we've matched him somewhat confidently to one news photo from 1989 and a more recent CCTV shot."

"And?"

"The first was taken in Potsdam right after the fall of the Berlin Wall. He was in the background. One of a group leaving the FSB headquarters. The second at a restaurant in Italy with Petrovich. Any idea who he worked for at FSB?"

Reilly ventured a guess. "Nikolai Gorshkov?"

"Absolutely right. And what does this have in common with Tokyo?"

"The bombing was a means to an end." *But to what end?*

PART TWO

THREAT ASSESSMENTS

28

MOSCOW, RUSSIAN FEDERATION

THE KREMLIN

Each of the men who sat around the huge conference table represented the views of the leader. Nothing less would be tolerated. Offering anything over and above came with its own risks.

The minister of defense, the chief of staff of the Armed Forces of the Russian Federation, the ministers of Internal Troops, head of Border Service, and the highest ranking generals from the Russian Ground Forces, Aerospace Forces, and the Navy were all present. Also, the director of the FSB. Intentionally absent was the president's full cabinet.

The most important man at the table was the man *Forbes Magazine* recently named the most powerful man in the world—Nikolai Gorshkov.

"Gentlemen," he began. There were no women in this inner circle. "We stand at a crossroads between yesterday and tomorrow. A yesterday from which Russia emerged from failure and embarrassment, greed and bankruptcy. Today we celebrate a rebuilt Russia. We are respected, we are powerful, and we are feared. But we have even greater steps ahead from which there will be no turning back."

Gorshkov sat at the large conference table adjacent to his opulent presidential office in the Kremlin. He kept an even tone, giving each of his men eye contact, but never looking for approval because he demanded as much from them—in addition to their lives.

"It is the Rubicon to cross for us to restore Russia to its full glory. We *will* become the leader in space again, a race Khrushchev gave up."

Gorshkov raised his voice, and his eyes flared.

"We *will* have the strongest military on the face of the earth again, an advantage Yeltsin forsake."

The louder he got, the more the veins in his neck bulged.

"We *will* be an international economic power broker again, a designation that was shamefully frittered away by Kosygin."

Finally he stood and with a commanding staccato delivery barked, "And *we will* be safe again."

Nikolai Gorshkov slammed his fist so hard on the conference table that water and coffee spilled from one end to the other. Now, commanding everyone's absolute attention, he explained how he would make it all happen.

MINISTRY OF ENERGY OFFICE

"Minister Kang, you beat my most optimistic expectations with your request for a follow-up meeting," Anton Nechayev said, welcoming his Chinese counterpart. "Thank you for coming to Moscow."

"I sensed urgency in your proposal and thought that our mutual interests could benefit from another discussion."

Urgency? Nechayev thought. If he had conveyed that, it had been a mistake in tactical negotiations. He would have to be more careful. To address it now would only reinforce the point. But there was another item worth acknowledging. *Mutual interests.* It was the essence of the agreement, and completely necessary to secure the loan and help stabilize Russia.

The Chinese minister continued. "The very fact that the principal pipelines transporting Russian hydrocarbons have been laid on Russian and Chinese soil helps both nations avoid third-party contracts and conflicts. It is the cornerstone of our twenty-first-century cooperation. Anything that will further cement our relationship strengthens us both."

Nechayev read between the lines of Kang's position, now realizing that Kang had done the same with him. Left unsaid was Russia's NATO strategy and China's policy in the South China Sea. Given the unpredictable, shifting political sands in the Middle East, increased oil from Russia would guarantee a market for its reserves. On Beijing's side of the equation, having Russia as a strong trade partner would bolster its posturing in the Strait of Malacca where China was island-building and island-arming.

But there were two even more important considerations. With 39 percent of Chinese oil imports passing through those waters, China needed more global muscle, or at least the threat of it. Additionally, and tacitly understood by both negotiators, but not brought to the table: the expansion of the accord between Russia and China would buy China time.

The China National Offshore Oil Corporation had invested some $20 billion on research to confirm that seven billion barrels of crude oil and 900 trillion cubic feet of natural gas were below the ocean floor. For a country that currently pumped a mere 1.1 percent of the world total, yet annually burned through 20 percent of the entire planet's reserves, the South China Sea offered a solution for ultimate energy independence. Tap it, refine it, sell it, and defend it. Together, China and Russia could control much of the world's oil.

Nechayev and Kang shook hands. The deal, like the current political borders on the map, wouldn't last forever. It didn't need to. As long as it worked to the aspirations of their regimes, there'd soon be signatures on paper. As diplomats, they'd done their part.

29

"So do we promote that we're upgrading safety? Seems like a surefire way to get sued."

This was a perfect question from Chris Collins. It had legal ramifications, but created marketing issues as well. It was also a perfect way to lead off the reconvened security committee.

"In a word, no," former CIA director Carl Erwin answered. "Travelers are used to seeing a higher level of security, especially in metropolitan areas. So don't worry them. But visibly heightened security is as much for the bad guys to see as it is for your clientele."

"How do we prioritize? What countries? What cities?" asked COO Tiano.

"Basically we break the world down into risk zones: high, medium, and low," Erwin stated.

"Are there any no-risk zones?" PR VP June Wilson asked.

"Not anymore," Erwin said. "Those days are over."

Wilson looked deflated.

"And when it comes to high risk, don't limit that to Iraq, Egypt, Yemen, or Afghanistan. Depending on active intel, France and England could be at the top. Brussels for sure these days. They're right up there on the UK's Joint Terrorism Analysis Centre lists. Plus key American cities and, of course, your Asian properties.

"Beyond that it's really quite simple. Terrorists focus on soft targets where people assemble—airports, train stations, restaurants, nightclubs. In your case a hotel or resort. More often than not, they'll pick a place where satellite news coverage can quickly pump out live video. They want that. They want to control the news cycle."

"Good lord," Wilson said. "No one's going to ever feel safe again."

"Safe? Maybe not," Erwin replied. "Safer, yes. I'll explain. You need to develop a plan."

"That's what we're here for, Mr. Erwin," Dan Reilly noted.

"Educate your core customers," Erwin continued, "develop relationships with local governments, and subscribe to advisories. Cultivate intelligence sources. You absolutely must have inside information."

Reilly smiled inwardly. He was doing exactly that.

"And for God's sake," the ex-CIA chief added, "drum this into your managers. They have to train their staff to report. Don't wait. And be ready to go to DEFCON 1 without question on a moment's notice."

Lou Tiano was beginning to feel this was not the business he had signed up for or a world he thought he'd ever be in. "How can we possibly succeed?" he asked quite honestly.

"How do you eat an elephant?" General BD Coons countered.

"What do you mean?" the COO replied.

"Very simply, how do you eat an elephant?"

"We don't."

"Come on, if you had to."

Tiano straightened up in his chair. "I suppose one bite at a time."

"Exactly," said the retired general and former number two in the previous president's national security team. "That's how. Look," he stood up and crossed over to a whiteboard on the conference room wall, "there's a method to the process. You probably do it yourself and don't even think about it."

General Coons drew a square and then divided it into four quadrants.

Over the top left box he wrote URGENT. Over the box on the right he wrote NOT URGENT. Then to the left beside the first box he scribbled IMPORTANT. Below it and adjacent to the bottom left box, NOT IMPORTANT. The next thing he did was number the boxes 1, 2, 3, 4, and inside each box he jotted down some terms.

"Ever see this?"

Reilly and Cannon had, along with all of the other consultants.

"It's an organizational chart," Tiano ventured.

"Yes," the general confirmed, "but much more. It's a critical management tool to develop strategies, time/duty analyses, and battle plans."

"Battle plans?" Brodowski nervously asked.

"Too strong a description, Ms. Brodowski?"

"I just don't understand."

"For now just write it down."

The KR team followed the general's directive.

"You fill in the blocks yourself. Whatever you plan, your plan will inevitably change. Whatever you change, you'll constantly reevaluate. You're not in control until you seize control. This basic organizational chart will help you. Before we leave today, we'll review our work. Tomorrow you'll start the day revising it."

"Any idea who came up with this tool and its significance?" Coons asked.

"Yes, sir," Reilly said. "Dwight Eisenhower. It's called the Eisenhower Method. He used it to lay out the strategy, one bite at a time, for D-Day."

"Correct. And it's exactly what we're going to do to get you operational." The general tossed the marker to Reilly. "You start."

Reilly joined the general at the whiteboard. He began by filling in boxes 2 and 4, with the team calling out suggestions. Quadrant 4 was the easiest to fill. Distractions. Too much email, too many people copied on those emails. Facebook, Instagram, YouTube, and all the other interruptions that interfere with the day's work. From there they went to quadrant 1: URGENT/IMPORTANT and 3: URGENT/ NOT IMPORTANT.

The KR team pitched in ideas. Some were shot down. Others led to lengthy discussions, requiring further evaluation. Over the next three hours they adjusted their priorities and formulated an initial strategy.

"Very good," Coons observed as he considered what they had developed.

"We'll see," countered Don Klugo, the private security consultant. "Now, I've got a hundred bucks for anyone who can tell me where the term terrorism originated. Worth knowing your history."

He removed a crisp new bill from his wallet and slammed it on the table.

"Come on. Someone must know."

But no one did.

"Like I tell my men, you have to know history to be in the fight and understand the enemy's tactics and motives. Here it is, plain and simple," the mercenary said. "The root is from a Latin term that means 'to frighten,' which later became part of the phrase *terror cimbricus*. Ancient Romans used this idiom to describe the intense and overwhelming fear they would inflict on their enemies. Centuries later, during the French Revolution, Robespierre executed thousands in what became known as the 'reign of terror.' The notion has worked damned well for brutal dictators and terrorists ever since."

"That's not our strategy," Pat Brodowski exclaimed.

"Of course not. But you are going to have to think like the enemy to beat them."

KIEV

Miklos reviewed the target report, which he would burn shortly thereafter. Security was typical. Completely lax. This was all the more surprising given the threats to Ukraine.

The operative laughed to himself. *Incompetents. They'll never learn.* He recalled the expression, which he thought was American in origin: *Like shooting fish in a barrel.*

He concluded that the surveillance report gave him carte blanche.

- Blackout areas on CCTV cameras

- Hotel security unarmed

- No active scanning devices

- Young, inexperienced staff

- No outside barriers or stanchions

- No bomb-sniffing dogs

- No additional security measures at the delivery entrance

So easy, he thought. *But never too easy.* He would check more himself before going mission active.

WASHINGTON, DC

"General, you brought up DEFCON 1, the highest state for America's defensive posture. We also need a way to differentiate threat levels," Reilly said. "Numbers, colors, probability. A system where we can determine the risk and act on preestablished procedure."

"Very good, Mr. Reilly," General Coons replied. "Spoken like someone with skin in the game already."

"We're all here because of it," Reilly said.

"But coming to the realization is another thing. So is the money it will take."

Lou Tiano spoke up. "The money will be there."

"Excellent. We're moving along more rapidly than I imagined. Most organizations don't get as far as you have already."

"It's no longer an option," Cannon interjected. "The toothpaste is out of the tube. No way to squeeze it back in."

KIEV

He left his room as Richter, the visiting German. In the elevator, which was not wired for cameras, he reversed his jacket, donned an insignia cap and wire-framed glasses, slung an ID lanyard around his neck, and removed a clipboard that he'd tucked into his belt at the small of his back. All in fifteen seconds.

He emerged from the elevator as Yarik Danko, a credentialed inspector from Kiev's building department, the kind of authoritarian figure everyday workers avoided. Andre Miklos acted the part, and hotel employees steered clear. He'd give himself ten minutes. No more, to access visible weaknesses. He figured that weaknesses would not be hard to find.

WASHINGTON, DC

Cannon proposed that Reilly take the key position as crisis team leader, and he accepted on the spot. The other stakeholders on the Kensington Royal side of the table took specific duties in keeping with their own positions.

"That's a first step," Erwin stated. "You're owning problem areas, but you'll need to delegate and supervise. Under you, regional supervisors will have to report up. People in food services must become experts in foodborne illnesses. Your chief architect needs to evaluate construction issues. Risk management to work with legal and PR. That's just off the top of my head. I'll prepare a full list for the committee."

KIEV

There's something intimidating about a man strutting around taking notes on a clipboard. It's even more intimidating when that man has an ID that's feared. For the Klovska Classic Hotel, it was a city inspector. Any city inspector. Cash usually kept them away, so when one showed up, it probably meant a shake-up, some finger wagging, a few citations, and a possible firing. So for the sake of their own jobs, the staff working in the subterranean floors steered clear of the bureaucrat. That included the chefs and cooks, electricians, housekeeping, maintenance, and even security. No one wanted to be asked a question and written up.

The clipboard was a powerful weapon and a ticket to anywhere

Miklos wanted to go. He quickly made his rounds, thinking to himself that a real inspector should have written the damned hotel up. In the electrical office door keys to every critical area hung from an open box. Every one of them were properly labeled; all easy to take. There was no sign-out book; no means to keep inventory. Electrical had to have access everywhere. And with multiple copies of most keys, they were literally there for the taking.

As soon as the office secretary saw him, she busied herself filing, or pretending to file folders. Her back was turned, and he removed two keys, leaving the rest. Even if she saw him do it, she wouldn't speak up, now or later.

Miklos loved when he could operate totally in the open while everyone else desperately tried to remain invisible.

WASHINGTON, DC

"Your enemy is smart," Don Klugo declared. "If it's a suicide mission he'll send expendables. If it's a political strike, he'll have a true exit strategy for himself and everyone on his team. So you start with respect for those conspiring against you. They have scientists and chemists and all types of technical experts at their command. Never doubt that they're deadly. Think like them. Be brave enough to make the hard decisions. Listen to your instincts and act. Better yet, prepare. Don't ignore the signs, and keep experts on speed dial who can handle things like the CIA, the FBI, and when you need some muscle, people like me. So, who's got a plan for a tiered approach?"

"I do," Dan Reilly piped up. "Or at least an initial framework."

"Let's hear it," the mercenary replied.

"I've been thinking about four categories of threat levels. Instead of numbering them, because people are often confused as to whether DEFCON 5 or 1 is the most serious, I've gone for a color code, much like the US approach."

He returned to the dry erase board. "Green, Yellow, Orange, and finally Red."

"Nope," General Coons immediately barked.

Reilly cocked his head questioningly.

"Green. We spend our lives at traffic lights waiting for the green. Green means go. It's an actionable word. Don't start off confusing people."

"Okay," Reilly said. "White."

"Bland. Says nothing," Erwin, the ex-CIA director, complained.

"Blue?" Brodowski offered.

Erwin nodded.

"Okay," Reilly said writing it on the board. "Blue will be normal. No intelligence, no apparent threats. The property is out of a critical area. But there will be a modicum of upgrades and training."

"Like?" Chris Collins asked.

"Like staff members posted in all public areas, on two-way radios. Hell, if you can ask anyone anything when you walk into Office Depot, why don't we equip our staff the same way? This will also encourage them to be to be more vigilant and share any suspicious activities. It's an easy upgrade for sure."

"Who would they report to?" the attorney followed up.

"Security at monitoring stations."

"Not all of them are that equipped," Tiano explained, "in terms of equipment and personnel."

"I know. That's another change for Blue."

KIEV

Real weaknesses, Miklos thought. *And blind spots.* The few cameras that covered critical areas were caked in dust. Miklos reasoned they probably hadn't been cleaned in years, and consequently it was easier for security to ignore them than wipe them.

WASHINGTON, DC

"Threat condition Yellow," Reilly continued. "We trigger this alert status when intelligence returns unspecified threats to US citizens and

US businesses in hot spots. The crisis management team will have the authority to advance to threat condition Yellow with consultation from our regional field president and the general manager of the hotel, but our crisis management team will have the final say. This moves all decisions above any local politics not to act."

"Run through the basic changes to come with this increased level," requested Tiano.

"I'll have printouts this afternoon, Lou, but here are the key points from subtle to obvious."

The KR chief operating executive put his pencil to paper as did his colleagues.

"First, the US flag is removed."

There was a gasp from June Wilson.

Don Klugo cut right in. "Look, there's a good shot you're being targeted *because* you're an American company. The flag becomes a powerful propaganda tool for terrorists. So take the fucking visual away," the mercenary said, not mincing words.

"I got it," Wilson replied. She returned to writing.

"Next, in relative order," Reilly continued, "review evacuation plans, increase security patrols in public areas, be alert to suspicious persons or packages, require positive photo ID of guests at check-in, remove all large containers like waste receptacles, restrict roof access, inspect public restrooms hourly, keep meeting rooms locked when not in use, and all outside vendors must display IDs at all times."

Reilly waited for people to catch up.

"Now even more serious procedures. All, and this means ALL suspicious packages must be treated as explosives and reported. ALL abandoned vehicles must be towed away. Protect and secure ALL water systems. ALL fuel trucks must be stopped before entering the property and not allowed to deliver until inspected and cleared and drivers' identities confirmed. ALL engineering areas, including heating and air-conditioning plants, boiler, electrical, and pump room must be restricted. A real must. We got hit hard there in Tokyo. Secure ALL fuel supply tanks."

"And this is just for one step elevation above normal?" Pat Brodowski asked.

Reilly answered with an unmistakable, "Yes."

KIEV

Two minutes left on his timetable. Miklos moved on to the electrical station, but not via the basement entrance. He studied the floor plan. There was an unlocked door off the ballroom. In fact, it was worse than unlocked. It had no lock. It opened to a hall that led to a flight of stairs. Down one flight was another unlocked door to the power plant and the boilers.

WASHINGTON, DC

Coons took Brodowski's concern a step further. "This second threat condition should be a response to actionable warnings from credible sources. As we discussed, any one of these procedures could dissuade terrorists who are putting their target report together. Seeing elevated defenses generally reduces their percentage of success. Unless . . ."

"Unless what?" Brodowski asked.

"The target isn't the *hotel*, but someone *in* the hotel."

KIEV

Miklos walked the entire power plant unseen. He had his ID and his clipboard and made appropriate notes in case he was stopped, but that never occurred. At best, someone from management might quietly offer him 13,000 hryvnia or more to ignore any issues. That would get him roughly triple in rubles or 500 in euros and US currency. He thought about whether he'd take it. Would it create more visibility or less? But what did he need easy money for? His boss had taken good care of him.

WASHINGTON, DC

The last comment silenced the room. Reilly let the thought settle, then he cleared his throat and moved onto threat condition Orange. As he saw it, the threat level included ramped up security at the swimming pools and spas, chemical tests of drinking water, checking fresh air intakes, and securing any supply louvers accessible to the public.

"I hesitate to think what Orange could possibly lay on top of these deterrents," Brodowski said.

"Well, you're right to use the word deterrents, because Orange moves us into more active steps," Reilly explained. "We activate this higher condition when there are specific threats against us. That means we've been threatened either in media or as reported to KR through our intelligence partners. We activate when a highly controversial political figure stays at the hotel during a time of regional terrorism."

Reilly stopped for a moment and thought about what he'd just said. *A highly controversial political figure.* Or as Coons had stated, "Someone in the hotel." A name came to him, a name of one of the victims of the Tokyo attack. He wrote it down.

KIEV

The assassin decided not to take any more chances. Before leaving at just under nine minutes, he made a few more observations in the hotel lobby, more than satisfied that his work as Yarik Danko was over. He'd return as he had checked in, and then complete his stay.

A few more days, he thought.

WASHINGTON, DC

"Orange goes further. Much further. Everything under Blue and Yellow plus this. June, public relations will have to plan the spin, and there's more on your shoulders, Spike. In anticipation you'll need to create new interactive computer programs to handle the constant flow of information and critical checks."

"I've been making notes all along. I'll need a dedicated person for a month."

Reilly looked to Lou Tiano.

"Done," the chief executive officer said. "Cost it out for Pat and add a contingency. I'm sure our experts here are going to up the stakes more."

"For certain," former CIA director Erwin added.

"Definitely," General Coons and mercenary Klugo chimed in together.

"Back to threat condition Orange," Reilly said, referring to his notes. "Nothing stays in storage, including luggage. And anything coming in, all arriving packages have to be inspected in the presence of the guest. No exceptions."

Even Alan Cannon looked surprised. "That's going to be hard."

"Yes, I expect it will be, Alan. But there's more. I propose that we restrict access to the hotel with guards checking all guests' IDs. No vehicles in parking lots unless they've been registered and cross-referenced to guests. Barricades should be installed to restrict parking close to the building. For that we'll have to work way in advance with local authorities. It might require a *special* undefined line item."

With that comment he turned to Collins and Wilson.

"You mean . . . ?" the lawyer asked.

"Let's just keep it undefined. A political contribution."

Collins shook his head. Wilson wrote down, *Contributions.*

"Guys, we've got to be proactive," Reilly continued. "Barriers stop cars and trucks. We didn't have any in Tokyo. Any vehicle sitting around or abandoned has to be seen as a potential weapon."

Reilly heard a pencil break. It was June Wilson's. Reilly slid a sharpened replacement down the table.

Jay Reardon, the retired FBI agent, had been quiet through most of the meeting. He raised his hand.

"I understand your ongoing concern," he said. "You don't want to hassle guests."

"Correct."

"And you're right. But trained security officers can usually distinguish between innocents and others. They can pretty well tell who's taking harmless family shots and selfies versus pictures and selfies that are more focused on the background."

"Thank you," Wilson replied.

Now Reardon's voice changed. "But it takes training. And I'm willing to bet your people aren't trained."

"They aren't," Cannon replied. "At least most of them aren't."

"Then get them trained fast, and by people who know what they're doing!"

More note-taking. More money to spend. Brodowski's list was already four pages long.

"One more on my list," Reilly said. "At shift changes, department heads will supervise work areas to see if any suspicious boxes or packages were left."

"Won't that suggest that we don't trust our own people?" Tiano wondered.

"Jakarta," Klugo responded. "The hotel's flower vendors planted bombs. So, to answer your question, damned straight. Trust no one. Check everything and everyone."

"But we're in the people business," Wilson replied.

"Yes, you are. But now you're also in the keeping people alive business."

KIEV

First the badge came off. A half block later, the hat. Around the corner he took off his jacket and slung it on his arm. A few minutes later, he casually reversed the jacket and put it back on. Yarik Danko was gone. In his place was the visiting businessman, Karl Richter.

He continued walking, checking traffic patterns and the best ways to escape into the city if he needed to.

WASHINGTON, DC

"Just to be clear, we do all this and never communicate that we care about safety?" June Wilson asked.

"Correct," replied Carl Erwin. "This is not a public relations exercise, Ms. Wilson. You let your actions speak for you."

"He's right," Alan Cannon added. "We presume the bad guys are smart enough to spot our defenses. Anything that adds risk to their operation increases the possibility of their failure. Terrorists don't like failure. It doesn't further their cause."

"I don't mind saying I hate this new normal," Wilson said.

"No one likes it," Erwin replied. He turned to Reilly. "Now to your top threat level measures."

"Threat condition Red," Reilly said. "If we'd had this in place we might have averted the Tokyo attack."

KIEV

Miklos was empowered to act *if and when* he was assured of success. Nothing he saw deterred him. Now, a simple one-word text to his team—five members for this assignment—confirmed the time and place of their final meeting before going mission active. The clock was running. He could almost smell death approaching.

WASHINGTON, DC

"We activate Red with a specific, serious threat toward the property, persons, or US interests in the region, particularly if the threat comes from known terrorist organizations or individuals."

"A clarification," General Coons offered.

"Certainly."

"The word *serious*. Your crisis management team could get bogged down debating what was serious enough to activate this level. This can't ever be misconstrued. It must be an automatic trigger based on the intel. Enough boxes checked, you go to red. No equivocation."

"You're right," Reilly replied. "If and when a threat meets the minimum standards, we suddenly have ourselves a *Red Hotel*."

It was the first time he used the term. It suddenly sent shivers up his spine.

KIEV

Miklos checked his watch and picked up his pace. He had to pass a man on Zhilyanskaya Street in three minutes. If he showed up on time and on the correct side of the street, it signaled all was well. If late and on the opposite side, then the mission would be scuttled. *Go or no go.* That simple. No coded messages at dead drops. No other intrigue than passing a man on the street.

WASHINGTON, DC

"This is the highest level," Reilly continued. "On top of all the previous safeguards in Blue, Yellow, and Orange, threat condition Red adds mandatory hotel entrance through metal detectors for all guests, all luggage inspected in a room off the main lobby, vehicles thoroughly inspected before entry in parking lots, and IDs required for cars, trucks, drivers, and passengers. No vehicles left unattended within fifty feet. Cement bollards installed and deployed to prevent full vehicular access to the hotel."

Reilly waited for reaction.

"Anyone have any thoughts?" he finally asked, breaking the silence.

Nothing from the KR side. They were still absorbing the steps.

"I do," Klugo said. "Pick a city. Then let's run through how unprepared you are today and how long it would take to implement each threat condition, including all the negatives you'd expect to find on-site. Worst case scenarios based on management egos, limited staff, local law enforcement and political relationships, and where you are with active intelligence in the region."

"I'd like to think we're not completely unprepared," security chief Alan Cannon volunteered. "Dan and I have been working with our regional offices on basic preparedness and we have open dialogue with intelligence contacts."

"Who?" snapped Chris Collins.

"Come on Chris. I worked at the FBI. I have regular conversations. And Dan was in army intelligence. He knows people."

The retired CIA director interrupted. "Mr. Collins, there are some things you don't want to inquire about. Suffice it to say, you're lucky your security chief and senior international executive are not starting from zero. We've talked to people who are at zero. Believe me, they don't have a clue what's out there. Your team is demonstrating they do."

"Yes, but . . ." Collins didn't finish the sentence.

"Maybe this will help," Don Klugo said. "It's a quote on a plaque I keep framed in my office. 'It often happens that I wake at night and begin to think of a serious problem and decide I must tell the Pope about it. Then I wake up completely and remember that I am the Pope.' Pope John XXIII said that," he added. "And the sooner you grasp your responsibility, the more lives you'll be able to save."

KIEV

Miklos passed the designated man at the designated time on the designated side of the street. That man would, in turn, send an innocuous one-word text to a friend in Paris who would forward it. Two people later, it would be read with a smile in the Kremlin. Andre Miklos calculated that the message would be received by the time he'd be enjoying dinner at Goodman, by reputation, one of the best steak houses in Kiev. Tonight he'd order his meat extra rare.

30

Edward Shaw read Reilly's entire document while sitting on his office couch. Reilly watched, looking for a raised eyebrow, a cocked eye, a frown, or a nod. But Shaw telegraphed nothing. Once finished, the chief executive started again from the beginning, this time making notes.

Ten minutes later, the KR founder lifted his head and sighed. "I grew up in the fifties. It wasn't a perfect world then. Lord knows discrimination in the South was horrible, and even here in Chicago. When we watched the news, we would see what happened yesterday, or maybe a week ago. It took that long for film to get back to the networks. I remember *The Camel News Caravan* with John Cameron Swayze. It was a fifteen-minute nightly news roundup sponsored by cigarettes." He laughed. "You can be assured there was no coverage of the health hazards of cigarettes. Now we have news—or is it noise?—24-7. Endless, and half the time mindless.

"The main fear kids had back then was whether hiding under a wooden school desk would protect us when the Russian planes or ICBMs dropped their nuclear bombs on our neighborhood. As if duck and cover would save anyone. But the Russians never came. We watched kids' shows full of heroes and imagined ourselves as cowboys, jet pilots, and astronauts. Roy Rogers. Captain Midnight. Colonel Ed McCauley. And we had our music. You know the song "Telstar"? The instrumental?" He hummed a little of it.

"Yes," Reilly replied, actually wanting to get to Shaw's assessment. "Love oldies."

"Well it was named for the first telecommunications satellite. I watched a live broadcast when they threw the switch. 1963. They cut between signals from Mount Rushmore, England, New York, and more. In that one moment, the time between an event and the public's awareness of it decreased. Telstar told us the world was shrinking. TV ads for nonstop 707 jet service to Europe demonstrated how quickly we could get there in person. That created global opportunities no one could have imagined just a few years earlier. It also brought news of wars home quicker. Vietnam, Granada, and Panama."

Shaw placed Reilly's proposal on the coffee table between them.

"Now you have a plan we couldn't have fathomed a decade ago. It recognizes today's dangerous world and how we have to conduct business. What did you say when you testified before that crackpot in Washington?"

"Essentially that our business has expanded beyond hospitality. Circumstances dictate that we're also in the anti-terrorism business."

"Your plan addresses that quite thoroughly. Has Pat put a dollar figure on it?"

"She's working on it. But there's no doubt that it's going to cost a great deal in IT and security, training, facilities, and travel."

Shaw checked a note he'd made. "And with all this we don't derive any public relations or advertising benefit?"

"No, sir. None at all."

"So bottom line, we develop this plan and the only people who might know are the terrorists?"

"Not completely, people will see enhanced measures. If they're traveling to danger zones, they've already gotten travel warnings from the airlines and State Department advisories. When they walk into our facilities, the visible measures will be in accord with their own expectations. Plus, we'll have more that aren't so apparent."

"I understand that Chris was concerned about certain relationships you and Alan have. And you still want more, according to your testimony."

Reilly smiled. "Yes and yes."

"Care to discuss it."

"Actually, no. You've hired us to deal with information and advise you. Best we leave it at that."

Reilly intentionally stayed with the *we*. It was his own cover.

"If we ever feel the need to share anything specific," he continued, "we'll give you the opportunity to decline."

"Is this my Senior VP of International speaking? Sounds like some other experience is coming through."

"Just putting you first," Reilly offered.

"You sure that's it, Dan?"

"As long as it works for you," Reilly added without expression.

Whatever Shaw might have been thinking, he dropped it. "Give me a few days to circle around to the team. We'll talk after."

"Absolutely," Reilly said.

He stood ready to leave.

"Wait, Dan. Before you go, let's debrief on Tehran, and I have another meeting for you."

"Where?"

"*Where* is only part of it. It's the *who* that's really interesting."

KIEV

One more night at the Klovska Classic Hotel. Miklos wanted to confirm that the shift changes were correct and deliveries remained unchecked and stored.

As Karl Richter, he walked freely throughout the building, amazed by the lax security from both a technical and personnel perspective. This made a hard job easier, but by no means anything to take for granted.

While strolling, Miklos recalled the days of Soviet oversight. There was an order to life. Everything in its place. Everyone understanding his purpose. Then came the unraveling. Order replaced by disorder. In place of a system that worked, a rush for personal material gains. This brought forth the oligarchs, the nouveau riche capitalists who nearly ruined the Motherland.

What would life have been like if there had been a different outcome in Potsdam? By that he meant, what would have happened had Nikolai Gorshkov not been reborn with the resolve to return Russia to greatness. Andre Miklos would die for his commander. Yes, he'd earned millions to retire on, but everything he did, he did out of loyalty. He believed in the greater good. Russia deserved to reclaim its rightful place as *the* dominant world leader.

CHICAGO

Shaw called in Alan Cannon and Chris Collins for the rest of the meeting.

"Are the Iranians committed to what it will take to build?" Shaw asked.

Reilly laughed. "They use gold and marble like it grows on trees. But American tourists are still reluctant to go. Too many unknowns."

"Let's find out," Shaw said. "We'll set up focus groups with multiple sessions in each city."

"I think they'll reaffirm what we already know," said Reilly. "If anything, we should evaluate the business market. Commission a couple of independent, confidential surveys through *The Wall Street Journal* and *Forbes*. They've already done stories on tech and textile firms that have feelers out to Tehran. Textiles, in fact, is Iran's number two export. They see US importers as potential partners. So, if the US corporations are willing to go, they might feel more comfortable staying in a hotel managed by an American brand."

"What's Europe doing?" Shaw wondered.

"Different history, different strategy," Reilly explained. "They're jumping at the opportunity. France in particular. Their attitude is if you snooze, you lose. We're different. There's deep distrust and potential political fallout."

"We turned Vietnam around," Collins offered.

"Yes," Reilly replied. "But it took decades. We're not at the same place with Iran."

"Dan's right," Cannon said. "You can't draw a comparison."

"Okay. Stand pat and get the data," Shaw instructed. "But, Dan, keep polite dialogue going. Now to the next item, and why I want all three of you here."

Reilly noticed that Chris had opened a file. Whatever the agenda, he was on the inside.

"Moscow," said Shaw. "It's back on."

Cannon reacted first. "Come on boss, we've taken this off the table twice already."

"I know, but there's an extra dimension with some high-level participation."

"But the Russian market is iffy," Cannon protested. "The West hasn't let up on all the sanctions. Besides, we'd need an investment company or a sovereign fund willing to commit."

"I may have someone," Reilly said.

"Oh?" Collins inquired.

Reilly briefed them on the Barclays executive he'd met in Tehran.

"Possibly," Shaw replied.

"No," Cannon said. "Not a good idea. "I don't trust the Russians."

"Just hear it out," Shaw said. "We have a specific opportunity, and Chris has some numbers that Brodowski ran."

"The Moscow Excelsior Hotel is going to come on the market," Collins began.

"To buy?" Reilly interrupted.

"To manage with an option," the lawyer relayed.

"It's a shitty property. It needs a fortune to bring it up," Reilly argued.

"Yes, at least 150 million, from soup to nuts, for the 300 rooms," Collins noted.

"Have you been there?"

"No."

"Better count on 300 million before all's said and done," Reilly said, correcting the lawyer. "I doubt any lender would . . ."

"Dan, much less," Shaw interjected. "Word is Russia is talking with China on multiple levels. New money may be coming into the country. They could potentially underwrite part of the investment. And they want us."

"Maybe so, but I'd wait for at least another year. We need to put our energies into our security plan."

"Agreed," Cannon said. "We should have one focus right now."

"I appreciate your thoughts, gentlemen, but we can do more than one thing at a time. President Gorshkov announced he's holding an economic development summit that starts with a state reception. I received a call from the state minister myself. And Dan, I said you'd show and consider the opportunity. Alan and Chris can carry on here with the security assessment."

"Edward—" Reilly began, realized it was a done deal, and stopped.

"Meet, be nice. Make friends."

"Come on. This isn't like an M&E or management arrangement here," Reilly argued. "Everyone's on the take in Russia. Hell, you can't make a business deal in Russia without cutting a side deal with the mayor. He'll demand 5 percent of all hotel receipts. That's how it works there. You'd never approve it. I sure as hell wouldn't recommend it to you. Besides, it violates America's Foreign Corrupt Practices Act."

"Dan's right," Collins said. "No businesses can make or pay bribes to a governmental agency. You saw what happened when one US hotel corporation was caught. Big fine and their stocks fell."

Reilly cut back in. "If we're even thinking of doing business in Moscow, I'll have to meet with the mayor and—"

"Meet with the mayor," Shaw said declaratively.

Reilly blanched. "I was speaking rhetorically."

"And I'm serious."

"Sir, with all due respect, he's corrupt in a corrupt system."

"You give him the message, maybe it'll work its way upstairs. Besides, you might have the opportunity for the message to go top-down."

"I don't understand," Reilly responded.

"The session kicks off with a reception. Tell it to Gorshkov yourself." Shaw smiled.

Cannon broke in. "You're kidding?"

"Nope. Great opportunity."

"And what the hell do I say to him?"

"On behalf of Kensington Royal, I'm honored to meet you, Mr. President. But I have a concern . . ."

KIEV

Sex was for sale everywhere in Kiev, a by-product of the fall of Communism. Once Russia seized all of Ukraine, the business would become a tool of the state, as it had been under the KGB. After all, sex was a means to secure information, recruit operatives, and blackmail enemies. However, for now, it was simply available, and Andre Miklos had the money to get what he wanted. Anything he wanted was sitting at the Klovska Classic bar.

Officially prostitution was forbidden in Kiev, but police looked the other way as long as the hooker didn't appear to be underage. Of course, that only made child prostitution all the more exciting. Though Miklos found that idea intriguing, he wanted someone as experienced and talented in her profession as he was in his.

The prostitutes began assembling every night after nine. The real beauties arrived later. Despite Miklos' desire to live on the edge, he never took chances. Ever. He'd play it safe. In fact, the hotel helped. The Klovska Classic, soon to be out of service, thoughtfully stocked condoms in each room free of charge.

"Hello," he said, in character with his German accent. The tall blonde smiled. Minutes later she smiled more in his room when he counted 51,000 hryvnia out onto the bed, about 2,000 US dollars. She was really going to work hard tonight.

31

WASHINGTON, DC

THE WHITE HOUSE

"Let's have it, Gerald," said the president.

This intelligence briefing could shape American policy in Europe. The topic was Russia. President Alexander Crowe expected his newest CIA director, Gerald Watts, to be brutally blunt. He counted on Pierce Kimball, his national security advisor, to be direct as well. Secretary of State Elizabeth Matthews, the most plugged-in, would remain cautious. Meanwhile, General Jeffrey Jones, Chairman of the Joint Chiefs, would undoubtedly advocate for the strongest possible military presence.

President Crowe was a moderate Republican in a polarized world; a veteran who had served under a ready, fire, aim president. He vowed not to do the same.

The president was known and lampooned for wearing turtlenecks and T-shirts with sports jackets. He wasn't conservative money's first choice, but the first choice was unelectable on a national scale, so the party intervened in a heated convention. Crowe, a Colorado governor and chairman of the Republican Governors Association, brokered the debate, then agreed to run. Now well into his first term, he governed with that same sense of reluctance—acting tough when absolutely necessary, avoiding confrontation whenever possible, but often surprising those in his own inner circle.

Director Watts began. "Gorshkov, Mr. President. His annexation of Crimea in 2014. His ongoing support for pro-Russian separatists in Ukraine, his seeding of anti-NATO opposition in Poland, Czechoslovakia, and Hungary. It's a pattern."

The lanky intelligence chief, a former Boston chief of police, looked the president squarely in the eyes. "He's increased submarine patrols in the North Sea, the Pacific, and even off the coast of Martha's Vineyard, for God's sake. He's tested western border weaknesses with helicopter flyovers. Quick ins and outs. It's unsettled former Eastern Bloc nations, NATO members, our allies."

Elizabeth Matthews amplified the point. "They're asking for more protection. More protection they say, while there's still time."

"Time?" the president asked.

"Time before the Kremlin makes its next move," she stated unequivocally.

"Mr. President," General Jones added, "our allies will only be our allies as long as they are still under NATO protection. There's growing concern that neither NATO nor the US will be there if and when they are needed."

"That's absurd," the president responded.

"Are you so sure?"

"What did we do for Georgia? For Eastern Ukraine? Turkey?" Jones continued. "We're losing their trust."

"Jesus. We could just as easily become the provocateur. A justification for Gorshkov."

"Yes we could, Mr. President. But a capital increase, not an increase in a military presence, would underscore our support," Secretary Matthews maintained.

"Ridiculous," Jones countered with emphasis on the *us*.

"Hold it, General," the president interrupted. "They're in Elizabeth's ear. What are they saying?"

"Money, sir. Four times what we're spending annually to date. It raises the threat, but not the way that troops would be seen."

Now the president pivoted. "Money and troop exercises? I've met the man. He'll consider anything as an escalation. So we better be prepared."

"Mr. President—" Matthews began to argue.

"Steps, Elizabeth," the president continued. "Nothing dramatic. We set up a new chessboard. We establish the agenda for the upcoming NATO summit and leak the proposals."

"Poland and the Baltic nations will want more than gamesmanship," General Jones argued. "Deterrence, Mr. President. Visible. Unmistakable. I recommend that we preposition equipment and troops in Central and Eastern Europe. It'll send a clear message of determination."

"Jeffrey, we're in compliance with the NATO-Russia Founding Act of 1997. That's where we stay. Troops rotate according to the agreement. It'll work for now. Pierce, are you in accord?" President Crowe asked, turning to his national security advisor.

"I'm with Secretary Matthews. For years both sides have stood by the promise not to station large numbers of troops at borders shared by members of NATO and Russia," Pierce Kimball explained. "If we add troops, Gorshkov will do the same. He'll meet your escalation, and you'd be jeopardizing the status quo. And right now, the status quo works."

"I disagree," Jones stated. "The Polish leaders believe that Russia's aggressions have already violated the 1997 accord. They need our help, and so do the other nations in the region."

"Is that true, Elizabeth?"

"Yes, substantively, Mr. President. But to acquiesce, to station more permanent troops, will be viewed as intimidation at best and a threat at worst."

"I understand that," the president said, letting his displeasure show. "But right-wing factions are taking more seats in the ministry, and not just in Poland. They've made the deployment of NATO troops a battle cry."

"Yes, but a battle with the Russians?" Matthews put in. "Think about it. Do you really want to provoke Gorshkov, Mr. President?"

Crowe did not immediately speak. National Security Advisor Pierce Kimball did.

"Have Secretary Matthews take your proposal to NATO," he said. "Float the idea. The Russians may publicly bark, but we'll state that our policy is to resupply and update equipment. As far as troops, we conduct routine training exercises as we've always done. At established troop strength," he added. "Nothing that would escalate or inflame. We move some of the pawns around on the board."

"All well and good until we discover that we've lost our knights and put our queen and king in jeopardy," barked General Jones.

President Crowe stood, signaling the end of the meeting.

"Thank you everyone. I'll get back to you in due time."

32

BUCHAREST, ROMANIA

Nikolai Gorshkov, a senior member of the current president's inner circle, wearing a black suit and a black and white striped tie, faced the press following the NATO-Russia Council held at the Palace of the Parliament. Reporters were there to score good quotes, but they got more than that. Gorshkov bluntly expressed his view that NATO's influence over Russia's former satellites seriously threatened mutual trust, which was rapidly a diminishing commodity.

"Mr. Gorshkov," one reporter asked, "looking forward, how would you sum up relations between Russia and NATO?"

There was absolutely no reason for Gorshkov to evade the question. In 1999 NATO warplanes had bombed Belgrade. American troops stormed in, securing territory in Kosovo, and pushed back Yugoslavia's military. At the time, Gorshkov saw the intervention as NATO's first step toward the Balkans. *Glavny protivnik*, he thought, the main enemy. The West pushing its own politics and policies at Russia's expense. NATO, with its Washington provocateurs, hadn't even referred the issue to the United Nations. *Relations. Here's my answer about relations.*

"NATO was created at a time when there were two blocs confronting each other. But today? There is no Soviet Union, no Eastern Bloc, and no Warsaw Pact. So NATO exists to confront exactly whom?"

Gorshkov bore down on the reporter, but had a message for Washington and the lame duck president. "We have eliminated bases in Vietnam and Cuba. We have called back our troops deployed in Eastern Europe, and withdrawn almost all large and heavy weapons from the European part of Russia. What are we left with? A NATO base in Romania, one in Bulgaria, an American missile defense area in Poland and the Czech Republic. We are the ones who are threatened. The West is at our front door with their military might."

Gorshkov went further in his harangue to explain how NATO had just extended membership invitations to Croatia and Albania, two countries even closer to Russia. How US President George W. Bush had wanted to add Ukraine and Georgia, but the proposal was defeated by German and French colleagues who feared it would further upset Russia. The actions underscored Gorshkov's ever-increasing distrust of NATO and his belief that America was pursuing a self-fulfilling prophesy.

"The appearance of a powerful military bloc along our borders could be taken as a direct threat to the security of Russia," Gorshkov stated. "The claim that this process is not directed against Russia will not suffice. National security is not based on promises. And the statements made prior to the bloc's previous waves of expansion simply confirm this."

Gorshkov's comments buoyed his associate Andre Miklos, who stood well back and out of view of the cameras. And beyond Nikolai Gorshkov's public comments, Miklos would make his own special skills heard. He had more unofficial assignments to execute.

33

WASHINGTON, DC

PRESENT DAY

"Russia?" Brenda Sheldon asked.

"Yup, Russia," Reilly said. "Schedule change. Tomorrow." He explained on the phone.

She did a preliminary check of flights as they chatted about the sessions. He casually dropped the name of the dignitary he would be meeting at the state reception.

"Well then, let's get you there on time. There's a nonstop out of JFK on Aeroflot at 2:20 p.m. arriving 6:25 the next morning or an evening flight at 7:10 p.m. That'll get you in a little after 11:00 the next morning."

"The later one," he responded. "Book it up for Thursday. My visas still good?"

"For another six months."

Sheldon kept an up-to-date grid that tracked the status of all his travel documents. It was critical to his international travel. She regularly renewed his 72-hour visa-free travel passes to countries like China and the 90-day visas for Japan, Singapore, Australia, and New Zealand. He had ten-year visas good for most countries friendly to the US. And for Russia, his invitation, signed and sealed by the Ministry of Internal

Affairs, was in force.

"Can't imagine any problem considering who you'll be meeting," said Brenda with a laugh.

The last thing Reilly wanted was personal scrutiny. But he wouldn't be surprised if the FSB had a dossier on him, if only for his work with Kensington Royal, and possibly his service and State Department record. Nothing specific, but enough for them to keep an eye on him.

"I can get you into the Ritz or would you prefer a European property?"

Reilly considered the optics. He was going to move a deal along, so staying at another American hotel wouldn't be right. Checking into a Russian hotel would be wrong from a security standpoint.

"Let's go neutral. The Swissotel Krasnye Holmy. I liked what I saw when I had a meeting there a year ago. Find out who the GM is, just in case. No suite, but you can arrange an airport pickup. I don't trust the cabs there. All in all, I want to keep a low profile."

"Some low profile. You're meeting Nikolai Gorshkov for God's sake."

"Well, yes. Basically I'm glad-handing."

Glad hand. He'd once looked up the term. It suggested a warm greeting prompted by ulterior motives. A gladhand connector, on the other hand, worked by interlocking two air hoses, providing a secure but easily detachable link.

What kind of link would this trip bring? he wondered.

"It'll be interesting," Reilly added.

34

MOSCOW, RUSSIAN FEDERATION

Reilly thought about the proper attire for the event. He settled on a conservative three-piece black suit, white shirt with French cuffs and gold cufflinks, a Movado black and gold watch, Gucci belt, solid black socks, and glossy black oxfords. All business, some class, but no one-upmanship. It would be appropriate for the reception and state photographs. Back at his office he had photographs on the walls of him with President Crowe, his predecessor Morgan Taylor, and the presidents of five other countries. He wasn't sure if he'd display a photo of him with Gorshkov.

At the hotel entrance the valet asked Reilly in English where he was going.

"The Kremlin," he said not raising an eyebrow.

The valet gave his whistle four quick blasts and then a fifth. Rather than the first taxi in the queue coming forward, the fourth car in line pulled out. The valet told the driver where Dan was going, but he already seemed to know.

None of this was wasted on Dan Reilly. He was being watched. *All business?* he wondered. *No way.*

The taxi driver immediately engaged him in conversation. Reilly kept to basics. He was a hotel executive meeting with the minister of industry and trade, and perhaps others looking for possible business. He was excited about going to the Kremlin for the first time.

The cabbie then began to probe a little further: "Will you buy or build? Will you own or will you franchise? So how did you get into this line of work anyway?"

His English was too good, his questions too probing. Reilly deflected them all with friendly replies. "Too early to tell. Depends. I like travel." Then he asked for the radio.

Ten minutes later they were waived through the Kremlin gate all too quickly and drove directly to the Palace entrance in Cathedral Square. Reilly paid the driver and gave him only an adequate tip, certain he was drawing another salary from the FSB.

Reilly stepped out and gave his name to the Kremlin guard. Though he assumed they had known it from the moment the cab cleared the gate.

"Welcome, Mr. Reilly. It's good to have you here," the officer said. "Please follow the usher up the steps."

Steps was an understatement. These were not just any steps. This was the Red Staircase, the brick, limestone, and red-carpeted entry to the most elegant reception rooms in the palace.

Reilly's knowledge of political history from graduate school professor Colonel William Harrison served him well. This wasn't the original staircase where Ivan the Terrible had killed the messenger with the bad news, where as a ten-year-old the future Peter the Great watched as Kremlin guards slashed his uncles to death during a failed coup, or where Napoleon Bonaparte was said to have watched the burning of Moscow.

Stalin destroyed that staircase when he cut through the palace walls to construct a dining room for Soviet delegates. However, the newer staircase, re-created to original specifications for Moscow's 850th anniversary celebration in 1997, was making its own history. The bright red carpet cushioned the last footsteps of the old guard, the Soviet leaders, and the heavy foot of the new regime. This was where Gorshkov stood to review the parade after his inauguration.

Before he walked up, the usher announced him with dramatic flair in English and again in Russian. "Representing the Kensington Royal Hotel Corporation, from the United States, Mr. Daniel Reilly."

Another usher repeated it midway up the grand staircase. A third when he reached Georgievsky Hall, one of five elegant rooms named for orders of the Russian Empire. There, Reilly was greeted by a Kremlin representative. He was immediately offered a glass of champagne, which he gratefully accepted.

Georgievsky was used for state and diplomatic receptions. No wonder. The hall was more magnificent than any he'd ever seen. Reilly took a first cautious step forward on the highly polished floor that reflected light from hundreds of bulbs set in the elegant chandeliers that hung like grand necklaces. The room was awash with white and gold. Drapes covered two windows two floors high. Cushioned benches lined alcoves that jutted out from the hall. At the far end was a frieze of Saint George, the Roman soldier beloved by the Russian Orthodox Church.

Reilly was surprised to see so many people at the reception. He'd been led to believe by Shaw that it was going to be a smaller event.

"Where is everyone from?" Reilly asked an usher, not even thinking English would be a problem. It wasn't.

"Government ministers, the mayor, tourism officials, international bankers, local businessmen. We had been scheduled for a smaller reception room, but we moved here. Georgievsky Hall is the largest and most impressive."

He looked around. "Absolutely beautiful." But Dan Reilly wasn't talking about the hall now. He'd spotted a woman in an elegant black cocktail dress some twenty feet away.

"Excuse me," Reilly said.

When he was halfway there the woman caught his eye and smiled. In turn, she excused herself and came over to greet Reilly warmly.

"Mr. Reilly, I had no idea."

He kissed her left check, then her right.

"Ms. Babbitt, delighted to see you. Apparently we move in similar circles."

The Barclays bank executive slipped her hand onto his arm. "Well then, let's explore together."

They strolled through the hall, pointing out people they knew and wondering about those they didn't. Reilly recognized representatives from other hotel chains and executives from the major credit cards, telcos, and three airline presidents. Babbitt pointed out the people she could identify from the banking community.

"Quite the bash," she quietly observed.

"Perhaps a little bait and switch to create more competition?" he mused.

"It wouldn't be the first time. Tell me, what is your schedule?"

It was a pointed question, bordering on the personal, as Babbitt so often tread.

"Tomorrow I'll be with the mayor of Moscow. He's across the hall now."

"That'll be fun," she said.

"Oh, a barrel of laughs."

She was familiar with the way Mayor Tyomkin conducted business. "He's a tough negotiator." Babbitt leaned into Reilly's ear and whispered, "With his own Swiss bank accounts."

Reilly pulled back. "Really now?"

"Hey, this isn't my first Russian rodeo."

"I guess not, Ms. Babbitt."

"I think we can progress to first names, Dan," she said.

"Okay. Marnie it is."

The pair continued to talk as they sampled the Russian *zakuski*, or appetizers: herring under a fur coat, which was herring mixed with boiled potatoes, beets, carrots, and mayonnaise; red and black salmon caviar; salmon pâté; and shots of vegetable borscht.

Occasionally they stopped for polite conversations with others they knew, but mostly they kept to themselves. A few times she gave a greeting in more than acceptable Russian.

"I hoped we'd see one another again," Babbitt said as they took a seat on one of the benches against the wall.

"I'd hoped the same thing. Suppose I could have initiated."

"Yes, Mr. Reilly. I'm a little old fashioned. I was waiting."

"Sorry. I've been busy. Back and forth between DC and Chicago. A lot going on."

He dabbed her lip with a napkin. "Don't think you want caviar lipstick when you meet the president."

"Ah, well, you've got a job for the evening. Keep me all aglow."

He felt that *intimate* just elevated to sensual. Her long gaze moved it one step further. Sexual. But the moment quickly came to an end.

A brass band opposite them began a fanfare. Reilly and Marnie automatically straightened. Next came the opening notes of a classical piece that Reilly recognized. He whispered it to Babbitt. "'The Patriotic Song.' A Russian composition by Glinka."

Dan Reilly looked up and down Georgievsky Hall. To his right he saw another guest point to the near entrance off the Red Staircase. Two guards in ceremonial garb marched along the red carpet with huge, high steps, perfectly in sync. It was grand theater, with more to come. The guards passed their vantage point and soon stopped at two gold doors at the opposite end of the hall. The music reached a crescendo. The two guards turned to face one another and did a quarter turn to the huge gold doors. Each guard reached for a doorknob on either side. Still in absolute sync, they opened them as the music swelled.

Twenty feet beyond them, a man exuding ultimate confidence, walked precisely on the center of the long carpet toward Georgievsky Hall. Applause began closest to the doors, then spread to the opposite end. The man stood out from the white wall behind him and hit every step precisely in time with the music.

It was the most regal, presidential, or dictatorial entrance Dan Reilly had ever witnessed, rehearsed and timed to perfection.

Ten steps inside the man stopped and raised his hands, welcoming everyone. Then he lowered them, palms down, a signal for his guests to stop applauding. Reilly and Marnie Babbitt hadn't realized that they'd also been caught up in the moment, clapping enthusiastically. Such was the power and charisma of Nikolai Gorshkov.

The president of the Russian Federation walked to a microphone that had suddenly appeared in the center of the room. He gave a two-minute welcome in Russian that was partially understood by his gestures.

Reilly glanced at Marnie. She was nodding and laughed with the Russian guests at a poor joke that Gorshkov made in Russian before switching to English.

"I am pleased to see so many members of the international business community here tonight. Together with your vision, your help, and our partnerships, Moscow will become the greatest global hub for conferences and a true and open travel destination. My poor English prevents me from saying more to my guests, but I look forward to meeting everyone before the evening has ended. Welcome and thank you."

As everyone applauded again, Marnie leaned into Reilly's ear. "He scares me."

But it wasn't fright that Reilly felt, it was a sense of unease. Like the moment he stepped onto Afghan soil for the first time.

He watched Nikolai Gorshkov welcome a few members of his retinue and then be led to a chair for photo opportunities. Just then, a man tapped him on his shoulder.

"Excuse me, Mr. Reilly."

Reilly pivoted. "Yes?"

An usher with an earpiece and a wire fed down his jacket addressed him. Reilly came to an immediate assumption. *Russia's version of the US Secret Service.* The man had been standing behind Reilly and Babbitt awaiting instructions.

"The president would be honored to meet you," he said. "Please come with me."

The man spoke with a military preciseness. It was not an offer or request. It had the tone of an order.

"Certainly. May Ms. Babbitt join us?"

"Of course, President Gorshkov would enjoy meeting . . ." there was a pause and a nod—he'd gotten Marnie's name in his ear, ". . . the representative from Barclays."

Marnie remained by his side and, for the second time that night, slipped her hand around Reilly's arm. This time she squeezed.

"This way," the officer instructed.

"How long was he standing near us?" she whispered.

"Later," Reilly said, patting her still clinging hand.

As they walked across the room, people Reilly had thought were guests opened a clear path. Now on closer review he saw that they all had earpieces. They were all connected. *The new Russia,* he thought. *Not so new.*

Four other people were waiting for their photo op with Gorshkov. They were quick with little conversation beyond a polite hello.

Now it was Reilly's turn. His handler walked him forward while another agent held Babbitt back.

The president had a chair, but he stood well to the side. From a psychological point of view, a photograph of anyone standing over him was not good.

Reilly expected the same speedy chat and snap—a glad hand memorialized with a framed photo sent to his office a month later. Instead, Nikolai Gorshkov reached out with both hands to greet Reilly. Dan automatically extended his.

"Mr. Reilly," Gorshkov said. "I have looked forward to meeting you."

"Why thank you, Mr. President." Reilly was caught off guard.

"Please, first, a photograph."

The two men stood side by side. Gorshkov joked, "And another one for your wall." They smiled. The photographer took five quick pictures. "Now that that's over with . . ." The president turned and faced Reilly, away from the camera, and continued, "A few moments with you. I will try my best English."

"Thank you, Mr. President. You're doing fine."

"We want very much your business. I have seen interviews you've given in *Forbes.* Insightful. You know your business."

"Well, thank you. I do." Reilly swallowed hard and decided that if this were the only opportunity he might have, he better raise the issue. "But if you'll allow me perhaps an imprudent notion, I am also aware of business practices in Moscow."

The president laughed. "Ah yes. Our beloved mayor."

"In fact, yes."

Gorshkov put his arm around Reilly's shoulders and brought him closer. "A man of action," he said. "I am aware of your American laws, and that is good enough for me. You have my word that no problem will impede our business."

"Mr. President, thank you. Your personal assurance means a great deal to Kensington Royal. Of course there are many steps."

"Yes, yes, yes. But we can," he struggled for the right phrase, "fast . . ."

"Fast track?" Reilly suggested.

"Thank you. Fast track. We can make this work. Then perhaps expansion into other key cities in the Russian Federation." He laughed broadly. "Tourism. Don't we all look toward expansion?"

Gorshkov squeezed his upper arm—just a little too hard.

A warning? Reilly wondered. *Don't fuck with me?*

Before he could give it another thought, Gorshkov released his arm and added, "Remember. You have my word."

As Reilly shook Gorshkov's hand and the photographer clicked away, Reilly played back the last statement. *You have my word.* He'd report that to Shaw after seeing how the meeting with the mayor went. But it was another line that perplexed him. *We all look toward expansion.* That one would go to Langley.

"That was pretty amazing," Babbitt said enthusiastically after her moment with President Gorshkov. She earned a kiss on both cheeks and a photograph.

During the exchange Reilly, who had stepped back, was aware that she'd spoken Russian with the president.

"And he knew my name. I didn't see anyone tell him."

"They say he has a photographic memory," Reilly commented. He also tapped his ear to indicate how they were communicating.

"Well, pretty amazing either way. I'm impressed."

They walked away from the staging area, her hand back on his arm.

"So, Mr. Reilly," she cooed, "you had quite the conversation with the president. Care to enlighten me?"

"Our years in Boy Scouts together, favorite Bond movies, the usual."

"Stop it. What did he say?"

Reilly shrugged his shoulder. "He's eager to do business."

"Well, that's great news coming from the president. Means he'll clear the forest."

"Seems that way."

"Then why don't we talk about Barclays making this even more possible? I'm prepared to discuss terms."

"Well aren't you the sly fox?"

"Eager beaver," she quickly responded. "Let's go to dinner."

* * *

Reilly chose Varvary based on recommendations that Brenda had provided. Reservations would have been difficult, but a woman at the desk spoke English and had gone to Emerson College in Boston. The Boston connection earned him an 8:45 p.m. reservation.

Arriving, Reilly and Babbitt took in the opulent décor, reflective of tsarist Russia, with lace, plush carpets, heavy silverware, and the color red everywhere. Following cocktails they started with black bread pudding served on a silver spoon with sunflower oil gel that dissolved in their mouths with a sensual intensity. Next, a bewildering borscht, unlike any Reilly had ever had, infused with slivers of beets with garlic ice cream. There was an unforgettable veal shank with horseradish, a play on herring under a fur coat, and so much more. The meal proved to be a gastronomical explosion of flavors, with foams and gels that were as much fun to see as to taste.

Three hours of delicacies. Three hours of getting to know one another. Three hours with an undercurrent of desire.

They talked about their marriages: both over.

They talked about children: none

They talked about work: all-encompassing.

"What went wrong with your marriage?" Marnie inquired. The second bottle of wine made it easier to ask and answer.

"Lots of things. My lack of commitment."

"Oh, bad boy."

"We met after I retired from the service. Things were good when I was consulting some in Washington." He didn't get into any other details. "But when I joined Kensington Royal I was on the road three weeks a month, twelve months a year. Two years of that was enough for Pam, and I couldn't blame her."

"Didn't she ever travel with you?"

"A few times early on, but remember it was anything but vacation for me when we traveled together. I worked. She waited. I came back to our rooms exhausted."

"Are you still in touch? I'm sorry. That's none of my business."

"That's okay," Reilly responded. "Circumstances keep us in touch. She's living in Virginia, went back to her maiden name, and working high up in Veterans Affairs. Her boyfriend is a CNN producer. He's always after me for a quote whenever there's a related story."

"Like recently?"

"Absolutely."

"Uncomfortable?"

"Only when I dodge him."

"How often does that happen?"

"Constantly," Reilly laughed. "And you? How long were you married?"

"Four years. A starter marriage with no second in sight. All that practice going nowhere." She laughed, but only to cover her feelings. "A few affairs that flamed out. You know, last minute rendezvous canceled, plans that fall apart. The excitement wears off fast."

"And your ex? Still in your life?"

She laughed again, this time with reason. "The modern way. We're Facebook friends."

Reilly chuckled. It was the modern way.

They talked about their management style, which dovetailed into the work that brought them both together.

"You do know that Barclays had a controlling stake in Russia's retail Expobank," Marnie commented.

"I heard it was an unmitigated disaster?"

"Well if you consider we acquired it for £373 million in '08 and sold it for, shall we say an 'undisclosed amount.'"

"About a tenth of your purchase price," noted Reilly.

"My lips are sealed."

But they weren't. Reilly leaned over and kissed Marnie Babbitt.

"And it's not even the third date," Marnie said breathlessly as they disengaged.

"I forgot the rules," Reilly explained.

"Who needs rules?" she replied. Marnie leaned back in, this time initiating.

"I think we have three more courses coming," Reilly said, needing to breathe.

"We could write the Yelp review with what we had and with no regrets of what we're about to miss. Get the check, Mr. Reilly."

The only remaining decisions were which hotel room to go to and top or bottom or a lot more.

35

As far as Nikolai Gorshkov was concerned, Ukraine embodied the failures of the Soviet Union. Moreover, a union between NATO and Ukraine, and for that matter, any other former Eastern Bloc nations, represented the ultimate threat to the Russian Federation's economic and political survival.

It had to do with energy. Natural gas and Gorshkov's own power as a president. Energy was the commodity that fueled both. Oil shipped out globally on tankers and train cars. Russia's enormous gas reserves ran through pipelines that connected much of Europe to Russia. The resource was the foundation of the entire economy, but the lifeline lay under Ukraine, where most of Russia's gas flowed.

Retaining control of the network was fundamental to Gorshkov's goal of restoring Russia's formal glory under his command. However, in the new century elections in Ukraine had gone against Moscow's interests and NATO was constantly knocking on Ukraine's door.

Seven former Soviet Bloc nations and other spin-off countries had already joined the pact: Albania, Bulgaria, Czech Republic, Hungary, Croatia, Slovakia, Slovenia, Romania, Lithuania, Latvia, Estonia, Poland, and of course East Germany, now unified in the Federal

Republic of Germany.

Moscow viewed NATO's encroachment into Russia's sphere as a violation of the pledge Mikhail Gorbachev secured during the reunification of Germany in 1989—a pledge that stated *NATO would not expand to the east toward Russia.*

Now, Gorshkov vowed that Ukraine, the skies above and the gas pipelines below, were not going to go west.

"Gentlemen!" The president addressed his ministers of Defense, Internal and Foreign Affairs, Energy, Emergency Situations, Finance, Natural Resources, and Crimean Affairs. They sat across the large conference table adjacent to the president's Kremlin office. "The future is upon us."

His cabinet had heard this declaration time and again. It was embedded in Gorshkov's very being. The real evidence was the dramatic visible steps he had already taken to undo the perceived mistakes of the past. The impact also served to advance his own image in the world.

It began with Chechnya and extended to Georgia. The annexation of the Crimean peninsula demonstrated the depth of the Kremlin's strategy. Now that Gorshkov was in charge, he sought to restore the historic concept of the Russian nation and establish the Russian Federation as a reinvigorated world power. The new Russia would be safe within borders Nikolai Gorshkov alone defined. The new Russia would be economically secure in the energy-driven economy.

"Millions of our fellow citizens and compatriots, native Russians, and Russian loyalists live as second-class citizens outside Russian territory," he continued.

The president abruptly stood, commanding complete attention. "No more! NATO expansionism continues. It is a violation of trust. Do you remember the words of NATO General Secretary Wörner in Brussels on May 17, 1990? I do."

He saw well-mannered nods, not the fervor he expected.

"Do you?" he shouted.

"Yes!" they replied in unison.

Gorshkov scrutinized his ministers for any sign of disunity. Satisfied, he continued.

"Wörner declared that no NATO army would threaten the USSR outside of German territory. Well, we are no longer the Soviet Union, but where are the guarantees? Where?"

The ministers grumbled in agreement. "Nowhere."

"Nowhere!" Gorshkov echoed. "The stones and concrete blocks of the Berlin Wall have long been distributed as souvenirs as far off as California. The physical representation of the dividing line between East and West is gone. But now they are imposing new dividing lines and walls on us. These walls cut through the continent. They build the walls, not us. And then they send their troops to defend them. Where are the guarantees?" he repeated.

"Nowhere!" they exclaimed.

"Where are the promises our Russian-speaking brothers and sisters in neighboring countries, former Russian protectorates, heard that they would be given rights, privileges, and citizenship under NATO dominance?"

Once again Gorshkov's question was answered with a chorus of "Nowhere!"

"Nowhere," Gorshkov said quietly, heightening the drama in the room. "The end of the Cold War left us emasculated, disheartened, and all but disarmed. What did they leave us with?" He didn't wait for a response this time. "Disaster. Rather than reducing conflicts, global tensions have increased. There's more war and more death than in the world where a wall symbolized a political divide.

"One state, one nation has overstepped its national borders in every way. One country. It's apparent in the economic, political, cultural, and educational policies it imposes on other nations. One government: the United States. And with its influence and through its surrogates, we are at greater risk today than any time since Russia was viewed with fear and respect. We will protect our interests and citizens in countries who owe their allegiance to Mother Russia. And once again, we will have our borders back."

His ministers pounded the conference table in enthusiastic support. Gorshkov again scanned the room, judging how sincere the others were in their affirmation. He was uncertain about one member of his cabinet. If the feeling persisted, there'd be more work for Andre Miklos when he returned.

The president looked at his watch. It was time. He turned on a 52-inch Chinese-built television monitor and said, "I suspect there's some relevant news coming on any moment."

36

MOSCOW, RUSSIAN FEDERATION

Reilly and Marnie were walking hand in hand toward Marnie's room on the seventh floor of the Swissotel Krasnye Holmy when his phone vibrated. Incoming texts.

He automatically put his palm over the inside jacket pocket and read the vibration. He programmed incoming messages different ways. A general, unspecific number would produce a series of two vibrations separated by two-second pauses. Nonstop, almost annoying pulses meant a text from his ex-wife. He usually ignored them. Brenda's *important but not urgent*, as in the Eisenhower grid, carried vibrations to the first notes of Beethoven's Fifth, in Morse code, the letter Q. A fourth vibration, indicating *important and urgent*, was also identified by Morse code. No matter what he was doing, Dan Reilly checked his cell phone when this alert triggered.

It was that fourth defining signal . . . / _ _ _ / . . . cycling three times. SOS. SOS from a special cell phone Alan Cannon used in emergencies.

Reilly stopped short of the door.

"What? You're not getting cold feet, Mr. Reilly?" Marnie asked mischievously.

"No, but . . ."

He removed the phone as the vibration began again.

She nibbled his ear and whispered, "You can turn it off."

Reilly opened his messages.

"Oh my God." The words were more somber than exclamatory.

"What is it, Dan?"

"Another hotel bombing." He read further.

"Where? How bad?" She asked, but Reilly was absorbed in Cannon's message.

"Not one of ours," he finally said. "Not anymore. It had been, but we sold it a few years ago. The Klovska Classic Hotel in Kiev. But I know many of the staff. Good people." Reilly stepped back. "I'm sorry, I have to go. I'm really sorry."

"No, please come in. I'll order coffee, we'll put the TV on. You can make your calls. No pressure. Trust me, I'm used to work coming before me." She smiled. "Well, I didn't mean it that way."

Reilly pulled her close and kissed each of her eyelids and then her lips. But it was a kiss that said *Goodbye.*

"I want to, but I'll be on the phone all night. We *will* pick up where we left off. I promise."

Marnie returned to his ear and whispered, "I'll hold you to it." Then she pulled back, put on a professional face, and said, "Get to work, Mr. Reilly."

He nodded and smiled. *A woman who understood.*

* * *

Twenty minutes later, Reilly was in his room. Bugged or not, he openly used his phone to call Brenda in Chicago and Alan Cannon for updates, but right now he was getting more from CNN International on his TV than they had.

He considered dialing Heath's cell. While there might be no immediate exposure by calling, there'd be a number on record through a Russian tracking system.

Damn! He wanted to find out more. *But how?*

There was a way. Reilly left his room and took a cab to the US

Embassy in the city center at No. 8 Bolshoy Devyatinksy Lane.

The new American Embassy building had a checkered history. Construction of the glass and cement structure began in 1979 by Soviet builders. Under Kremlin orders, covert listening devices were laced throughout the columns. Upon detecting the spy equipment, the US had to traffic all classified information through the old embassy. The political Cold War fallout hit Washington. In retaliation, Soviet diplomats weren't allowed to occupy their new embassy in DC.

That's where the diplomatic row remained until well after the fall of Communism, when an American construction team was permitted to dismantle part of the new embassy and add four floors. The building, never deemed completely secure, reopened in 2000. Classified matters were conducted on the upper floors, while other embassy business was relegated to the lower, security-vulnerable floors.

Reilly showed his KR identification to the guard outside the embassy. After a check on his status, he was allowed in and ultimately permitted upstairs.

A marine lieutenant politely led Reilly to an office and gave him a piece of paper with a one-time dial-out code. This would get him to a secure line at Langley. He had no doubt that his friend would be in the building, even with the eight-hour time difference. Kiev was in Ukraine, and Ukraine was a flashpoint between US and Russian relations.

Heath came on the line after five minutes. He wasn't surprised that Reilly had gone to the embassy.

"It's bad," the CIA operative admitted. "And based on the reports, it'll get worse."

"How so?" Reilly asked.

"Death estimates are ninety to a hundred, maybe more. You know how it goes. At night more people are in the hotel, so there's a bigger rush at exits of people trying to escape. That's where timed secondary devices exploded."

"Anyone taking credit?"

"That's where it gets complicated and even more worrisome. A group of pro-Russian separatists were at Klovska Classic Hotel with a delegation from Moscow. They were meeting into the night."

"And?"

"A bomb went off in their conference room. Russians and pro-Russian separatists are among the dead."

"They were the target," Reilly surmised.

"That's our initial assessment. You can bet that's going to be Moscow's as well. We'll track whether it's enough of a provocation for Gorshkov to make a move and fulfill his wet dream of expansion."

"Jesus!" It was only five hours earlier that Reilly had been struck by the same word Heath had just used. *Expansion.* He relayed his conversation with President Gorshkov.

"Bob, play that thought out. What would Gorshkov do?"

"Well, if there's proof that Ukrainian nationalists wanted to take out the separatists and retaliate against Russia, Moscow could launch a full-scale attack. Hell, even if there isn't real proof, Gorshkov could gin up the possibility and still act. Or he could bring troops closer and keep the threat alive for a long time."

"And if it's one of the usual terrorist groups?" Reilly asked.

"Then why would they have picked this specific target on this specific night? This feels like it was a strategic inside job to take out pro-Russian separatists."

A thought came to Reilly. "And not the first at a hotel." He jotted down a name on a piece of paper.

"What? I don't know of any others," Heath responded.

"Tokyo," Reilly replied.

"What are you talking about? There were no Ukrainian separatists there."

"No, there weren't. But there was a pro-Russian Romanian separatist. A singer." He read from his note the name "Janusz Kretsky."

"Spell that."

Reilly slowly spelled the Romanian singer's name. "There's been an outcry of support for Kretsky from Russian nationals in Romania.

And still no one's come forward. Call me crazy, but what if there's a connection?"

"I'll never call you crazy, but it's likely more of a coincidence."

Reilly hated the reference, but he didn't push the point. Heath had the name now and could check.

"Will the SBU help any in Kiev?" Reilly asked. "CCTV cameras, hotel check-in info?"

SBU stood for the Security Service of Ukraine. The Sluzhba Bezpeky Ukrayiny, the country's leading anti-terrorism and counterintelligence agency.

"Working on it," Heath replied. "Too soon to know what kind of cooperation we'll get."

"Send them the screen grab of Smug," Reilly recommended. "See if anybody saw him."

Heath thought about it and replied. "Long shot, but I'll kick it upstairs."

"Worth a try."

Before they hung up, Heath had a warning for Reilly. "I'm glad we talked, but you've got to be careful leaving. You start the night with a private conversation with Gorshkov and end it with a trip to the US Embassy. It has the appearance of you reporting in. Better than an even chance you'll be followed back to your hotel and thereafter. There's been an uptick in harassment of our people. Windows in their rooms left open in the winter, for instance."

"It's warm out."

"Arrests for jaywalking"

"I cross at corners."

"Overt tailing."

"They already have my schedule."

"You get what I mean. They're going to be on you."

"Here's what I'll do. Play it head on. I'm scheduled to meet the mayor early. I'll tell him I checked in at the embassy to find out about Klovska Classic staff I knew since it used to be in our portfolio. No mention of separatists and politics. Only business, which is why I'm here."

"Why wouldn't you have just called your own office?"

"I did. They didn't have anything. I figured the embassy could make appeals to Kiev."

"Okay, then make sure you speak with someone who can do that. But still watch yourself."

"I'm sure they'll be much more interested in having me recommend the Moscow deal than in thinking I'm a spy."

"I hope you're right buddy," Heath said.

At 3:45 in the morning Reilly hailed a cab passing the embassy. He immediately noticed a car pull out of a parking space and follow him back to his hotel.

37

The next morning Dan Reilly arrived at Moscow City Hall, the office of the mayor, ten minutes before the appointed time.

The red brick building in Pushkin Square, built and rebuilt over 250 years, housed the executive branch of Moscow's political system, an arm of the Kremlin. Hundreds of city bureaucrats oversaw the administration of police, fire, and public property. Many had direct access to Gorshkov's ministers, but no one had quicker access than the mayor. The reverse was also true, but at a more intense level. The Mayor of Moscow reported to and served at the pleasure of the president.

Reilly's own reading suggested that Vadim Markovich, the latest mayor, was a puppet Gorshkov crafted, manipulated, and tolerated. When Gorshkov told Reilly that there'd be nothing to impede the Moscow hotel deal, Reilly understand it to mean that the mayor had been instructed not to ask for, demand, or even count on any kickback as part of the deal.

As a result, Reilly predicted the meeting would be pro forma. But then again, this was Russia, where power and money were intertwined.

Vadim Markovich stepped from behind his desk to greet Reilly. He was a short, stocky man with bushy brown eyebrows that made up for the lack of hair on his head. His brown suit was anything but stylish, and his tie too wide for today's fashion. Reading glasses hung from a red lanyard around his neck. If Reilly hadn't known he was the Mayor of Moscow, he'd have guessed he was some thug who hung out at a local bar.

He would have been right about the thug part. Vadim Markovich was anything but metropolitan. He was Gorshkov's appointee, in office for as long as Gorshkov desired.

"Mr. Mayor, so good to meet you," Reilly said. According to his research, the conversation could be conducted in English.

"Indeed, Mr. Reilly. I trust this will be the first of many such meetings, though I had come close to canceling. You've heard the news from Kiev."

This provided the perfect opportunity for Reilly to explain his late-night trip out of the hotel, a report which undoubtedly had been passed along to Markovich.

"Absolutely. Shocking. I went to our embassy as soon as I heard to check on associates and colleagues who worked at the hotel. My company had managed it until fairly recently."

"I didn't know that," the mayor lied.

Reilly lowered his eyes. "I'm still waiting to find out whether I lost some friends in the explosion." He bowed his head and continued. "The news reported that Russian diplomats were there. I hope . . ."

"A terrible tragedy. Ten members of our trade delegation. Maybe more."

"I'm sorry. If my company can be of any help . . ." Reilly feebly offered.

"Thank you, but no. Let us move on to making some good news and talk about how we can turn the Moscow Excelsior Hotel into one of your brand operations."

"We are very interested, Mr. Mayor. However you must realize we have not come to terms, nor considered financing options." He was thinking of Barclays, and that made him smile. "But Moscow would be a wonderful addition to our Kensington Royal luxury brand."

"I suppose we should talk unofficially about aspects of the approval process."

Reilly straightened up, surprised by Markovich's sudden detour.

"I'm afraid I don't understand."

"Traditionally Moscow participates."

This was in direct contradiction to the assurance the president had given him. *What's he trying to do?* Reilly thought. *Going rogue?* Reilly decided to see where it went.

"Please explain, Mr. Mayor?"

Markovich waved his hand as if to dismiss the seriousness of the point. "Call it a luxury tax. A small percentage that helps the city. Not at all unusual. Capped at 10 percent, but negotiable. Perhaps on a sliding scale over ten years. You just pass it on to your clientele. Nothing out of the ordinary."

"I'm sorry, but I need to get this clear." Reilly proceeded to tickle the tiger. "I've had assurances that *officially* the city VAT will not apply to this transaction. Are you proposing something different?"

"Well, in fact, yes, but—"

Reilly interrupted. "Sir, in April 2015, the Moscow City Duma adopted amendments that provide for special *tax benefits*, not additional taxes for, among other business ventures, hotels. Are you proposing something different?"

"Perhaps tax is not the correct word. It's my English," the mayor said with feigned sincerity. "Call it a service charge."

Reilly decided to end the chess game. Vadim Markovich not only revealed himself as a thug, but a stupid thug.

Reilly stood. He now towered over the sitting mayor who, with one additional conversation with Gorshkov, might not be the sitting mayor any longer.

"Mayor Markovich," Reilly said angrily, "your English is not failing you at all. So I'll use some English vernacular. To be kind, you're proposing a sweetheart deal, with Moscow the sweetheart. There's another term, however, less kind: a shakedown. If that doesn't translate, try side deal." For impact, Reilly said it in Russian. *"Pobochnaya sdelka."*

The Russian blanched.

"For the record," Reilly continued, "our legal department will not permit it. Moreover, the U.S. Department of Justice will prosecute us for entering into such a relationship. And here's the bottom line, which should end this discussion once and for all. I met with President Gorshkov last night. It was a short conversation, the substance of which included his personal pledge to me that you would not make the very proposal you've just made. And I'm being polite when I call it a proposal."

The mayor tried to recover, but Reilly would not allow him the time to pull an excuse together.

"As I see it, I have four choices," he pressed on. "I agree to your *pobochnaya sdelka* and subject myself to prosecution. I walk away from an important management opportunity in Moscow and you stumble through an explanation. I consider this conversation never to have happened. Or my favorite, I notify President Gorshkov that his promise to me was subverted by you. I know current circumstances in Ukraine have made this a busy day for him, but I'm certain I can get the message through."

Then Reilly added insult to injury, turning on his heel and starting to walk toward the door.

"Mr. Reilly, wait!"

"Yes?" Reilly did not immediately turn.

"You spoke of another choice. The third, I believe."

Reilly remained facing the door.

"We met and I agreed to help you in every way," the mayor continued. "No impediments. No special agreements."

"No *pobochnaya sdelka?*" Reilly said coldly.

"No side deal," Markovich said in English. "Do we have an understanding?" His voice cracked. "Your assurance that this will not go beyond my office?"

Reilly slowly pivoted and faced the corrupt bureaucrat. "Yes."

He waited for the mayor to cross the room to him. Markovich shyly put out his hand. Reilly took it.

"I'm glad we understand each other, Mr. Mayor. I look forward to seeing you at our grand opening should the remainder of the negotiations be fruitful."

"I will do everything to make it happen with the current owners."

The current owners of the Moscow Excelsior Hotel were his friends. He would make it happen at all costs. Even a loss, if necessary.

38

KIEV, UKRAINE

Russian press dropped its normal coverage and ran with the attack in Kiev. With 93,000 media outlets, 27,000 newspapers printing 8.2 billion copies, 330 TV channels, and hundreds of online news outlets, not to mention Twitter and other social media portals, Russians couldn't escape the news.

The government-owned daily *Rossiyskaya Gazeta* had access to Kremlin sources and leaks.

> Last night, terrorists intentionally targeted Russian nationals and pro-Russian supporters in a brutal attack at the Klovska Classic Hotel in downtown Kiev. Authorities report 72 dead and more than 100 injured. Among the dead are ten confirmed members of a delegation from Moscow who were meeting with pro-Russian sympathizers. Local Kiev police are heading the investigation. The Ministry of Defense is sending its own team.
>
> President Nikolai Gorshkov stated, "This cowardly act, obviously directed at Russian diplomats and freedom loving supporters, has echoes of the Moscow apartment bombings that took so many lives years ago. I join with the nation in expressing our sorrow to the families of those killed."

Izvestia added:

No group has taken responsibility, but a source at the Klovska Classic told *Izvestia* that interior hotel diagrams and what could be a detailed timeline were recovered by housekeepers from a waste basket in a guest's room. Police have not confirmed the report.

Gazeta.ru put out quicker online updates.

In response to fears of Russian loyalists residing in Ukraine, the Ministry of Defense has deployed an undetermined number of Mikoyan MiG-31 to Kursk Vostochny Airport. The ministry also acknowledged that troops were assembled across the Russian border with Ukraine.

Russia 1, Channel One, and Rossiya 1 TV dropped normal programming in favor of live news from Kiev, taped reactions from Moscow and other Russian cities, and Kremlin statements.

Russia 1 has just learned that Kiev police, acting on evidence found at the Klovska Classic Hotel, have begun a search in the Lukyanivka district of the city. We have no further information at this time.

Thirty minutes later:

We're at a police barricade in northwest Kiev where police have instructed residents to leave neighborhood buildings. They've taken up positions across the street from an apartment building where the Kiev bombing suspects are said to be held up. Channel One and other news organizations have not been permitted closer.

At 1545 hours Rossiya 1 went live with long lens helicopter coverage.

It's been four hours since police and now Ukrainian armed forces set up a perimeter around the apartment building where we have uncon-firmed reports of gunfire. As you can see from our overhead cameras—

Suddenly, the camera shook as the helicopter banked. The sound of an explosion, delayed a second by the half-kilometer distance to the building, was audible over the reporter's microphone. The pilot steadied the helicopter and the camera zoomed in on a dark plume rising over where the building had stood. The reporter for the Russian-owned TV station vamped the best he could, not knowing if Ukraine armed forces had fired on the presumed stronghold or suspects had detonated a bomb.

39

THE WHITE HOUSE

"What the hell's going on, Gerald?" The president didn't mince words. He wanted it straight from his CIA director and national security advisor, both of whom had been summoned to the Oval Office.

"Frankly we don't have enough to go on," CIA Director Gerald Watts admitted.

"Not enough?" National Security Advisor Pierce Kimball exclaimed. "How about Googling the 1999 apartment bombings that led Moscow to move against Chechnya? Looks an awful lot like that."

"You believe this could be totally scripted?" the president asked. "Gorshkov's not that crazy."

"Not crazy, Mr. President. Tactical," Kimball clarified.

"But killing his own delegation?" Gerald Watts said, sounding skeptical. "Too politically dangerous for him if his fingerprints are on it."

"Who's going to investigate Gorshkov? Gorshkov?" Kimball replied. "You forget he controls the press, Gerald. Like the old days. No one's brave enough to dig anymore. The people who tried are all dead. But what's the expression? I read it in a thriller a while ago . . . 'The absence of evidence is not the evidence of absence.' Just because it can't be proven doesn't mean it isn't true."

"You could apply that to any theory," the CIA director countered.

"Right, I could, but I'm not. I'm specifically talking about Kiev."

"To what end?" President Crowe hadn't yet taken a position in the argument.

"Moral high ground to move in and finish what he started in Ukraine, Mr. President," Kimball explained. "The reason to invade."

"There's no evidence yet that . . ." The president didn't complete the sentence. He caught himself on *yet*.

"Correct. Not *yet*," Kimball added, emphasizing the last word.

Crowe thought for a moment. "What are we hearing from Moscow, Gerald?"

"We're monitoring reports and getting firsthand updates from our assets. Sources report that there's activity at Russian Aerospace Defense Forces bases. Particularly the 4th and 5th brigades in Moscow and the 6965th aviation base at Vyazma Airport."

"Where the hell is that?" the president asked.

"Western border. Just before Belarus. More to the point, close to Ukraine."

"Jesus. Time Gorshkov and I talked," Crowe said.

* * *

After the meeting broke up, the CIA director responded to a text from Bob Heath. Heath explained that Reilly was in Moscow and perhaps could provide more intel, considering who he'd just met.

"He saw who?" Director Watts was flabbergasted to hear where Reilly had been.

"The president. Hotel business."

"And you said he works for us?"

"Informally," Heath replied.

"Well then get him the fuck in gear!"

Heath called Dan Reilly's office. He gave Brenda just enough information to patch him through to Reilly. All of this occurred before Director Watts even reached his car.

"What, Brenda?" Reilly answered the phone. "I'm packing."

"Not Brenda. It's your old army buddy. Been looking for your sorry ass. Tracked you down. Your assistant was kind enough to connect me."

Reilly stopped packing. This was a dangerous call. He had to handle it carefully.

"Oh my God. How the hell are you? It's been how long?" Reilly said, trying to be upbeat for the listening devices.

"Seven years, buddy. Seven stinking years. Looks like you're doing okay."

"Oh, I'm fine. And you?"

"The same old. They'll probably bury me in my suit."

Reilly feigned a laugh.

"Brenda said you're in Moscow. Jesus buddy, don't you ever sit still?"

"Never," Reilly replied, still not knowing where this was leading.

"Too bad. Thought we could get together. I'm only in town for today. Would have loved seeing you. But since you're halfway around the world, that's not going to happen. You might as well stay put a few days and meet a nice Russian bride to bring home."

The message. *Stay put a few days.* Reilly heard it loud and clear. Descriptive, yet unspecific.

"Damn. I would have loved getting together with you, too," Reilly replied. "When will you be back?" Reilly hoped to get more specific, but cryptic information.

"You know me. I never know. When business wraps. But you know the company."

Company, not corporation, Reilly thought. KR was the corporation. The CIA was the Company. *He wants me to look into things.*

"Lots of decisions to make high up."

How high up? Reilly wondered. *The director?* He'd pursue.

"Your boss?"

"If only. My boss's boss. It's going to get me an ulcer."

Reilly ended the call with small talk and the promise to get together next time it was possible. In the meantime, he interpreted the call to mean that he was the closest thing the CIA had to Nikolai Gorshkov. And they wanted him even closer.

* * *

"Sir, the connection is good. President Gorshkov will be on the phone with his interpreter in a moment."

Alexander Crowe thanked his assistant Dorothy and picked up the phone. His National Security Advisor, Secretary of State, and Chairman of the Joint Chiefs were also listening.

"Mr. President," Crowe began once Gorshkov was on the line, "thank you for joining me on this call. I trust you are well."

Crowe immediately realized it was a stupid remark.

"I am not well!" Gorshkov shouted after he heard the translation. "Russia has lost loyal, good, dedicated men. Fathers and husbands. Their only mistake was in accepting an invitation to meet with other freedom-loving men and women."

"Mr. President, the police action on the apartment building in Kiev should be a step toward ending it. The alleged perpetrators are dead."

"It ends nothing!"

The call never improved from there.

MOSCOW

Reilly called the front desk and extended his stay. He was about to leave the room when his cell phone rang. Marnie.

Damn, he thought. *Should have called.*

"Hi there," she said. "Missed you last night."

"Me too. Sorry."

"Hey, like we said, business comes first. But you can earn some points back by sharing a ride to the airport. When's your plane?"

Now he had to be careful.

"I have to stay for more talks"

"Well," she softly replied, "I could too. Without the talking."

Babbitt was certainly eager.

"I wish, but it's gotten more complicated.."

"Well, you sure know how to disappoint."

After promising to make up for it next time, Reilly ended the call. Then he caught a cab back to see Moscow Mayor Victor Markovich.

"Highly unlikely, Mr. Reilly," the mayor stated after hearing Reilly's request. "I have very little access to the minister of defense."

"Very little or none, Mr. Mayor?"

"Well, some. But the steps they make us go through can take days. Besides, it's highly usual."

"The Kiev bombing was unusual, and I can't reach some of my former associates," Reilly asserted. "I'm worried, and since your people are on the ground, I thought that in the spirit of the *understanding* we established this morning, you could make a most personal appeal for me."

Markovich blanched. "I will try."

"I'm sure you'll succeed given the circumstance," Reilly countered.

"It must be today?"

"Today. I'm extremely concerned. And given our mutual interests in Moscow . . ." Reilly left the rest of the sentence hanging.

"The terms between us will not change?"

"Get me in to see the minister," Reilly stated emphatically.

"Would you mind waiting in the outer chamber while I make a call?"

Reilly stood and smiled. "Not at all."

Fifteen minutes later, Dan Reilly was on his way to the Kremlin to meet with Nikolai Gorshkov's minister of defense.

Holy shit, he thought. *What have I gotten myself into?*

40

MOSCOW, RUSSIAN FEDERATION

OFFICE OF THE DEFENSE MINISTER

Crimes that brought many oligarchs down extended into the Red Square. The fastest revolving chair in the Kremlin? The defense minister's office. One minister was implicated in an embezzlement scheme to sell off outdated military buildings to the private sector below market value. Another lost his job because he skimmed the military housing budget. Still others were accused of misappropriating or outright stealing Kremlin and contractor funds. If appointees thought they could survive Gorshkov's wrath, they needed only to look at his record.

Dan Reilly cleared metal detectors and waited in the lobby of the magnificent gold and white three-story Defense Ministry headquarters in Red Square to meet with the latest—and likely temporary—job holder. A uniformed guard at reception dialed the minister's office in his Kremlin office. "Fifteen minutes," he said in passable English.

Fifteen became thirty. Thirty stretched into an hour.

"I'm sorry to impose, but my meeting was set up by Mayor Markovich. Will you please check with Minister Lukin's office again?"

"I will inform you when he is available," the guard said dismissively.

Over the next half-hour Reilly simply stared at the guard, who avoided eye contact. At ninety minutes, even the officer grew impatient enough to make another call. Five minutes later, a military aide to the defense minister approached.

"Mr. Reilly, I'm Colonel Borodin. My apologies. It has been a busy time for us."

The armed officer, in his mid-40s, was curt, but polite.

"Thank you, Colonel. I will be respectful of the minister's time."

"This way," he said.

They walked by busts and portraits of Russian tsars, conquerors, and dictators and marble statues commemorating famous battles over the centuries. *Impressive, historic, militaristic, patriotic*, Reilly thought.

"I see you're admiring our heritage," the colonel volunteered. "The works have been recently returned for display. President Gorshkov takes great pride in embracing Russia's history, especially in *narod*."

"*Narod?*"

"Yes, the collective people of Russia, the bearers of our national culture."

Their walk through the corridor ended at a door that opened to a wood-lined waiting room. A uniformed receptionist, probably in her early twenties, looked up, but did not speak. While the colonel addressed her, Reilly perused the space. Straight ahead was the tricolor Russian flag, with equal horizontal bands from top to bottom of white, blue, and red. On the walls were military citations, photographs of the minister with the president and other dignitaries, and war relics from ancient to contemporary battles.

The receptionist typed something before nodding to Borodin.

"Follow me," the colonel said. He led Reilly to another door beyond and to the right of the receptionist. After two knocks and a pronounced *"Da"* from within, Borodin reached for the handle.

The colonel ushered Reilly into an expansive office appointed with more flags and war memorabilia. He crossed over a carpet woven with an illustration that commemorated the defense of Moscow during the Great Patriotic War—World War II by Western standards. At the far end of the room sat the austere, decorated Minister of Defense Colonel

General Yakov Lukin, reading a file.

The newest minister of defense was an officious-looking and equally officious-sounding general of the Russian Federation, with a buzz cut and a cold stare.

"Mr. Reilly, apparently you have friends in high places," Lukin said, barely looking at him.

Borodin remained to translate.

"World events move at such eclipsed rates that business must react quickly," Reilly offered. He stood directly in front of Lukin's desk. "I reach out to public and private contacts to compete and survive. But I also work with governments."

The general considered this worthy enough to grant him more time. He closed a file on his desk, which Reilly eyed, convinced it was a brief about him. Undoubtedly it included a report on his conversations with the president and the mayor. Lukin straightened his blue military tunic, embroidered with gold leaves on each collar. The shoulder boards were festooned with three gold stars indicating his high rank.

"Well then, tell me, what do you need? You must need something otherwise you wouldn't have pulled such strings to see me. Sit," Lukin said through Borodin.

Borodin pointed to a chair across from Lukin's desk.

"Thank you, Mr. Minister. First of all, please accept my sincerest condolences for the loss of your countrymen in Kiev."

He waited for the translation before continuing. The general simply nodded.

"I'm concerned about the lives of associates who may have also been in the Klovska Classic Hotel when it was attacked. The company I work for owned the hotel until a short time ago. While we have no interest in it today, we still have friends who work there, some we can't reach."

He waited for Borodin to relay what he said.

"That is a matter for the Ukrainians," Lukin replied.

"The news reports your government is investigating."

Lukin listened, but did not respond.

"Should you hear anything, I would certainly appreciate knowing."

Again, no response.

"There is another matter," Reilly said. He stopped to see how Lukin would react.

"Oh?"

"We have other properties we manage in the city. Accordingly, we are deeply concerned about possible future events." Reilly paused for the general to weigh the meaning of his statement. He was certain this is what Heath wanted him to gauge.

"If the Russian Federation takes any retaliatory action, we want to be able to prepare and arrange for safe passage. I'm sure you can understand."

Lukin leaned back in his chair. For the first time he studied Reilly while considering a response. He tapped the closed file and began slowly. "Mr. Reilly, citizens of the Russian Federation were killed by the explosion as were Ukraine nationals repressed under the current regime. This was an unforgiveable act of terrorism."

"Yes, and again I extend my sympathy. But subsequent reports have stated that those responsible presumably died in the apartment building explosion." Reilly had his doubts. He wondered whether the real perpetrators were actually safely back in Russia. He returned to his immediate question. "Does that mean there will be no reprisals?"

Lukin grimaced. "Mr. Reilly, you have had your meeting. I have fulfilled the mayor's request. We have met. I must return to my work."

"Sir, will you guarantee the safe passage out of Ukraine for my company's personnel should hostilities ensue?" The Romanian singer came to mind again. "Or for that matter, safe passage out of any other nation the Russian Federation has interest in?" he added.

Colonel Borodin began the translation, but before he finished the defense minister responded in English, "Good day, Mr. Reilly."

Reilly rose offering a simple, "Thank you, Mr. Minister. I do appreciate the time."

The colonel led Reilly back down the hallway, past the paintings of

Peter the Great, Catherine the Great, Alexander, and surprisingly even Lenin and Stalin. This time the meaning of the art on display became abundantly clear. Gorshkov was restoring a sense of history—the good, the bad, and the ugly. Despots and dictators. Partisans, presidents, and premiers. All to rekindle the nationalistic spirit in the Russian people, in the *narod*.

Halfway down the busy hall, a group of men and women scurried about, some uniformed, some not. Some maneuvered around others, respectful of rank. Others stopped to chat, making passage tighter. Colonel Borodin loudly cleared his throat. Those in military uniforms saluted. Civilians nodded.

At the same time, a man dressed in a grey sports jacket, blue shirt, and jeans exited a room a few steps ahead. He walked toward them. The crowd made for narrow passage. He traded quick eye contact with Borodin and sized up Reilly in the manner that comes with field experience. Reilly did the same.

Because of the congestion they came close to one another. The man felt Reilly's gaze linger. He turned away, cut inside and around two officers, and was gone.

Reilly stopped and peered back.

"Something the matter?" Colonel Borodin asked.

"No." Reilly hesitated as he watched the man disappear. "Nothing. Just thinking of that word you mentioned. What was it again? *Narod?*"

* * *

Minutes later, Andre Miklos burst into the defense minister's office.

"Did you just meet with someone?" Miklos demanded.

Lukin stammered, "The American?"

"Yes, the American! Who is he?"

Throughout the highest Kremlin circles, rumors abounded over Miklos' reputation and curried favor with the president. He was Gorshkov's protégé and confidant, his fixer and enforcer, the president's personal spy and assassin. No one really knew everything, but a direct question from Miklos required an unflinching answer, no matter the rank.

"He's a corporate hotel executive."

Hotel triggered an immediate visceral reaction for Miklos and a follow-up. "Who does he work for?" he questioned.

Lukin opened the file and read from a brief. "Kensington Royal."

The minister saw Miklos visibly stiffen, which put him on guard, suddenly aware he had made a mistake taking the meeting.

"Is there a problem?"

"There is a problem. Now tell me everything you talked about. Everything. And give me that file!"

Miklos' next stop was at Mayor Markovich's office. He flashed his FSB identification as he brushed past the mayor's assistant.

"Who the hell are you?" Markovich shouted.

"Your worst enemy if I don't get straight answers."

Markovich hesitated, which prompted a tirade from Miklos.

"Let me put it this way. My interests are the interests of the Russian Federation, the security of the republic, and the determining factor as to whether or not you make it home alive tonight. Tell me everything about your conversations, conversations *plural*, with the American Daniel Reilly. Verbatim. Do we have an understanding?"

THE KREMLIN

"Yes, yes. I met the American at a reception last night," Gorshkov explained to Miklos several minutes later. "A large trade group. He was representing his company's interests in managing the Moscow Excelsior Hotel. Why?"

"Did you know he met with Lukin an hour ago?" Miklos asked.

Gorshkov, who had been sitting, now also stood. "What?"

"I saw him in the hall. He stared long and hard at me, as if he thought I looked familiar."

Andre Miklos was one of only a few privileged people allowed to pose a direct question to the president. He used that privilege now. "What was his business when you talked?"

"The hotel. I assured him that there would be no obstacles to the deal. He should have gotten the same message from Markovich."

"Who passed him on to Lukin?"

"What an idiot. What could he possibly want from Lukin?"

Gorshkov reached for the phone. Miklos interrupted him.

"I'll save you the trouble. I went right to Lukin. Reilly insisted on an introduction to Lukin from Markovich. He claimed he was concerned for his company's Eastern European corporate friends in Kiev. Up until a few years ago they had managed the Klovska Classic."

The president pondered the point.

"There's more," Miklos added. "I learned this from Markovich's secretary, not Markovich. Reilly met with him twice."

"What!"

"Once on the Moscow hotel, the second time about meeting Lukin—specifically Lukin."

"And Markovich was vague about that?"

"Vague? He didn't even tell me," Miklos replied. "He used Markovich, and the fucking mayor had no reason to help him unless Reilly was holding something over him."

Gorshkov's eyes flared, then slowly relaxed. "All of this could simply mean he's effectively representing the interests of his corporation after the bombing," the president said.

The assassin thought about lighting a cigarette, but Gorshkov hated smoking.

"Perhaps, but now what worries me was his stare. It felt like he recognized me."

"How?"

"Tokyo. It's the same company. Kensington Royal. And as chief executive of an international hotel chain he must have relationships with the American intelligence agencies. Somehow he could have connected me. I don't know how—yet."

Gorshkov fixed his eyes on Andre Miklos. "Find out."

41

Two days later Reilly was back in the states leaning over a computer screen at CIA headquarters. "Go blond," he told Veronica Severi.

She moved the curser over the man's hair, selected a lighter color from the palette, and clicked.

"A bit lighter and shorter." The facial recognition expert made the changes. "Okay, now give me blue eyes. Piercing blue."

Reilly studied the reconstructed picture. "Put him in a blazer. Light grey."

That directive took a little more time while she searched for the right clip art.

Reilly continued with more tweaks.

"How's it look?" Severi asked.

Reilly examined the image on the computer. He shook his head. "I don't know. It's close, but not dead on. Give him a few day's growth. A little salt and peppery."

Five minutes later she stopped and turned to Reilly. He sat shaking his head.

"What? What's wrong?" she asked.

Reilly whispered, "Nothing."

"Nothing?"

"Print this, grab the original from Tokyo and come with me."

* * *

"Bob, I saw him!"

"Whoa, you don't knock anymore?" Bob Heath complained when Reilly and Severi burst into his office.

"I was within a few feet of him."

"Who?"

"Smug. In Moscow."

"Impossible."

"I did and here he is."

Reilly laid both photographs on Heath's desk. "Tokyo and Moscow!"

Heath examined the second against the first. "How'd you get this?"

"Veronica rendered it from my description. I swear to God, Bob. That's him, alive and well."

"Where in Moscow?"

"In the fucking Kremlin!"

Bob Heath reached for his phone. This would be Reilly's first meeting with CIA Director Watts and he was about to lob in a potential political grenade without knowing the ultimate impact.

"Be specific with the director," Heath warned while they walked. "Don't hesitate. Don't speculate unless he asks. I'll cover the backstory. You pick up with what you saw."

"Does he have a clue who I am?"

"He's aware of our relationship."

They reached the director's office. "Okay, let's do it," Reilly said, taking a deep breath.

As they were led in, Reilly reflected on the past few days. *Meeting with Gorshkov, standing up to the Moscow mayor, spying for the CIA in the Kremlin. Fuck*, he thought. *Now the CIA director . . .*

"Mr. Reilly, good to meet you," Watts said. He met them halfway across the office. "Coffee?"

"Wouldn't mind that at all, Mr. Director."

"Bob, you?"

"Thank you, yes."

Watts crossed the room to a bureau on the left side of a door that led to what Reilly presumed was either a private bathroom or a conference room. While Watts poured the coffee in CIA logo mugs, Reilly scanned the space. Brown wood-paneled walls, a framed American flag behind the director's desk, white carpet, and simple white chairs. Reilly had more memorabilia in his own office.

The director served Reilly and Heath and invited them to sit in the chairs facing his desk.

"Bob, what has you moving at light speed?"

"We'll start with the attack at the Kensington Royal Hotel in Tokyo. Dan Reilly is the senior VP of International for the corporation."

"Got that."

The comment told Reilly that the director had enough of an understanding of who he was that he wouldn't have to go into his relationship with the agency.

"We have a screen grab of a possible suspect who we've been unable to identify."

"Got that, too. Mr. Nobody."

"We call him Smug," Reilly interjected.

"Because?" Watts asked.

"His expression caught on a Tokyo CCTV camera," he replied.

"Do you have the shot?"

Heath removed the photograph from a manila envelope. "Here."

The director examined the photo. "Smug it is. And . . ." He let the sentence trail off.

"Well, that and another earlier photo from Germany just after the Wall fell was all we had," Heath continued, "until Dan's recent trip to Moscow to represent his company. While he was there, I asked him to gauge Moscow's intent in regard to Kiev—of course in the context of his corporate position. He was able to wrangle a meeting with the defense minister."

Watts shifted his attention to Reilly. "Lukin? You were able to see Lukin? How the hell did you do that?"

Reilly cleared his throat. "Well, sir, the night before I had a conversation with Gorshkov."

"Oh, this just gets better."

"It was at a reception for executives doing business in Moscow. The next morning I met with Moscow Mayor Markovich. Let's say it turned somewhat contentious when he tried to circumvent business assurances I had from President Gorshkov."

Watts looked at Heath with a raised eyebrow. Reilly caught the skeptical look.

"I called Markovich on his fast one, coming a hair short of exposing him. Hours later, just before I was set to leave, Bob asked me to size things up."

"On an open line?" Watts asked.

"Yes, but cryptically," Reilly answered.

"And not from the agency," Heath assured the director. "A phone conferenced through his office. Safe."

"Go on," Watts requested.

"I returned to Markovich's office and upped the stakes. Considering I could expose his end run to Gorshkov, I played a card. I told him I needed to meet with Defense Minister Lukin to express my concern for our associates in Kiev if Russia moved against Ukraine."

"Holy shit. And we don't have you on salary full-time?" Watts exclaimed.

Reilly laughed uncomfortably.

"What did Lukin say?"

"Nothing and everything. When I pressed him he abruptly ended the meeting."

"And your assessment?"

"It's going to get worse before it gets better, if it ever gets better. It might not even be just Ukraine."

Watts didn't reveal what he already knew—that Russia was already bolstering troops at key border crossings up and down the continent.

"Why do you assume that?" Watts asked.

"Because he promptly ended the meeting after I asked."

Director Watts nodded as though to say *interesting*.

"Well, thank you for going into the lion's den, Mr. Reilly. Most impressive."

"I don't know. Maybe stupid."

"Let's stick with impressive," Watts replied. "So where does that leave us?"

Heath pointed to the photo. "Back to Smug. He's our suspect. But a suspect who seemed to fall off the face of the earth. Until . . ."

Heath handed Director Watts the second image. He examined it against the first.

"Who took this?"

"No one, sir. It's a workup from Veronica Severi," Heath said.

"Based on?"

Reilly jumped in. "My description after seeing him in the Kremlin. Mr. Director, if you'll look closely at the two, the Tokyo photograph and the computer generated image, it's the same man."

"How close were you," Watts demanded without lifting his eyes from the two printouts.

"Closer than I am to you now. We had direct eye contact and he got a good look at me, too." Reilly paused, and then offered something he hadn't even mentioned to Heath. "And I'm willing to bet he had a similar discussion about me with the FSB that I'm having with you."

The CIA director focused on Reilly with real concern. "The FSB or even higher, Mr. Reilly. Even higher."

42

MOSCOW, RUSSIAN FEDERATION

FSB HEADQUARTERS

Miklos' growing apprehension came from the basic fact that the man, who took more than a passing glance at him in the Kremlin hall, did so with a sense of recognition. His unease was amplified because that sense of recognition, a dead-on stare, came from the head of the international division of a hotel he attacked. Now Miklos explained his encounter to the FSB's deputy director of operational reconnaissance.

"How difficult will it be to get eyes on him?" Miklos asked Alexandr Vasilev in the directorate office at Lubyanka Square.

Vasilev pursed his lips. The career officer, with scars on his face that made him look as fearful as any KGB agent from the Cold War, didn't like to be told what to do. He especially didn't welcome it from an operative who, according to the record, had no current FSB assignment, yet retained high-ranking privileges.

"He must travel a great deal for his work. It won't be a problem."

"Hack into his computer," Miklos insisted. "Track his routine. Check out his family."

"That's a lot of work. But if you're worried . . ."

"I *am* worried. And if I'm worried, you should be worried, too."

Vasilev bristled, but Miklos gave him no quarter. "I want everything there is to get on this Mr. Reilly. Whoever he talks to, wherever he goes, and who he fucks. Get into his goddamned life."

"I will need the authority to do so."

"Authority?" Miklos bellowed.

"Yes, some goddamned authority! Otherwise . . ."

"You want a number?" Miklos asked sharply.

Vasilev responded rudely, clearly under the impression that he was the senior of the two. "Not want. I demand a number."

Miklos reached for the closest document on Vasilev's desk. Ignoring the importance of it, he flipped it over, grabbed a pen from Vasilev's pocket, and scribbled a private telephone number. He underlined it three times and whipped the paper back around to face the deputy director.

Alexandr Vasilev didn't recognize that it was *that* number.

"Who the hell does this belong to?"

"Someone who will likely fire you on the spot for questioning my authority. You'll recognize the voice. For your own well-being, I recommend you don't dial."

Miklos kept the pen and stormed out, muttering exactly what Gorshkov had in Potsdam all those years ago: "Functionary!"

Vasilev's first reaction was to report the belligerency, but that meant paperwork. The better course of action was to lay it off on the directorate's research department, get some preliminary information, and call it a day. After all, if it were really important, it would have come from FSB Director Nicolai Federov.

Alexandr Vasilev looked at the number Miklos had rudely written down.

"Fucking asshole," he proclaimed. He examined the other side of the paper. A file on a dissident. At least that was important.

43

WASHINGTON, DC

Reilly had work to catch up on at his office. More acquisitions, a quarterly report that would be due soon, a birthday present for his ex, and the endless requests for interviews. He could parse out some to Brenda Sheldon, but most of it fell to him.

He began to create a list of priorities and assignments, however the computer rendering he'd created with Veronica Severi interrupted his thought process. *Smug*, or as Director Watts called him, *Mr. Nobody*. He couldn't get him out of his mind.

Reilly rose from his desk and focused on various items in his office. All of them related to his world travels and his experiences. There were carved marble elephant figurines from South Africa and India, boxes inlaid with turquoise and quartz from Vietnam, photographs he had taken at each of the Seven Wonders, a captain's chair with the logo of his alma mater, and a framed commemorative US Army citation accompanying his Bronze Star Medal.

Reilly read the text. "This is to certify that the Secretary of the Army has awarded the Bronze Star Medal to Captain Daniel Paul Reilly for exceptionally meritorious service."

He stood back from the honor and recalled the event that led to the decoration: saving Bob Heath's life in Afghanistan.

It filled him with pride, but now also dread. His military record was easily researchable. How long would it take the FSB to make the connection that the man he rescued was a career CIA officer and that they likely maintained a relationship?

Reilly went back to his desk and called KR's IT wizard, Spike Boyce, with questions that sent shivers up the young executive's spine.

"How secure are we from the most sophisticated international hacking possible? And how do we prevent it from happening—fast?"

Next, Reilly called Heath's cell. He didn't get through, but he left a message. "Hi buddy. Looking at that wonderful honor in my office and thinking of you. It'd be great to see you again."

Reilly didn't need to go into more detail. Heath would decipher the intent. His next call was to Brenda.

"Yes?" she answered.

"I need you to set a time for me at Harvard."

"Harvard? Sure. Who?"

"Colonel Harrison. William E. Harrison, my old grad school professor. He's in my contacts."

"Will do. I'll call you when I have him."

"No," he said, correcting her. "A meeting. I'll go to Boston. Also when Spike Boyce calls back, I'll take it no matter what."

44

CAMBRIDGE, MA

The next afternoon, Reilly knocked on a familiar door, though he hadn't been there in years. A booming voice came from inside. "Mr. Reilly, if that's you, you're late with your paper!"

Colonel William E. Harrison kept a strict calendar and had a wonderful sense of humor. Reilly was indeed on time to the minute now, but he *had* missed a paper deadline in his graduate school history class.

Harrison, dean emeritus of the Harvard history department, retired US Army colonel, and former advisor to President George W. Bush, maintained his office at his last college teaching post. No one in the faculty or administration had the wherewithal or the guts to ask him to give it up. Instead, Colonel Harrison came to campus every day to write newspaper op-eds, forewords to history books, and blogs. Rumor also had it that he often advised the current Joint Chiefs.

"How about one more extension?" Reilly offered as he opened the door.

"Another, what, twenty years, Mr. Reilly?" Harrison laughed. "I suppose the world can wait a little longer for 'Why the Romans Fell Despite Their Superiority.'"

"You don't miss a beat, Colonel."

"Not when it comes to history."

"Thank goodness for that," Reilly said. He gave the octogenarian a warm hug.

"Sit, sit," said the colonel. "We'll get caught up, then walk across the yard to dinner."

Reilly obliged. They recalled the years since they'd last talked, which principally covered Reilly's career at Kensington Royal and Colonel Harrison's full-time non-retirement. After forty minutes Harrison looked at his watch.

"We have a twelve minute walk to the restaurant. We will be on time for the reservation if we leave now."

Reilly responded the best way possible. "Yes, sir."

Once standing, Harrison sized him up and down. "You're no worse for the wear, Mr. Reilly."

"Thank you. I try to keep fit. Most of the time in gyms on the road."

"Keep it up, young man. You never know when you'll need to turn up the juice," Harrison advised.

"Doing my best."

"Well, what's really on your mind?" Harrison asked as they began their walk across Harvard Yard to the colonel's favorite Cambridge restaurant, Harvest. "I suspect something urgent."

"Chalk it up to current affairs."

"I live in the present, Mr. Reilly, with eyes on its relationship with and relevance to history. More specific."

"Russia."

"Ah, very current."

"In particular, two questions. Would you consider Russia a terrorist state?"

"Interesting. The second?"

"What's Russia's biggest threat?"

Harrison smiled. "You thinking of joining the Foreign Service?" He stopped and looked at Reilly. "It'd be a perfect complement to all your travel."

Reilly deflected his comment. "No, just need to know more about the countries we're in, and . . ." he paused to weigh the importance of the next thought, "the dangers."

"Well then, let me address your second question first with some background. What's Russia's biggest threat? There are actually two threats, one internal and one external. With the migration of Muslims from Syria and the high birth rate among Arabs in Europe, many countries are experiencing a dramatic surge in their Muslim populations. Taking Europe as a whole, demographers predict the Muslim share is expected to increase by nearly one-third over the next twenty years. Of course, that doesn't mean that it will, in the majority, be fundamentalist or radical, but it will affect governments, laws, representation and accommodations, and eventually borders. Russia is not immune to this cultural and religious wave."

Reilly listened as they continued toward Brattle Street.

"For the sake of argument, stepping outside of Russia, this could most threaten Ukraine, Romania, and Poland, and for that matter the Baltic countries to the north, which all border Russia. What worries Moscow is that those former Communist nations contain populations of fiercely independent ethnically-Russian minorities. In Gorshkov's mind, these peoples suffer discrimination and indignities at the hand of the democratic governments. And in truth, some do. That said, Moscow's growing inclination is to use the argument to support Russian partisans wherever they are. In a nutshell, that opens up a wide door to Russian land grabs in the name of humanitarianism and ultimately a way to reestablish satellite states loyal to the Russian Federation. A new Soviet Union, if you will."

Colonel Harrison delved deeper. "Gorshkov is irate about how Russian minorities are treated in the Baltics. Take Latvia for example. Within the population of two million, 10 percent—more than 250,000— are Russian-speaking former Soviets, many of whom have not been granted Latvian citizenship. A second-class country within a country.

"Here's how it works," he explained. "Anyone whose ancestors weren't living in Latvia before 1940, which includes the majority of

Russians there today, must pass an examination on Latvian history, culture, and language as a path to citizenship. Gorshkov has railed against that and the absence of an official status for the Russian language in Latvia.

"So, my tardy student, how does this affect the price of eggs in Russia?"

"If ethnic Russians voted in the majority, they could open a back door for Moscow to enter," Reilly answered.

"Almost right, Daniel. Except it would be the front door with the NATO membership left out in the cold. When you stop to think about it, it's actually an elegant approach. Gorshkov uses nationalism as a means to imperialism. And when that doesn't work, there are always other means."

"Military?" Reilly suggested.

"Too noisy. Try espionage, followed by military action," the colonel continued. "Not too long ago, an Estonian Internal Security Service officer, intelligence grade, was abducted by Russian agents and charged with spying against the Federation. Add to that the list of assassinations on Moscow's streets, the disappearance of a Latvian movie producer who was going to produce an anti-Russia film, and all the oligarchs thrown into jail. You get the picture. But Moscow's incursions into Georgia also qualify. Punishment for its NATO membership aspirations. And after annexing Crimea, I have no doubt Russia has a parallel strategy for South Ossetia and Abkhazia. Moldova is in the Kremlin's crosshairs after Moldova moved too far and too fast into the European Union. And then there's Ukraine, very much in the news now. When it was close to joining NATO, the Kremlin risked losing its Black Sea port, critical to tactical and timely military maneuverability. It also put the historically ethnic Russian population on the ropes. No surprise Gorshkov snatched Crimea."

"What country might be next? Poland?"

"Too large, too visible."

"Bulgaria?"

"Perhaps."

"The rest of Ukraine," Reilly suggested.

"Certainly possible. Very possible, but try again."

Reilly pictured the map. "Romania?"

"Also vulnerable. We should be supporting Bucharest far more than we have. But too many people in the administration who know nothing claim that Gorshkov is merely posturing for the cameras. In my mind, anyone who believes that is a fool."

Romania. Reilly focused again on the singer in the Tokyo attack. *Kretsky, the Romanian separatist.*

"Gorshkov sees all of this as yet more evidence that the West is attempting to economically and politically limit the new Russia, and that brings us back to your initial question. Is Russia capable of terrorism? Is it a state capable of terrorism? The answer is possibly—as a means to an end, considering they truly view NATO as threat."

Colonel Harrison gave Reilly a further history lesson. Some he knew from the news. The rest was eye-opening.

"Let's go back to the period immediately following the fall of the Berlin Wall. Order throughout Europe depended on whether the reunified Germany would be in the pocket of the West or the East. NATO or the Soviet's Warsaw Pact nation. The former head of the CIA made the decision which way it would go."

"President Bush?" Reilly interjected.

"Well, the first one. In February 1990 the US, through Secretary of State James Baker, gave Moscow, and now I quote, 'an iron-clad guarantee that in exchange for cooperation on Germany, NATO would not expand one inch eastward.' End quote. Within the week, Soviet President Mikhail Gorbachev accepted the terms. Germany would align with NATO. Later that month, Bush and his policymakers secretly reconsidered what they had given up: the possibility of NATO claiming ground in Eastern Europe."

"A double cross."

"Call it a change of heart," Harrison laughed. "By October the State

Department signaled 'the new democracies of Europe,' and I'm quoting again, this time from a National Security memo, 'NATO's readiness to contemplate their future membership.' And along came Poland, Hungary, the Baltic States, the Czech Republic, and others. Yeltsin and even Gorbachev were infuriated. They screamed bloody murder through public and private channels and feared that NATO would press further east to Ukraine and Georgia."

"Which brings us to Nikolai Gorshkov decades later," Reilly exclaimed.

"Precisely. Everything validated his basic belief. The West, and the United States in particular, was determined to dominate Europe."

"So now he's ready to make strategic moves."

"Wouldn't we?"

"What can he do," Reilly asked, "either legally or . . . ?"

"*Law* is not *rule of war*. Look at recent events and at history," the old professor replied. "Russia has carried out small-time killings and mass murder, incursions and invasions with little in the way of international reaction beyond tongue lashings. Gorshkov, like his forerunners, has boasted he could be in downtown Kiev in two days if he wanted, or if provoked. With a similar time frame he could take Riga, Vilnius, Tallinn, Warsaw, and Bucharest. Two days, mind you.

"Actually Daniel, I see him employing more of a hybrid approach to warfare. Daring military strikes intended to surprise, combined with infiltrating countries through political means."

"Which is why the Baltic States are important."

Harrison congratulated Reilly. "Definitely. Good student. Gorshkov constantly throws opponents off, wearing them down and confusing them. He's demonstrated his willingness to use force and deploy troops or mercenaries with little notice."

They crossed Harvard Square and soon turned right onto Brattle. Harvest was still a block ahead.

"Colonel, what do you think would happen if Gorshkov does make a move?"

Harrison's eyes narrowed. "He wins. Because he can. Gorshkov and his fellow KGB henchmen emerged from the Cold War as losers. Not that they personally were, but their government lost. That fact alone makes his Russia even harder to deal with than the Soviet Union. During the worst of it, the West was still able to have substantive and pragmatic negotiations with the Kremlin on issues ranging from conventional arms to nuclear stockpiles. Not so today."

"Would anyone in the region defend themselves?" Reilly asked.

"Would or could? It's a complicated question. Not long ago, the Belarus president proclaimed that no matter who threatened Belarus, they would fight back. But could they really stand up to Gorshkov for long? I doubt it."

"And the US?"

"I'll rely on what Zbigniew Brzezinski said regarding Russia, pre- and post-Cold War. As you well know, Brzezinski was a Lyndon Johnson counselor, national security advisor to Carter, and foreign policy advisor to Obama. He warned that unless the US supplies weapons and troops to the nations Russia seeks to control, Moscow will invade. I'll say it again. Moscow *will* invade. Crimea proved Russia's intensions. If we consider that a preview, what does the future hold?"

Reilly took it all in.

"And Brzezinski didn't believe it would take two days for Russia to seize Kiev or other former Eastern bloc capitals. Not two," the colonel emphasized. "Just one. And why? History. The Russian Federation watched the West fail to respond to their invasion of Georgia. And we did nothing after the downing of the Malaysia triple seven over Ukraine. Downed from a missile certain to have been fired by Russian separatists, or . . ." He let the last notion linger.

"So without the United States or NATO answering Kremlin aggression, what's Gorshkov left to think?" Harrison rhetorically asked.

"He has every incentive to act."

"Correct. We're not prepared to storm ashore in the Baltic or the Balkans like Normandy. Or march across Germany to regain ground in Poland, Hungary, or Romania. And we're not going to be willing to start a nuclear war in defense of those nations. The only way to avoid the former Soviet states falling into Gorshkov's hands is to send in troops and weapons early as a deterrence. And we may have missed that deadline."

Harrison was painting a bleak picture. They stopped at the front door of Harvest.

"Look, Daniel. Russia constantly overflies NATO states borders. NATO is averaging more than 400 intercepts of Russian aircraft a year now, with 150 incidents over Latvia alone. Hell, a few years ago, two Russian strategic bombers flew right down the English Channel. Why?"

"To prod, to test. To taunt."

"Exactly."

"Would Gorshkov ever stage an act of terrorism?"

Colonel Harrison was thrown by the question.

"For what purpose?" Harrison asked.

"To create a provocation. A reason to act."

They were at the front door of the restaurant now. Harrison stopped and faced his former student.

"There was, of course, the Cuban Missile Crisis. But then Soviet leaders answered to the Politburo. Today, every decision, including the use of nuclear weapons, will be Gorshkov's, with the blessing of the Russian people."

"That's not quite where I'm going. The missiles in Cuba demonstrated Russia's influence, but it wasn't intended as a provocation. I've got something more specific in mind. Something on our balance sheet—the Gulf of Tonkin."

The history professor frowned. Reilly had made a point that even Colonel William E. Harrison, United States Army retired, could not deny.

They entered the restaurant, Reilly and the colonel sequestered themselves in a back corner, Reilly taking the out-facing chair. More than ever he wanted to have a good view of everyone coming and going.

The only interruption came when it was time to order. Reilly held up two fingers to get the attention of the waiter. Colonel Harrison ordered his seasonal favorite, Maryland striped bass and a mushroom pasta. To make it easy, Reilly had the same.

"Did you realize that Russia has more nuclear weapons today than in the Soviet era?" Harrison asked.

"No way. I thought—"

"You thought wrong. Try around 2,000 operational battlefield nukes, thousands of more in storage, and 1,700 deliverable nuclear warheads able to reach us right here at this table. Though it'd be a waste of a great restaurant," the colonel joked. "It's all so unstable, and aside from the typical hawk/dove rants, it hardly causes a blip on the national consciousness. Yet Russia is a true threat if we're so foolish as to take the bait. In truth, as I suggested, we helped regenerate this angry Russian bear."

"Explain?" Reilly prompted.

"Ah, not so fast. You travel everywhere. What's your worldview?"

"Always the student?"

"You better be. There's always more to learn," Harrison declared.

"I've seen tensions grow over the past fifteen or twenty years," Reilly enumerated. "The US and our European allies built a post-Cold War security zone with NATO's expansion. Nation by nation, Russia saw its own sphere of influence diminished. This created an unstable balance of power along Russia's western borders."

"Correct and as I've covered, that put the Russian Federation in the sights of NATO guns. The situation worsened coming out of the Bucharest summit in 2008. Russia felt more cornered when Bush Two pressed for Ukraine and Georgia's membership. A nail in the coffin, if you will. In response, we saw the Russo-Georgian War, which was the Kremlin's response to NATO expansionism. So consider everything from Russia's point of view."

Reilly realized he knew far too little about Gorshkov's psychological makeup, which was key to understanding what moves he would make. He made a mental note to learn more about the man he met just days ago.

"It was risky for NATO to sign up those former Soviet nations that border Russia," the historian continued. "It was particularly risky when NATO accepted Estonia, Latvia, and Lithuania and put them under NATO's Article 5 that requires all NATO-member states come to the defense of others if attacked. Would we do such a thing if Russia moved against those countries?"

"Doubtful," Reilly replied.

"Damn straight. What about for Poland, Romania, or Hungary?" Harrison continued.

"I just don't know."

"Well, I'll tell you. The Chicago Council on Global Affairs did a survey to gauge public support for the use of force in response to Russia's move into Ukraine. Any idea the level of backing?"

"A guess," Reilly said with his concern about Kiev growing. "Low."

"It was 42–44 percent. Less if Russia were to mount an invasion on the Baltic States. Truth be told, I cannot envision an American president on either side of the aisle who would be willing to go to war with a nuclear-ready Russia over any of those countries, especially when member states are spending less than 2 percent of their GDP on defense. But still, we pose a threat to another threat-maker. NATO has rotating ground forces in Bulgaria, Poland, Romania, and those three little countries, Estonia, Latvia, and Lithuania. You tell me how pissed that makes Gorshkov."

"Very pissed."

"There's more that you won't find on the front pages. The army has pre-positioned limited armored vehicles and troops from the 1st Armored Brigade Combat Team, 1st Cavalry Division out of Fort Hood, Texas, to the United States European Command."

"Very, very pissed."

"You bet."

Dinner came, and with it one last question from Colonel Harrison for his former student.

"And what does a very, very pissed cornered bear do?"

"Rise up and defend itself."

45

CHICAGO, IL

REILLY'S OFFICE

Reilly caught the 9:00 a.m. American Airlines flight from Boston to Chicago. It beat the projected two hours and forty minutes by fifteen and got him to his last security committee meeting only a few minutes late.

The team had copies of the color code system and a prioritized list of cities to rank in potential danger zones.

Reilly excused himself for being late. He took his seat and listened. They were discussing the likely pushback to the costs from regional management and franchise managers. Donald Klugo, the private security consultant, engaged CFO Brodowski in the debate.

"You have car insurance?" he curtly asked.

"Of course."

"Homeowners?"

"Yes." She didn't like being cross-examined, especially by a mercenary. Her answers were getting as brusque as his questions.

"Life insurance?"

"Yes, damn it. What's your point?"

"Well, your company needs terrorism insurance. Not the kind we collect on if something happens. It's the upfront money it will take to help prevent attacks."

"None of it's in our fiscal year budget."

Klugo slammed his fist on the conference table. "Well find it then. Because the bad guys are sure out there spending their money to bring down your buildings and thinking about ways to kill people while you're sleeping in your comfortable lakeside bed."

Brodowski was aghast and visibly violated. "I never told you where I . . ."

"Don't worry. I'm just making a point. If I can find out where you live, there's no limit to what the bad guys can do to your company."

She exhaled, getting the message loud and clear.

"Okay," Reilly said with his palms down, trying to restore calm. "The money's not currently allocated. So yes, we need to create the funding." He glanced over to the KR COO who nodded to Reilly.

"Pat, send me your projections," Lou Tiano said. "We'll create the line items."

"Projections, line items? You think the enemy is talking this nonsense?" Klugo interrupted dismissively. "Open your goddamned checkbook and make sure you have a lot of zeroes at the end of the figure."

"Mr. Klugo," Tiano stated. "We are committed. But I would appreciate it if you brought the tone down."

The COO's comment ended the exchange. "The real problem," Tiano honestly admitted, "will be getting our managers comfortable with the decision-making process."

"Oh God!" Reilly exclaimed as he wrote two letters on his pad.

"Is there a problem?" Klugo asked.

"No. Well, yes," Reilly said correcting himself as he circled *US*. "Right here. Typically American owners and operators are even more complacent than those abroad."

"Well then I'd say you better bring in another few chairs," Klugo declared.

Tiano nodded agreement. Reilly texted Shaw.

"And to the larger point," former CIA director Carl Erwin added. "You'll have to audit your properties."

"What do you mean?" June Wilson asked.

"Surprise visits to make sure they're in compliance. Believe me, you can't trust an email missive to guarantee success."

"My God!" Chris Collins exclaimed. "We turn our friends and employees into our enemies?"

"No," General Coons said, joining the discussion for the first time that day. "You make them responsible partners."

"And if they disagree?" the lawyer asked.

"Fail once, they're warned. Fail twice, they're gone. This is not a game. You don't have the luxury of being polite. Lives are at stake."

The heated exchange was an inevitable part of the process, particularly on this last day. Reilly's plan needed teeth. He was about to offer a thought when Brenda Sheldon unceremoniously interrupted the meeting and waved for him to come out.

Reilly shot an inquisitive look.

She mouthed the words. "Phone call. Important."

* * *

"Get me Boyce," Reilly said as he returned to his office and closed the door. Seconds later Sheldon rang him through.

"How'd you know?" Spike Boyce asked.

"Know what?"

"That we'd be getting a whole helluva lot more knocks," he lowered his voice. "Knocks at our back door."

"Hacks?"

"Attempts. Thwarted, but the number's gone up exponentially."

"With any success, Spike?"

"So far, no," the IT executive offered.

"Oh man. Will they get through?"

"Might help if I knew who 'they' were."

"For now, keep it at 'they.'"

"All right. How technical do you want me to get?"

"So I can understand with the fewest questions," Reilly replied.

"Okay, one level up from the basics. Because we have transitional sites and online reservations, we have a door that assholes from around the world with sophisticated software try to wedge open. In computer terms, it's buffer overflow. The hacker uses our online interrogatives, the form fields, as entry points. Take a zip code line for example. The field is programmed to expect five to nine characters, but a sharp hacker can use a complex code that provides an alternate way in. Any idea how many times a day people try to fuck us up?" he asked.

"Can't imagine."

"Try."

"A hundred," Reilly ventured, thinking it was a high guess.

"Think bigger."

"Shit. Five hundred?"

"Bigger."

"Two thousand?" This time Reilly really posed it as a question. A number like that was scary.

"Are you sitting down?"

"No, for God's sake. How many hacks do we get?"

"Hundreds of thousands," the IT chief exclaimed.

"A year?" Reilly responded with amazement.

"No, a day. Robo on automatic."

"Holy shit!"

"Remember, we're talking about computers around the world programmed by geeks and governments that are constantly feeling out for soft spots. A hacker turns his PC on us and it keeps on going like the Energizer Bunny!"

"Jesus Christ. So how the hell do we block them?" Reilly realized he needed to learn more, and not just because of his personal concerns.

"Well, like other firms, we have unified threat management technology, UTMs, that can help stop attacks like that. The problem? As hard as we try to stay ahead of the hackers, they're working twice as hard to trip us up and get to our proprietary content."

Reilly realized Spike Boyce was telling him the same thing he had heard in the conference room.

"Of course," Spike continued, "if they're trying to freeze us up or wipe the memory, we've got backup."

"In house?" Reilly followed up. "Aren't we still exposed?"

"Way out of house. In a bombproof location."

"Where?"

"Can't tell you," Boyce admitted.

"Really?"

"Honestly, I'm not allowed." Boyce didn't even hint at the location, which was a retired Utah salt mine. "You can't even get it out of Alan Cannon. He's not on the list either."

"So what are the hackers after?"

"Most of the time credit card info, which we have to further encrypt, but they also probe for accounting, rewards, and corporate email."

Corporate email. Boyce hit Reilly's direct fear.

"Tell me about that," Reilly said.

"Which?" Boyce asked.

"The email. What do you use to protect it?"

"UTMs again and something we call fault injection techniques."

"What the hell is that?"

"We outsource with a number of 'white hat' firms that constantly test our systems at the hardware and software levels for 'black hat' penetration."

"We trust them?" Reilly asked.

Boyce laughed. "We vet them," was all he explained.

"Are we safe?"

"Today. For a while, yes. But 100 percent safe forever?"

"Try tomorrow," Reilly said. He was becoming increasingly worried.

"We'll never be 100 percent safe against cyberattacks. In fact, we're most vulnerable through outside portals that do business with us."

"Like?"

Boyce ran through a list. Reilly was not pleased with what he heard. "If it's any consolation, we have antispyware protection that's updated daily; multiple times a day, in fact. But that only allows us to play a zero-sum match. Any of us can click on an attachment that has a virus or a worm that wiggles its way through the system and compromises everything."

"I don't think that's the case," Reilly volunteered. "What would it take for someone to hack into my email and contacts?"

"Finally something I can work with."

"Come on, Spike. What would it take?"

"Someone very smart. Someone like me."

MOSCOW

Andre Miklos took the stairs two at a time up to the Operational Reconnaissance office. He waited ten minutes before being allowed to enter and speak to the deputy director, which annoyed him all over again.

"Talk and make it count," he demanded as he walked through the door.

"The cybersecurity division has been working on access," Vasilev explained defensively. "Some road blocks."

Miklos wondered if the American was onto him.

"Deputy Director, what don't you understand about my request?" Miklos stared long and hard at Vasilev.

"I understand completely. The directorate's chief IT officer has prepared an interim brief and we're diligently—"

"Show me!" Miklos demanded.

Vasilev handed the brief to Miklos.

Daniel Paul Reilly. Age 39. Former Army Major, served in Afghanistan, South Korea, and European posts. Decorated for saving a fellow officer. No details of the specific action. US Army retired. Accepted post in the US State Department. Research analyst. Washington office. No information on assignments.

"Of course," Miklos whispered.

"Of course what?"

"Nothing," Miklos said. But his mind went back to the Kremlin hallway as he continued to read the brief.

Employed by Kensington Royal Corp., Chicago, IL, USA. Senior vice president of the international division. Worldwide travel. Principal full-time office in Washington. Married. No children.

Miklos looked at the date. The last entry was two years old.

"What is your opinion?" The assassin wanted to see how committed Vasilev was to the inquiry and if he had even read the report.

"Definite military background that he parlayed into a cushy government job, likely taken to secure a second government retirement plan as Americans do. Used that position as a jumping-off point for a corporate job. A third retirement option. He keeps pretty public," Vasilev said confidently. "So there's little to hide."

"Are you so sure?"

"Would you go on TV and expose yourself if you were trying to stay in the shadows?"

"What do you mean?"

"You can watch him on TV," Vasilev proclaimed in a superior voice. "Here." He gave Miklos a thumb drive. "The subject recently testified in the US Congress. We translated what he said, but you should listen to his tone. He's defensive. A corporate shill under the lights. Entertaining viewing."

Miklos took the external drive and the limited dossier, which included photographs from the KR website.

"He comes across serious, though," Vasilev concluded.

"So am I," Miklos said. "So am I."

CHICAGO

Reilly didn't immediately return to the meeting. He and Brenda worked on an Excel spreadsheet listing specific hotels around the globe, regional heads, and general managers. Before printing out copies, he gave it a final review. "God almighty," he said. "We've got a lot of work to do fast."

Back in the conference room Reilly distributed his latest work.

"What's this?" Lou Tiano asked for the group.

"Hotels in cities where we have to step up security now."

Members of the committee scanned the sheet. Alan Cannon remarked first. "Interesting grouping."

"Yes, they are," Reilly replied.

Chris Collins finished looking over the list and noted, "Some of these cities haven't been cited as terrorist targets."

"You're absolutely right, Chris. They're not. But they should be." And Reilly explained why.

46

CHICAGO, IL

KENSINGTON ROYAL CORPORATE HEADQUARTERS

A week later, Edward Shaw requested that Tiano, Reilly, Collins, and Cannon brief him. They could bring endorsements and objections from the other stakeholders, but he wanted to keep the meeting manageable.

The executives waited in the corporate conference room for Shaw's arrival. It was agreed that Reilly would take the lead with Cannon covering operational plans, Collins legal and Tiano financing. Tiano had notes on the 30,000-foot view, and what it would mean to the entire industry.

Prior to the meeting, Reilly placed two stacks of documents face down on the long conference table. One included five copies of a twenty-page bound PowerPoint deck. The flyover. The second contained an equal number of full plans, detailed in 120-pages. They'd start with deck.

Shaw entered with a hearty greeting for everyone. "Okay, jackets off. Let's roll up our sleeves and see what you have."

Before handing out the PowerPoint presentation, Reilly delivered a preamble.

"We are targets. We must fully recognize that yesterday's embassies are today's hotels. Hotels and resorts are targeted by rouge nations, terrorist groups, and lone wolves. Some seek to disrupt and kill simply to say 'look at us.' Others attack to destabilize sitting governments. But there are other untold, unconsidered, and so far unimagined goals that terrorists of any stripe hold. The common denominator that puts us in the crosshairs? We're vulnerable."

Reilly turned over the deck. "You know I prefer these things one page at a time, right across the table. So let's go through our initial assessment and what it means to Kensington Royal."

He handed out the copies titled *Crisis Management Plan: Possibilities, Procedures, and Prevention.*

Alan Cannon, head of security, paraphrased the objectives. "Our first objective was to create a coordinated and effective handbook to deal with crisis situations—direct threats to our brand and personnel. These include kidnapping or hostage taking of any of our staff, their families, or guests; extortion against any associate; civil disturbances; bombing or the threat of bombing; biochem attacks; and even natural disasters. Having done that, as you'll see in the detailed plan, we have two immediate goals. One, implement a four-tiered color-coded threat-assessment program that can be raised from low to high as threats demand stronger responses. Two—and even more immediate of a need—place a number of our properties on the top two threat levels now."

Next, Alan Cannon summarized the third page of the deck. "Our plan represents a paradigm shift for us and the industry, taking existing precautions further than anyone has to date. It puts Kensington Royal in a go position, ready to move quickly to prevent loss of life and loss of property. Building on Dan's introduction, we must operate on the principle that terrorist strikes will continue. Inevitably, we will be hit again."

Shaw internalized the warning. He couldn't hide the alarm it sounded.

"So we must invest at a substantial capital level that Lou will soon cover," Cannon continued. "Failing to do so will put us at even greater risk. Now from a security point of view, a key component in launching an effective plan is establishing strong liaisons with local, regional, and national law enforcement departments. These include government intelligence agencies here and abroad. Dan focused on this at his Congressional hearing. We'll need access to current and credible intelligence to vet risks, to determine whether our defense posture can stand up to perceived threats, and whether we have enough active protection in place to deter attacks."

"How are we doing with NSA and CIA channels?" Shaw asked.

Reilly remained intentionally quiet. Cannon took the question.

"I'm working with my bureau contacts and having informal conversations with the other agencies. To be honest, we could use a friend to make some calls."

Shaw smiled. "Like someone in this room who donated to the president's campaign?"

"Precisely," Cannon said smiling.

"What about you, Dan? Your State Department years give you any access?"

"Some, sir. I'm working on it."

"Okay, go on," Shaw said.

Cannon nodded. "Page four. Western-branded properties, luxury or not, are a symbolic target of American's influence and affluence, our strengths and weaknesses. We house tourists, business executives, and diplomats. Facilities host celebrations, meetings, and conventions. We provide open, principally unfettered environments with multiple access points that create relative ease for pre-attack reconnaissance runs. Finally, we offer a virtually guaranteed high death toll."

"Alan, I know the problem. Cut to solutions. How are we going to accomplish this? And then, I hate to say it, give me the cost."

Cannon went through the threats: Blue, Yellow, Orange, and Red. Upon hearing each escalation, Shaw realized how lucky they'd been to date.

"Sir, launching our proposal will also require paid analysts," Cannon continued. "We first thought Washington, Hong Kong, and London. Given instability throughout the world, we're now recommending an even larger team that will include Brussels, Istanbul, and Buenos Aires. But we'll need more expert intelligence to assess and evaluate security conditions on a worldwide basis; to determine where and when potential and active threats exist."

"Lou, what's the sticker price?" the august owner asked COO Tiano.

"Year one, we're asking for $12 million as a fund to hire, instruct, build, and supervise."

"Asking, Lou? What will it take to really *do*?"

Tiano had another number that they'd debated. Start lower with marked increases year-by-year, or higher from the start? Shaw's question was right. *What would it really take?*

"Dependent on our future acquisitions or sales, a better number that comes with more confidence is $18.3 million, maybe rolling off two million over the next five years. We have snapshots of both starting on page twenty."

"In all good conscience," Reilly interrupted, "it could go up. It depends on what happens in the world. No one ever expected what we've been seeing on a global scale."

Shaw read the Excel spreadsheet included in the PowerPoint deck. While he did, Reilly wrote a short note, ripped it off his pad, and folded it once.

"Dan's right," Tiano said. "Read the second chart, which has the escalations."

Shaw's tone of voice markedly changed. "To the best of your knowledge, are we today, right now, this minute, facing any threats?"

Tiano looked to the KR head of security.

"None that we know of," said Cannon. "But we have no way to know without implementation of the committee plan."

"Jesus," Shaw exclaimed. "What is this world coming to?"

At that point Reilly slipped the note across the table to his boss. Shaw opened it and just stared at Reilly.

MOSCOW

Anatoly Zherdev sat in a virtual command center of his own design in the Lubyanka building, the FSB headquarters. He selected an interior room with no windows, thumbprint locks on his equipment, and a bank of ever-improving American computers. He preferred working on PCs, a combination of HP, Dell, and more that he had built from scratch.

Anyone who passed Anatoly Zherdev on the street, with his thin black tie, blue shirt, and jeans, would likely peg him as a bookish computer nerd. However, unless he was seen entering or exiting the FSB offices, which included the prison on the first floor, no one would ever think he was the Russian Federation's smartest hacker.

Zherdev grew up in the service. He was recruited as a teenager by the FSB in the late 1990s. Now he was a decorated, though plain clothes, FSB officer. He didn't carry a pistol—his battlefield was the internet, his weapon of choice, computer code. The FSB hacker was fluent in multiple computer languages: C, Python, Ruby, Perl, Bash, and a dozen others only in the beta stage.

He relished opening doors to other people's private lives. He did that when they were poorly protected or when they hid behind complicated barriers. Some were so simple they were boring. But he lived for the challenges provided by individuals, corporations, and governments. He was as silent as a stealth hunter stalking a deer. And he had killer instinct.

Just for fun, he'd hacked successfully into Wall Street financial houses, American movie studios to screen movies long before release, the Queen of England's email, and Las Vegas oddsmakers.

For work, Anatoly Zherdev penetrated the White House, 10 Downing Street, and even the Kremlin. He always proceeded patiently and methodically, searching targeted computers for ways to unlock ports and find acceptance as a user with administrative privileges.

So far Zherdev's direct attacks on the Kensington Royal system were frustrated. Then again, he didn't expect easy entry. Any corporation operating globally had to have multiple rapidly changing defenses. The Sony hacking and the breaching of the *New York Times* firewalls had upped everyone's game. Cyberattacks against the US State Department and the Democratic National Committee and Russia's game playing in elections around the globe put governments on ever higher alert.

"So," he said aloud, "perhaps you've left another door open for me."

To find out, Zherdev went to Hoovers' and *Forbes'* public websites using a system of his own design that didn't leave a trail of cookies or other traceable footprints. From there he checked out American SEC filings, legal actions on LexisNexis, plus a wide swath of newspaper and magazine article search engines. Zherdev had immense faith in his own special abilities as an FSB agent. He'd find a way into Kensington and prove they weren't so *royal*.

CHICAGO

"What's so important we couldn't discuss it in the room?" Shaw asked, holding Reilly's note.

"Relationships, sir. Confidential relationships that should be kept that way," Reilly announced. He paused to see if Shaw even wanted to proceed.

"Oh boy. Take a seat. I have no idea what the hell you're talking about, but it's obviously important."

Shaw sat on a leather chair in his office while Reilly settled onto the couch opposite him.

"We already have a well-placed contact with American intelligence services."

Shaw raised an eyebrow. "I'm confused. During the Washington hearings you sought intelligence. That was your testimony."

"Yes, it was, sir." Reilly decidedly remained formal. "It's developed since. I wanted to create an official route which, for now is only . . ." The next word was critical. "Unofficial."

"How unofficial?" Shaw leaned forward.

"Extremely."

Now silence. Reilly thought it would be up to Shaw if he wanted to learn more.

"Relationships that go back to your State Department work?"

"I'd prefer not to say," Reilly volunteered.

"You're being very careful with your words."

"Yes, I am."

Shaw stood and walked to his refrigerator. "Water?"

"No thank you."

Shaw removed a bottle for himself and returned to his chair.

"I have to understand the level of the relationship. Please think carefully about the answer."

Reilly read this as cautionary statement with legal implications for Kensington Royal.

"Dan, will you be receiving active intelligence that could potentially help our company assess threats against our properties?"

"That is what I've asked for."

"And is there anything else to this relationship?"

He's looking for deniability, Reilly realized. He would give him an answer he could live with.

"I initiated contact with members of the intelligence community in the course of investigating the Tokyo bombing. Suffice it to say, my contact will expand through the development of our strategic plan. What I argued for in the Washington hearing is absolutely true. We need information that is current and critical to our operation. I figured I might as well make the call. But your outreach to the White House can help, too. Let's just keep them separate."

Reilly stopped there. If Shaw wanted a real answer he'd go back and break down his question into the two essential parts.

Shaw straightened up.

"Well then, I'm pleased that your relationships are communicating with you. And Alan has his own?"

"Yes. Long-standing."

"So what are the two of you hearing?"

Reilly felt it was a fair question, but he was still learning.

"Japan, open and friendly. I've found South American officials to be dicey. As for Europe, my impression is that Great Britain, France and Germany will cooperate. The rest of the continent? No idea. Remember, this is why we'll need our own analysts."

"You must have a sense of the danger," Shaw said.

"I have a greater sense of the void we're in. Shared intelligence is a huge problem. The truth is that each country is more willing to talk to the US than one another. That's no secret. I experienced that at the State Department. But it does mean the NSA and the CIA are in the lead. The fastest, most efficient way to circulate intel around Europe is to tell the Americans."

Reilly saw an opportunity to develop distance and deniability. "That's why it's important Alan and I cultivate direct channels inside the intelligence community. It should give the company greater confidence that we're not going this alone."

"Does Alan know about your outreach?"

"Not specifically."

"You're planning on telling him?"

Another carefully chosen word, Reilly perceived.

"Planning. Yes."

"Good. Then let's get back to work."

Just before leaving the office, Edward Shaw touched Reilly's arm and held him back.

"One last thing, my boy. You're going to be very busy over the next few weeks. London, and then back to Moscow and Tehran."

Reilly's eyes opened wide. "Yes."

"Promise me you'll be careful."

Reilly smiled. It was pure Shaw.

"I promise."

47

The Times

ADVANTAGE GORSHKOV

Ukraine continues to devolve from crisis to crisis. The death of pro-Russian separatists at the Kiev hotel attack, ongoing endemic graft within the parliament, and the growing loss of patience in Washington and Brussels hands Nikolai Gorshkov an advantage in the region.

"Ukraine will implode," cautioned UN Secretary General Forstin Heildelberg. "Russia, working through its oligarchic interests, will be able to chip away at Ukraine's infrastructure from the inside out." Heilderberg further warned that if Ukraine failed to enact meaningful reforms, the West will wash its hands of a no-win situation, leading to a breakdown in which separatists sympathetic to and sponsored by Moscow, will seize control. "The Kremlin will then step in to protect its economic interests and its supporters, the culmination of its Crimea strategy."

Evidence of this inevitability is seen in the East, where pro-Russian rebels have intensified their fight.

Dan Reilly read the day's paper on his trans-Atlantic flight to London. Chris Collins and Alan Cannon were already asleep. He put the paper down, reclined in his first-class seat, and closed his eyes. *There must be smarter people than me thinking about this.* He pictured the map of Europe. It was a memory exercise he'd done since elementary school to identify countries. It had served him well in the military, too. He memorized safe havens and enemy posts, city streets and mountain trails. Top to bottom from the Baltic Sea, he envisioned the nations that bordered Russia.

Estonia, Latvia, Lithuania. Then Belarus, not part of the Russian Federation, but home to Russian military bases. Below Belarus, Ukraine. Sharing borders with those countries: Poland, Slovakia, Hungary, and Romania.

Kiev? Is Kiev part of something bigger? he thought. *Another move toward . . . what?*

Reilly tried to doze off, but couldn't. After fifteen minutes, he brought his seat back up and opened another newspaper. He focused on a page 5 article.

Reilly ripped the page from the newspaper and recovered the previous article. He looked across the aisle and decided to wake Cannon.

"Alan," Reilly said, kneeling in the aisle of the spacious new Airbus A-380.

Cannon awoke. "I figured you'd be coming my way." He checked his watch. "Almost an hour. More than I thought I'd get."

"Sorry, but I wanted to run a thought by you," Reilly said softly while his colleague raised his seat.

Cannon took a long swig from a water bottle. "What's up?"

"Russia."

"The deal?"

"Partly. The deal, the political landscape, the future."

"It's a good market for us to be in."

"Unless there's war," Reilly whispered.

Cannon's eyes widened. "War? With who? Ukraine?"

"Possibly, but not exclusively."

"Not Turkey," the KR security chief said.

"No."

"Then?"

Reilly gave Cannon the articles he'd ripped out of the papers.

"I've seen stories like this for years. It makes for scary headlines. Red meat for elections. It adds to the political narrative."

"Absolutely, but there's a common denominator. Pro-Russian separatists targeted, right down to the Tokyo bombing. I'm no conspiracy theorist, but I am a conspiracy realist."

"It's a long way to go to make a point that's barely reported. The death of a fringe singer halfway around the world part of a bigger plan? I don't buy it. Not enough."

"Maybe not one. What about two stories that have a familiar ring?"

"Two?" Cannon asked.

"Kiev. And that's two that we know of. Two in the news now in Western press. I'm also curious what's being reported in Russia and pro-Russian press where there's sympathy for historically Russian populations."

"Well, looks like you just created a new research project. In the meantime, you know how much Shaw wants to make the Moscow deal work and he likes the idea of financing through your Barclays contact." Cannon pointed to the sleeping Chris Collins. "Chris brought his Montblanc signing fountain pen with him."

"Just think about it, Alan."

"I will, but don't you take your eyes off the work ahead. Shaw greenlit the plan and Chris can draft the paperwork. I don't think you'll see home for quite a while. You've got enough in your urgent and important boxes to last a year.

Reilly stood up and smiled. "You're right. Thanks." He took back the clippings, returned to his seat, and pressed recline. As he fell asleep, he kept thinking that this time Alan Cannon was not right.

48

MOSCOW, RUSSIAN FEDERATION

FSB HEADQUARTERS

Anatoly Zherdev generally felt that private industry did a better job protecting its interests than governments. That's why he smiled when he discovered Kensington Royal's weak spot. Some of its resort properties around the world had casinos. Macau, Monte Carlo, and one in a US territory.

He focused on the American location, the Kensington Resort and Casino along Condado Beach in San Juan, Puerto Rico.

He made the decision to dive into Puerto Rico because the island government controlled gaming. That meant his potential entry point would be government computers, running on life-support in a financially-strapped bureaucracy. Likely they were maintained only part-time and by IT people who had more pressing duties than setting up more firewalls while Puerto Rico's economy was crumbling.

He expected he'd be able to slip through weak defenses and find a virtual side entrance into Kensington Royal's mainframe. From there, he would grant himself root user privileges, hop across the Caribbean to the KR computers stateside, and accomplish his mission to develop a dossier on his target subject, Daniel Paul Reilly.

"Here we go," Zherdev typed code and hit send, reciting the line from "Ali Baba and the Forty Thieves," "Open Sesame."

HEATHROW AIRPORT

Three men were in position at Heathrow Terminal 3 as the British Airways flight from Chicago arrived. One, dressed casually in jeans, a solid black T-shirt, and loose jacket, was outside the customs release door. He kept rising on his toes, peering forward, smiling like a husband or boyfriend anxiously searching for a sweetheart. Except romantic airport man had no passion in his eyes and he wasn't looking for a love.

A second man stood even closer to the same automatic door. He wore a plain black suit and held an iPad with a name on the display. The name of his airport pickup was as fake as his role in the crowd of drivers.

The third man, wearing all black, was outside the terminal in a Lincoln. He had an actual executive chauffeur license, one of his many covers.

The two men inside were low-level spies, most days assigned as couriers and trackers. The third man, the one in the Lincoln, kept the others on an open conference line. For now the mission was to identify and follow. He expected further instructions.

* * *

Reilly, Cannon, and Collins cleared customs and walked briskly side by side through the open sliding door to arrivals. They pulled their single suitcases and laughed at a joke Cannon had cracked.

Collins spotted their limo driver in the middle of the waiting crowd holding an iPad sign with his name on it.

"Over here!" he said waving. "Kensington!"

This made it very easy for an FSB agent posing as another driver to spot Reilly. He spoke in English over the Bluetooth microphone in his ear. "Party of three. Green." It was code that he'd spotted the group and ID'd the specific target.

Reilly came close to bumping into the man as he passed him in the public area. The limo driver kept looking forward and avoided direct eye contact. Not so for another lookout.

Reilly saw a man on his toes. On first blush it appeared as if he were trying to peer over the crowd, but instead of looking for a friend, he locked onto Reilly just a little bit longer than normal. Reilly caught the stare. It was not the warm look of an excited husband or lover. It was steely and cold, and it lingered as he walked by.

Reilly elbowed Cannon and tilted his lead to the left.

"Seven o'clock behind me," Reilly whispered. "Check him out."

The Kensington security chief casually patted his pockets, as if he forgot something. He stopped, turned around, and patted front and back. The forgetful move, likely repeated by hundreds of travelers a day, appeared completely ordinary. What was unusual, was the man intently observing them.

Cannon continued his sweep. He saw the tail. To finish carrying off the ruse, he pulled his wallet from his jacket pocket and gave a relieved sigh strictly for effect. He turned, caught up with Reilly and Collins, certain he hadn't given himself away.

"Good eye," Cannon said.

As Collins walked ahead chatting with their driver, Reilly and Cannon each took quadrants left and right. They kept their vigil through the parking lot and into their town car.

"Clear," Cannon said as they drove off.

"Clear," Reilly agreed.

"What?" Collins asked, completely oblivious to situation.

"Nothing," Cannon said.

"Probably nothing," Reilly added. He turned again to see if anyone suspicious was following them. An empty limo was.

LONDON

After checking into the Kensington Royal London Towers in Mayfair, Reilly showered and shaved, sipped coffee he'd made in his executive suite, and dressed in a light blue shirt with a forward point collar, a dark blue silk tie, and a charcoal grey three-piece suit, more British than American. Downstairs he joined his traveling associates and COO Lou Tiano, who had flown in separately. They took their waiting car to Churchill Place for the day's meetings at Barclays headquarters.

As they approached the drop-off, Reilly fixed on the massive bank headquarters. The building shouted money. Barclays' magnificent new 32-story, one-million-square-feet, steel-framed corporate campus towered over Canary Wharf. Inside, he immediately felt that the airy design was meant to encourage communication among staffers, though most business, by its very nature, had to be conducted confidentially behind closed doors. Still, the open floor plan and glass paneling provided ample natural light, impressive views of London, and room for the bank's ever-expanding departments.

The Kensington Royal contingent was welcomed into a spacious conference room on a high floor. They accepted the offer of coffee and muffins from the greeter as they waited for the Barclays Hotels Team to enter. This gave them the chance to savor the extraordinary view of the Thames and London to the west.

"Good morning," Marnie Babbitt graciously welcomed them a few minutes later. Two other Barclays executives followed her.

"Good morning, Marnie," Reilly said extending his hand, completely professionally. "So good to see you again. Thank you for putting this together."

"Absolutely, Dan."

Everyone went through the formal introductions and exchanged business cards. In addition to Babbitt, the other attendees on the Barclays side of the table were Charles Perry and Todd Brymmer.

Perry was the most senior representative at the table, a mid-level president. He wore an immaculate three-piece suit, de rigueur for the job and close to Reilly's choice of wardrobe. Todd Brymmer was introduced as a director of finance. Not *the* director of finance. *A* director of finance. He gave a cursory hello.

Reilly took him to be a level or more below Marnie. *The contrarian who would have to be sold. Right out of the playbook*, Reilly thought. He also assumed Brymmer was making up for insufferable years as a child when everyone called him "Toddy."

In the realm of corporate diplomacy, Brymmer was there to challenge. Reilly would ignore the bait and play to Perry, ultimately the quiet deciding voice, and Marnie, the avowed advocate.

The roles for Kensington Royal wouldn't be that much different. Tiano would listen, Reilly was there to speak in favor of the relationship, and Chris Collins would frown and be the tough negotiator. Cannon's job was to ask questions outside of the roles the others had.

On the surface, this looked like a good opportunity for both corporations. KR still lacked a Moscow hotel. The management arrangement would change that. Even though most of the incentive would be coming from Russia, a Barclays loan could erase the need for KR to write a check. The drawback in the negotiations was Barclays' insistence of tying Tehran to the deal. Reilly strongly recommended against it.

The fact that Perry was in the meeting spoke to Barclays' interest in moving forward one way or another. As head of the bank's Hotel Finance Division, he brokered deals throughout Europe. A relationship with Kensington Royal would further strengthen its aggressive position as an investment and equity partner in the ever-expanding leisure market.

Reilly began the session. "First I'd like to thank Ms. Babbitt for her overtures in Tehran and Moscow. Hopefully they lead somewhere beneficial for both Kensington and Barclays. So how about we all get to work?"

* * *

His name was Leonid Klenkov. Bald, five-eleven, and without an ounce of body fat, he was the perfect operative. No romantic entanglements. No family.

Klenkov was the third member of the Heathrow team—the field leader who had driven the empty limo from the airport. He had served with the 45th Guards Spetsnaz Brigade within the Russian Airborne

Troops, in both officially sanctioned and secret assignments. Special forces with special talents. Now Klenkov did the same work and more for Russia's secret service, the FSB.

Usually Klenkov took orders from command. Other times, they came in a roundabout way. His current assignment was the latter.

Such surveillance often came with additional instructions. He expected to get an update sooner rather than later, which he'd be prepared to carry out. But it wouldn't be here. In fact, he considered the day's work a waste. He knew where his subject was staying and he could pick him up later. But his orders were explicit. *Remain with target.* And he knew not to fuck with orders that came *roundabout.*

MOSCOW

"Nailed him," Anatoly Zherdev told the FSB deputy director.

"Took long enough," Alexandr Vasilev retorted.

It put Zherdev on the defensive. "My apologies, sir, but there was no easy way in. I actually had to find an alternate route."

"Yes, yes, yes," Vasilev said with little interest in the process. "So, what do you have?"

Zherdev handed Vasilev a file.

"Personal information, business contacts, background. Salary. Bank accounts. Divorce filing. Of course, if I had more on the subject . . ."

"Not necessary."

"Yes, but if—"

"That's all, Zherdev. I'll let you know if I require more from you."

Zherdev loathed the current boss who oversaw the Operational Reconnaissance Directorate. He considered him an egomaniac, which on the surface often worked at the FSB. But it also led to mistakes, errors of omission, and ass covering.

For his own job security, Zherdev had dug deep into Vasilev's own life and career. In the process, he had amassed a most *interesting* file full of hookers' names. They alone could compromise the deputy director. But the real dirt was Vasilev's foreign bank accounts and his visitations to explicit sexual websites, including video chat rooms. Dangerous blackmail material in the hands of the CIA, if they found out.

"I think you'll want me to stay on this after you really read the dossier," Zherdev said as he prepared to leave the deputy director's office. "I'm just beginning to—"

"You have other assignments?"

"Of course."

"Do them."

Zherdev, even more frustrated than ever with his boss, didn't move.

"Is there a problem, Zherdev?"

"No."

"Then back to work now!"

LONDON

The deal talks expanded and contracted depending upon whether or not Moscow and Tehran were bundled. Moscow was a management takeover, with yet unanswered questions about rehab costs. Tehran, a build from the ground up.

Reilly had doubts about both for reasons he didn't share in the meeting, though in discussions he remained positive and patient. Collins scowled and mostly looked annoyed. He played with his Montblanc signing pen, but it never touched any paper. They were a long way from agreeing to agree on an initial term sheet.

The workday ended with Marnie Babbitt passing Reilly a handwritten note. He leaned back in his chair, suspecting it was personal.

Dinner, Mr. Reilly?

Reilly smiled and made a sign that he'd call. Cannon raised a curious eyebrow, but Reilly waved him off mouthing, "Nothing."

Outside, the KR team took stock.

"Well?" Tiano asked.

"The money's there," Chris Collins said, "but the number of years they're proposing is way out of line. Plus they're still stuck on bundling."

"Can't do that," Reilly said. "The deals will move at different speeds, if they move at all. We'll be paying interest for longer while we wait to break ground on Tehran."

"We can separate, with an option to revisit in say eighteen months," Tiano countered. "Dan, even you reported Iran is going to be big business."

"Yes and there will be lots of opportunities to acquire. I still say no to a build."

"What about Moscow?" Alan Cannon asked, recalling their conversation on the plane. "How are you feeling after today?"

"Keep them talking, but my vote is bifurcate or push away from the table. But," his manner lightened, "I may get a better understanding tonight."

"Oh?" Tiano questioned.

"Marnie Babbitt slipped me a dinner invite," Reilly said as professionally as he could.

"Well, good for you," said Tiano.

"*Very* good for you," Cannon agreed, suspecting there was more to their relationship.

* * *

"Indian? Continental?" Marnie asked on the phone an hour later.

"Hmmm," Reilly said. "Thinking more Indian tonight."

"Good. Spicy," she said. "How about Masala Zone? "

"New to me."

"It's wonderful. Street food to fine dining. One of London's best. If you don't believe me, check Zagat."

"I believe you, but it's probably too late to get a reservation."

"Not if they want their refi to go through," she laughed. "Connections."

"When?"

"As soon as possible. I have plans for us later!"

* * *

While Klenkov rested at his flat awaiting new orders, another FSB agent watched Reilly leave his hotel and get into a black cab from the queue. He waved to his associate driving another cab, joined him in the front seat, and followed Reilly from Park Street to his next destination, a restaurant across London in Covent Garden.

MOSCOW

Anatoly Zherdev ignored Vasilev's orders. He worked on hacking into other secure computer sites behind his own closed, locked door. He quickly found footprints, footprints from when Daniel Patrick Reilly worked at the US State Department. Footprints leading to a nondescript functionary's job. Footprints that disappeared for a time in Pakistan, Egypt, and Libya. Footprints that he left the State Department but had friends in American intelligence agencies.

Government, travel, and an unremarkable title. "What were you really up to?" Zherdev asked the screen.

Zherdev cross-checked the periods of time when Reilly disappeared against news coverage from the regions. He set up a spreadsheet of dates and locations. Pakistan lined up with Secretary of State Condoleezza Rice's June 2006 meeting with President Musharraf and Foreign Minister Kasuri; Egypt occurred at the same time presidents Obama and Hosni Mubarak conferred before Mubarak's fall in June 2009; and Libya was just prior to Gaddafi going into hiding in fall 2011.

Each time Reilly went off the grid. Each time overlapped with important global developments.

"Got you!" Zherdev exclaimed.

LONDON

"Well, where do we begin?" Reilly asked Marnie Babbitt.

They were seated at the far corner of the golden-lit restaurant with Reilly facing out—his choice, and not just to take in the warm atmosphere of Masala Zone, reputedly one of the hottest restaurants in all London. He was in surveillance mode.

"Exactly where we left off," Marnie Babbitt proposed without an ounce of business in her reply.

She leaned across the table and kissed him. Not a casual kiss, but deep and personal. *Exactly where they left off.*

Small talk took them to drinks. Marnie ordered for them.

"The tasting menu," she said with double meaning.

As their Indian waiter brought the first course, pao bhaji, a spicy potato mash, and Goan crispy fried prawns, Reilly peered around him and saw a man enter, take in the entire restaurant with a thorough sweep, but wave off the hostess. Instead of going to a table, he sat at the bar. On first blush, it was not out of the ordinary. But there was more.

Reilly's impression was that the man was Eastern European. He judged him to be in his late twenties and extremely fit. Extremely. Tough, bald, and beyond health club fit. Also to Reilly's thinking, he had scrutinized the surroundings a little too meticulously before settling in at the bar. And once there, he ignored people next to him and stared straight ahead.

"What?" Marnie asked, concerned that her comment about the tasting menu hadn't received the intended reaction.

"Sorry," he replied. He shifted his gaze back to Babbitt.

"That's better."

But it wasn't. Through the smiling, the flirting, and delicious courses, he was completely aware that the man at the bar never touched his drink. More importantly, he could see Reilly's reflection in the mirror just as Reilly could see his. He sat like that for the next hour.

They finished four of their eight courses. Little work was discussed. Just enough to suggest that Barclays might ultimately separate the two deals with an option for a longer term relationship—enough to keep Kensington in the conference room. It might not be enough for Collins to uncap his fountain pen, but Reilly would have to let it play out in real time in order not to expose their relationship.

After lamb roghan josh, a wonderful slow-cooked lamb curry, Marnie announced, "Let's get the rest to go."

"Perfect," Reilly agreed.

Marnie asked for the bill and everything remaining to be put in takeout containers. They talked for another ten minutes, both eager to leave. The check and the food arrived, and while Marnie made good on her promise to pay, Reilly watched the man at the bar. He'd already slapped down cash so he could leave at any moment. Reilly suspected it would be shortly after they stepped outside.

The only real decision still to make was Marnie's house or Reilly's hotel. Reilly wasn't completely sure they should even spend the night together. But despite his heightened awareness, he felt no immediate danger. Nonetheless, while Marnie was in the bathroom he texted Alan Cannon.

"Company again," he wrote.

Cannon texted back, "Who?"

Reilly sent a quick reply: "Def not friendlies."

Marnie returned to the table. "Ready?" she slowly asked with a long sigh that punctuated her intent.

"Oh, yes."

For the sake of decorum, dealing with the morning after, they mutually decided on her row house in Notting Hill.

"But I'll have to wake up early," he said.

"That's assuming you get any sleep at all."

They left the restaurant and hailed a cab.

Leonid Klenkov left without concern for his overpayment. His car and driver were waiting for him down the street.

* * *

The London-based Russian spy had a *no go* order. But Klenkov hung close to his target as Reilly drove across town to where Klenkov concluded the American would enjoy a good fuck.

Klenkov's driver took the first watch while Klenkov remained in the car. The operative stood across the street from the woman's two-story home. He watched as the lights went on in the first floor and, a few minutes later, off again. Then lights went on and off on the second floor, which he surmised contained the woman's bedroom.

He saw the flickering of candlelight and two silhouettes pass before the window. Two minutes later the form of a man, possibly naked, stood at the bedroom window. He closed the shades almost completely.

The spotter watched the man at the window linger. *Shit,* he thought, crouching behind a parked car, hoping he hadn't been seen. After a minute, certain all was fine, he texted Klenkov in English, "Lights off."

* * *

Marnie enticed Reilly from under the sheets. "Come to bed now."

Reilly pulled the curtain tight. He had seen a shadow move at ground level across the street.

Nothing or something?

Before stepping away he opened it again, just enough to peer through the slit. He *had* seen someone, and there was an illumination from a cell phone.

* * *

Klenkov read his text. It was not the one he was really waiting for. He wanted word from Moscow.

49

Zherdev worked through the night. Thanks to the access he created through the Puerto Rico gaming site, he had found his way deep into Kensington Royal's mainframe. He learned that the American corporation was exploring a management takeover of a famous Moscow hotel. Zherdev concluded that was the business that brought Reilly to the attention of the FSB. Vasilev could have saved him time and effort with that detail. Financial terms were not available, but he discovered that Kensington Royal was currently having meetings in London regarding the deal. While he couldn't get into Reilly's own email, which frustrated him, he did discover that his subject was part of the London delegation.

All of this was worthy of sharing upward, but Zherdev decided not to hand it over to Vasilev. *Screw you*, he thought.

LONDON

Klenkov had taken the watch thirty minutes earlier since he was eager to bring this job to a conclusion.

Sleep wasn't important when he was on alert. Besides, adrenaline pumped him up as he worked out details: how to pop the lock, defeat security measures, and eliminate Reilly, whoever he was. If necessary, which would be likely, kill the woman, too. Plant evidence that made it look like a deadly lover's quarrel. Leave. There might be other details to deal with depending upon the moment. But it was well within his skill set.

However, the Russian was also trained not to act on impulse. He couldn't move yet. So he returned to the shadows and considered how good he'd feel when it was all over.

Soon, he hoped.

* * *

Reilly's cell phone wake-up musical tune sounded precisely at 0300, only 45 minutes after they had finally collapsed into a deep sleep.

He quietly slipped out of bed, showered, opened the BBC app on his phone, and toweled down. The radio presenter was in the middle of a report. Reilly quickly gathered trouble.

Moscow was railing against Warsaw for treatment of pro-Russian separatists who had mounted a rally against the government. Fifty-five protesters had been arrested overnight. Two had been severely beaten by locals. One was shot dead. Police were investigating who had fired the shot. The Kremlin blamed locals. Polish officials countered that Russia had provoked the incident.

A slight rustling behind him took Reilly out of the broadcast. *A cautious footstep?* He tuned his ear. The floor creaked.

He casually reached down for something on the bathroom vanity that could serve as a weapon. Reilly touched a small bottle. Marnie's perfume. *Alcohol.*

Using his body to shield his maneuver, he unscrewed the bottle top with his thumb and index finger.

Another creak along the wood floor boards. Closer.

To anyone approaching, Reilly hadn't telegraphed any awareness. But with the sound of another step closer, Reilly stepped left toward the bathtub, leaned, pivoted around, and swung his arm wide to the right, ready to splash the stinging liquid in an assailant's eyes.

"Whoa, be careful there," Marnie said, thinking Reilly was just slipping on the wet floor.

She saw the perfume in his hand.

"And watch it. That's my Jo Malone. I try to make that bottle last."

Reilly looked at his hand.

"Grabbed it when I started to . . ."

"Well, put it back, mister. It's far too feminine for you."

Reilly laughed. "Yeah. I suppose so."

He returned the expensive bottle to the vanity and screwed the top back on with the same dexterity he had used to remove it.

Marnie lowered her hands and found him.

"Ooo," he said as he lifted her hands up. "Sorry, but I really have to go."

"You're no fun," Marnie replied.

"That's not what you said last night . . . or was it just a little while ago?"

Reilly took a deep breath and raised her hands to his lips. He kissed them both. "To be continued."

"I'll hold you to it," Marnie added, reaching down one more time. "That's a promise."

"Accepted."

Marnie sighed deeply as she saw the news on Reilly's phone.

"Oy, what now?" she asked.

"Poland. Riots. One dead."

"Seems like every day there's something else," Marnie said. She reached for her toothbrush.

"Every day," Reilly replied. But to him it wasn't just something else. This story played into a pattern.

"What do these people want?" Marnie asked as she brushed her teeth.

"It depends. Which people?"

Reilly pressed play on a news video on his phone. The anchor was introducing a live phone call from an on-scene *London Times* reporter, who actually got to Marnie's question.

"What set off the conflict?" the anchor asked.

"For the past few years," the reporter answered, "Poland has been an outspoken critic of Russia's aggression in neighboring Ukraine. It's one of Europe's most hawkish countries, willing to be consistently tougher than other EU members. Yet at the time, a Polish political party has emerged which seeks a friendly partnership with Nikolai Gorshkov and rejects the position that Russia has taken an aggressive posture in the region. The party, *Zmiana*, which translates as *change*, supports Kremlin policies, has strong anti-American positions, and speaks for the pro-Russian constituency in Poland and Romania. In particular, it's a separatist movement which would realign Warsaw and Bucharest with Moscow rather than NATO."

Marnie finished brushing and wrapped her arms around Reilly from behind. He felt her warmth. Together they continued to listen.

"Then the attack on the separatists could be an attempt by the government to limit the party or instill fear in its members?" the anchor proposed.

"Too early to speculate, but the emergence and growth of *Zmiana* demonstrates once again the lesson of history that European borders are drawn more in pencil than ink."

Dan Reilly sighed. "That may be the most prophetic comment of all."

Marnie was tired of listening. She silenced his phone and checked the time on the display.

"Well, I've got my own idea about things."

Her fingers went back to work. "Let's go to the meeting with a better outlook."

"I really have to go," he weakly offered.

"No," she whispered. "Just the opposite."

MOSCOW

Zherdev barely slept an hour on a couch in an office. Not his office. Vasilev's. Months earlier he'd cloned his boss's ID card. After today, he'd be surprised if Vasilev himself would be using the office much.

The FSB hacker awoke at 4:30 a.m., took advantage of Vasilev's bathroom, and returned to his computer station. Two hours later he had everything in presentable form. Presentable for Nicolai Federov, Director of the Federal Security Service of the Russian Federation.

Zherdev stood outside Federov's door, waiting for the intelligence chief to arrive.

Federov was as prompt as he was deadly. Forty years of spying for the FSB and its predecessor, the KGB, and his unwavering loyalty to Nikolai Gorshkov gave the 74-year-old Federov power worthy of the old Cold War years.

Zherdev had earned Federov's respect when he produced compromising intelligence on a British prime minister, an American real estate mogul running for a high political office, and the wife of a former French president. In each case, FSB operatives let the principals know what Russia had, how they'd use it, and most of all, what they wanted in exchange. Classic blackmail and sheer thuggery, old-school KGB style.

Anatoly Zherdev waiting outside Federov's office meant that he had something special.

"Well, has the early bird caught a new worm?" Federov asked.

Federov proudly wore his crisply ironed uniform with medals and emblems emblazoned across his chest. He removed his hat and tucked it under his left armpit.

"Actually two worms, sir. Do you have a few minutes?" Zherdev lowered his voice. "Inside?"

"Enter."

Federov sat at his desk. Everything was so neatly arranged it screamed obsessive compulsive. Current files were in alphabetical order and pencils were all the same length, sharpened to fine points. The telephone was positioned squarely in the near right corner with equal space to the edges. The phone cord had no knots.

To Nicolai Federov, order was a sign of character. Everything in its proper place; everyone doing his job as required.

Zherdev took a chair across from the director and removed two folded pages from his inside jacket pocket.

"Sir, I have disobeyed a direct order."

"Oh?" Federov asked, his face neutral. Instead of reacting, he arranged anything he thought was out of place on his desk.

"Deputy Director Vasilev gave me a research assignment on an American businessman who had met with the president. I turned in a preliminary report, with more to follow. Surprisingly . . ." Zherdev drew out the word, feeling it would turn Federov's head. It did. He continued the sentence, "The deputy director insisted I forego further investigation in favor of other duties. With all due respect to the deputy director," this was a complete lie, "I said there was more intelligence to glean."

Federov bore down on Zherdev with a threatening stare. "And you disobeyed his order?"

"I did. Willfully, Director. I continued all day yesterday and through the night."

He phrased his next thought all the more carefully. "Fearing that Deputy Director Vasilev would bring disciplinary action against me for disobeying his order," he paused for a confident breath, "I decided to come to you."

"To be pardoned?"

"To present the rest of my report." He raised the paper and held it tight. "If the director wants to . . ."

"Give it to me!"

Zherdev felt he had played Federov perfectly.

"Yes, sir." He handed it to the director. "The subject is an American corporate executive. His title is International Senior Vice President of Kensington Royal Hotels. It's a global chain. They're currently discussing the possibility of managing the state-owned Moscow Excelsior Hotel. Prior to his present job, he worked for the US Department of State. Before that he was an army intelligence officer."

"And your assumption is that he continues to work in that field?"

"I have every reason to believe that's possible, sir, especially given his recent trip to Moscow. I need to dive deeper."

Director Federov alternated his view through his progressive lenses, reading the document and peering at Zherdev. Once finished, Federov returned to an earlier comment. "Vasilev ordered you to stop?"

"Yes sir."

"Do you have any idea why?"

It was time to take Alexandr Vasilev down.

"May I speak freely?" Zherdev asked.

The FSB director's eyes narrowed. "I suspect that's not a failing of yours. But remember where you are and the liberties you've taken."

Zherdev suddenly wondered if he had gone too far. Maybe there was a relationship between Federov and Vasilev he'd failed to uncover. But it was too late. He had to proceed.

"In my mind Deputy Director Vasilev exhibited gross incompetence, Mr. Director. And it was not the first time either." Now to put his career on the line. "I have another file for you."

"Oh?"

Anatoly Zherdev leaned down, unlocked, and opened his brief case. "At the risk of losing my job . . ."

"Or worse. Far worse," the FSB director replied.

"Read this." Zherdev handed over the research he had done on his reviled boss. "Information you likely don't know."

Federov took it with great interest. He immediately saw Vasilev's name and disturbing photographs.

"We will continue our conversation," Federov said. "I will notify you. Do not discuss this meeting with anyone."

"Thank you, Mr. Director."

"Wait to thank me until I decide your future."

Zherdev left with a polite nod. He had one more thing to do once he returned to his office. A very important phone call to another very important person he routinely reported to. However, even Federov didn't know this man. Few did.

"He's everything and possibly more," Zherdev began. He recounted his findings, his conversation with the deputy director, and his follow up with Federov.

Andre Miklos was extraordinarily pleased that he had recruited Zherdev a year earlier. It had taken time, but he had delivered. Zherdev was his inside mole reporting on Vasilev's ineptitude and Federov's political posturing. He'd be due for a reward for this new work, but first Miklos sent a three-word text to his waiting operative in London:

The message simply said "*Stay on him.*"

LONDON

In London, three hours behind Moscow, Klenkov got the text not long after the lights went out in the woman's apartment again.

* * *

Marnie reluctantly let Reilly leave. He quickly dressed and stepped out into the darkness at 4:15 a.m., first to check if he still had a tail, and second, to hail a cab.

He stretched his arms wide on the steps to her house on Cornwall Crescent. The move gave him an opportunity to surveil the street. Reilly didn't see any threats. He bent down to tighten his shoelaces. It was an awkwardly transparent move, but quite intentional. It might let anyone in the shadows know he was on alert to danger.

For now, no one appeared. When Reilly felt it was safe, he started up the sidewalk, hoping to flag a ride. But it was still too early and Marnie lived on an exceptionally quiet street. Reilly had to walk to a more commercial area.

* * *

Diagonally across the street, Klenkov signaled for his driver to hang back. He'd take his quarry on foot. While he walked, the Russian threaded a suppressor onto his Beretta M9A3 pistol and thought time and opportunity had come together.

Stay on him? he thought. *A quiet kill would be so much more satisfying.* Like he had done to a British member of parliament and former FSB agents who had turned.

Wishing he had the kill order, he pictured the scenario. *Hit him on the street. One bullet through the back of his head. Quick. Efficient. Then drive away, and go to sleep.*

In the ninety meters to the corner he halved the distance between himself and his target to roughly sixty steps. The assassin calculated Reilly would follow the traffic flow at the corner, make a left, and look for transportation.

Considering it was still dark he could act and quietly leave with no one even noticing. But that wasn't the directive.

Klenkov continued to close the distance, walking on his rubber soles. Thirty steps. Twenty-five. Twenty. Close enough. The subject, whistling to himself, turned the corner from Cornwall Crescent to Ladbroke Grove.

He thought again how easy it would be. *One shot and leave.* But now it was too quiet. No footsteps ahead. The Russian automatically removed his Beretta.

Without warning, Klenkov saw a large fast moving object appear out of the darkness in front him. It registered. A metal trash can top.

The first impact knocked the Beretta out of his hand. The second smashed his head. Klenkov crumbled to the sidewalk. The fall broke his nose and cracked his chin.

* * *

Reilly was about to bring his improvised weapon down on the assailant again just as a car careened around the corner. The driver slammed on the breaks and shouted in Russian. Reilly turned and saw a gun aimed at him through the car window some twenty feet away. He turned his body sideways, creating a smaller target. The bullet missed by only inches. Reilly dropped the trash can top and ran. For a few seconds Reilly had the advantage. The downed man would be slower. The car, inefficient. But he had to gain real *strategic* advantage to defend himself.

* * *

"I'm okay!" Klenkov yelled to the driver. "Go!"

The Russian fought through the pain. He spotted his subject cut sharply across the street. Klenkov retrieved his gun, rose, and ran. His prey had built some distance, but in no way was it insurmountable. Getting the American had suddenly turned into revenge.

The Russian in the car began a fast U-turn to join the chase. That's when he made a foreigner's mistake, looking the wrong way for oncoming London traffic. Midway into his turn, a sixteen-ton lorry plowed into him.

* * *

Reilly heard the crash but ignored it. Escape and time were his only options, especially considering there was one man left who was again on his feet and running at full speed.

Reilly rounded another corner onto Elgin Crescent. Two blocks further he saw a construction site on Kensington Park Road. It was a high-rise office building, structurally about 30 percent completed, partially enclosed, and with no apparent overnight activity.

* * *

As Klenkov sprinted, he sniffed hard to stop his nosebleed. He had only two thoughts. Catch up and kill.

Fifty meters ahead the American vaulted a metal fence into a work area. Klenkov followed, reducing the distance with every purposeful stride. *Soon,* he thought. *Soon, soon, soon.*

Klenkov ran faster and took the fence easier than his target.

* * *

Reilly scrambled up the first of the unfinished stairs within the building. He didn't get a good count of the floors, but it looked to have at least ten or twelve. *Enough to work with,* or so he hoped.

The floor plan was about 20,000 square feet. Temporary work lights lit the way. He dodged shipments of plate glass for still uninstalled interior windows, crates with building supplies, and skids containing lumber. To survive, Dan Reilly needed to find a weapon. So far nothing.

He ran up an inside flight of stairs to the next floor. Again, a quick look around under the limited light revealed nothing he could work with. The sound of heavy footsteps on the wood floors got louder. The killer was still on him, and Reilly felt his advantage, if he ever really had one, was slipping.

Reilly assumed the man had recovered his gun. *As soon as he had a clear shot . . .* He pushed past the thought. Another flight up. The fourth. And then another.

On the fifth floor he saw a box of construction supplies: loose tools including hammers, screwdrivers, and saws. Short of throwing them, they were no help. Ahead were loose rebars, but they would only be good in hand-to-hand combat, which was not going to work against a man with an automatic.

Reilly was winded by the time he got to seven. He scanned the area. The floor was partially completed. Only one wall was up. The other sides opened to a straight drop.

He spotted a few places to hide. Not many. Then he saw something he might be able to use. Reilly ran diagonally across the open expanse to what looked like a toolbox with an orange logo set against a black background. A logo he recognized. *Ramset.*

Reilly took the entire kit and ducked behind a wooden shipping container in an unfinished office. The crate was the size of a refrigerator, lying lengthwise. Beside it were a stack of cardboard boxes, which offered no protection, and multiple plate glass office windows, upright and in a wood base. He crouched low, away from any overhead light, opened the toolbox, and did a quick inventory of the contents. The sound carried.

* * *

Thirty seconds later, with a sliver of daylight beginning to slice over the horizon, Leonid Klenkov took the last steps up to the same floor.

"Ah, I hear you," Klenkov said as he slowly approached. "Now where are you hiding?"

Reilly distinctly caught the Russian accent, but he was more focused on going through the toolbox, hoping it was complete. It wasn't.

Damn, Reilly said to himself as the footsteps got closer. *Where the hell . . . ?* The Ramset tool was there, but it was missing . . .

Klenkov moved stealthily closer, looking left and right, his gun making turns around boxes and obstructions before his body.

"Not here . . . or here," the Russian said.

Reilly calculated the distance between them. He was halfway. Little time and nowhere else to run. He felt around the floor, hoping to find the one thing he still needed.

"You have no weapon, or you would have used it," Klenkov continued. "And there are so many ways you can hurt yourself at a construction site, so why don't you just come out. We can just talk."

Reilly shifted and felt around the floor. *Come on*, he silently mouthed. *It's a fucking construction site. There's got to be . . .*

He saw what he needed about a body's length away. But it was out in the open. Now he thought, *Just keep talking, Ivan.*

Seconds later, Reilly heard the killer's voice reverse direction away from him. He used the moment to lunge forward, grab the single small item, and return to the crate.

But the shuffling gave him away. Klenkov pivoted and got a bead on Reilly's hiding place.

"Oh, now I have you."

Reilly didn't respond.

"Are you certain you don't want to come out and talk about this?"

There would be no talking. Klenkov's Beretta was up and aimed at the horizontal crate.

"All right then. Let's see how well-protected you are," the Russian said brazenly.

Klenkov fired his silenced automatic. There were two sounds: the suppressed thud from his gun and simultaneously a muffled hit.

"So," he said, "what could possibly be in the way? An appliance?"

Taking a single step forward he fired again.

"No. Definitely didn't hear metal. Did you?"

Klenkov took another step.

"Bricks?"

Another shot.

"Bricks? I don't think so. Maybe sand."

He fired again.

"Did you know it would take only seven inches of sand to stop a 9mm round?"

Another shot. Closer.

Reilly was listening, but busy at work.

"Of course you did. You're much better trained than I expected. That's why you're hiding behind something strong. Hoping I'll run out of ammunition. But I won't."

He shot again. Another thud.

"So what does that leave us with?"

Reilly concentrated on what he was doing. He calculated Klenkov was within twenty feet. That was good and getting better.

"Did you know that a few jugs of water can stop a bullet?"

The Russian fired twice more.

"But if it had been water, we'd know it."

Klenkov laughed.

"You'd be soaking wet by now. Maybe you'd drown in the process and I could save a bullet."

Now Klenkov swept wide about fifteen feet beyond the six-foot-long container that the American had hidden behind.

The toolbox Reilly found contained a thin device less than two feet long. It looked like a small jackhammer, but was light and deceiving. On one end, a narrow black tube; on the other, what looked like a half of an orange colored cup. The generic name for what he held in his hand was a PA, a powder-actuated tool. This one was a Ramset Hammershot, sold for only around thirty dollars. It had a unique property which Reilly knew well from his trips to construction sites around the globe and volunteering on Habitat for Humanity builds in the United States.

The Hammershot was a rudimentary tool to drive pins and threaded studs through wood into concrete or steel. This version was the most basic. It required a sharp hit on the cup side by a mallet or hammer while the tube end was placed up against wood or whatever surface needed to be secured by a nail.

The toolbox had three of the four things required to make it work. The Ramset itself, the mallet, and a half-filled red box labeled STRONG. The fourth item, the thing Reilly had just found, was a 2.5 inch nail.

Klenkov continued to circle. As he did, Reilly adjusted his position around the crate.

The Ramset was almost ready. He opened the box labeled STRONG and removed what appeared to be a bullet casing. It was, in fact, a .22 caliber explosive shell without a bullet at the end. But once inserted into the Ramset chamber and cocked, the .22 would become the charge that fired the typically-used threaded studs.

But the tool kit was missing a box of threaded studs. That's why Reilly had to find something else. The 2.5 inch nail fit perfectly into the barrel.

He took five deep breaths and listened for the footsteps. Now he needed opportunity and the correct trajectory.

"Ivan," Reilly said mockingly.

"He speaks," Klenkov replied.

Reilly shifted somewhat to the right, closer to the stack of standing plate glass windows.

"What's this all about?" Reilly asked. He pulled back the steel spring mechanism on the Ramset.

"That's a good question. They just tell me what to do and I do it." He laughed. "And I do it very, very well."

"Who?"

"Oh, I can't say."

"You're never curious?"

"Oh sometimes, I suppose."

"There's an old saying about curiosity," Reilly continued.

He took another deep breath. Though he couldn't see, Reilly calculated that the Russian was almost opposite the glass beside him.

"Oh?" Klenkov sniffled hard to keep his nose from bleeding.

The sound came from the right of where Reilly was. He rose behind the glass, not showing his full body to the killer. In his right hand and to his side was the mallet. In his left, the Ramset.

The Russian was actually surprised to see Reilly stand.

"I suppose you think it's bulletproof glass?"

In one smooth move, the one chance he had, Dan Reilly raised the Ramset, put the barrel end squarely against the glass, directly facing the Russian at midbody height. Without another word he slammed the mallet against the orange cup end.

The power of the mallet transferred into the .22 caliber casing that transmitted the energy to the nail. Instantly, the glass shattered with a flash. The nail continued straight on 15 feet at 223 miles per hour into Leonid Klenkov's chest.

Klenkov stumbled and looked down. Utterly confused, he watched his blood gush out. The Russian tried to raise his gun arm, but it didn't listen to his command.

Reilly read Klenkov's shock, ran over the broken glass and drove his head into the Russian's stomach.

The force sent the killer backwards.

Reilly went after him again. This time he led with his right shoulder, knocking the Russian further back, more off balance until . . .

For a second, Leonid Klenkov felt a chill on the back of his neck from the light breeze that flowed through the open construction site. Then he was weightless, feeling the rush of air all around him as he tumbled off the side of the building, down seven floors.

Reilly peered over the edge. The dead Russian resembled a broken marionette with arms and legs splayed across the cement foundation.

Dan Reilly inhaled deeply to get his heart rate down and clear his head. Twenty seconds was enough. He had cleanup. He recovered the man's pistol and scoured the crime scene for any other clues to what had occurred.

Construction site CCTV cameras below, if working, would have a record. He decided to turn that problem over to Donald Klugo and his private security company. If necessary Klugo could reach out to Langley through Carl Erwin, the former CIA director on the Kensington team. There was also his friend Bob Heath.

On his way out, Reilly patted the wooden box that had saved his life. *Definitely a bullet stopper*, he said to himself. He read the stenciling that fortunately had not been facing outward: *Marazzi: World Leader in Ceramic and Porcelain Tiles.*

He put the Ramset back in the kit and left with it. Looking back at the building from the ground he let out a much needed laugh. Ramset had a well-deserved nickname. Bang gun.

50

Reilly called the mercenary and explained what had happened.

Klugo took the information down and told Reilly that what he couldn't take care of, others would. The *others* were not identified. Klugo said he'd also check with his global contacts for intel on the hit team sent after him. All signs pointed to Russia, but Iran wasn't out of the question either.

"Just watch your back," the private contractor said. "Oh, and this will cost you more. Considerably," he added laughing.

After agreeing to terms, Reilly ended the call, wrote a note to legal advising the department of the new terms, and showered and changed before joining his team downstairs for a breakfast strategy session.

Cannon intercepted him in the lobby. "How'd it go last night?" he asked.

"Killer," Reilly stated dispassionately.

If Cannon thought Reilly was joking about his sexual exploits, his manner said otherwise. He pulled Dan away from the others.

"What happened?"

"The guy following us out of the airport—"

"Yes?"

"Gone."

306

"Good."

"I mean gone, gone. Car crash in Notting Hill. It'll be on the news."

"Jesus Christ, Dan. What . . .?"

"And another, less delicately."

"Oh my God! And you're—"

"Fine. All things considered. Talked to Klugo this morning about the clean-up."

The Kensington security chief did not need a definition of *clean-up*. He put his arm around Reilly and whispered in his ear.

"What the hell have you gotten yourself into?" Cannon asked.

"Apparently condition Red."

Reilly and Cannon caught up with the rest of the Kensington negotiating team in the restaurant. Over breakfast, Collins reported on an email he'd received from Brymmer, the junior executive from Barclays.

"They want to come away with an initial deal memo today," he said. "Tomorrow at the latest. Brymmer indicated another hotel group has—"

"He's dumber than I thought," Reilly said. "We take our time. This is too big for Barclays to rush or blow up. It's a freshman tactic. Ignore him."

Tiano agreed. "We're the biggest. They want us."

With that, they ordered breakfast and Reilly only excused himself once to splash cold water on his face.

* * *

Ninety minutes later they were back in the Barclays conference room. Babbitt greeted Reilly with a firm handshake.

"Dan, good morning. Thanks again for dinner last night."

"Thank you. It was your check."

"By all means. Good to get to know one another," she replied.

Keeping it professional, he mused. "Likewise."

This was to be Tiano and Chris Collins' day. A day to drill down more. Reilly took the back seat as planned. He had leverage, patience, and what Marnie leaked to him on his side.

Not surprisingly, Barclays' first proposal presented by Todd Brymmer didn't go anywhere. The rates on the term sheet he passed out were high with key points tipped to the bank's full benefit. Most importantly, the Kensington team said the two deals—Tehran and Moscow—had to be separated.

Brymmer argued his position for nearly two hours until a hand signal from Charles Perry ended his efforts.

"I believe we can move on now, Todd," the senior president stated for the room. "You concur Marnie?"

"I do," she replied, stifling a smile.

"Good. I'd like to hear a serious offer," Collins stated with an undisguised sarcastic tone.

Perry smiled. "Todd, slide me your top sheet."

The executive took pencil to paper, crossed out rates, and replaced numbers. He passed it to Marnie. She scanned and approved it, then handed it to Brymmer. Without comment he ran the math on his laptop and wrote computations on the page.

Perry examined the revised top sheet back, initialed it in the lower right corner, and handed it to Lou Tiano

"I think we're ready to have you look at our first offer," he said laughing.

"Thank you," the Kensington chief operating officer replied. "I'm glad to see everyone's come to work."

They did just that for the next six hours. Over coffee. Over lunch. Over more coffee and snacks. Over dinner. The negotiation ended with handshakes and initials. Collins got to use his pen, but the document was not a final agreement with full signatures. After two days, it was their official starting point. Tehran was out for now. Moscow was in with appropriate caveats, mostly lodged by Reilly.

* * *

For Reilly and Marnie the night didn't end at dinner. This time they went to Reilly's hotel room. They made love and they talked.

"How about this?" Reilly asked.

"Only if I can return the favor," she cooed, negotiating in bed. Five minutes later she did. They continued to playfully parlay sex like a business deal. More this for that.

An hour later they ordered room service but hungered much more for each other.

"You realize, if we keep this up we're going to have to recuse ourselves." Marnie emphasized the point by reaching down. "But you'd be very *hard* to give up."

Reilly was too lost in his feelings to reply.

They returned to the discussion early in the morning. Marnie was right. If they actively participated in any negotiations, they'd have to put their relationship on standby, and even then risk creating animosity over deal points. Conversely, if they admitted they were seeing one another, who would believe they weren't trading secrets over pillow talk?

Privately, Reilly felt that Moscow was fraught with political problems and Iran had its own set of geopolitical issues. So instead of discussing it more, he moved under the covers and gave Marnie Babbitt reasons to lose her mind.

Suddenly he stopped.

"What's the matter?" she whispered.

"Nothing. Just catching my breath."

But there was something else. A thought. *Tehran and Moscow.* Was it odd she had been at both locations, seemingly waiting for him?

51

Two days later back in DC Reilly had a busy day ahead with Kensington Royal duties and attention to the greater geopolitical world.

First, his paying job. He called Brenda.

"I need a holiday calendar."

"The main ones are already on Outlook and your phone," she offered.

"Deeper. Can you include the Muslim and Jewish holidays and anything that's celebrated in a number of specific countries?" He rattled off a list.

"Sure. How soon?"

"Today. Copy Alan and Chris on the calendar and send it to each of the members of the crisis committee."

"With any comment?"

"No."

Reilly reminded himself of one of his favorite beliefs. *Some people who follow politics and world news get the* New York Times *and don't read it. Others read it but don't get it.*

"They'll *get it*," he added.

Cannon would view the dates as operational goals in critical cities. Furthermore, he'd work with his contacts to get relevant intelligence and develop new relationships with national intelligence agencies as he had proposed in the meetings.

"I'm on it. Glad to have you back. Oh, your ex called today. She needs to talk."

"About?"

"Don't know. It was on voice mail, but she sounded stressed."

"Okay. I'll call." But he didn't right away. Reilly turned his attention to contacting Bob Heath and meeting him at a safe location. Safe meant unobserved, off the beaten path, and a normal part of his routine. He was concerned about the uptick in hacking and felt he couldn't see Heath in the open. So he needed a place with multiple access points, one that he could come through, while Heath used another. A restaurant? A museum? The Capitol? Each offered possibilities, but then there was the question of where to talk.

Instead of a building he settled on the Metro. He would get on the Red Line at Farragut North heading to Bethesda. Heath would board at Union Station, taking the same train after Reilly texted him the number. If followed, he would not make contact. If clear, they'd both get off at the Walter Reed National Military Medical Center and stop for presumed health examinations. Once cleared inside, they'd speak in a prearranged room.

It was well beyond what might be necessary, but certain things were beginning to nag him. Reilly was thinking more like an intelligence officer.

Now for an even more immediate problem—how to surreptitiously contact Heath? He didn't consider any of his phones all that secure, so he decided to stop at the Office Depot on Connecticut Avenue and picked up a pay as you go phone and a prepaid credit card.

Heath wouldn't know the number, but the text would contain enough touch points for his friend to recognize the source.

While walking, Reilly dialed Marnie on his regular cell. He reached her in her office. She sounded thrilled that he had called. They talked about their schedules and their work. He heard her close her office door. Then they talked about rendezvousing.

As busy as he was, she was equally busy. And as much as he wanted to see her, she sounded like she wanted to see him more. Reilly felt a connection, but he also felt probed.

Marnie began suggesting places to getaway. "Southern France, Bermuda, St. Lucia." She stopped when she got a text. "Hold for a second."

Reilly heard her gasp.

"What?"

"I'll call you back."

LONDON

Minutes later Marnie Babbitt turned on CNN International in her London office. A Paris correspondent was in the middle of a report. The wide shot of the scene showed officers laying out plastic barricades and police tape. Sirens wailed in the background. The woman reporter had to speak loudly over the noise.

"According to a spokesperson with Barclays Bank as many as thirty people have taken control of the branch on Boulevard Raspail. There are hostages. Bank officials and customers. What's not known—and is why the police are cautious and moved us a block away—is whether the perpetrators intend to do any harm or if they're just there for the cameras. What we do know is that they've chained themselves to one another and are hunkered down with their hostages."

"We've seen demands they posted on the internet in French and English," the CNN anchor noted from the studio. A cell phone video appeared on a split screen between the anchor and the reporter.

"Correct. Those videos were shot inside the bank. They're calling for Barclays to divest itself of shares in NATO-supported arms manufacturers. They claim these companies make missiles and drones that are currently deployed in Poland and threaten the Russian Federation, Belarus, and pro-Russian forces in Crimea. Barclays has not issued a statement beyond the initial confirmation, but we're very early into this situation. The group also linked the US to their complaints, citing a Russian poll that the United States now tops the list of countries

Russians view as most hostile."

As the reporter continued, the video switched to B-roll of the area. "With more satellite news trucks arriving, the protesters are definitely in control of the message and the moment. Though there have been no threats of violence, the *Police Nationale* and the *Gendarmerie Nationale*, the French armed forces, have secured the area, evacuated business and residential buildings, and stationed emergency vehicles, fire trucks, and ambulances nearby. We've also seen GIGN teams, Paris' SWAT, take up positions. It's a developing situation here, unlikely to end anytime soon."

WASHINGTON, DC

Right after he hung up with Babbitt, Reilly checked his phone for news alerts. There were two. The *Washington Post* and the *New York Times*. He suddenly understood why Marnie had ended the call so abruptly. Reilly reversed direction and returned to his office, running most of the way.

Back inside and before he could say anything, Brenda told him that Alan Cannon was on hold.

"I'll take him. And turn on the news!"

Cannon had more details. "This is probably going to impact Barclays' investment decisions. I recommend you back channel with your . . . friend." Cannon's pause and intonation on *friend* indicated he definitely knew they had a relationship.

"That obvious?" Reilly asked.

"Well, to me, buddy."

"We were talking when the news broke."

"Call back. Find out what they're thinking. No reason to suggest they'll pull out. But deals are going to slow down."

"Agreed." However, thinking beyond the business deals, Reilly saw a scenario that was far more troubling.

Then his cell rang with a very familiar number.

"Pam," he said, shyly greeting his ex-wife.

"Didn't Brenda tell you I needed you right away?"

"Yes, yes. I'm sorry. There's a lot going on. What's the matter?"

Reilly expected to be chastised about alimony or trouble with the car.

"The house was broken into last night."

"Oh God, were you there?"

"No."

Reilly took a deep breath. "Good. Good. Anything taken? Did you call the police?"

"I don't know," she shot back. "And yes, I called the goddamned police."

"Okay, Pam. Easy. Insurance?"

"If you've paid."

"Yes, I've paid. I meant did you call the insurance?"

"Not yet. You might want to."

"I don't understand."

"They didn't touch my jewelry, at least not that I've seen yet. But they sure tore through some of your boxes in the basement."

He tightened his grip on the phone. "What boxes, Pam?"

"Your stuff. I don't know. Some of your old army memorabilia."

"Christ! I'll be right over!"

VIRGINIA

Reilly still found it odd to knock on the door of his own Virginia house, or what used to be his house. Now it was Pam's.

Pam Reilly was a statuesque blonde who had taken Dan's breath away when they met at a party ten years earlier. In the eighteen months since their split, she'd taken a good deal of their savings. Reilly still cared about Pam and hadn't made their settlement a negotiation. It was more of an apology for things not working out.

Pam opened the door and allowed him an inconsequential hug.

"I'm sorry, Pam. Really."

"Come on. I'll walk you around. I haven't put things away yet."

Drawers had been pulled out. Closets torn apart. But as Pam had said, her valuables hadn't been touched. After taking stock and looking around, the only thing of real concern was one particular cardboard box strewn across the basement floor.

He bent down and began to sort through the items.

"What's missing?" Pam asked.

"Not sure yet."

Reilly went through a mental inventory.

"It's seems like it's all here," he said.

But that really wasn't the problem, he reasoned. If he was the target, there was no need to steal anything. On one hand, they could have snapped photographs of specific items contained in the box. On the other hand, the break-in served as a visible threat.

"So things are okay?" she asked hopefully. "Maybe they just got spooked and took off."

"Right. Sure," he said dismissively.

"Then we're okay, Dan?"

"No. We're not okay. I'll call the alarm company and have them install cameras and motion detectors."

WASHINGTON, DC

Reilly phoned Marnie on his way to Office Depot.

"What's the latest?" he asked after explaining that he'd caught the news, too.

"Right now, quiet. Surprisingly quiet. Hostage negotiators are talking with the protestors. So far no movement. They've got what I think they want. Press. Hell, there's a report that three women super glued themselves to the vault. Others are chained. They're tweeting, calling themselves activists, not protestors or terrorists. They've even got a name. NOT-O Nations, a play on NATO Nations."

"Cute," Reilly replied.

"Bottom line is they want Barclays Global Investors UK Holdings to dump more than eight million shares in two missile manufacturing companies and a drone company, and to cancel loans to transportation companies doing business with those manufactures."

"Like the 2014 demands against Barclays in Cardiff." Reilly recalled a similar assault on a Barclays branch in Wales.

"Yes, but bigger this time," she added.

"If it's like the last, it'll grind down. They'll walk out."

"That's what we're hoping."

* * *

Reilly returned to his own one bedroom condo at 1150 K Street after filling his shopping list at Office Depot.

He lived in a relatively new high-rise residential building at the corner of K and 12th. The building had a front desk manned twenty-four hours a day with standing orders from Reilly that no one was permitted in his apartment without his approval. Still, he questioned the security officer on duty and asked for all others to report if anyone attempted to enter. But knowing what was still possible, he made a thorough search of his apartment, looking for anything out of place or the tell-tale signs that listening or viewing devices had been installed.

The apartment appeared to be clean. As an extra precaution, Reilly took the elevator up to the rooftop deck to activate his prepaid cell phone. Once done, he texted Bob Heath with a message that couldn't be misconstrued.

52

MOSCOW, RUSSIAN FEDERATION

"Two brothers," Gorshkov explained to Andre Miklos.

The president told him about Mairis and Sandis Gaiss, beneficiaries of the new Russia and members of the billionaire Russian class. Post-Cold War investments had paid off handsomely for the ruthless Gaiss brothers, Latvian by birth, but fiercely loyal to Russia by expediency. They had turned 20,000 US dollars into a fortune with a combination of shrewd stock plays, strategic takeovers, and friends who had wanted them to succeed—at least at the time. But that was about to come to an end.

Mairis and his younger brother Sandis were not just dedicated to winning. They were champions of absorbing and destroying competitors and eliminating enemies. They were equally adept in the boardroom and the back alleys.

They forged political alliances and agreed to the Kremlin's terms, thinking they had the better end of the deal.

For the past two years they ate and socialized with the president with outward smiles, all the while banking on a lifelong relationship with Gorshkov. They thought it was a mutual feeling. But they were mistaken.

"Two brothers," Gorshkov said again as he finished his story. "Do the math. They can afford to lose one. And then who knows?" The president laughed at his own joke and proceeded to outline his agenda.

The assassin listened. It was complicated, creative, challenging, appealing to native emotions, and calculated to stir patriotic fervor. There were multiple moving parts with ultimate public relations benefits—a critical payoff and a prelude of things to come. The next steps in the master plan.

"The fuse?" Miklos asked.

"Yes. And you'll light it."

53

BRUSSELS, BELGIUM

ONE WEEK LATER

A middle-aged Hungarian architect passed through the revolving doors of the four-star Kensington Diplomat Hotel a day before the business meetings on his calendar. Jani Bakó pulled a single suitcase and stopped mid-lobby to survey the magnificent late nineteenth-century art nouveau design. The area opened to a high curved ceiling with painted intertwining motifs of plants, birds, and curvaceous female figures. He marveled at the detail and the beauty.

"*Bonjour,*" he said in French as he approached check-in.

Brussels was a diplomatic city. Accordingly, the receptionist, a blonde German beauty, was fluent in six languages. She read the name on his passport.

"*Szervusz, Bakó úr,*" she replied in Hungarian.

"Well, thank you. I'll speak French and some English if that's easier," Bakó replied in English.

"Whatever you prefer."

"English then," he said, struggling somewhat. "My tutor said I can use the practice."

"Very good then. I see we have you in for five days."

"Yes, that is correct," the architect replied warmly.

They continued to talk through the check-in process. She recommended the restaurant in the hotel, told him how to gain access to the gym with his key card and what to see in the area if he had time.

He appreciated the suggestions. "I'm here for a series of cultural tours. I'm an architect and Brussels is renowned for its design. It's my first visit. So much to photograph, including your exquisite hotel. Late 1880s?"

"1895," she replied. "It's a treasure trove of art nouveau."

"Abundantly apparent in the lobby. May I ask, is photography permitted?"

"Absolutely," the receptionist said. "We've been featured in many art books. I'd be happy to have someone give you a tour."

"Really? That would be wonderful."

Jani Bakó thanked her and took the elevator to his floor, admiring the craftsmanship along the way.

Once in his room, the Hungarian architect unpacked. He took out a blueprint of the hotel and area street maps. Soon he'd return downstairs to take pictures, but Jani Bakó, née Andre Miklos, already had captured a great deal of video through his lapel camera.

In the bathroom he removed his glasses, which had no prescription, stroked the rough artistic stubble he'd grown over the last week, and smiled into the mirror.

Despite his new looks, it was the same menacing, smug smile, recorded weeks earlier on a security camera in Tokyo.

BETHESDA, MARYLAND

"What do you need?" Heath's offer came with money, manpower, and the resources of the CIA behind it.

They had successfully coordinated their Metro travel to Walter Reed according to Reilly's instructions and now wasted no time talking strategy.

"A couple of things. Tap into the extra security I ordered at Pam's house. It'll be installed in the a.m. You can follow ADT in right after they leave. I'll give you the passcode. Next scrub any record of me at the Company. Anything and everything. Fast. And make sure there's nothing traceable about us, in Afghanistan, in the army, or at Langley."

"There shouldn't be."

"Make sure."

BRUSSELS

Jani Bakó walked with the Kensington Diplomat General Manager, Liam Schorel, occasionally lingering to compose a photograph. "Astoundingly beautiful. I can't thank you enough. You could have assigned someone on your staff to assist."

"No, no. The pleasure is all mine."

"I've long admired Victor Horta's work and his influence."

"Yes, one of Brussels' most inspiring architects," Schorel noted. "A true perfectionist, often inspired by music, particularly the violin. You can feel the influence in the lobby."

"Most certainly."

Bakó appeared to admire the interlocking wrought ironwork over marble, which soared to interior stained-glass balcony windows surrounded by fauna and flora scrolls and arabesques. He snapped another succession of photographs.

"Isn't it true that the Conservatoire de Musique expelled Horta because they viewed him as a pupil who lacked discipline?"

"Truly. You know your history well."

"How ridiculous," Bakó said.

"How fortunate for us. Horta's dismissal from the conservatoire has been a lasting gift to Brussels. To honor him, all of the furniture is either Horta's original work or recreations based on his designs."

"Such detail!" the Russian spy exclaimed between pictures. "Incredible attention to every aspect, everywhere." More shots. "The table tops, the door frames, right down to the door handles. The buttons on the elevator?"

"Everything," Schorel proudly responded. "Horta was so meticulous that the tiniest details were as important to him as the most open, airy, and flowing aspects of his design. Just breathe in the life he gave the lobby with the curved lines and the light from the windows."

"Magnificent. You can almost feel the building's heartbeat." The visitor snapped more pictures before switching to video to pan across the lobby.

Liam Schorel stood out of the way.

Bakó zoomed in on the hotel flower shop between the elevator bank and lobby entrance to Bistango, the ground floor hotel restaurant.

"I see you're taken by the window design on the shop."

"The floral metal work over the glass—extraordinary," Bakó declared.

"Horta carrying his organic touch forward," said Schorel. "He intended the space as a flower shop in keeping with his vision. It's always been that. Let's go over. I'll introduce you to Madame Ketz. She's getting a little hard of hearing, but it doesn't take away from her character. You'll see. After, be my guest at Bistango. Our chef is renowned for his Flemish cuisine."

"Oh, I truly wish I could, but I'm much too tired," the spy replied.

Bakó smiled outwardly to Schorel, but his alter ego, Miklos, laughed inwardly.

BETHESDA

"Why are you so worried?" Heath asked Reilly.

"After the divorce, Pam let me store boxes in the basement that I had no room for at my condo. Some clothes, stuff from when I was a kid, and a box of war memorabilia. Whoever broke in went through it all," Reilly explained.

"So?"

"So, there were photographs of us together in Kabul."

"So what?"

"It won't be hard to find a match for you," Reilly said.

"It's no secret where I drive to work every day."

"Granted. But if our association comes out, there'll be a shitstorm.

Shaw's adopted a 'Don't see, don't tell' attitude. But if it's leaked, Congress will have me in the hot seat with a whole new set of questions coming my way and KR stock will be in trouble."

"Got it. Give me a few minutes."

Heath stepped away to make two calls. One was to a memorized number at INSCOM, the Army Intelligence and Security Command at Fort Belvoir, Virginia. The other was to the CIA director.

"Okay, in the works," he said upon returning.

"Good," Reilly responded.

"Your record is disappearing, but we'll create a record of 'official' hotel inquiries, just as we have with other US corporations doing business around the world. Nothing untoward or out of the ordinary."

"Let's hope," Reilly sighed.

"Anything else?" Heath asked.

"Yes, I want an appointment with a shrink."

BRUSSELS

Madame Ketz was born in another era. Miklos thought she was probably in her mid-70s, perhaps closer to 80. She wore a chic ivory period fascinator hat accented with a white rose—a grand dame dressed for the 1895 opening ball for Horta's hotel.

Schorel handled the introduction. The spy was gracious, taking her hand and kissing it almost royally.

Johanna Ketz spoke with a Dutch accent and happily shared her knowledge of how Horta brought the outside in to his buildings, creating a sense of openness.

"It's been said that he came in daily to buy a flower for his lapel. Although I've never seen such a photograph, it makes for a wonderful story. I shall give you one in his honor, Mr. Bakó."

While she went to the refrigerator, Miklos photographed Horta's architectural touches in the shop, catching Ketz's assistant building floral arrangements in the background. He whispered to Schorel. "I see she has help."

"Yes," the general manager said. "Frederik is very new. Madame Ketz's long-time assistant suffered a heart attack only a week ago. Frederik is a temporary replacement."

"Too much for her to do alone?"

"Yes. Far too much. Frederik is quite responsible, and that lets Madame Ketz do what she loves."

The spy smiled. "Flirt with her customers?"

"Correct. And here she comes now."

The old florist brought the Russian spy a vibrant pink orange rose for his lapel.

"For you, my handsome friend."

"I shall come in for one each day before I leave," he said, kissing her lightly on each cheek.

Back in the lobby, the general manager thanked Bakó for his graciousness. "We often get inquiries to tour the hotel, but not from architects with your passion."

"Oh, it's my on honor. Thank you for all your time. A few more photographs?"

"Of course," Schorel graciously extended. "I failed to mention that the Kensington Diplomat is seriously being considered as a UNESCO World Heritage site. The process is long and complicated, but we're hopeful."

"I'm quite familiar with all that it takes. We have multiple sites in Prague, including the Historic Centre. But I must admit the magnificence here, Victor Horta's talent and touch, surely set the standard for neoromanticism."

"Precisely. I feel great responsibility for maintaining its character."

The Russian had an opening for his next question.

"Speaking of that, you must take extra precautions against theft or vandalism."

Andre Miklos planted the thought very casually through his guise as the Hungarian architect. He was rewarded with a very specific response.

"We do. We have twenty-four cameras in the lobby constantly

recording in our security office behind reception and six independent sprinkler zones, although we could us some structural upgrades. Someday. Never know when we'll get another earthquake," Schorel joked. "The last significant one to hit was 1692."

"Dangers rarely come with a warning," Bakó noted.

"True, but for all other things, we're buttoned down. We've taken exceptional precautions."

Miklos cleared his throat to stifle a laugh. In fact, he'd never had such open access. In return, he decided to send the manager a 2014 Chateau Mouton Rothschild Pauillac and a vase of flowers from the old florist. *Lilies?* he thought. *No, too dead on.*

"I understand that Horta's design lines, colors, and ironwork often continued beyond the public areas."

"Oh, most definitely. Would you like to tour the basement?"

"Anywhere you'd like."

54

TWO DAYS LATER

"Thank you for seeing me on such short notice, Doctor."

Reilly shook Dr. Chadwick Ellis' hand.

"Please, I'm much more comfortable with Chad. Besides it's less formal here."

For convenience sake, Ellis had recommended the Washington Harvard Club. Both were members with access to a private room.

"Well then, let's begin." The 56-year-old psychiatrist closed the door, picked one of the two deep burgundy leather chairs, and invited Reilly to take the other.

Reilly settled in and thought the doctor looked the part with wavy salt-and-pepper hair, a light blue and red checkered shirt, grey slacks, and a navy blue cardigan jacket with felt elbow patches.

"Nice not to have to fill out medical insurance forms," Reilly lightly joked.

"Fortunately I never had to process any. Besides, my subjects are never even aware I'm evaluating them."

Dr. Chadwick Ellis was not the typical psychiatrist. He was Harvard educated, with a minor in political science, and spoke Russian and Arabic. The CIA had recruited him his junior year and fully funded his medical school tuition. Now thirty years later, he was the CIA's senior shrink, writing detailed political prescriptions.

"Bob Heath tells me you want to understand what makes Mr. Gorshkov tick."

"If possible."

"You've met Gorshkov?"

"Yes, briefly."

"And your opinion?"

"Powerful. Calculating. We only spoke for a few moments. All in English, and something was probably lost for that reason, but I had the distinct feeling he was sizing me up."

"Why did you feel that way?"

Reilly felt this was a classic psychiatrist question. He smiled. "You're good. You turned this back on me."

"It's what I do," Ellis said as he leaned into his chair. "So, tell me why."

"It was in his eyes. The coldest I'd ever seen with a smile that said, 'Don't fuck with me.'"

Dr. Ellis laughed. "Go on."

"I thought you'd be filling me in."

"Soon enough. Please."

"Well, I had a sense he was probing for my weaknesses. Oh, and his handshake wasn't a greeting. It was all about control. I couldn't get the thought out of my mind that this was the most dangerous man I'd ever met."

Ellis removed his glasses, raised them to the sunlight, and looked for smudges.

"You got an impression and interpreted it," he said, replacing his glasses. "Was it what you felt or what he wanted you to feel? Do you know the story of the blind men and the elephant?"

"No, I don't believe so."

"It's Hindu lore, but retold and popularized by the nineteenth century American poet John Godfrey Saxe. Forgive me, if you will. It's worthy of our discussion."

The CIA psychologist began the story.

"Once upon a time six blind men in a village encountered an elephant. Of course they had no idea what an elephant was. Perhaps by feeling it they'd understand better. One at a time each of the men stepped forward to touch the creature. First came the blind man who touched the elephant's leg. He claimed an elephant was a pillar. The second touched the tail and argued it was like a rope. The third felt the trunk. He described the animal as a thick tree branch. Remember," Ellis said, "these are blind men."

Reilly nodded.

"The fourth reached higher and touched an ear. He claimed the elephant was an enormous hand fan. The fifth man ran his hand across the elephant's side describing it as a wall. Finally, the sixth blind man, after feeling the tusk, said an elephant was a pipe.

"All the different experiences led to a debate, with each blind man insisting only he was right. But a wise man passed by and asked why they were arguing. They explained they couldn't agree what an elephant was. They had no consensus and clearly couldn't reach one. They recounted their individual impressions.

"The wise man calmly observed that each blind man touched a different part of the elephant. They were all correct in their own way, just as you were. It's all about perspective and what we are allowed to experience, either through circumstance or manipulation. You weren't in control. Gorshkov was. He projected, through a false smile, a stronger than comfortable handshake, a greeting void of any emotion, the cruelty he wanted you to feel."

"Part of the elephant or the whole elephant?" Dan Reilly asked.

"For you, it was the entire elephant," Dr. Ellis stated. "The Russian people have an entirely different impression."

"Am I so wrong?"

"At Langley we share your impression. You felt you were in the presence of a dangerous personality. He may very well be the most dangerous predator you or anyone has ever met in the modern era.

"I have to confess, I really have an interesting practice. The patients I've analyzed over the years? Kim Jong-un, bin Laden, Bashar el-Assad, Gaddafi, Hussein. Never met any of them. Haven't needed to. Same with Netanyahu and even our presidents from Clinton forward. I've evaluated them all—through impressions like yours and actions by them. Reading news reports, viewing interviews, studying photographs, debriefing field agents and political figures, researching their childhoods, understanding their purchases and their predilections.

"I develop analyses and what I like to call *personality predictives*—hints into who they are and how they may act in 'what if' scenarios. It helps us wage a better diplomatic chess game."

Ellis locked onto Reilly's eyes to underscore his point. "Chess, being the alternative to war."

"I imagine you have a real success rate," Reilly offered.

"Imagine all you want. It's classified." It was a joke, but it had the weight of truth. "For the sake of this discussion," he continued, "let's get into the weeds with Nikolai Gorshkov."

"I'm ready."

"First a little background that suggests a developmental pattern. He was born in Leningrad, now St. Petersburg, Russia, in 1957, the year Sputnik launched the space race. Gorshkov was a baby boomer whose parents survived the siege of Leningrad, the Nazis' push into Russia, which left nearly one million people dead. His father was a factory worker, a laborer, and a janitor. He grew up with little materially in Soviet Russia, but was ingrained with the spirit of Mother Russia, a life force that continues to flow through him today.

"He's a smart man with a PhD in economics and a law degree from Moscow State University. But it's the KGB that truly shaped the man we see today. Gorshkov was in his twenties when he was recruited by the Soviet spy agency. It was KGB Director Yuri Andropov's idea to bring in younger operatives who hadn't risen through the typical military track. However, Gorshkov either felt like an outsider or was judged as one. As a result, he didn't earn top postings. He was assigned to Potsdam and charged with doing what the KGB did—surveil, collect data, and potentially detain and interrogate. But this was as perestroika was taking hold, the period that brought reforms and ultimately seismic changes to Russia and its relationship with the West. In my estimation, this new world order was counter to his nature as a thug."

Ellis' manner and delivery changed. He straightened up in his chair, his voice deepened, and his eyes narrowed.

"The Nikolai Gorshkov of today is still a thug who envisions himself as the leader of the country for the rest of his life . . . a contemptible dictator who has maneuvered upward with virtually unchecked power. Mr. Reilly, you were right to feel threatened. The leaders of countries around Russia should take heed as well."

Reilly exhaled. Chadwick Ellis had turned on a dime and what began as an analysis now became a warning.

"Do I have your attention?" he asked

"A hundred percent."

"Then more history. From an historical perspective, Gorshkov was angered and humiliated by the collapse of the Soviet Union. He felt little allegiance to Russian leadership that had all but abandoned him in Potsdam following the fall of the Berlin Wall.

"Biographers reported that the Kremlin ignored his requests for assistance. He and his aides were left to destroy files on Germans the KGB had deemed enemies of the state. He viewed this as surrender, capitulation, and defeat. Not quite the Russian tradition. In that abandonment, the young KGB operative was reborn with a certain historical destiny—the destiny to one day rebuild respect for Russia, and yes, rebuild the Russian empire. That set the course which Russia and the rest of the world is on now."

Ellis smiled. "Am I giving you too much or going too fast?"

"No, not at all," Reilly replied.

"Clearly you're getting *my* interpretation. But for what it's worth, the man is not hard to read. You walked away with a strong first blush reaction."

"Yes, a visceral feeling, but without an understanding."

"Quite so. Going a little deeper, from a clinical point a view, I'm of the opinion that Gorshkov projects multiple identities. Don't take that as schizophrenia. He's anything but. While he's not a communist today, he's a statist—one who believes in the concentration of a highly centralized government that extends into government ownership of industry. He sees himself with a sense of manifest destiny, returning order to the country and legitimacy to the Russian Orthodox Church through autocratic power. His autocracy."

"How did he consolidate so much power?" Reilly asked.

"Over a long period of time and with a great deal of money," Ellis replied. "After the dissolution of the Communist union and the end of Soviet Russia, he entered politics and, with proper influence, was given the post of deputy mayor of Novosibirsk. There, he realized that to succeed in politics—to win—it was completely acceptable to exploit the weaknesses of others. In the emerging capitalistic state it was also a practice that Gorshkov embraced for his own gain. He manipulated many financial scams. Businessmen became his focus, his *targets*. They were permitted to conduct high-level transactions in his city so long as he benefited as well. To guarantee that business worked in his favor, his KGB training came into play. Remember, he was a case officer. The tools of the trade included identifying suspects, cultivating sources, and running operatives. But in Novosibirsk it wasn't tracking down Cold War spies or traitors. He now collected critical personal financial records on Russia's regional and national oligarchs, which ultimately made them dependent on him. That dependency brought Gorshkov untold wealth."

Reilly shifted in his chair. He had to ask the obvious question.

"How much?"

"Untold. Unknown."

"Any estimate?"

"Lot of digits. Lots of commas," Ellis stated. "Wealth that he has continued to build."

"Multimillions?"

"Multibillions. But back to the timeline. It's important to follow. In 1998, he was invited to Moscow to investigate corrupt business practices. Imagine that. A man who went from poverty to great fortune based on his own corrupt practices was suddenly brought to Moscow to root out fraud. Again, he relied on proven lessons from his old KGB playbook. As the saying goes, he won new friends and influenced new people. And those he viewed as either political or financial enemies he jailed. All of this led him a step closer to the Kremlin. A step closer to fulfilling his destiny."

"History is his constant," Reilly observed.

"Correct. Gorshkov wears a coat woven with threads of Russian history. He cites leaders from tsarist Russia to Lenin as inspirations and invokes nationalism and patriotism as means to justify his very malevolent ends. He's a megalomaniac and a perfectionist, with perfection equating to a Russia of his design. And yes, he still operates like a spy and is wary of everyone's motives. That makes him unpredictable and dangerous."

"And power hungry."

"Absolutely, with absolute power," Ellis continued. "He's stepped over everyone in his way. And as a survivalist, a statist, and a nationalist, he fits the Russian profile of a leader. He lives a private life, but with a theatrical public façade. Big, bold, brash. Certainly, the shrewdest in the room. A classic Machiavelli."

"Manipulative," Reilly added.

"Among the best," Ellis emphasized.

"Sane or crazy?" Reilly asked.

"Completely sane and crazy like a fox. Nikolai Gorshkov's overarching goal has been to rebuild Russia's belief in itself, then restore Russia as the ultimate power broker in the world. To achieve this he will test the weakness of adversaries, whether they're in the Kremlin, across Russia's immediate borders, or beyond Europe. And he counts on America's lack of resolve.

"One of my jobs is to look for hints of what he might do next. It's harder with Gorshkov than anyone in memory. He's a trained spy who holds all of his cards tightly. He telegraphs little or nothing. The aides he confides in are equally guarded ex-KGB. They communicate in small groups and watch one another for missteps. As far back as fifteen years ago CIA analysts concluded that Gorshkov created a tough environment for intelligence. It's gotten tougher since."

"So, what's he likely capable of doing next?" Reilly asked.

"*Likely.* Gorshkov likes to echo his predecessor who said, 'Only a sick person in his sleep can imagine that Russia would suddenly attack NATO.' He also said, 'There's no need to be afraid of Russia.' Two statements meant to misdirect concern. And yet his planes buzz American ships in the Baltic Sea and test defenses in the Western Hemisphere. NATO nations on Russia's borders nervously look east."

"And Ukrainians wake up every morning wondering if this'll be the day Russia launches a full-scale attack."

"Correct. In the short term, the goal is to create chaos; a favorite tactic of dictators. Designed to keep adversaries off balance. They benefit from chaos. They create external threats to hide internal problems, warn citizens that the enemy is at the gate, and stir up patriotic fervor to discourage and derail any regime change. Chaos kicks up so much dirt it clouds our ability to act effectively," the CIA psychiatrist continued. "Yet our inaction feeds the monster's id and diminishes our standing in the world."

"And the monster is Gorshkov," Reilly asserted. "But Gorshkov more than Russia?"

"Gorshkov's at the top. He isn't just the face of the new Russia, he is its brain, body, and soul. Beside him, or rather under him, are his former KGB associates. They serve at his pleasure and discretion so long as they obey. Loyalty comes with its benefits: wealth, homes, women. Disloyalty? I think you can fill in the blanks."

"All too well," Reilly whispered.

"Nikolai Gorshkov is father and leader. His purpose is to rebuild the old Soviet Empire. He doesn't view it as an impossible task. But his tendency is to sell it in as a means to protect Russia, its sovereignty, its territories, its values, and its people."

"Using propaganda to establish firm foundation for political gain," Reilly noted.

"Not just political gain," Dr. Ellis maintained. "Land. And this quickly gets to the larger issue of Western influence. Gorshkov isn't frightened or threatened by any single European country. But in his mind, NATO and the EU are driven to expand and under the control of American presidents. In even harsher terms, he sees those countries as occupied by the United States, with Russia our next commercial trophy."

"That's ridiculous," Reilly proclaimed.

"Not for a narcissistic Machiavellian with millions of followers. And because of who he is, what he believes, and the power he's amassed, Gorshkov operates in a world of duplicity and deceit reminiscent of the old Soviet Guard before Khrushchev."

"Two questions," Reilly said. "How responsible is the West for his ascension? And even more important, if Gorshkov believes in his own manifest destiny, then beyond all the cloak-and-dagger stuff, what does he want?"

Dr. Chadwick Ellis took a deep breath. "Questions with alarming answers, Mr. Reilly. We are not blameless. Our geopolitical missteps, and those of our allies, contributed to the creation of Gorshkov, or at least helped his ascension. After the end of the Cold War, we dismissed Russia as a third-rate player. The country was struggling to rebuild a national identity and ascertain international respect. The Kremlin saw NATO expanding, pushing its boundaries up and down Russia's western frontier. Even though we invited Russia to have an unofficial say in NATO, we didn't allow it to become a member. Whether that would have been a good idea is another thing. But it did serve to isolate and neuter a former super power. In my estimation, this gave Russia's leaders permission to stand up to the West, to restore the pride and patriotism to a nation that had been stripped of both.

"To your second question, Nikolai Gorshkov believes that today *he alone* has the wherewithal to reclaim Russia's rightful place in the world. *He alone* has the draconian authority to create a new Russian empire. It is his destiny to become the most powerful person in the world."

"The ultimate egoist," Reilly concluded.

"Probably none greater. He is cunning, diabolical, and deadly."

Again Reilly thought about Gorshkov's end game, wondering how it would play out.

55

Without realizing his complicity, the Kensington Diplomat's general manager had aided a Russian assassin in compiling an extraordinarily detailed target folder. It was replete with sixty photographs, the location of load-bearing structural supports, and virtually complete intel on the CCTV system and what hotel security could see. The research included traffic patterns and times of neighborhood gridlock, typical police response times, alternative exit routes, and weak spots within the hotel power plant.

Liam Schorel hadn't expected any gifts, but the architect thanked him with a surprise, a expensive bottle of Chateau Mouton Rothschild Pauillac.

"You've made my stay wonderful," the man named Bakó said as he gave him the fine Bordeaux.

"Thank you. This is wonderful and it has been my pleasure. I hope you'll return."

"Oh, I promise I will," the spy said with an expression that Schorel couldn't interpret.

"Let me walk you out," Schorel offered.

At checkout, Schorel reviewed his guest's bill and reduced it to the family and friends rate. Miklos almost thought it would be a shame if

Schorel was in the hotel the appointed moment. Almost.

Before departing, he kissed Madame Ketz again, which earned him another boutonniere. As she pinned it on him, he noticed Frederik busy at work putting flowers and plants in the large cooler. *What a good helper*, he thought.

MOSCOW

FSB Director Nicholai Federov solved the Alexandr Vasilev problem the old-fashioned way. Vasilev, a widower of eight years, went to join his wife. Pravda reported that he had died quietly in his sleep. The Federal Security deputy director was cremated and quickly honored with a military burial. All within one day. Inefficiency eliminated. An irresponsible intelligence officer removed from service before he became a bigger problem.

LANGLEY

Bob Heath read the CIA summary with skepticism. Vasilev was one of Russia's veteran intelligence officers. There'd been no evidence that he'd had significant health problems, though a company psych workup on him by Chad Ellis suggested he had authority issues. *Could he have come down with a fatal case of advanced discord?* Heath mused. He contacted the Moscow desk with a simple query: Vasilev. Top-level assessment.

Sudden deaths like this were rarely what they seemed. Under Gorshkov's authoritarian command, they always pointed to either political changes or political fuckups. To Heath's thinking, Vasilev had been taken out the way dissident journalists were, though with fewer theatrics.

The CIA operative began to speculate. He wrote down possibilities:

1. Ego conflict with Federov. How big?

2. Bad managerial decision. If so, what?

3. Operational failure. What nature?

4.   Liability going forward. Worthy of elimination?

Heath added one more item on the list he wasn't prepared to share.

5.   Any connection to a Reilly inquiry?

MOSCOW

Now meeting with President Gorshkov, Federov took a deep breath, ready to review the findings on Reilly. He began with the bungled surveillance in London which led to agent Klenkov's death.

No more than two sentences in, Gorshkov screamed. First at Federov, then the FSB in general. Federov feared for his own life when the president took a Luger from his desk and waved it around maniacally. But minutes into the rant the president suddenly calmed. Federov believed it was because Gorshkov knew Klenkov had been operating under orders from his own right hand man in the Kremlin—Andre Miklos, not directly under FSB orders. However, it was a point he did not pursue.

"Continue," Gorshkov said as he returned the gun to his top drawer.

"The subject appears to have retained some contacts from his military career and a Washington post, but the contacts are consistent with his international job. It's also in line with comparable executives from Marriott, Hilton and other corporations that have ongoing relationships with US Homeland Security, the State Department, and private security firms. Their holdings are soft targets."

"But is he an American intelligence officer?"

"So far we have no evidence of that," Federov replied.

"Do I hear *yet* in your voice?"

"If I may, our chief researcher, through his exploitation of the corporate website, has discovered that Kensington Royal is developing a multitiered threat-assessment plan. That is also in line with other American corporations operating on a global scale, though theirs appears to be more comprehensive. That would explain his trip to the US embassy the night of the Kiev bombing and his meetings with Markovich and

Vasilev. But . . ." Federov trailed off.

"But what?"

"This photograph from his service in Afghanistan."

The FSB director showed the president.

"And?"

"Reilly on the right. The man on the left was a compatriot. He now works for the Central Intelligence Agency."

"How did you acquire this?"

"A break-in to his ex-wife's house."

"Do you have any knowledge that Reilly and this agent remain friends?"

"We're working on that."

Gorshkov narrowed his eyes to slits, a sign not to be mistaken for anything but unflinching resolve.

"The clock is ticking. He worries me. If he worries me, he should worry you. I want a report every day, detailed and thorough."

"Yes, sir."

Gorshkov stood. The meeting ended, but not the president's apprehension.

LANGLEY

Heath's inquiry returned a reply from the Moscow station chief.

> Nothing specific beyond cited OSINT. Asks out to friends and Joe.
> Street talk—poss personality conflicts with his number one. No one
> in mourning.

The memorandum reinforced Heath's initial suspicions. Vasilev was taken out quickly, probably because he'd more than pissed off someone important. Likely his boss, Federov. Considering it was FSB, this added to his concerns shaped by Reilly's London encounters, the break-in at Reilly's wife's home, and the increased probing of the KR network. Although there was nothing specific from OSINT, Open Source Intelligence, the agency was still checking with the British, other friends, and "Joe"—the generic name for a deep cover agent.

Aside from Reilly's work with the State Department, there was now no record of his CIA contacts remaining.

But . . .

But, the perfect rejoinder. *But.* As troubling as *yet, unless, except, on the other hand,* and *nevertheless.* Heath ran through them all. Each of the synonyms set off a spy's senses. Each pointed back to Dan Reilly's own instinct and the reason he wanted to speak with a Company shrink.

Heath called Chadwick Ellis.

"Doc, I haven't followed up with you about Reilly. Can we talk?"

Ten minutes later the agency psychologist was in Heath's office.

"What was Reilly fishing for?" Heath asked.

"A psychoanalysis. He was full of questions about Gorshkov," Ellis offered.

"What kind?"

"The kind that can connect dots."

"Connecting the dots creates a picture."

"Yes," Ellis continued. "In this case, it isn't a face. Reilly was reaching for an understanding of Nikolai Gorshkov's psyche, where his motivations lie, and ultimately what he is capable of doing."

"Did he explain why?"

"No."

"Jesus. What the hell?"

"He didn't explain why," Dr. Ellis interrupted. "That doesn't mean I wasn't able to make a determination."

Heath bore down. "Explain."

"Whatever he suspects, it seemed imminent."

56

CHICAGO, IL

KENSINGTON ROYAL HEADQUARTERS

THREE DAYS LATER

"As we expected, there's pushback from regional directors," Alan Cannon reported to Shaw in a meeting also attended by Dan Reilly. "Not all the managers on the priority list were eager to make all the changes."

"You're going to have to see them one by one," Shaw stated. He looked at Cannon and Reilly. "Split the toughest ones up."

"Will do," Cannon agreed. "Part of the problem is that some GMs are resisting the idea of surprise audits. Others are nervous about the optics and how they might chase away business. Same for a couple of our domestic managers."

"I'll be happy to show them footage from Tokyo." Reilly was frustrated and showing it.

"Actually," Shaw replied, "that's exactly what we should do. And not just the attack against our property. Think about how to add Egypt, Mali, and Tunisia. Run it for them. Sit with them. Let the images make the argument. Leave the video, and before you go, spell out that this initiative comes from *me*."

This was the Edward Shaw Reilly admired: a thoughtful manager and a decisive leader.

"Okay then," Shaw continued. "You two hit the international properties. I'll deal with the US. And tell each and every one of them that if they disagree and want to kiss their pension goodbye to call me! That's the only thing I'll want to hear from anyone not in accord."

"Yes, sir," Reilly said.

Next they went to the financial impact and the locations that were making headway.

Following the meeting, Alan Cannon and Dan Reilly divvied up the destinations and laid out an aggressive travel schedule to cover the next three weeks. Before wrapping for the day and returning to Washington, Reilly went to the corporate media office.

"Len, what do you have archived from the Tokyo attack?"

Len Karp's primary job was surfing the internet and the cable news channels for anything company related. He produced edit reels daily and forwarded them to the executive suites for planning and promotion.

"CNN, Fox, MSNBC, NHK," the 44-year-old Karp said. "I've been archiving everything I could since the bombing."

"Can I see what you have?"

"Sure. Pull up a seat."

For the next thirty minutes Reilly sat with his mouth open and silent. He had seen the initial reports on TV and walked through the debris in Tokyo, but Karp had compiled additional footage. Graphic, powerful, sad. Truly sad. Much of it was social media postings.

It was like a minefield explosion at its worst. Body parts separated from bodies. Blood flowing into drains. A child's burned stuffed animal clutched in an equally burned hand. A leg sticking out from under a pillar, the rest of the body still smoldering under a white cloth. Strewn pearls. Workers carrying covered stretchers to the parking lot where victims were lined up and tagged. Hardened first responders crying. Survivors staggering out the door, covered in ash. A family that had been swimming, lying dead two floors below where the pool had been.

He recognized some of the young staff, who only seconds before their deaths had been on promising executive tracks with the company.

Security officers who would be easier to identify because of their name tags. Kitchen workers burned beyond recognition.

"That's enough." Reilly had to stop.

"It's awful," Karp offered. "Tokyo, but it could be anywhere today."

"That's why I came by, Len."

"You want to show it around?"

"Yes, to some of our GMs who don't recognize the risks."

"Whatever you need."

"A four-to-five-minute edited reel. Raw, no additional announcer track. Real sound and maybe powerful music underneath."

"I've got just the piece. Tomaso Albinoni's 'Adagio in G minor.' It'll help me organize the shots and build to the music."

Reilly didn't know the composition offhand, but he trusted Karp's instincts.

"And at the end, add a graphic," Reilly added. "White letters over black with the location and date of the attack and the names of the victims. After that, the names and dates of other hotels that have been attacked. I'll email you the information."

"And the ultimate impact?"

"Scare the living bejesus out of anyone who watches it."

* * *

The urgent and important boxes on the Eisenhower Method suddenly had a new priority: bringing the Kensington Royal general managers into line.

Reilly conferred with Alan Cannon on the assignments. Cannon chose the Asian, Middle Eastern, North African, Eastern European, and Scandinavian destinations. Eleven in all. Manila, Singapore, Istanbul, Dubai, Cairo, Athens, Belgrade, Budapest, Zurich, Prague, and Copenhagen.

Reilly had twelve hotel cities to visit, from South America to Europe. Bogotá, Rio de Janeiro, São Paulo, Cancún, San Juan, then Paris, Brussels, London, Vienna, Rome, Lisbon, and Amsterdam.

"Bring enough underwear," Reilly joked

"You've got that right," said Cannon. "I figure we can do it in twenty days if the weather cooperates."

"Might want to give it twenty-five. Some of the GMs may take more than one conversation. I'd rather we help them find the reason to sign on. I think most will."

"Not so sure about Athens because of the money crunch. We may need to look at fine-tuning the management there," the security chief noted. Fine-tuning was KR-speak for firing.

"The video will help. Len Karp will have a cut for us to screen by nine tomorrow."

"Any rethinking on which properties go Orange and which go Red?" Reilly asked.

"No change based on today's State Department alerts and the other outside daily briefings we're subscribing to now."

"I'm afraid from here to eternity we'll be living in a day-to-day world," Reilly sighed. "We have to be able to respond immediately. It'll take the financial incentives from Chris. Money will ease the pain and speed up the process."

But Reilly and Cannon both understood it would take more than money. The real underlying hurtles were grounded in religious practices, local politics, and, to insure success, even potential payoffs.

After discussing these challenges Reilly revised his travel estimate. "Let's plan on thirty days."

* * *

Three days later, both men shook hands at O'Hare and took off in different directions—Cannon to Asia, eventually working his way to Europe, and Reilly to South America, with his last stop in Brussels.

Reilly's first meeting was in Bogotá, Colombia, a city and country that had improved its security profile in recent years. However, US State Department advisories still warned tourists to be aware of "the existence of criminal organizations that operate independently and may cooperate with insurgent or paramilitary organizations in the narcotics trade and other illicit activities such as prostitution and extortion."

This was nothing new to Reilly. He'd learned an important lesson in dealing with local drug lords who still used kidnapping when necessary. The cartels took a dim view of a hotel executive firing an employee for trafficking in drugs or prostitution. But they understood booting an employee for not working hard, not meeting the hourly requirements, or providing bad service. All would be justifiable causes for dismissal.

Reilly understood these unique cultural and social rules and followed them. That's why he convinced KR to allow for more local hires in global hot spots.

One of those important local hires, the Bogotá general manager, Jorge Suarez, agreed to the upgrades to Orange without debate.

There were no active threats to Rio de Janeiro, São Paulo, and Cancún beyond local crime and the fair warnings for tourists not to venture off the beaten path. Reilly designated those hotels Blue, the lowest level.

San Juan, Puerto Rico, was another issue. Reilly was told the Kensington Royal island resort had been hit by cyberattacks, a disturbing report that he relayed to Spike Boyce in Chicago. That was enough for Reilly to move it up a notch to threat level Yellow.

Alan Cannon's initial meetings were much harder. While Manila was safe, not so for travel to other parts of the Philippines. The State Department advised, "Separatist and terrorist groups continue to conduct bombings, kidnappings, and attacks against civilians."

The team elevated Singapore to Yellow status because the US military gateway to Southeast Asia was based there.

Further along, Cannon upped the status of Istanbul to Red due to Syrian and ISIS threats as well as its own internal political turmoil. Cairo, a danger zone since the fall of Hosni Mubarak in 2011, also rose to the highest alert and protective category.

Cannon moved on to Dubai and Copenhagen—both Yellow. The remainder of his meetings required much more convincing.

Reilly found the same issues in Western Europe. The general managers appreciated the company's concerns, but didn't want to give into what they considered hysteria.

Both Cannon and Reilly presented a powerful rebuttal on video. It took Cannon five extra days to get through Zurich, Athens, and Belgrade. Reilly was ahead of him, finding more corporate cooperation.

Cannon still had to contend with reluctant teams in the former Eastern Bloc capitals of Prague, Bucharest, and Budapest, cities where it was utterly important to adopt changes. Local management didn't immediately buy in. Cannon explained that the program was nonnegotiable and would actually provide defensive measures which, up until now, had not existed.

The general managers in Prague and Bucharest agreed. Tired of the back and forth with the head of the Budapest property, Cannon finally explained he had twenty-four hours to either get on the train or find himself under it. Twelve hours later, he agreed.

Meanwhile, only Brussels and London remained on Reilly's list. He hoped Brussels would go quickly so he could get to London to see Marnie.

57

WASHINGTON, DC

THE WHITE HOUSE

The president read the PDB, the president's daily briefing, prepared by the national security advisor. The top secret document was a synthesis of CIA, NSA, FBI, and Defense Intelligence reports and analysis. It was the president's primary source of raw intel and it usually ranged from not so bad, to really bad, to worse. Though there might not be any hard data on *where* or *when*, the *what* would stir up bile in any president's stomach. It did just that for President Alexander Crowe.

"Jesus H. Christ," he said aloud to Pierce Kimball, his national security advisor.

"Yes," Kimball replied, breathing in hard.

"But they're not even countries!" the president exclaimed.

He was referring to overnight statements from the unrecognized president of the nonexistent country of South Ossetia, arguably a disputed region in northern Georgia, and the similarly separatist leader of the nonexistent state of Transnistria, a fraction of Moldova. Both men were calling for their regions to "become part of Russia." Their pleas had been covered in Moscow's Gorshkov-controlled press. But there was more. Pro-Russian separatists had taken to the streets in Kiev and Bucharest.

"What they really want is to be absorbed by Russia," Kimball stated.

"Meaning an invasion."

"Yes, sir," the national security advisor agreed.

"Gorshkov can't," the president argued.

"Can. But I don't know if he will."

"And Nagorno-Karabakh?" Crowe tapped the report. "Where the hell is that?"

"Azerbaijan, Mr. President. "East of Armenia, south of Georgia. Asia on the Caspian Sea."

"Right, right. Please, get them to include maps next time," the president said. "What's the real stake there?"

"NK is part of Moscow's poker hand in the oil trade. It always comes down to oil. The separatists are poker chips that Gorshkov plays well. He backs Armenia while selling weapons to Azerbaijan and stirring up Russian nationalism."

"All of this goes on, but most of the press in the US still just focuses on Ukraine. And even then, very little."

"It's too confusing for the public and Congress," the president replied, "and barely understandable to me."

"Mr. President, that's precisely what Gorshkov is counting on. He has you focusing on the pretty girl in the magic act to miss what the magician is doing. It's a diversion."

"And the real trick?" Crowe asked.

"Possibly Romania. Russia could move against Romania. That's the prize."

"Are you certain?"

This was the question military strategists and national security advisors hated to answer. Political calculation, deniability, and obfuscation could mean the difference between the beach and the high tower, invisibility or a post-White House career as a cable news contributor.

Pierce gave himself rhetorical wiggle room. He would write his response in a diary right after the meeting.

"I can only advise based on the latest intelligence community reports. Moscow appears to be doubling down on separatists loyal to Russia. The most vocal are the Romanian, but there are others. And in each case, a provocation could push them over."

"What about NATO?"

"Not watching the store either."

"And our principal source to back up the assumption?"

Another question to field correctly.

"Multiple sources. Inside and out. Some hints from the Tokyo hotel attack as well. Enough to trigger alarms. The Joint Chiefs are recommending we mobilize NATO forces to Romania."

"Shit," the president said.

"But Gorshkov will see that as an escalation," Pierce said for his own version of the record.

"He damn well should!" an energized president declared. "I want the Secretary of Defense and the Joint Chiefs in for a meeting. Tomorrow at the latest."

"The agenda, sir?"

"To show Gorshkov we still have some balls in this country."

58

RIGA, LATVIA

TWO DAYS LATER

Mairis Gaiss celebrated his 50th birthday in high style. Champagne, caviar, and hookers. All premium. The celebration lasted all night in his penthouse three blocks from his ArtiCom Energy International corporate headquarters on Elizabetes Street in Riga, the capital of Latvia.

ArtiCom Energy was a leading oil and gas exporter with rigs in the Baltic Sea and expansive explorations in the ever-melting Artic from which the company took its name. ArtiCom Energy enjoyed favorable business dealings with Russia's Gazpron through a deal completely facilitated by the Kremlin. This gave the Gaiss brothers sway in Riga's government to get their way and promote Moscow's interests, which included representation for the ethnic Russians in Latvia. The only thing left to irony for the fossil fuel family was that their name meant "air," the polar opposite of their business.

By daybreak, the party was over. Gaiss rose from the bed, but not before kissing the lips of all that had pleased him for so many hours. He showered and shaved, and then returned to his bedroom to dress. By then the women were gone, but the musky scent lingered. It had been a great party. His brother had gone above and beyond throwing him a true blowout.

Gaiss donned his newest three-piece black pinstripe suit from Volpe, one of London's hottest tailors. The white bespoke shirt fit his trim body, the same body that four hands had pawed over just a short time ago.

When he was ready to leave, three bodyguards met him at his front door. "Good morning, sir," the head bodyguard said. "Walk as usual?"

"Yes," Gaiss replied. "I need to stretch." He didn't explain, but his security team knew full well why.

They took his private elevator down twenty-one floors. Gaiss held back inside while his men checked the street. All clear. It was always all clear. There was never a problem. They believed no one would fuck with the Gaiss brothers in Riga. That's why the guards, as trained as they were as former members of the Latvian Special Tasks Unit, didn't see it coming.

They walked along Elizabetes Street in tight formation. The head guard, a 6'2" moose of a man, led the way, then the oil magnate, followed by the two other imposing men, each with a 4.5" barrel on their Heckler & Koch USP semiautomatic pistols holstered under their suit jackets.

Midway down the street in front of Vērmanītis, a popular bistro, a motorcyclist swerved, then skidded in a move that had been rehearsed in another part of the city for days. The biker fell off and rolled to a stop directly ahead of the ArtiCom Energy contingent.

The head bodyguard slowed his pace, reached backwards to protect his boss, and then went to the aid of the downed cyclist who was writhing in pain. It was a breach of protocol—and a mistake.

The other guards stayed close to Gaiss, pulling him from the scene. But invariably a crowd was quickly forming. This worried the bodyguards. They steered Gaiss away from the street and along the large Vērmanītis ground-to-ceiling windows. Another mistake.

Now they quickly walked single file with one of the bodyguards taking up the rear. He watched Gaiss, who was moving a few steps ahead of him. Then he saw nothing. He went through the window pane, but not of his own accord.

Gaiss grabbed the other guard's jacket as the man turned and saw his colleague on the inside of Vērmanītis with a hole through his head.

Four thoughts instantly flooded the guard's mind. *No sound. Suppressed gunshot. Short range. A setup.* He tried to reach for his H&K, but he had no sensation in his hand. He couldn't move his arm either. He was suddenly aware of a warm wetness on his stomach. He looked down and saw the ground quickly coming up. A new thought. A last thought. *How strange.*

Andre Miklos had come upon his targets swiftly. His first shot sent one man through the restaurant window. His next bullet ripped open the second guard's chest and severed his spinal cord. Quite by chance, on exit, the bullet still had the force to bring down the man directly behind him.

Mairis Gaiss gasped. Not just at the horror inflicted on the others, but at the realization that he had also been shot. The billionaire stood and stared into the eyes of the man who stepped over his bodyguard.

"Why?" he asked.

The man simply said, "Expediency."

Gaiss didn't understand—and he never would. A last bullet ended this short and final discussion of his life.

People rushed away from the pool of blood, giving the lead bodyguard a clear view of what had happened. He unholstered his H&K, tuned out the screaming, and scanned for a target. Nothing in front of him, nothing across the street. He pivoted. Nothing behind him. Even the injured biker was gone.

The accident had been a diversion. Had he not bent over to check the cyclist, he'd be dead as well. That fact was clear. But with his boss murdered on the street in broad daylight, he wondered how much his life would be worth when the surviving Gaiss brother found out.

* * *

Ninety minutes later police responded to a suicide call not more than a kilometer away. A nurse returning home from her shift at Riga

Maternity Hospital reported that she had found her husband dead. But this was not just anyone. Her husband had been a deputy in the Riga Municipal Police Department. A controversial, outspoken deputy who was fiercely pro-Latvia and even more vehemently anti-Russian.

Two hours later, Latvijas Radio 1, one of Riga's news stations, which was already covering the murders on Elizabetes Street, received a tip that police were investigating a suicide of a yet unnamed police deputy who may have been involved in the attack. This tip led to anonymous leaks at other media outlets. By noon, reporters were speculating as to the identity of the deputy based on the public anti-Russian statements he'd made.

An hour later hundreds from Riga's Russian community had amassed at the steps of the Riga Municipal Police Station at Lomonosova Street. By 1400 hours, the crowd had doubled, and it doubled again by 1500. Now some 1,200 angry protesters, many armed with Molotov cocktails, fueled by ongoing breaking news that linked the suicide weapon with the murders on the street, moved toward the police station.

Riot police took up positions. Television cameras were on the scene, not only broadcasting to Riga and the rest of Latvia, but feeding CNN International, which in turn went to TV sets in Russia.

Protesters taunted police. The recitation grew into a deafening roar that spurred some young men to throw rocks at the building. At first their aim was off. Then far better. Windows smashed. They overturned one police car, then another and another.

A line of twenty-five heavily protected police officers advanced using truncheons to disperse rioters. They were followed by another line of police with Mace and billy clubs.

For a few minutes there was a clear standoff. That changed when the sound of a gun cut through the chanting. No one knew who fired or where it came from, but a young woman who had been drawn to the excitement dropped.

"They're shooting!" yelled a man near her. Screams replaced the chants and Molotov cocktails replaced the rocks.

Andre Miklos, wearing a T-shirt, jeans, and hoodie, drifted back, tucking away a Glock—the same model and type used by the Riga Municipal Police.

By nightfall, Russian television, print, radio, internet, and unaffiliated bloggers ran with the story. They relied on attributable and anonymous sources, live interviews, Riga's hourly municipal police press conferences, and directives that originated in the Kremlin. Directives with biting specificity. Directives that had to be followed to the word.

Beyond the political rhetoric, the explosive adjectives, and the active verbs, one phrase carried the most meaning. It was widely reported in *Izvestia,* Rossiya 1, First Channel, and NTV, and thereafter was reinforced, echoed, and heralded around the world.

Co-opting the French expression of unity, it simply and effectively translated to "I Am Russia. We Are Russia."

International journalists picked up Russia's broadcasts and the impact. The Kremlin viewed an attack on its business interests, its business partners, and ethnic Russians as an attack on Russia itself.

59

ROMANIA

FOUR DAYS LATER

DECEMBER, 1989

"Gentlemen, are we in accord?" asked Lieutenant Colonel Whit Ellsworth.

The ranking Romanian officer, Major Constin Tomescu, responded for his team. "Yes, Colonel."

The operational plan, developed by the US Army Training and Doctrine Command (TRADOC) was intended as a highly visible exercise. Highly visible to the Russians, that is. Romanian Land Forces would participate, but this was an American-directed mission with some light fingerprints from NATO command. Rumor had it the mission came straight from the White House.

"Observers will be assessing critical response time, capability of your troops, and your ability to react in the moment to tactical changes. Operation Pressure Point-South is an expensive war game. Make sure you play to win."

"Sir, a question?"

"Yes, Major."

"Russia will be watching in real time."

"Undoubtedly. What's your question?"

"Given what's going on, the protests in Latvia, is this the US's way of drawing a 'do not cross' line? Considering the lack of any military response in Ukraine . . ."

"Major Tomescu, may I remind you, Ukraine is not in NATO. Moreover, I'm not a politician. I follow my orders. My orders are to prosecute Pressure Point-South to the best of my ability. When we're through, we'll toast our success with a glass of tuică and solve all the world's problems. Until then, Major, get your forces ready."

"Yes, sir."

The conversation didn't relieve the Romanian officer's underlying concerns. *Was NATO drawing a line in the sand? Would NATO actually be willing to commit in Romania to repel a Russian attack?*

* * *

Dawn the next morning found fifteen transports flying over a training area near Babadag, Romania. Two hundred paratroopers dropped to join the fifteen hundred ground troops already there. The mission: to retake an airfield captured by a "fictional enemy."

A Russian spy satellite watched from its orbit. But live video on CNN International told the Kremlin what was going on at ground level.

Meanwhile in Moscow, Nikolai Gorshkov watched the coverage in his living room. "More of a good thing," the president said to himself. "More of a good thing."

PART THREE

THREAT CONDITION RED

60

BRUSSELS, BELGIUM

THE KENSINGTON DIPLOMAT

ONE MONTH LATER

Liam Schorel strived to make the Kensington Diplomat the foremost hotel in Brussels for international dignitaries and world travelers. Thanks to both the visible historic architecture and the unseen state-of-the-art infrastructure upgrades, Schorel had succeeded. Moreover, as a rising star in the company, he was proud of his achievement, securing industry awards for KR and cover articles in major travel magazines.

Now he hoped to impress the corporate executive who had just arrived.

"Dan! Wonderful to see you again." He gave Reilly a warm handshake.

"Thank you, Liam."

"You picked the perfect week. We're at maximum capacity. Lots going on."

"Congratulations."

"Height of the season and it'll be busy through the end of the year."

Schorel led Reilly into his well-appointed office where they could talk. Reilly sat in the center of a brown leather couch that perfectly matched architectural touches from floor to ceiling—all in keeping with Victor Horta's original art nouveau design.

"Anything to drink? Water, wine, coffee?"

"Maybe wine in a bit, but for now I could use a coffee Americano."

Schorel stepped out to give the order to his assistant. Reilly took the time to gaze around the manager's office. French woven rug on the floor, period garden tapestry, framed awards for the building, some dating back to the heralded opening, others from recent honors, and photographs of Schorel with notable guests. On his desk, commemorative Lalique glassware, more photos, a bottle of wine with a note attached, and an eighteen-inch computer screen.

"It'll be just a few minutes," Schorel said upon returning. "In the meantime, I've read your proposal and—"

Reilly interrupted. "Actually, Liam, it's not a proposal. It's an action plan."

"Of course, but I thought we could talk about the need to put the Kensington Diplomat through all the pain of all this . . . planning."

"Liam, perhaps I'm at fault for not explaining this better in my email. Given the risks in Brussels, we want to be able to protect our guests without hesitation. That means the building needs to be threat ready."

"Of course, of course," Schorel said. "But surely you have to realize the difficulty of pulling new permits and getting approvals from the city, let alone the impact the," he paused to find the right word, "adjustments will have on our guests."

Reilly stood. "Liam, I want to show you something."

The general manager agreed, not certain he had made a convincing argument to his direct boss.

Reilly removed a thumb drive with a KR logo from his interior jacket pocket.

"What's this?" Schorel asked with enthusiasm.

"A video. Watch it."

Schorel offered to turn the monitor around.

"Not necessary. Just put it in. It's under four minutes. Make sure the sound is up. Up good."

Schorel inserted the USB drive into the computer and clicked a file with a date that didn't immediately register. Twenty seconds into Lenny

Karp's edited video, it did. The day of the attack on the Tokyo property.

Reilly watched Schorel. His upbeat, jovial, all-fine-with-the-world manner dissolved away. His mouth gaped in horror. The impact of the images was inescapable.

Schorel's assistant came in with coffee, but Reilly waved her away, whispering, "Not now."

The final shot was of the corpse of a little boy clutching his burned teddy bear. It faded to black, but the music continued. Liam Schorel couldn't turn away. He read a series of facts in bold white letters. The number of deaths. The number of injuries. The types of injuries. The names of the dead. This was followed by the names and dates of other hotels attacked within the past two years.

The final chord rang out, but Schorel continued to stare at the blank screen. Reilly had seen the same reaction in many other screenings around the world.

"I'm sorry," Schorel said. He started another sentence but it didn't form.

"Liam, every day hundreds of people come to your hotel. Fathers and mothers, couples, executives, politicians, officials, tourists, students far from home. They're not thinking about anyone intent on killing them. But now you must.

"They check in believing the room will be clean, the mini-bar will be full, the pay-per-view channel is working, and there will be chocolates on their pillows when they come back after a night on the town. These are the visible services we provide that are traditional to our business. But today, we have another job: to protect our guests and our employees," Reilly intoned.

"The faces in the video are the faces of people you see every day. Only they're gone. In this world, Liam, in this day and age, in this new reality, you share the responsibility to keep them safe. Brussels has been targeted. Only blocks away. Tragically. How could you possibly feel immune?"

In a matter of minutes, Liam Schorel had become a changed man.

"You have my word, Dan. I will make this work for you."

"Not for me, Liam. For the people we are responsible for."

"Yes," he said softly. "But there are still many practical considerations."

"Go on," Reilly encouraged.

"First of all, it's not easy dealing with city codes. It takes time."

"Time may not be on our side. We have no way of knowing who may strike next or where. But we are a soft target, the softest. So let's deal with the problems one at a time."

Reilly retrieved his briefcase and handed the general manager a single-page checklist. Next, they moved to a small round table in the office. Their conversations took them through the coffee, and an hour later, a fruit, cheese, and charcuterie plate.

Schorel was honest with the problems he faced, while Reilly proposed solutions. Some would come from political pressure applied by the US State Department officials in Brussels, others through donations to historical cultural funds. "And," Reilly said, "you'll have a fair share of wining and dining to cut through the red tape."

The comment prompted Schorel to return to his desk.

"Should have thought of this when the charcuterie came out." He raised the bottle of wine. "I've been saving this for the right occasion. I think I need it now."

Reilly leaned back in his chair, quite ready for a drink. The last ninety minutes had been productive. They'd covered the checklist and were poised to review basic CAD drawings of exterior prevention measures the consultant committee had developed.

Schorel popped the cork and poured two glasses. "Quite a bottle. A gift from a guest. A fine, fine wine." He examined the label. "2014 Chateau Mouton Rothschild Pauillac."

Reilly held it up to the light from the period chandelier. "A beautiful deep red."

Schorel swirled his glass and sipped. "I get warm blackberries and chocolate covered cherries. Maybe a hint of violets."

Reilly followed. "Well, you have a more finely-tuned palate than I have."

Schorel raised his glass in a toast. "Here's to successfully working together."

Reilly spun it differently. "Here's to beating the clock."

They relaxed and talked about the wine. Reilly was impressed with Schorel's knowledge. He explained that this particular Bordeaux had real flamboyance and depth. "A real treat and a special present from a grateful guest. A most grateful one. This bottle is more than the equivalent of a night's stay here."

"Pretty impressive."

"Funny thing is I wrote a really nice thank-you letter, but it was returned. Got it back a few days ago. Nicest man, though. A Hungarian architect. He loved the Diplomat. You know me. I'll talk about it all night long. I ended up giving him a tour of the whole hotel. Top to bottom."

Reilly stiffened. The aside that the letter had been returned hit him hard. The inside tour even more. "Liam, did he take pictures?"

"Certainly did. Everywhere. He really appreciated the work that—"

"Exactly what did you show him?"

The general manager put his drink down. "Why? What's wrong?"

"Where, Liam? Where?"

The general manager still wasn't getting Reilly's point.

"Everywhere there was relative historical relevance. The lobby, the offices, the elevators. He wanted to see it all. Even the classic design that's carried along the stairway and into the hallways. Not usually seen in most art nouveau buildings. He was even interested in the foundation. The bones of the building."

"Where security, the electrical and heating plant, and storage are housed."

"Yes, but—"

Reilly stood. "I want to see the security camera recordings, Liam."

"I don't understand—" Schorel stammered.

"Did you read the memorandum that said watch out for people taking photographs of the property?"

"Well, yes, but he's an architect—"

"With a fake mailing address. Jesus Liam! You gave a terrorist a first class tour of *my hotel!*"

The color drained out of Schorel's face. "Oh my God, I had no idea."

"The security video. Now!"

Five minutes into screening the CCTV video on the hard drive, Schorel stuck his finger at the monitor. "Stop. There!""

The young uniformed security officer froze the image.

Reilly asked if they could zoom in. The computer couldn't.

"Can you print it out?"

The officer, already annoyed with a stranger looking over his shoulder and disrupting his day, shook his head *no.*

"I'm not a technical whiz," said Reilly, "but don't you have a screen grab program?"

Again no.

Reilly removed his cell phone and took a succession of shots of varying focal lengths.

Thinking he was able to get back to other things, the security officer pushed away from the computer.

"Oh no. There's more." Reilly tapped the man's shoulder. "I need to see video of what he's taking pictures of. All of it."

"Can I ask what this is about?" the security officer asked in adequate English.

Reilly quickly shook his head to make sure Schorel didn't say anything.

"We think the guy was casing the hotel in advance of a robbery," said Reilly. "It might involve a guest. I'll let you know if and when you can say anything. Until then, not a word. Do you understand?"

The guard looked at Schorel for approval.

"Whatever he says goes, Pietor," the general manager replied.

"Are you Interpol or something?"

It was a fair question. Schorel had only introduced Reilly as someone who needed to view archived footage.

"Worse than that, Pietor," Schorel said. "He's my boss."

* * *

They worked well beyond the shift change. By 1:00 a.m., Reilly had sixty-seven photographs on his cell. But rather than emailing them stateside from his iPhone, which he couldn't trust, he went to the Kensington Diplomat business center.

There, he disconnected the computer from the internet. Taking it offline was his first line of defense in case it had been hacked. Next, he connected the cellphone to the hotel PC via a USB cable. For the next hour he download, cropped, and uploaded the best of the photos in high-resolution jpegs to his own thumb drive. But before attaching them to a succession of emails, he had an afterthought. It was a simple one. *Don't trust this computer coming back online.*

Reilly shuddered. He deleted the photo work he'd done on the PC, handwrote a *BROKEN* sign and taped it to the HP monitor. For good measure, he unplugged and disconnected the hard drive, and carried it out of the business center to his room.

Reilly fully intended to walk the half mile to the American Embassy on Boulevard du Régent. But it was after 2:00 a.m. and he was exhausted. He decided to lie down on his bed and close his eyes, thinking he'd rest only for a few minutes.

* * *

A warm breeze blew across the bay, but Reilly couldn't feel it. The waves washed across his feet, but he didn't get wet. Reilly looked at the sun blaring down on the beach. He squinted and blinked. The moon appeared in its place.

This was a familiar place. *But where?* he thought. Reilly turned around. He saw a mustard yellow building in the distance glistening in the moonlight. In front of it were smaller structures painted in the whitest white. He stepped forward onto the sand, yet he had no sense of walking. He was only aware of the emptiness, which now included the buildings. *Mexico? Mazatlán?* He blinked and tried to remember. Daylight again. *Yes. Mazatlán.*

Reilly entered the resort from the beach. Couches, chairs, a coffee station, concierge, and check-in desk—all empty. He could hear his footsteps echo on a highly polished marble floor, again without awareness of his feet touching the ground.

An elevator. He pressed the button. The door opened. He stepped in, turned around, and the door immediately reopened to a hotel room.

Somewhere else. Where am I?

Inside the room, the wide-screen TV was on, displaying a KR logo. Reilly picked up the remote on the dresser. He changed the channel. A CCTV camera appeared, showing the lobby and a man taking pictures as he walked through. He changed the channel again. Another closed-circuit camera. The same man in the basement snapping shots of the hotel boiler.

Now another channel. The video displayed the security office with the photographer on all the monitors, each covering a different area of the hotel. Then, the man appeared full frame in the CCTV camera. He smiled directly into the camera. It was a cold, heartless smile.

With one hand, the man removed his glasses. With the other, he stroked his stubble, which flaked off.

Reilly knew there shouldn't be any audio on the closed-circuit cameras, but he distinctly heard laughter. Cruel mocking laughter. Then a comment directed through the TV to him.

"There's nothing you can do," the man said with a Hungarian accent.

He stepped closer to the camera.

"There's nothing you can do." He now spoke with a distinct Russian accent.

The man was Jani Bakó. Then he suddenly became Smug in Tokyo, and with a blink of his mind's eye, the Russian he had seen in Moscow.

Reilly hit the power button on his remote. The screen went to black. He heard the sound of rustling sheets behind him. Reilly turned. There, in bed, was Marnie Babbitt, kicking the covers off, sexy, naked, and inviting.

She smiled. But it wasn't the smile he knew. It was the man's smile, ice-cold.

Marnie spread her legs, and he moved forward.

"Come to bed," she said. She opened her arms beckoning and repeating her invitation. "Come to bed." Then, "There's nothing you can do."

Reilly stopped. She said it again with Bakó's voice in sync from the TV set.

"No!" Reilly heard himself say.

He ran out of the room, but instead of the hallway, he found himself back in the lobby. Now the area was a battle zone. Bodies were everywhere. Blood spilling from severed body parts. Fires still smoldered. A cacophony of wails and cries mixed with moans and last gasps.

Reilly stumbled through the wreckage, eventually tripping over a fallen beam. He landed hard on the ground, facing the entrance. There, he saw Bakó standing and smiling.

He turned away, discovering he was lying next to the little boy from Tokyo who was clutching his teddy bear. The boy's eyes were open, but with no life behind them. And yet, he spoke in a whisper.

"There's nothing you can do."

He said it again, this time mixed with the man's voice and a third time with Marnie's.

It repeated again and again until a loud scream cut them off. It was Reilly's own cry that awakened him from the worst nightmare of his life.

* * *

Reilly bolted upright, shaking and covered in perspiration. He was awake, but the dream remained completely vivid. Every disturbing image. Every detail.

It was 5:45 a.m. A shower would help cleanse him emotionally.

Reilly shaved, all the while seeing Bakó's eyes peer through the fogged bathroom mirror. He had to find out if Bakó was Smug. The dream told him they were one and the same. If there was any chance in hell, Veronica Severi would confirm it.

He dressed in a black T-shirt and jeans, slipped on loafers, and grabbed a black sports coat. The thumb drive was in his pants pocket along with his passport.

Reilly was finally out the door at 6:30 a.m. and at the embassy twenty minutes later via a circuitous route. He was certain no one had followed him.

Talking his way in was not difficult. Convincing the CIA station chief that he had important files to email to Langley was another. It required a call to Bob Heath at home and Heath going to work. All of this took another forty-five minutes. Under the eye of the overnight desk agent, Reilly emailed the photographs on his thumb drive.

Reilly passed on the offer of breakfast at the embassy. He had to work with Liam Schorel on accelerating the Diplomat to Red Hotel status.

61

YALTA, CRIMEAN PENINSULA

UKRAINE

Andre Miklos sat with his feet up on an ottoman on the third-story veranda of an Airbnb rental. He had a magnificent view of the Black Sea and was enjoying a break from his preparations. The assassin puffed lightly on a hand-rolled Cuaba Exclusivos Cuban cigar and sipped a glass of Russian Standard Vodka. He held a yellow pad with a to-do list on his lap, but hadn't looked at it in the last twenty minutes. Only four boxes remained unchecked.

Miklos listened to a movie that was on the living room TV. The sound was amplified through a larger five-point Bose system. The score swelled. He waved his hand through the air as if he were conducting. It was a soundtrack he knew well. As it began to crescendo he got up and went inside, continuing to conduct the rising score to the action scene in the film.

While doing so, he studied photographs, notes, and maps he'd taped to the wall. His eyes scanned the photographs, a timeline, and a city street map with three routes highlighted in different colors.

Miklos stood back and admired his planning, his hand still leading the orchestra. He took all but five photos down, each in time with the music. Then the schedule came down and finally the map. He stared at the remaining pictures, photographs he had shot in the guise of the Hungarian architect. They were certainly worth the three hundred euro bottle of wine. Perfect photographs of the Kensington Diplomat Hotel's most vulnerable areas—the street-side entrance, the lobby, the basement power plant, and the elevator banks. What interested him the most, however, was another part of the hotel. *Maybe the plan could be scaled down*, he thought. *Make it easier, more efficient, and eliminate any confusion over the actual objective.*

Miklos went to his laptop computer and ran off new photographs through a portable printer. *Yes*, he told himself. *Better.* Especially considering he already had an asset in place.

The music shifted tempo to an adagio passage, a momentary lull that he knew would build to his favorite part. He turned to the television screen and stood for the climax of the movie, one that hadn't been regularly scheduled on Ukrainian TV for years, but now played regularly on the Russian-held Crimean station.

The film, a silent classic, *Battleship Potemkin*, included a score added in 1950 comprised of three Dmitri Shostakovich symphonies. It dramatically depicted the 1905 proletariat uprising against the Cossack army and a mutiny aboard the tsarist ship that sowed the seeds for the Russian Revolution.

The music, one of many scores composed or inserted in the film over the years, swelled as the tsar's troops approached the top of the Odessa Steps behind the citizens cheering the mutineers who had overthrown the tsar's ship commander and crew. Suddenly, a woman screamed. People turned to the danger.

Tension built. Would the Cossacks shoot? *Of course*, Miklos smiled. *Martyrs must die to light the revolutionary fuse.*

One row of white jacketed soldiers was followed by a second. Scores of panicked citizens began running down the steps.

The first tsarist soldier aimed and shot. Then more.

A cripple bounded down the steps. A baby carriage rolled out of control. A student with broken glasses stared at the inevitable slaughter.

Men, women, children, and the elderly died as they ran. A mother picked up her dying child and faced the Cossacks. The caption read, "Don't shoot!" But the soldiers did.

Stopping the inevitable? Miklos thought. *There is no stopping the inevitable. I am the messenger of the inevitable.*

Miklos watched the magnificent poetic violence unfold in the 1925 Sergei Eisenstein movie, as powerful today as when it was filmed.

Now all the Cossacks fired. The good people of Odessa fell. *Necessary casualties*, Miklos said to himself. *Just as others must die.*

The massacre on screen would have continued had the crew of the *Potemkin*, moored in the Black Sea harbor, not mutinied. But they had. Heroically and for the sake of the people. *Comrades.*

Now the huge cannons aboard the battleship, in the hands of the mutineers, aimed at the Cossacks massacring the citizens.

One of the big guns discharged. The first volley of the new order.

Then another, and another.

The strings pulsed. The timpani pounded and the brass blared in sync with the ship's cannon fire. The Cossacks showed no mercy for the oppressors.

Miklos heard Nikolai Gorshkov's voice in the trumpets and his own calling in the rhythmic beat of the drums.

This was the story of the revolution that overthrew the hated tsars in the twentieth century. This would be the story of Russia's renewal in the twenty-first century.

Andre Miklos was the great cannon on the *Potemkin*. The tsar was NATO.

Miklos placed five new photographs on the wall. "Yes," he said aloud, admiring his planning. "Yes."

The film's score built to a final emotionally charged climax. He imagined the soundtrack playing against the destruction he would soon create and the spark it would ignite.

"Yes," he said one more time.

62

"Hi buddy, sorry about the sleep deprivation," Reilly apologized to Heath.

"Comes with the territory," Heath answered. "So does bad news."

This threw Reilly. "Not a match?"

"Oh, Veronica got a match all right. That's the bad news. The very bad news. The good news would have been if you had nothing to worry about. But she came back with a reliability factor of 100 percent. No equivocation."

Reilly exhaled deeply into the phone.

"We'll work with you. Whatever you need," the CIA agent said, recognizing his friend's apprehension.

"The first thing is figuring out when," Reilly said.

"Any ideas?"

"Perhaps. How do you spell NATO?"

* * *

Reilly was waiting for Schorel when he came into work.

"Liam, do you have a NATO schedule covering the rest of the summer through the fall?"

"Ah, good morning. Yes, a general one."

"Get it, please."

The hotel GM produced a document showing upcoming NATO conferences. There was the military committee conference in August, ministers of defense meetings in September, and ministers of foreign affairs meetings in October.

"And bookings for these events."

"Usually a lot. We're on the approved list."

"Check."

Schorel had to dig into reservations to see who had already booked with NATO discount codes. He came back after an hour with the names of 394 guests over the three conference dates.

Reilly examined the portfolio, but nothing jumped out at him.

"Do you still have avails?"

"Yes, and there are always changes and additions."

"Do you know who these people are?"

"Officials and their staffs, if they're using the discounts. Beyond that, no."

"Damn," Reilly said. He thought about the dead Romanian folk singer again and the Ukrainian separatists in Kiev. "I'll take these, but it may be too narrow. What about all the bookings right through the end of the year?"

"Thousands. Tens of thousands, Dan. They'll be on your registration portal, too."

* * *

Reilly wrapped up with Schorel and immediately called Heath on his cell. The CIA operative reminded Reilly they couldn't assume the Diplomat was the only target or even the best one in Brussels. Proscribed practice would suggest Smug had cased other locations as well.

"True, but he spent an extraordinary amount of time and effort here," Reilly said. "In my estimation, we're at the top of the list."

Heath listened to his friend's concern and vowed to circle around to all of his sources.

Reilly's next call was to Spike Boyce in Chicago.

"Spike, I need you to press F7 or whatever the hell you do to output all the reservations for the Kensington Diplomat in Brussels from now through the end of the year. Flag any that look hinky to you."

"Hinky? If you're asking me to profile by name?" The IT executive voiced a definite exception.

"No, I'm not. Hinky in terms of obvious targets. People or groups that might make especially big headlines if *something* happened."

"Oh input our guest list into a crystal ball, that's all you need?" Boyce asked sarcastically.

Reilly had no appetite for humor.

Boyce realized his *faux pas*. "When do you need it and in what format?"

"Immediately and on an Excel spreadsheet with names and addresses."

"You kicking it up somewhere? Is that kosher? Because if you are . . ."

"Spike, we ended our conversation one sentence earlier."

* * *

Reilly studied the list Schorel provided. Ministers, aides, and their plus-ones, all credentialed by a diplomatic billing code. None of the names meant anything to him. He cross-checked their nationalities against the twenty-eight members of the NATO alliance. *No outliers from other nations using NATO discounts*, he concluded.

Of course, he didn't think an answer would come that easily. He hoped Boyce would have more.

There was one more call he had to make. The hardest one.

"Edward, sorry to bother you at home, but it's important."

"All okay, Dan?"

"Afraid not. Brussel's has been cased thoroughly. Top to bottom. Confirmed photos."

"Jesus," the Kensington Royal president exclaimed. "How did you find out?"

"In the course of briefing Schorel."

Shaw mulled over the comment. "Care to explain?"

Reilly decided not to torpedo Schorel for now, since he needed him to carry through on the security upgrades. "Let's just say we got lucky, but there's more."

"I'd expect so."

"We know who it is," Reilly added. "The bomber from Tokyo."

Reilly heard Shaw gasp.

"You're certain?" he asked.

"100 percent."

"I can assume that percentage comes from some pretty well-connected friends of yours." It wasn't really a question.

"Yes. But I can confirm it as well."

"What?" Shaw asked.

"I saw him myself. In Moscow. Inside the Kremlin. We have every reason to believe that this is a Russian mission and has been from the beginning."

"Against us?"

"Not directly."

"Then how?"

"Our guests."

"Who?"

"In Tokyo it may have been just one person and although not our property, we believe a similar attack in Kiev targeted a visiting delegation. We're looking into who it could be in Brussels. But considering NATO, we've got a lot to consider."

"Dan, you keep saying *we*."

Shaw was right. Reilly wished he had been more careful with his language. There was definitely a bigger *we* than Kensington Royal.

"Yes, sir. This is going way up the ladder."

"Way up?"

"Way up."

Reilly got another incoming. He asked to put his boss on hold. Shaw obliged.

"Hello, Daniel." Marnie Babbitt had that certain hunger in her voice. It had been more than a month since their last rendezvous. "When can I see you?" she asked.

"Soon. I'm so sorry. It's been nonstop." He automatically gathered up the papers even though she couldn't see them.

"You go to bed every night?" she asked.

"Of course."

"So do I. Shame I have to make mine when I get up in the morning."

Reilly laughed. "Yeah, tough not having room service."

"My point exactly," she added.

"Hey, can I call you back in a few?" Reilly pleaded. "I'm on with Chicago."

"Sure."

Reilly returned to Shaw.

"Cannon up to speed?" Shaw asked.

"Completely. He'll be getting photographs he can distribute to all the GMs on our lists."

"Okay. Beyond whatever you're doing, engage that special committee of yours. They may have some worthwhile ideas."

"Will do."

"And daily updates."

"Right," Reilly said.

"Daily, Dan," Shaw emphasized in a sharper tone.

They said goodbye. Reilly breathed deeply. He needed a moment before calling Marnie back, but she beat him to it.

"You realize anywhere in Europe is a puddle jump away," she said.

"Oh yeah."

Marnie's pitch was having the desired effect.

"Hours. Maybe minutes."

"I'm sorry. It's been busy."

"Sure would love not to have to make the bed tomorrow."

"I may be in London soon."

"Soon? Too long. I'm thinking right now."

"Now?"

"Yes! I'm in the lobby. On my way to Bonn for a meeting tomorrow. Just figured . . ."

"Oh, you figured wonderfully."

"Then how about giving me your room number or risk me taking the wrong man down, if you get my drift?"

Reilly got the message and put away all his work. *After all,* he thought, *Spike Boyce had work to do before he could make his next move.*

* * *

For the next twelve hours Reilly dealt with varying forms of pressure. Marnie took care of some. The rest Reilly dealt with in the adjacent living room area of his junior suite.

"I need you, buddy. Serious shit here in Brussels," he told Alan Cannon on the phone.

"Which box?" Cannon referenced the Eisenhower Method.

"Upper left. Number 1. URGENT and IMPORTANT. It knocks everything else out."

"I'll get a flight as soon as I wrap up Stockholm."

"Thanks."

More calls.

Shaw phoned for an update, then Heath called in with news.

"Severi's still working on Smug's identity. And we're checking if any of our older agents recognize him. Or retirees. The hard part is tracking down decommissioned agents. You know, they often like to disappear. Spain, Portugal's coast, the Caribbean. If they stick around, chances are they'll get a fat offer from a security consulting firm, write their novel, or find their way to Fox News. Sometimes they're willing to help us out." He paused, "Sometimes they won't."

"The Caribbean is beginning to sound pretty good to me."

"In another life," the CIA agent joked. "You like your frequent flier miles too much."

Reilly pushed the bedroom door open. The sight of a beautiful woman asleep in his bed made him think.

"I don't know. Three retirement checks and no calls in the middle of the night. I could live with that."

When he hung up another notion nagged at him again. *Was there more to Marnie Babbitt?*

He hated having the suspicion and finally put it to rest at 1:14 a.m. when he returned to bed.

Reilly quietly crawled under the sheets and pulled Marnie Babbitt into his arms. He thought it would have to be their last night until the crisis was over. She moaned softly, but didn't wake. At least she was right. She wouldn't have to make her bed in the morning.

63

WASHINGTON, DC

THE WHITE HOUSE

"Let's have it," the president ordered.

Alex Crowe expanded the scope of the intelligence briefing to include Secretary of State Elizabeth Matthews, a senator he had defeated in the primary.

Crowe considered himself lucky that he had knocked Matthews out early. The 55-year-old Nebraskan knew much more about international relations than he did. It was her stiff, relatively humorless personality that hurt her with voters on the campaign trail. But Matthews's personality served her for the job at hand.

She was the last to enter the situation room in the basement of the White House. Already around the table were the president's leading military experts, collectively the Joint Chiefs. Army General Jeffrey Jones, Chairman of the Joint Chiefs, along with Admirals Steve Hirsen and JJ Koehler, and Air Force General Ed Stuckmeyer. Also present was CIA Director Gerald Watts.

Crowe went to the CIA director first. "Gerald?"

"Mr. President, we don't like what we're seeing. All indications point to Gorshkov attempting a repeat of Crimea, or worse, one not so covert. He could respond to a direct provocation to justify ground troops, or he could inflame tensions between ethnic Russian minorities and the standing governments of Russia's former satellites to create a moral imperative. He sees those countries and the Russian minorities living a second-class status as the 'near abroad,' well within his sphere of influence."

Admiral Koehler raised his hand. "Sir, it could happen in one or more nations quickly. I'd be lying to you if I said NATO was prepared across the board. Some countries more, most less. Romania and Poland are among the best defended. But against a full-scale assault, they'd all be pushovers. Gorshkov bragged he could take Warsaw or Bucharest in—"

"Yes, yes, yes. Two days," the president said. "Tell me something I don't know."

"I think he's testing NATO," Secretary Matthews said. "And he's testing you, Mr. President. He'll move on one nation, and depending upon what you do, another and another. He's expecting you'll do nothing."

"Not we?"

"No," she declared. "It really does come down to you."

"Come on, we don't offer any threat," Kimball interrupted.

Matthews continued. "We, and by we, I now mean the United States and NATO, continue to do nothing. Russia's flights over the English Channel? His submarines in the North Sea, the joint operations with China in the South China Sea. His attacks against our interests in Syria, and the sleepers that he still sends to the US? What have we done?"

"Nothing," General Jones interjected. "He's checking for our resolve and our appetite for engagement. Unfortunately, no one in Congress will want to put his—"

"Or her," Matthews interrupted.

"Or her signature on a war authorization vote. Once again, he's counting on that. The same from EU nations, which will invariably argue that a regime change won't matter. We'll still trade with Russia. Sure, there may be renewed sanctions, but he'll have his spoils. Then game over."

"So unless the president of the United States, pardon the third person," Crowe said, "leads the way, Gorshkov will restore the old map just the way it was."

"More or less," was Matthews' response.

"Come on Elizabeth. Which is it?"

"Both. After his land grabs, those nations will project a modicum of independence, greater than they had under Stalin, Khrushchev, or Gorbachev. But they'll be the buffer to the West that Gorshkov seeks, locked into his power grids, his oil and gas reserves, or whatever resources come from a new Chinese-Russian consortium that's developing."

"Authoritarian at its core, Elizabeth?"

She paused. "The Syrian immigration issue and Islamic terrorism will be the deciding factors. To contain both, it will take an authoritarian regime. A dictatorship makes for a much more effective policeman than a parliamentary or democratic rule of law."

The president wasn't hearing anything new, including solutions.

64

Miklos welcomed his men with hearty handshakes and bear hugs. One had the look of a salesman, another a college professor, the third a tourist on a Canadian passport. They were all ex-KGB and loyal to Andre Miklos. It was their first meeting since Kiev. They'd have more, but never at the same place. Today's was at a $144 a night Airbnb on Rue St. Bernard.

They spent the first half hour trading stories about their travels over the last few months and the women they had had. With the second glass of vodka, Miklos brought them to the business at hand. He'd prepared a detailed map of the area on a poster board. It was everyone's job to memorize the one-way streets, the locations of known CCTV cameras, and the likely trouble spots.

Once everyone was ready to move on, Miklos introduced another board, this one with photographs.

"Jesus," said Miklos' man, the one dressed as a salesman. "You getting booked on a National Geographic photography excursion? Look at all those pictures!"

"I had a most hospitable hotel manager."

"I'd say," the salesman laughed.

"But this plan's different than the others," Miklos continued. He reviewed what he had come up with: an amazingly simple mission compared to their previous strikes. "The main challenge, getting the device in. Here's how we'll do it."

When he finished running through the plan, Miklos invited questions.

Miklos was so thorough there were none. The team liked the approach. It was elegant from an operational standpoint. Little exposure. Little risk. All the better to get back to spending their money.

"One more thing." Miklos produced an envelope from his jacket. It contained more photographs, all the same.

"Don't lose these," Miklos said as he distributed the pictures.

Now questions followed.

"Who's the guy?" the man posing as a visiting college professor asked.

"Someone to look out for. Someone who may be looking for me. For us. If you see him, notify me immediately. "

"A cop?" the salesman asked.

"Not a cop. He's an executive with the hotel company."

"We're worried about a suit?"

"Yes. This one."

"Does he have a name?"

Miklos' eyes narrowed. "Reilly. Daniel Reilly."

* * *

Schorel unfurled blueprints for the Kensington Diplomat Hotel. The business at hand: prepare active defenses against the anticipated strike.

As they spread the sheets out, Reilly asked about the subject. "Did he seem happy when he left?"

"I wouldn't call him happy. I'd say *satisfied*. Yes, he was satisfied."

"No shit. He got everything he needed."

"Not these blueprints," Schorel volunteered. "I didn't show them to him."

"Are these the only ones?"

"Yes, here," Schorel said confidently.

Reilly picked up on his answer. "Here, Liam?"

"Well," he hesitated. "There's a duplicate set at the Royal Library of Belgium and probably elsewhere. But that doesn't mean he got them."

"Trust me," the CIA-side of Reilly said, "he has a copy. Send over your head of security to ask if the librarians have any record of him coming in. Have him bring the photograph, but I wouldn't be surprised if he used a different disguise. If they come up with anything positive, I want a description, maybe even a sketch, and definitely a signature if one exists."

Schorel made the call. When he was off, Reilly reviewed more in his urgent and important boxes.

"Okay, first, pull together a list of all upcoming events in the city," Reilly continued. "Conferences, group meetings, everything related."

Schorel stammered, "I can get that. Or at least what we have."

"Everything! And then these." Reilly passed him a list of structural changes.

"These will be difficult because of city regulations," Schorel pleaded.

"Fuck the regulations. Start without permits."

Schorel looked nervous.

"Now, Liam."

Once out of his office and beyond Reilly's sight, Liam Schorel took two puffs of his inhaler. The last twenty-four hours had not been good for his asthma.

* * *

Reilly checked his watch, anxious to hear from Heath. Two hours now. No text. No calls. There was so much beyond his control.

He went to Schorel's computer and, not waiting for Schorel's research, he typed two key words into Google: Brussels, events. A series of music festivals came up on the search. Ommegang, Festival Musiq'3, Royal Park, and Classissimo. He also checked out a number of film festivals and the Belgium Beer Weekend. Nothing had the ring of politics.

* * *

Reilly's cell rang. Heath.

"Reilly, Severi's got some things for us," he said nonspecifically. "She aged our friend back to his early twenties. Multiple versions from the screen grabs, and the renderings generated from your description. She also put him in different outfits. Army, agency, and plain clothes. With shades, without. Moustache and beard, and clean-shaven. You'll get them in a bit."

"In a bit?"

"Yeah. Chain of command. Meeting with the director first. Then you."

"Okay," Reilly said. "At least everyone's taking this seriously. But for my money, Smug's proximity to the top is not coincidental."

"Step by step. And once we've got the go-ahead, we'll reach out to Belgium and other EU nations' customs to see if they ID'd Mr. Smug at transit points."

"Good luck, but I doubt they'll come up with anything. This guy's far too careful."

"We'll be working it, brother."

"Just hurry."

* * *

Schorel returned a few minutes later. "Our security chief is on his way."

"Good. Now let's pick up where we left off."

Reilly began with the easiest upgrades from threat condition Blue. "American flag?"

"Down."

"Review threat evacuation plan with staff."

"Starting today at 1400 and 2000. Hitting both the day and night shifts," Schorel replied. "I'll be there."

"Good, I'll join you. Next, increased security patrols in all public areas. And report anyone suspicious or suspicious packages."

"It'll be part of our meeting. We'll also drum that into all staff members including maintenance and housekeeping."

"Check all ID's at check-in, remove any large containers, restrict and lock roof access, all electrical, engineering and mechanical rooms, check public restrooms hourly, keep meeting rooms not in use locked."

"Understood. I'll issue those orders," Schorel said. "We'll also check outside vendors at entry and make sure fuel trucks don't have access until inspected."

"You may need more staff. Put them through complete background checks. No one gets hired without passing."

"Understood."

"Now onto the additional Orange upgrades. Since there's a higher level of protection in the final threat condition, this is a shorter list."

The basics included a ban on stored luggage, all incoming packages would have to be inspected with the guest present, all entrances would require ID's, and the hotel would enforce strict supervision at shift changes.

Finally, the changes that would make the Kensington Diplomat a Red Hotel.

"Everyone goes through metal detectors, Liam. Guests and staff."

"I'll order the equipment now."

"You'll need more security. We'll talk about covering you with a vetted outside company. I have a committee that can make solid recommendations."

"Thank you."

"No vehicles can be left unattended within twenty meters of the building. That means you'll need to have the police ban parking and immediately tow cars that do park."

"Harder."

"An absolute must," Reilly replied. "And we'll send you detailed construction plans that Chicago has worked up to install permanent rising bollards and delta barriers. The bollards probably the less offensive option."

"That's where we're going to have problems. You can't imagine the endless paperwork in such a historical city. Nothing moves fast here."

Reilly reconsidered what he'd said before about permits. "Then set a meeting with the mayor. Today. The video will make a convincing argument."

"It's not that easy."

"Neither is planning a bombing," Reilly said angrily. "But we're past that. It's been accomplished most efficiently, Liam, with your help."

"Damn it, Reilly!"

"Schorel. Tell you what. Set the meeting, we'll both go."

* * *

Mayor Lina Janssens was as unpleasant as they get. Grey-haired, thin eyes, hair in a bun, tailored black suit. It all telegraphed a purposeful coldness, reinforced by her decision to remain seated behind her desk when Reilly approached. To Reilly, all the signs said she was going to be trouble. The greeting didn't dissuade.

"Mr. Reilly, Mr. Schorel. What's so important that I had to alter my schedule?" she said in perfect English.

Reilly took the lead. "Thank you, Madame Mayor. I'm—"

"I've been told who you are. Get to the point, Mr. Reilly."

"This is an urgent matter."

"It better be," she chided.

"It is," Reilly replied, equally sternly. "We have to fast-track structural changes to the exterior of the Kensington Diplomat."

"There's a department that oversees this." She curtly addressed the person she knew. "Liam, you're familiar with the rules."

"Yes, Mayor Janssens."

"Then why are we meeting?"

Schorel prepared to speak. Reilly held his hand up. "I'll take this. Mayor, our hotel was surveilled by a terrorist. We're going to add hydraulic pop-up barriers street-side. Mr. Schorel informed me we need the city's approval. That's why we're here."

"As I said, we have a department. They have their procedures. That's the way it's done."

Reilly interrupted. "We don't have time for paperwork, Madame Mayor. You don't either. Brussels, of all places, grasps the danger. You must realize that given recent events. This threat is real. The subject has already pulled off a successful operation. We have connected him to the attack in Tokyo. He may be responsible for more bombings in other cities. And now that you know, Madame Mayor, you have the ability to help prevent another horrible attack in *your* city, at our hotel or other soft targets. But right now, my concern is the Kensington Diplomat."

"Don't lecture me, Mr. Reilly. When the Brussels police tell me there's a problem, then I'll deal with it."

"And you'll be too late, madame."

"Who is this mystery man who so worries you? We're hunting ISIS cells and you come to me with one man?"

"One man with a deadly team and a country behind him," Reilly hissed. "Cut your red tape and you'll never hear from me again."

"If you're trying to intimidate me, you're falling far short."

Reilly removed his business card and a USB drive from his jacket pocket. He deposited both on her desk.

"Put this drive in your computer. Call me after you watch the video on it. It'll look very familiar to you. Bloody terrorist attacks tend to have an unmistakable sameness. Death." He paused, but only for her to absorb everything he had said. "My cell number is on the card. I'll be at the Diplomat a few more days." He took a beat. "Overseeing the construction."

* * *

"Jesus, Reilly!" Cannon exclaimed when he heard what his colleague had done. The KR security director, now at the Diplomat, met Reilly at the Bistango bar off the lobby. "Trying to cause an international incident?"

"Figured if I could bully my way through the Kremlin, what's a Brussels mayor?"

"Pick your poison," Cannon added. "An injection from the tip of an umbrella or a bullet in the head down a dark European street." Alan

Cannon was only half joking. "There could be repercussions."

"Pile drivers bang away tomorrow. Bollards are on the way from Bonn. A row of eight ten-inch B3X's will be up and functional in seventy-two hours. Fast. They deploy in one second. We can have multiple proximity switches," Reilly explained.

"And if the city shuts you down?"

"The news will have her for breakfast. I'll provide the hollandaise sauce."

Cannon slapped Reilly on the back. "So what can I do?"

"Meetings. Introduce yourself to Belgium's intelligence forces."

"Coordinate the uncoordinated?" Cannon asked.

It was no secret that Belgium's security agencies were separated by language—French and Flemish—districts, and operational authority. They lacked the resources of other countries, and yet Brussels was the capital of the EU and the home of NATO. They were underfunded and even outmanned by the number of suspected terrorists living in the country, and they didn't have a unified army.

"Bring them into the tent," Reilly answered. "Gently. Put it in terms of a 'tip' that we received. Not Schorel's blunder. And emphasize that we're still investigating. Nothing to launch publicly."

"There is another option," Alan Cannon stated.

Reilly anticipated Cannon would raise the point. "Shut down the hotel."

"Correct. Take the target out of play."

"No," Reilly argued.

"It would legally shield us," Cannon affirmed. "The company. The stock."

"Yes, it would. But then the target checks in somewhere else. At least we know what's coming."

"Are you so sure?" Cannon questioned. "Standard ops are to surveil multiple potential targets, then select the softest. Elevating the Diplomat to Red could possibly take it out of play. Closing it down for a critical period will guarantee it."

Reilly exhaled deeply. "This *is* the target, Alan. I'm certain."

"You don't know that. And I think Shaw would back a closing."

"I disagree. It would hit the bottom line hard. Hell, you know how many bomb threats we get every day at different locations?"

"Crazies. Not credible. This is different," Cannon replied.

"Right. And I say we don't close down the hotel, we defend against the event."

"It'll make the problem go away."

"For us. But I believe this isn't an indiscriminate terrorist attack. It's strategic, Alan. Smug is targeting a specific guest or group for a specific reason. They check out of here, they'll end up somewhere else. And wherever they go, the fight will go to them. At least I believe they're coming and we have the best chance of stopping it."

Cannon shrugged. "We're at least obligated to run it by Shaw." He corrected himself. "I'm obligated."

"Alan, it could be weeks or months."

"Could be and sure, we'd lose a lot of revenue, but knowing what we know . . ."

Reilly couldn't win an argument with a feeling alone. "Okay, two things. We'll go to Shaw and present the argument. But before that, talk to the GMs of other hotels here. Find out if anyone has taken special or at least undue observable interest in their properties. Smug went to extra pains to analyze the vulnerabilities of the Diplomat. If he'd been seriously interested in another hotel, maybe someone would have spotted him."

Cannon didn't instantly reply.

"Alan?" Reilly asked.

"Just thinking about what I'd say and whether they'd cooperate. I could say too little or too much."

"It'll be pretty obvious what we're doing street-side at the Diplomat," Reilly explained. "Tell them Kensington Royal is taking a proactive stance after Tokyo. We're training our staffs to be vigilant. 'If they see something, say something.' Hell, share the basics of our tiered alert status. The more this becomes industry-wide, the safer the industry will be. Deal?"

"Deal," Cannon said. "But we still go back to Chicago and give Shaw the choice. Deal?"

Reilly shook his colleague's hand. "Deal."

Minutes later, Reilly was back in Schorel's office.

"Anything new?" Reilly asked.

"Going through the bookings again. Who's coming for what," the general manager offered.

"And?"

"I really can't say I understand what I'm looking for."

"Then try this. Any groups from Romania, Ukraine, or the Baltic states."

"Why there?"

"History."

65

BRUSSELS, BELGIUM

IXELLES DISTRICT

The next morning the man who looked like a college professor knocked on Miklos' door.

"Yes?"

"It's Petoir." Of course that wasn't his real name.

Miklos unlocked the deadbolt. "Is anything wrong?" Petoir was hours early for the next briefing.

He entered and went to the window, moving the curtain slightly aside. He peered up and down the street and stepped back.

"We have a problem."

Miklos studied his man. He was visibly nervously and worried that he had been followed.

"What's wrong?"

"I drove by the target this morning. They're installing hydraulic barriers outside. I saw dogs, too."

Miklos sat across from his operative and nodded thoughtfully.

"You're not worried?" the man asked.

"I plan."

"Getting a device inside is going to be nearly impossible. The security measures . . ."

"Will not be a problem."

"But?"

"It's already there." Miklos explained.

* * *

Andre Miklos had been an A student in theatrical makeup and disguises at the Soviet Andropov Institute, the KGB's highly secretive spy school.

So who shall it be today? He was partial to innocuous, sometimes gender-bending characters, both old and young. On the other hand, he could hide in plain sight and pose as a credentialed member of the Brussels police, a French NATO lieutenant, or a Belgium officer.

Brussels offered Miklos so many choices. The federal police answered to no fewer than six governments. The nation's constabulary was comprised of 196 individual police forces and brigades, working under the mayors of the disparate municipalities. In Brussels alone, roughly fifty police agencies covered the territory. The weaknesses were widely published in Russia's Sputnik news and reported around the world.

Hiding in plain sight. Nowhere better than Brussels.

66

THE KENSINGTON DIPLOMAT

For the fifth time Schorel reviewed all the locations where he took the man he presumed to be an architect. "I met him here in the lobby," he told Reilly. "We walked around the public spaces."

"Let's do the walk again," Reilly insisted. He was feeling increasingly frustrated with his GM. "Everywhere."

They walked around the lobby. Schorel retraced the steps through the lobby, outside, back inside to the kitchen, down into the basement, and finally the executive offices.

Reilly pictured what a terrorist would look for. *Structural weaknesses. The power plant. The fuel intake. Entrances and exits. Traffic flow.* Using Tokyo and Kiev as recent case histories, the Kensington Diplomat was an easy target. *An easier target,* in fact.

They ended where they'd begun. The lobby.

"Anywhere else, Liam?"

"That's it." He stopped. "Oh, and we stopped in the florist shop. I'm sure Madame Ketz would love to say hello to you."

"Let's do it."

They crossed the lobby to the old florist's small shop. Entering, they were engulfed by penetrating scents from the beautiful flowers;

the very things that surrounded Madame Ketz's life.

* * *

"Madame Ketz, so nice to see you again," Reilly warmly offered. "You look wonderful."

"Oh, Mr. Reilly, it is my pleasure." She remembered him from previous visits. "I hope you've been well."

Reilly noticed she had aged, but still exuded a timeless cultured civility and a compelling spirit that lived for making others happier.

"Definitely," he said. "And you?"

"All the better, seeing you."

As they chatted, Reilly surveyed the shop. *Nothing out of the ordinary.* Small bouquets in colorful glass vases on a counter display; a selection of cards, ribbons, and wrapping paper behind the cash register; and further back in the deep refrigerator, a variety of fresh flowers and a large plant in a deep metal pot. Nothing out of the ordinary. Of course when it was time to leave, Madame Ketz pinned a fresh yellow rose on his lapel.

"That's it," Schorel said back in the lobby.

Reilly corrected him. "The restaurant."

"Right. Sorry."

Bistango had two entrances. One near the florist, the other on the street.

The restaurant's actual footprint was carved out of older retail space. Its modern design had echoes of architect Victor Horta's work: art nouveau-inspired ironwork, downlit by golden spiral sconces, backed by glass and dramatic walls painted in a flat black. Modern copper wire statuary divided the dining areas and the bar where Reilly and Cannon got a drink. It all allowed for an open, airy environment. A floor-to-ceiling black wine rack stood at the far end of the restaurant, accentuating the restaurant's height. Bright red fabric chairs popped, giving the restaurant even more dynamic flair.

Reilly walked the length of Bistango, focusing on the public and semiprivate dining areas, the kitchen, and the bathrooms. He took a mental picture of the area, a lesson he'd learned in the army. Like everything in the hotel, he could now draw it accurately if he had to.

* * *

Belgium Malinois were well-suited dog breeds for police work, and they made great bomb-sniffing dogs—among the best in the world. They were more reliable than any devices yet developed for detecting and differentiating scents.

Those in service were rigorously trained and retested weekly to maintain a successful discovery rate. They worked best in thirty- to forty-five-minute shifts with success averages at 75 percent, and up to 90 percent when trained by the US Secret Service. But never 100 percent.

When a dog detected a scent it had been trained to identify, it would circle the object or area and assume an "alert" posture. However, poor training could lead to lower success percentages. Nervous or impatient handlers could completely throw a dog off. Telegraphing a gesture, an emotion, or a glance would travel right down the leash and lower success rates to 75 or 60 percent, or worse. As a result, dogs could completely miss a threat.

Natural diversions could also get in the way. If a dog was stressed or excited, it might overreact. Humidity level and air movement could also have a negative effect. If it were too hot, a dog's nose would dry up, while cold could kill scents.

Cold in the middle of summer. That was exactly what Andre Miklos was counting on.

67

LONDON

With Cannon on site in Brussels, Reilly decided to jump over to London to meet with his managers at the two London KR hotels. He'd make sure they were in line and be ready to move the properties up to a higher threat status if needed. It would also give him at least a night to put himself in Marnie's hands.

PORT ELIZABETH, GRENADINES

Heath took the ferry across the channel from Kingston to Port Elizabeth. The town was on the island of Bequia. From the port, everything was a short walk; the restaurants and pubs, the B and Bs and the galleries.

Port Elizabeth's population by the last count was 10,234. One of the residents was the owner of a small boat charter with a single 40' 3"-cabin Bavaria sailboat. Typically it sailed around the Grenadines to St. Lucia, Barbados, and Grenada. The owner was one of a crew of six.

Joe Lenczycki checked his email regularly. That's how customers usually contacted him. He also did background and credit checks of everyone. That was his training. He was ex-CIA, out of the trade for nineteen years.

For a few years, he'd belonged to CIRA, the Central Intelligence Retirees Association. But eventually Lenczycki dropped out. He cashed in his retirement, said goodbye to his friends, and quietly unplugged until he needed the internet for his business. That's how the agency found him.

Bob Heath sauntered up to a dockside office in front of a boat slip. Over the front door was a hand-painted but stylistic sign that read "Skip's Carib Cruises." *Simple. No frills*, Heath thought. *Straight and to the point.* Like everything he had read in his file.

Lenczycki's file covered twenty-seven years with the agency—from a recruit out of George Washington University with a poli-sci degree, to the CIA's rigorous training course in rural Virginia dubbed "The Farm," to his still classified field assignments

Joe Lenczycki was a standout, a personal discovery of CIA Director Richard M. Helms. He earned even more praise through the '70s and '80s from successive agency heads William E. Colby, George H. W. Bush, William Casey, and William Hedgcock Webster. Casey posted him to Russia, and Webster later assigned him to Germany in advance of President Reagan's visit. He was there when the Wall fell. For his last nine years, he supposedly sat at his Langley desk. *Supposedly.* Rumor had it that times he disappeared coincided with some significant breaking news:

- Crisis in Mindanao, Philippines, 1990

- Ten-Day War in Yugoslavia/Slovenia, 1991

- Georgian Civil War, 1992

- NATO's Operation Deliberate Force in the Bosnian War, 1995

- Sierra Leone Civil War, 1996

- Afghanistan, 1997

Joe Lenczycki was the real deal. As far as Heath could tell, his life was full of *didn'ts*. He didn't turn down tough assignments. He didn't talk about them with colleagues while he worked for the Company. He didn't spill the beans in a book after he left. He also didn't marry, he didn't take anyone up on the lucrative consulting offers at retirement, and he didn't tell anyone he moved away.

Lenczycki *did* get well out of the business. He returned to his favorite pastime growing up in Marblehead, Massachusetts. He bought a boat, sailed away, and became Skip Lenczycki.

Now in his late sixties, he was permanently moored in Port Elizabeth, and according to the limited information Heath could gather from his website, he had a girlfriend who helped him book guest cruises.

Heath opened the door to the cruise office. It was hardly an office, more of a small room with a desk, a phone, and a computer.

A sun-loving blonde in a loose-fitting floral muumuu sitting behind the desk smiled at Heath. "Hello there. Looks like you're ready to shed those duds."

Heath was dressed in tan slacks and a blue shirt. He carried a sports jacket on his arm.

"I wish," Heath said. He introduced himself. "I'm Bob."

"I'm Layla."

"Like the song?"

She smiled. "Yep, my parents were Clapton fans."

"Great song. You wear the name well."

By this time a man with a grey beard that hid years of hard living had spun 180 in his computer chair. He quickly sized up the visitor.

"I'll take it, Layla."

"Sure, honey."

"You didn't come here to rent my boat."

The comment was cold and not welcoming.

"No I didn't, Mr. Lenczycki."

"Boy, don't you guys ever dress casually?"

"Did you?"

"I tried to blend in with the natives. Care to tell me who you are and why you tracked me down?"

"I'm Bob Heath." He produced his agency business card. "Can we talk elsewhere?"

"Heath. Heath? A newbie?"

"Twelve years."

"Well, you're getting there," Lenczycki said. "Truth be told, I'm not interested."

Layla was pretending not to pay attention.

"A few minutes. I need your help."

"Of course you do."

"Please," Heath said.

Lenczycki looked at Layla. She shrugged.

"Let's take a walk," the sailor said. "And for Christ's sake, leave your jacket here and roll up your sleeves. At least try not to look like a goddamned stockbroker."

Heath had been briefed on Lenczycki. He was brash and bold, driven, and fiercely loyal. He also had a mildly sarcastic side that he often led with. The combination had made him one of the most liked agents at the Company. He was authentic then, and maybe more so now as a crusty sailor living the life in the Caribbean breeze.

Heath started, "Mr. Lenczycki—"

"No. Wrong. It's Skip. Nothing more. Nothing less. You're not at the fucking campus so chill a little. Take in the fresh air."

"I wish I could. But I'm not sure if time is on our side."

"Your side," Lenczycki replied. "I've heard that too many times before, so you can cut the crap. I'm retired. I moved down here to get away from the rest of the world. The last war here was in 1783, and it ended sixteen years later. The British and the French had their time owning and exploiting the Grenadines. In 1979 it finally got its independence. Sort of. Saint Vincent and the Grenadines remain part of the crown with the British monarch, the mother hen. That's the extent of my politics today. You're welcome to the rest of the fucked-up world. I'm happy. So whatever you're peddling, I'm not buying."

"I suppose you won't know until I get to it."

"Man," Lenczycki sighed, "I used to be like you. I took it all so seriously. And you know what? Things are worse now. But not to make this a total loss for you, I'll treat you to a St. Vincent Sunset Golden Rum." The ex-agent stopped to consider Heath, head to toe. "You look like you could use the Very Strong Rum. That's what it's called." He laughed. "And for good reason."

After a ten-minute walk filled with only small talk, they ended up at Basil's Beach Bar on Bay Street, a rustic joint that thrust out into the Caribbean.

St. Vincent Very Strong Rum was everything Lenczycki promised. They also ordered a delicious West Indian curry chicken and potato roti wrap. Heath returned to his agenda midway through their second drink.

"Skip, I need your help."

"Sure you do. The answer is no."

Heath lowered his voice. "Question for you. You automatically took the seat facing out."

"So?"

"So you could see everyone who came through that door." Heath nodded to the entrance. "Your eyes darted on our whole walk. You ushered me out of your office and away from Layla. You're thinking that whatever I have to ask you might be sensitive enough for someone to discourage you from answering."

"That kind of discouragement can prove permanent," Lenczycki said.

"And a bomb in a hotel? What kind permanent damage could that cause?"

"I stay away from hotels."

"Good for you. Other people don't," Heath remarked. "Families, kids, American diplomats."

Lenczycki eyes narrowed. "What's your point, Heath?" he said sternly.

"A simple one. I show you a few photographs, you tell me if they ring a bell."

"And if they do?"

"You help me out with some memories that come to mind. I listen, pick up the bill, and go away never the worse for the wear."

Lenczycki slowly glanced around the room. He recognized some of the patrons, but not all.

"Tell you what." He stood. "Different order. Pick up the bill, and we'll go to my boat. Then we'll talk."

* * *

Going to the boat meant sailing, or rather puttering out to sea under power without the crew. Fortunately Lenczycki had an extra pair of sneakers that fit Heath.

Twenty minutes off shore and beyond the reach of eyes, ears, or scopes, Lenczycki idled the 50hp Volvo diesel engine.

"This is my baby," he said. "Born in Germany, adopted by me nine years ago. $198,000. Expensive, but I don't have to send it college," he joked.

He spoke of the boat with real affection, from the teak decks to the solid fiberglass hull with a reinforced Kevlar shield. "Bulletproof," he added.

"Never can trust those gunner fish," Heath joked.

The sailor continued to boast about his boat, gushing over the three cabins, the salon, the wraparound dinette, the C-shaped galley, and even the head.

"Not sure it's on my bucket list when I cash out," Heath admitted.

"No, the suit fits you too well. You're more the consultant-type. Twelve years you said?"

"Yup. Hope to be out in another thirteen."

"That was a long time ago for me and a different world. You can have it," the former agent said.

"But it *was* your world and I need to dig back into it."

"Give me the goddamned pictures," Lenczycki exclaimed, exasperated.

Heath pulled a set of photos from his pants pocket.

"Here you go. Fifteen shots. A little crumpled," he noted.

Lenczycki quickly went through the first nine. "No." For each. "Don't know him. And can't you guys use real cameras? These shots are terrible."

"They're from an ATM and CCTV cameras."

"Hell, an iPhone would do you better."

"It would be easier if we knew who he was."

"I'm not going to be any help." He started to hand back the photographs.

"Keep going. There are only a few more," Heath implored. "Please."

Lenczycki looked at the next photo. Another screen grab from a Kensington Diplomat closed-circuit camera. "No," he said again, placing it on the bottom of the stack.

He was ready with another *no*, but paused. The ex-operative stopped and studied the photograph. It was one of Dr. Veronica Severi's age-regression outputs. The rendering depicted a younger man in plain clothes. It was enhanced and sharper since it wasn't real. The man had thicker hair, high cheekbones, and a thinner face. For this first picture Severi had given him a smile.

"No," he finally said.

The next image was the same, but without the smile. He held this one out at arm's length.

"Wait a second."

Lenczycki went to his cabin and returned with reading glasses.

"Better."

"Want to start over?"

"Nah." He studied the photograph again. "Maybe." Lenczycki compared it to the shot with the smile. "The smile's wrong."

He went to the next picture, the same face and body, but now photoshopped into a Soviet Army uniform. He discarded that. The last picture had him in a KGB uniform from thirty years ago: grey-brown, 4"x 2" lapels, four stars on shoulder board epaulettes, and a Russian star on each collar patch.

Lenczycki looked at the image. He went back to the previous photograph.

"Too many stars. You have him in a lieutenant colonel uniform. He was a lieutenant."

Heath sat up straight. "You recognize him."

"Yes, from East Germany. First saw him through binoculars, then closer. Yes, I know him. KGB. He did dirty work for his supervisor. Bad shit. Unnecessary stuff at the end. Beatings. Killed some. The last I saw him was in Potsdam. I was an undercover, quote, unquote, 'observer' with the Bundesnachrichtendienst, West Germany's counterpart to the East's Stasi. The Wall had just fallen and we were tracking the last remnants of the old guard. The problem? The Stasi was still flexing its muscles and the KGB had no love for them. Had we been caught, we would have undoubtedly become two more stars on the CIA lobby memorial wall. Two of the last in East Germany. Dead and honored anonymously."

Heath was grateful for the background but one thing was missing from the account.

"A name?"

"Miklos. Andre Miklos." He spelled it. "If he's still at it, he's probably better at the job."

"He is," Heath acknowledged. "He's moved way beyond killing just some. Try mass murder. Bombings. Hotels."

Lenczycki appeared puzzled. Then he suddenly dropped the expression.

"You didn't ask who his supervisor was back in the day," he noted.

Heath had missed that follow-up. "Who?"

"The man whose uniform you likely lifted from his KGB photograph. A former lieutenant colonel, now president. Nikolai Gorshkov."

Heath exhaled. Given where Reilly had spotted him and his subsequent suspicions, it now made absolute sense.

"I'm in no rush to get back to port," Lenczycki said. "If you're not, what do you say we hang here and talk about what those bastards are up to?"

"On the clock?"

"Consider it a freebie for old times' sake. Old times going back to Potsdam, 1989."

LONDON

Reilly had been divorced for a little more than eighteen months. During that time he'd hardly dated. Now, at a critical period, he was becoming involved with someone he knew nothing about. But the attraction was strong and more than just sexual.

He stroked Marnie's hair as she nestled up to him. She was beautiful and exciting. Emotionally available and considerate. They understood each other's work, but turned work off as they turned one another on. But now with his eyes wide open he saw what he had to do. *Focus on my job.* Then a greater realization. *Not job—but jobs!*

Reilly got out of bed and opened his tablet. He had new email: Brenda's updates on calls and meetings, a matter of fact request from his ex who wanted him to cover the cost of iron bars she had installed on her first-floor windows, and a late night note from Schorel that included an attachment. He clicked on the file. It listed all the relevant upcoming NATO and EU events and the people who were booked at the hotel for each of them.

This was just part of the puzzle. Spike Boyce's research would hopefully fill in the rest. In another three hours, he'd make the call.

* * *

"Well," Spike Boyce began on the phone, "this was one helluva assignment. Something like 35,000 names to cross reference. Do you have any idea what you put me and my guys through? Christ Almighty."

"I owe you."

"You sure do. You can start by telling some of your old State Department buddies not to put me on any watch list because of the websites I visited for you."

"Oh?" Reilly asked.

"American citizens are relatively easy to check. We do that as a normal course of action when the president or a foreign dignitary stays with us. Sometimes the Secret Service makes the request. Other times it's Cannon's call. International travelers are another thing entirely. I've learned how to tap into certain identity records and—"

"You mean you've hacked into— "

"I've got my ways, Mr. Reilly." The next thing Boyce said was fairly revealing. "You've got yours."

Reilly wondered if Boyce had actually stumbled upon something about him. "Point well taken."

"But not everything is so mysterious," Boyce added. "Interpol's databases in Lyon, France, for example. We routinely work with them. Some, like the Global Terrorism Database, are open-source research tools. Others require more finessing. Relationships count." Boyce didn't need to complete the thought.

"So what do I need to worry about?" Reilly asked.

"I'll email you the file when we're off the phone. The good news, no individuals on any no-fly lists. No known terrorists. Not a one."

This did not surprise Reilly. "And the bad news?"

"In exact numbers, the 7,554 people we need to research further. Of those, when we filter for the country parameters you gave me, we drop down to 845 subjects during the target dates. Further filtering out tour groups, we're at 465. Those are the ones we should both examine."

Reilly used the next ninety minutes to look over the file Boyce sent. He went back and forth between the names and highlighted those he personally questioned.

People were coming to Brussels for meetings with the governing boards of NATO and the EU. Some included conferences at the hotel, which he rated five on a scale of one to five. Off-site meetings that could include scheduled sessions at Kensington Diplomat were fours. And finally, uncategorized, possibly random bookings. They were threes or twos. He gave ones and zeros to those that just seemed too random. Then he rethought that decision.

In light of Kiev, Reilly went with another possibility. He searched for other Romanian individuals and groups. Then an epiphany. What about earlier attacks in or out of hotel sites? The kind that could be viewed as a *part* of something rather than *the* something itself.

From this came other questions. *Who died? What did the international press report?*

Most of Reilly's Google news searches were a waste of time. Except one. The assassination of a Russian government minister, blamed on pro-Russian Polish separatists.

Random or common factor?

Dan Reilly searched further using as key words: *pro-Russian separatists* and anything *anti-Gorshkov.*

With each find he drilled down further, finding a good deal of noise about disenfranchised Russians and threats to Russian-speaking citizens in former Soviet Bloc nations. What was most interesting? The consistent use of what he viewed as a coordinated message. The same phrases in the same order attributed to different people. Talking points that had been approved and widely circulated:

NATO pushes further east

NATO threatens Russia's border

Belarus threatened by NATO troops

Freedom-loving Russian loyalists singled out in Moldova

Increased NATO-inspired attacks against pro-Russians supporters in Lithuania

Moscow fears for Russian expats' lives in Latvia

Assassination of Latvian oil magnate Mairis Gaiss linked to anti-Russian plot

News or propaganda? The quotes were attributed to different people, but they were consistent in tone and content.

Reilly added another parameter to his search. Ukraine. The quotes were eerily similar:

NATO prepares to push further east to Ukraine

Russian loyalists singled out by Kiev police

Increased NATO-inspired attacks against pro-Russian supporters in Ukraine

Moscow fears for Russian expats' lives in border nations

Pravda, Izvestia, Russian State Television. Even Western press reports. The quotes were strikingly similar. The rhetoric was most fervent when it came to reporting violations of Russian nationals' rights. In each case, the equal sign equated to NATO expansionism.

Reilly sat back in his chair to contemplate the finds. For the first time, he looked at the issue from the inside out, from an internal Russian point of view rather than external.

Jesus, he thought. *Like business. Like managing a hotel crisis in Mazatlán or anywhere else.* His own rule. *Understand the culture.*

Then it came to him. He felt his heartbeat quicken. His fists tightened. He sucked in a deep breath and held it.

The answer was in the press reports. Strategic, spaced out over time, laying a foundation. It seemed obvious. *The Russian people were being prepared for another Crimea.* It was coming, and either Brussels was going to be the catalyst or a significant part of the plan.

Reilly reviewed the bookings again, this time with a new filter.

68

MOSCOW, RUSSIAN FEDERATION

The meeting was neither on the president's official calendar nor any of the attendees'. Admittance was limited to four fiercely loyal generals. Loyalty was demanded without question.

Under Nikolai Gorshkov, top lifetime military service ended one of three ways: honored retirement, swift firing, or unexpected heart failure.

Constant changes at the top of the military command represented the unmistakable sign that Gorshkov was serious about bringing the Russian military into the modern era. The overhaul not so coincidentally occurred around the time the president announced a new military doctrine that specifically focused on NATO expansion, Russia's main external threat. It established a joint missile defense pact between Russian and allied nations, specifically aimed at developing a missile shield around Poland.

The four generals summoned today—Valery Bakhtin, Gennady Titov, Alexi Kanshin, and Pavel Makarov—understood the price of loyalty and were ready to execute Nikolai Gorshkov's most ambitious plan yet. They rose to attention when the president entered the conference room.

After a short welcome and a rambling prologue on NATO, which they'd heard time and time again, Gorshkov added, "Of course, I welcome dissent," before signaling for General Bakhtin to comment.

Of course he doesn't, thought each of the generals.

Bakhtin served as chief of the general staff, having worked his way up from commander of the Baltic tank regiment. The 60-year-old, dark-haired, square-jawed general had benefited the most from Gorshkov's upper level house cleaning.

"Mr. President," he began, "the mess in the EU continues to erode cooperation. Financial crises are weighing heavily on weaker member nations. Frustration in the stronger countries grows with the burden of carrying them. We have studied multiple models of what will likely follow. More ruptures in the coalition. Germany, France, and Italy won't be able to hold it together. If one of them falls out, we can expect the Scandinavian bloc, and in our sphere, a union of the eastern countries based on shared trade, security interests, or root language, to splinter off. Our goal is to not wait for these changes to transpire, but to hasten them."

The general tugged at his jacket, commanding more attention. "Our first steps will cause a stir and cry, but little else. NATO will protest, but with no will to act."

"The United States still talks war," Deputy Minister of Defense General Titov noted.

"Yes, but conservative American leaders have walked back willingness to defend its allies in Europe and Asia. This actually has Japan more fearful than some of their European allies. It all plays well for us."

General Bakhtin opened a file. "According to a Stanford University analysis, the cost of maintaining US troops in Japan is only about 10 percent more than keeping them in Texas." He closed the file. "That's just one example and on a larger scale, it's really not about money. Americans increasingly feel they're being taking advantage of by foreign obligations. So, the prevailing mood is get rid of outdated treaties, especially when they seem meaningless to their lives. That means opportunity for us."

President Nikolai Gorshkov couldn't have put it better himself.

LONDON
THE KENSINGTON ROYAL TOWERS

After reviewing the file Boyce had sent over, an excited Reilly placed a call to Heath, who was still at work. He explained what he had been doing and the conclusions, still unsubstantiated, that he had come to.

"NATO," Reilly said.

"Not possible," Heath replied, waiting to be convinced.

"I'm telling you it's all about NATO."

"How, where, when?"

"I don't know. But you tell me whether NATO will enforce or wiggle out of its Article 5 Common Defense commitments if there's an attack on a NATO partner country."

Heath hesitated.

"My point exactly. And what about England and Germany? Did they move a muscle when France sought an authorization of Article 5 after the Paris attacks?"

"No," Heath admitted.

MOSCOW

"The EU has contributed to its own demise," Bakhtin argued. "It was sheer lunacy for them to ever think that our patriotism and national will could be reduced to a forgotten memory. Sheer lunacy to delegitimize nation states with hundreds of years of cultural differences. The very idea denied history itself."

Gorshkov nodded. This was just the conversation he wanted.

"And so," he continued, "a generation now exists in Europe that has little or no sense of national identity. Who there would answer the call for a war to defend borders when no true borders remain? Back to your notion about America talking war, General Tito."

The minister of defense tipped his head signifying he was in accord.

"Congress couldn't come together with Obama over his war authorization against ISIS," Bakhtin added. "They have no appetite for another war they can't win, a war that would quickly escalate if they entered. Who wants that? Certainly not the American people. Not even their president."

Titov nodded his agreement.

"Great Britain?" Gorshkov scowled.

"They'll step aside," Bakhtin stated. "They're against engagement. The EU's foreign minister is a Labor Party appointee to the House of Lords. She earned her stripes in the Campaign for Nuclear Disarmament. Their focus was on disarmament over defense, which firmly put them against engagement."

Gorshkov laughed. "Yes, yes, yes. The Campaign for Nuclear Disarmament was our special operation, founded in 1957 with the goal of making England indefensible."

LONDON

"Reagan took NATO seriously," Reilly told Heath over the phone from his hotel room. "And, in those days, the Kremlin believed that if they tried to seize other European nations, the penalty would have been a world war. But those days are over. It feels like NATO is from another era. And unlike Soviet Russia, today's Kremlin doubts that we have the stomach to fight for Europe."

"You might be right," Heath admitted.

"And no matter what official statements come out of NATO, the member nations also would find ways to avoid committing their young men and women to defend a border change that to them would only mean changes in the faces on foreign currency.

MOSCOW

"The growing separatist movement is succeeding, Mr. President," General Alexi Kanshin, head of the Western Military District located in St. Petersburg, stated. "Infusing Russian as a required national language throughout the region was one of the Soviet Union's smartest decisions. That single act instilled a passionate sense of loyalty to Moscow among the separatists. When called to protect and defend them, such as in Crimea, we will be acting on behalf of beleaguered, isolated friends.

Justified and authorized. In my mind," Kanshin added, "we could move on multiple fronts. Moldova's Transnistria region is an easy get. Bordered on Ukraine, it offers—"

Gorshkov slyly smiled as he interrupted him. "Be patient, my general," he said. He followed it with a sharp rebuke. "And don't ever presume you have permission to tell me what to do."

LONDON

Reilly continued his phone conversation with Heath. "A land invasion would be quick," he predicted. "According to my old Harvard prof, one or two days."

"Too quick for us to act with or without authorization. And the risk—"

Reilly completed the sentence, "of nuclear war would be too great."

"There's another geopolitical consideration," Heath added, coming around to the same conclusion. "In the global economy, European young people freely move for school, for work, for marriages. And they don't necessarily return home. Mass migration across Europe's old boundaries has killed the appetite among military-age citizens of any need to defend what used to be their homeland. Hell, in another decade there might not be many people left who even want to hold office in some of those border nations."

MOSCOW

"There are troops," warned a more contrite General Alexi Kanshin. "And some émigrés might come back to fight."

"They lack the training and the desire," General Bakhtin argued. "To return and die without a fervent patriotic calling would be pointless. They have their lives and families to think about, not a glorious death for their motherland. They have none of the need to protect their natural resources as we do. No desire to spill their own blood in the name of an antiquated notion of cultural history. They gave that up when they sold their identity to the European Union. But to your point about troops,

General Kanshin. Yes, they have them. But they are no match to the forces under your command and those of General Makarov's Central Military District."

LONDON

"What about our defenses in Europe?" Reilly asked Heath.

"Decades after the Berlin Wall fell, we figured what's the point of stationing 60,000 troops in Europe when most EU nations still don't make a substantial commitment of manpower and money themselves. So, despite the fiery rhetoric every four years in the presidential debates, our military capacity in Europe is little more than a placeholder."

A paper tiger, thought Reilly. *That doesn't scare Gorshkov.*

MOSCOW

General Makarov, commander of Russia's forces in Crimea and, as a result, the nation's most practiced military strategist, spoke next.

"America's war is with terrorism, not Russia. That's where they have committed their resources. Ukraine demonstrated that Americans won't commit their armed forces to Eastern Europe. We will have no opposition to speak of."

LONDON

"Okay, my friend, here's where I'm going with all this, and then I need to end this call," Reilly stated.

"Ready."

"Gorshkov is threatened by NATO and relying on our reluctance to get involved. He's planning on retaking one or more of Russia's former satellites."

"You better be wrong," Heath replied.

"Stay with me. He'll use a provocation to strike. A provocation of his invention. There will be an incident, the last in a series of unspeakable crimes against Russians or Russian loyalists. Incidents that they, in fact, are behind." Reilly went through his internet search again. "This will be the impetus for Gorshkov to come to the defense of one or more nations where a significant percentage of the population closely aligns with Russia."

"You really think so?" Heath asked.

"I do, and so should you."

MOSCOW

"Specifics now," Gorshkov stated. "At worst, what will be our target's response?"

Without hesitating, General Valery Bakhtin handed Gorshkov a document.

"Mr. President," the general read from a top sheet, "they have 13,000 national frontline forces. Active reserves, 11,000. Adequate, but not formidable. The Parliament abolished conscription in 2006. Those who volunteer are assigned to the home guard and the reserve."

"Equipment?" the president asked unemotionally.

"Tanks, zero. Multiple launch rocket systems, zero. SPGs, self-propelled guns, zero. There are 250 armored fighting vehicles, 20 towed artillery. Airpower, both fixed-wing and rotary from all branches of service, four fighters. Total Naval strength, eleven coastal defense crafts and six mine ships. They also bought three TPS-77 transportable Multi-Role Radars, which bring their defense capabilities up, but only marginally."

"Marginally?" the president asked. "Define marginally."

"It gives them a chance to act, sir, but they have little to act with. They recently increased military spending from 1.4 percent of their GDP to 2 percent, the absolute minimum NATO has mandated. But given their current economic problems, it's unlikely they'll make the number. Of course Germany could offer 54 of its stored Leopard 2A6 tanks, but it wouldn't be in time. France could send interceptors, but late."

"What about the resolve of the people, those not loyal to Russia?" Gorshkov asked.

"The answer is embedded in the debate they've had since the fall of Communism. It comes down to patriotism vs. nationalism," General

Titov explained. "Patriotism makes them stronger as a people. It defines their set of values. Before the internet and social media it actually meant something. But hundreds of thousands have gone to other countries to work. Patriotism loses to nationalism, the set of values that provided security to the people after the Nazis. The leadership that protected them. The pipelines that delivered oil. The wires that gave them electricity. For them, nationalism is Russia."

"And the practical reality," Bakhtin added, "they know they'll have to bring the fight to General Makarov's forces across the border. They'll have to scuttle our fleet equipped with missiles. That's not going to happen."

"But do they believe we would strike?" Gorshkov shot back. "Not a guess. Your professional judgment. "

General Bakhtin responded without a moment's hesitation. "As with other NATO nations, like Romania, they rate an actual invasion at 0.01 percent. To put it another way, the government is content to believe by 99.9 percent that Russia will not invade."

"Then bring your troops to full readiness," the president commanded. "The time is nearly here."

69

LONDON, ENGLAND

THE KENSINGTON ROYAL LONDON TOWERS

After ending his call with Heath, Reilly was suddenly aware he wasn't alone in his hotel suite living room. Marnie was watching him.

"How long have you been there?" he asked.

The question took Marnie by surprise. "That sounds awfully accusatory."

Reilly stared at her. Marnie closed her open bathrobe and tied the belt.

"How long?" he repeated.

"What the hell's your problem?"

"*Ty kto?*"

"What?" she replied.

"*Ty kto?*" he repeated in Russian.

Marnie pursed her lips and furrowed her brow.

"Who am I?" she answered in English. "What the hell are you asking? And why in Russian? I'm the woman you've been sleeping with." She pulled her belt tighter. "And I don't like what you're suggesting one bit. Why don't you just come out and say what's on your mind. *Ti chyertovski moodak!*"

"You're fluent," Reilly sharply replied.

"Damned straight. And your accent sucks," she said. "Maybe you should have studied with my professors at Oxford."

Reilly lowered his eyes and shook his head.

"School?"

"Yes. Want to hear my Mandarin, too?" she asked.

"I'm sorry. But—"

"I'm in international banking for God's sake. You actually thought I was, what? A Mata Hari?"

Reilly half laughed. "Well, seeing you in both Tehran and Moscow? You knowing so much about me. I guess I questioned how much of a coincidence it was. And then your Russian at the Kremlin."

"*Ti chyertovski moodak!*" she repeated with disgust.

"What's that mean?"

"Oh, you know how to ask 'Who am I,' but you don't know the expression 'You're a fucking asshole?'" She turned to leave. "And you want to do business in Russia?" she said over her shoulder. "Forget what you were thinking. What was I thinking? Forget everything!"

Reilly crossed the room and took her arm. "I'm sorry. I'm really sorry."

"Fuck you," she said with her back to him.

"I deserved that."

"You sure do."

He reached out, turned Marnie around, and quietly added, "I'm sorry."

"You should be!" she exclaimed. "Just tell me why? What's going on with you?"

Reilly took a long deep breath, reaching for some part of the truth.

"A combination of everything. The deals, which we shouldn't talk about and . . ." He stopped short.

"And what?"

Reilly suddenly wondered if her question was more probing than caring. He couldn't tell.

"Oh, this whirlwind trip I've been on. It's exhausting. And the personalities. Trying to get people on board with some new concepts."

"Like?"

Probing or caring? He still wasn't sure.

"Corporate policies."

He let the answer settle, hoping it would be enough.

"There's a lot happening," he continued. "I suppose I need help. I'm questioning everything, and I'm short on answers." He paused. "I shouldn't have questioned you."

"You sure shouldn't."

"I'm sorry," he quietly offered.

Marnie looked away. Reilly stepped up to her and put his arms around her.

"What are you doing?"

"Getting close."

"Then ask," she said.

"May I?"

"I don't know."

"Please."

"Yes."

After holding her for a few moments he nudged her chin up and moved forward to kiss her.

"Ask," she repeated.

"May I?"

"Yes."

As their lips met he reached down and slowly undid her robe.

"May I?" he whispered.

"Yes," she replied softly. "But I still say *ti chyertovski moodak!*"

Reilly slipped the robe off her shoulders and backed Marnie into the bedroom.

Da. Yes, he thought in Russian, having decided he would have the agency look into her past. *Da.*

* * *

Brenda warned Reilly that Shaw would be calling him from Chicago. She didn't know that it would involve most of the major management team.

"Sorry to blindside you, Dan," the company president began. "But I've got Lou, Chris, Pat, June, and Alan on with me."

Reilly figured that Alan Cannon had pushed for the conference call and wanted the CFO and heads of legal and marketing in his corner.

"I want to understand the problem better," Shaw said. "Alan is in favor of shutting the Diplomat down. You're not."

"That's correct, sir."

"Care to defend your position?"

Reilly hated the way his boss phrased his question. But he believed he had the best argument for keeping the Brussels' property open.

"Yes I would."

Reilly explained his recommendation, logically and unemotionally. He hit the points a devoted company man would, with the added perspective of a man committed to righting a terrible wrong. A man on a mission.

When he finished, Cannon took the opposing side. Collins lined up on the side of closing. Brodowski favored Reilly's POV. Wilson saw public relations problems either way.

Shaw called on Lou Tiano for his opinion. "Lou, you've been quiet. I'm not asking for a tie-breaking vote. In the end, this will be my decision. But where do you stand?"

"I think it comes down to trust. Can we trust the defensive measures we've implemented? Can we trust the people we've empowered to evaluate the danger? Can we trust ourselves that we're not simply going to make an economic decision that benefits us?"

The CFO sighed deeply. "A few questions for Dan and Alan."

"Go on," Shaw encouraged.

"Alan, have you gotten any indication that other hotels in Brussels have been subject to similar target surveillances?"

"No, Lou. I've talked to managers at the principal properties. They had no reports of having been cased."

"Will our Red Hotel emergency procedures deter an attack?" Tiano asked.

"More than if we hadn't acted. But nothing is guaranteed."

"Have we hired our own private security force? One we can fully rely on?"

"Yes. Dan and I actually subcontracted Donald Klugo's company. You'll remember he was one of our committee consultants. A few of his team are visibly on the ground now. More within thirty-six hours. Given Brussels' recent history, they don't appear out of the ordinary. Just tougher, better trained, and better armed than our in-house security."

"They're mercenaries?" Wilson asked, fearful of any negative marketing blowback.

"Yes, they are," Cannon answered.

"Thank you. Now Dan," Tiano continued, "you believe the potential assassin . . . we can call him assassin?"

"Yes."

"This assassin is the same individual behind the Tokyo bombing?"

"Yes."

"Supported by?" Tiano pressed.

"You mean who's behind him or where does the intelligence come from?"

"Since you bring up two points, both."

"The American intelligence community has been conducting a serious search, which started with the ATM image recovered in Tokyo. They believe they have a credible ID on the subject. We should leave it at that. But I believe our hotel is a collateral target. The true objective? A specific person or group of persons."

"And who does this person work for?"

Reilly cleared his voice. "Edward, Lou," Reilly said, directing his comment to the two executives in particular, "this is not something to discuss on an open phone line."

Chris Collins objected. "What? Why in hell would that be a problem?"

"It is," Reilly stated.

"You mean, 'could be,'" the attorney shot back.

"Is," Reilly reiterated.

This ground the conversation down to an uncomfortable silence. Shaw was the first to speak. "Respecting Dan's wishes, we should take care. Let's simply talk in general terms."

"What possible motive is there?" the PR executive asked.

"Publicity, June."

"To what end?"

"I don't know that yet," Reilly explained, preferring not to share his own thoughts.

"Any ideas?" the president pressed.

"I'm working on it," Reilly quietly replied. "Again, let's table that right now."

"Dan, you need to be straight with me."

"Sir, trust me. Not here. Not now."

"I get it," Shaw said, calling an end to the dialogue. "Just assure me that you're working for the best interests of the company."

Shaw had asked a very pointed question. But not *the* question. The question he could have asked: *Was Reilly also working for the best interests of someone else?*

"Yes, sir. I am. And if we have the chance to prevent a greater crime from happening, one that has immense geopolitical ramifications, I recommend that we keep the doors open in Brussels and help catch the bastard who murdered 115 people in Tokyo."

* * *

Shaw put the call on hold while he conferred with his Chicago team. Reilly in London and Cannon in Brussels were left speculating what he would decide. Five minutes later, the chief executive reactivated the line.

"There are risks on either side of the argument," Shaw stated. "Risks to the lives of our guests and staff, risks to our stock and our financial bottom line, and risks that, if I make the wrong decision, could shake faith in the corporation."

So far the company founder hadn't telegraphed his decision.

"But whether we like it or not, our industry has entered a phase with no end in sight. We are in two businesses today, as Dan reminded me not long ago, hospitality and anti-terrorism. We have the same challenges as an international airline carrier transporting people by air, or the city of New York protecting New Year's revelers at Times Square. It's the new normal. And as far as I'm concerned, I want us to be the leader."

Edward Jefferson Shaw then proclaimed, "We stay open. Now, Dan and Alan, make Diplomat the safest hotel in the world."

70

LANGLEY, VA

CIA HEADQUARTERS

Heath read the briefing paper titled "The Effect of Increased NATO Presence in Eastern Europe on The Russian Federation." It was dated and marked secret.

The assessment had been culled from field reports and those who were paid to interpret from the comfort of their Langley offices.

It began with a synthesis of news reports from AP, *The Wall Street Journal, The Guardian, The New York Times,* and Russia's *Izvestia*. The key bullet points:

- Pentagon rumored to increase American troops, armored vehicles, and tanks beyond even Q4 projections to deter Russian aggression.

- 4,200 troops annually rotated and divided among Bulgaria, Romania, Poland, Latvia, Estonia, and Lithuania. Total permanent US troop strength, 62,000. New equipment stockpiles to Germany, Belgium, the Netherlands.

- White House avoiding comment.

The report chronicled the largest buildup since the end of the Cold War. To Heath's thinking, it read like war footing and it played into Reilly's beliefs.

The report continued with the potential negatives. Big ones. Important ones.

- Creates exposure for NATO nations on the eastern flank.

- Fear the commitment could come too late.

- Moscow will view the strategy as a visible and dangerous escalation and a threat.

- Russia will cite a violation of the 1997 NATO-Russia Founding Act that stated the alliance would not position substantial, permanent combat forces at Russia's eastern frontier.

- It may motivate Russia to act first.

Underscoring the assessment about the Russian Federation was on record criticism from the Russian ambassador to NATO.

"NATO is moving its territory closer to Russia. It is using this territory to project military power in the direction of Russia." The ambassador had concluded his statement adding a counter threat: "Russia *is not* moving."

The report went on to outline moves and countermoves played out at the expense of NATO's smaller border countries, which resembled disposable pawns in a larger game of chess.

Heath requested and received approval to share the report with Dan Reilly. He also had more to discuss with Reilly. A name to put on the face of Smug.

71

DECEMBER, 1989

The angle was bad, but it wouldn't get any better.

"Fucking freezing out here."

"A little longer. Keep your eyes on your side."

The two men were doing double surveillance. One had binoculars on the drab three-story building from across the street. The second was tasked with watching a building to their right. Both targets were dangerous: the local KGB headquarters and the nearer Stasi outpost.

"They're shouting," the first man whispered. CIA agent Joe Lenczycki adjusted his focus. "Spitting mad over something. Hasn't slowed them."

They watched as the subjects threw file after file into the burn oven. The open window provided ventilation and allowed Lenczycki to see better. The two men, with holsters over their left shoulders, worked fast.

"Damn."

"What?" asked Taylor Roberts, the second agent.

"Wish I had the camera." A 35mm with a long lens would have helped, but it also would have drawn attention. Attention meant questions. Questions meant problems. So they had crossed the border without it.

Most Stasi agents were doing everything they could to disappear between the cracks in the pavement after the fall of the Berlin Wall. Yet some still patrolled the streets of Potsdam hoping to take down a few more enemies of the state. A last shot for Communism.

The two CIA agents had been stopped twice during their stay. Each time they acted appropriately nervous as their identities as college professors on holiday from Australia would suggest. It was a solid cover backed up in Melbourne thanks to cooperation from ASIS, the Australian Security Intelligence Service. And while their binoculars might be considered suspicious, Lenczycki and Roberts also had rehearsal tickets at the Neues Palais for *La forza del destino*, a Giuseppe Verdi opera, which explained away the gear.

Now safely observing from the roof, Lenczycki sharpened the focus on his binoculars. Through the glass, his subjects looked particularly cold. *No,* he thought. *Cruel.*

He made mental notes. Number One was perhaps five- to ten-years senior to Number Two. That suggested he was in charge, in addition to the way he strutted around the room. Number Two merely nodded and obeyed, but it was clear he was upset. He added files to the fire with increasing vehemence.

The CIA had limited eyes in Potsdam and other GDR cities, and scant intelligence on the KGB operatives and infrastructure. Lenczycki and Taylor's assignment, according to Director William H. Webster, was to gather everything they could before the goons got out of Dodge.

Given the age of One and Two, they could still have thirty or more years ahead of them in whatever would replace the KGB.

Damn, he thought again. *Wish I had that camera.* A moment later, "Whoa," Lenczycki whispered. "They're putting their jackets on. We're rolling."

Lenczycki tucked his binoculars under his jacket inside his belt, near his Taurus 850B2UL .38 special revolver.

They watched the two men turn off the office lights, but the glow of the burning papers backlit their exit. Outside, they split up.

"Shit," Lenczycki said. "You take the guy heading toward the river. I'll stay with the one to the left."

They raced down the old fire escape on the side of the red brick building that had been their perch. "Meet back at Alpha at midnight."

Roberts followed his man, but lost him after only four blocks, a combination of Taylor Roberts' inexperience and the realization of KGB station chief Nikolai Gorshkov that he was being followed.

Not so for the younger Russian agent. He remained unaware that he had a shadow.

The KGB agent wandered around the streets, occasionally bumping hard into drunken revelers who were dulling the pain of the Soviet years with cheap Russian vodka.

"*Bewegen sie assholes!*" he shouted. "Move!"

On the second encounter he knocked a man down. The third time he slammed an old man against a street light. The KGB agent was clearly furious, and Lenczycki feared it would get worse.

The agent entered a dive bar. In order to stay invisible, Lenczycki inserted himself into a barhopping group. Five steps in, they were back-slapping good friends. He pretended to listen to someone too wasted to realize Lenczycki had only a few German words in his vocabulary.

Lenczycki sat down with him and continued to nod politely and laugh. Meanwhile, he watched the KGB agent across the room down four vodkas in the time he pretended to have one. The alcohol appeared to do little to sublimate the Russian's growing anger. He was belligerent with his waitress and when the bartender told him that his uniform certainly wouldn't buy him any favors, he abruptly stood, ready to take him on. But two bouncers intervened and began to guide the stumbling Russian out.

Lenczycki dropped enough East German marks to cover his drink and those of his drunken companion. Then he left the bar ahead of his subject and turned right, hoping the man would do the same and pass him. If not, he'd double back.

With a 25 percent chance of choosing the correct side of the street and direction, the CIA agent played the odds and won.

The KGB agent staggered past him. Lenczycki hung back, feigning his own drunkenness. Four block later, the Russian eyed a couple in their early twenties loudly celebrating.

"*Freiheit!*" they shouted over and over. Freedom. Then they sang a two-line song that they delivered in English. "Fuck Russia! Fuck Russia! Fuck Russia!" followed by a chorus of "*Freiheit.*"

Lenczycki worried whether this would push the KGB agent over the edge.

A friend joined them in song. Then another celebrant.

"Fuck Russia! Fuck Russia! Fuck Russia! *Freiheit! Freiheit! Freiheit!*"

The singing got louder in volume and spirit.

The Russian stopped ten feet from the group and faced the drunken young revelers.

Even in the dark from thirty feet, Lenczycki could see the agent reach under his jacket with his right hand. He knew what was there.

What happened next occurred quickly. The KGB agent stepped forward. He pulled out his Makarov PM 9mm pistol and yelled in German, "*Verräter! Verräter!* Traitor! Traitor!"

"Fuck you!" The young woman was the first to respond and the first to be shot between the eyes at short range. Another bullet dispatched her lover, who would never know *Freiheit.*

Drunk one moment, now with adrenaline pumping, the agent realized what he had done. He also spotted the man down the street running toward him.

Seven rounds were left in his pistol. Two shots went wide, but they made Lenczycki duck behind a lamppost. That cost the CIA agent time and allowed the Russian to commandeer a car at gunpoint and escape.

Lenczycki went to the victims. They had been murdered for celebrating. Murdered for demonstrating their joy in front of a uniformed KGB agent drunk with power.

There was nothing for the CIA agent to do except to get away himself. For the rest of his years in the agency he searched for the assassin. But he never found him, and Skip Lenczycki finally retired.

72

PRESENT DAY

The next day Heath met Reilly at a designated London clothing and tailor shop on Bond Street, which led to a CIA safe house next door. It was right out of a Cold War novel for so many reasons, the name of the street being just one.

Without talking, Heath led him through the store, into the tailoring area, and to a door that opened to an apartment. Once inside he said, "Sorry for the cloak-and-dagger stuff, but your worries are on my mind."

"Thanks," Reilly responded. "What's up?"

"A good deal."

Heath summarized the report he'd read at Langley.

When he finished, Reilly smiled. "So I'm not so crazy?"

"No," Heath acknowledged, "you're not. But there's more. It goes back to Potsdam at the end of the Cold War"

"Oh?"

Heath backed into the account, starting with 30-year-old agency files, which led him to Port Elizabeth and a man with an intriguing story.

"He's a retired agent. Comfortable and happy, but with unfinished business hanging over him. He had a brush with your Mr. Smug in Germany in late 1989. For years he tried to track him down. He was unsuccessful. Smug was as elusive as they get. He vanished, but there were hints of his presence in highly suspect places."

"Like?" Reilly interrupted.

"Targeted assassinations and acts of terrorism around the globe."

"How do you know?"

A man stepped out from another room in the apartment.

"He doesn't. I do."

Reilly spun around. A weathered, tanned, and muscular man in a polo shirt and tan pants came closer.

"You're the agent?"

"Retired," Skip Lenczycki replied, "the one with unfinished business."

Heath introduced the two. They shook hands, and Lenczycki sat opposite Reilly.

"Heard some good things about you," Lenczycki said.

"Thank you. Feeling a bit out of my comfort zone, though."

"You are when it comes to Andre Miklos."

"Who?" Reilly asked.

"Andre Miklos. The man you're looking for."

Reilly felt all the muscles in his body relax. At last he had a name. Now he settled in and listened to Lenczycki's story.

The agent-turned-sailor saved his most striking comments for last.

"Andre Miklos is death. He lives for it. And as best as I've been able to surmise, when he's not listening to the devil inside him, he's listening to only one other person."

"Who?" Reilly asked.

"His superior in the KGB then and today, the president of the Russian Federation. Nikolai Gorshkov."

Lenczycki explained his history with Miklos.

Next it was Reilly's turn to share what he had garnered. He focused on Spike Boyce's IT search. "We discovered some bookings. Look at these."

Reilly removed a printout from his jacket pocket and handed it to Heath. As he read, Reilly went into more detail.

"A Romanian delegation has booked the Diplomat for an EU meeting on climate control. A Romanian minister of defense is coming in a week later, and a Romanian dance troupe will be performing at Théâtre National. That's at the end of the month. We're going to have to drill down further. If the singer killed in Tokyo was a Romanian dissident, then we should look into the politics of these guests as well."

Heath excused himself to phone Langley. Ten minutes later he came back into the room with a troubled look.

"There's increased chatter over the NATO maneuvers in Romania. The White House is seriously looking at it. So are the Russians. And yes, Dan, that singer Kretsky now has analysts wondering if you could be right."

Reilly felt vindicated.

"So play this out," Lenczycki said. "Miklos plants a few bombs at the Diplomat. They go off. A bunch of Romanians die."

"Along with dozens or hundreds of others," Reilly interjected, correcting him.

"Yes, more. What happens? The Russians say 'enough is enough' and they sweep into Bucharest."

Reilly allowed an okay but with a caveat. "I believe they're coming."

"Then start with the givens," the retired agent said. "He's already done his survey. He's got a plan. And so far he's partial to truck bombs."

"But if he's seen our barriers go up," Reilly noted, "wouldn't he adjust his strategy? Why risk a botched run? He'll go for bombs inside the hotel."

"Security makes it harder," Heath replied. "Dogs and metal detectors even more difficult."

"Harder, but not impossible," Reilly responded. "Especially if devices are already there."

"You could be right. When's the first group due?" Lenczycki asked.

"Ten days," Reilly said from memory. He thought they had better start searching.

"Okay," Heath said. "Let's see where these three leads take us."

* * *

Two hours later, a call from Langley provided a strong connection for one booking.

"The Romanian dance troupe," Heath explained. "Their artistic director, Ionela Soryn, was the longtime girlfriend of Kretsky."

"She's pro-Russia?"

"Big time. She's singing her dead lover's chorus."

"When will she check in?" Lenczycki asked.

Reilly had the dates. "On the eighteenth for five nights." Then another thought. "We should see if there's been any unusual activity at the venue. Excessive photography. Impromptu tours. Circulate Miklos' photo."

"Good," Heath replied.

Lenczycki stirred. "I want the room next to hers."

"No," Heath said without equivocation. "You're not going."

"Of course I am. Besides, I'm not talking to you. You're not the one with the free rooms."

Heath jumped in before Reilly answered. "Agent Lenczycki—"

"Former," he replied again. "Former."

"Former Agent Lenczycki, I appreciate your help and your contributions. But your involvement in this case will end here and now."

Heath stood, signaling the argument was over and his word was law.

"Has your buddy always been such a dick?" Lenczycki asked Reilly. It wasn't a joke.

"As long as I've known him," Reilly said with the same tone.

"Then I guess it's time for me to leave."

Lenczycki rose and shook Reilly's hand. "Nice to meet you." Then to Heath he added, "Thanks for the trip to London."

Without another word, Skip Lenczycki walked out of the room.

73

Risk was an evitable part of the job. The way to mitigate risk? Outthink the opposition. Since a drunken night in Potsdam, which he never reported up, he only went operational if he could control the variables. This required painstaking advance planning, strict control of information, development of principal, secondary, and tertiary exfiltration routes, and the experience to pull the plug on the mission.

As far as he was concerned, even with the additional defensive measures at the target, he had complete confidence in his plan. The time, the date, the precise location. All were in order.

It wouldn't be the biggest explosion. Not as big as Japan or Ukraine. *But,* Andre Miklos thought, *it'll be a shot heard round the world.*

Long ago he learned the historical references. *The shot heard round the world.* The original context celebrated the first volley fired by a line of colonists the night of April 18, 1775, in Lexington, Massachusetts— the beginning of the American Revolution. It was also applied to the bullet fired by a Serbian assassin that killed Archduke Franz Ferdinand of Austria. The launch of World War I.

Yes, the shot heard around the world. Only louder.

* * *

Reilly checked back into the Diplomat and reviewed the precautions. Donald Klugo, president of GSI, Global Security Initiatives, had arrived with five of his team. Twenty-two members of NRF, the NATO Response Force, were posted throughout the Kensington Diplomat Hotel. The CIA had dropped in a ten-person team headed by Bob Heath. Joe Lenczycki was not among them.

Most hotel guests, diplomats especially, took little notice of the various security personnel roaming the public spaces with ear pieces and ceiling CCTV cameras pointing down from corner installations. The units, visible and hidden, watched everyone, everywhere.

Other Red Hotel measures were in full force. X-ray machines scanned all suitcases and deliveries. Bomb-sniffing dogs made rounds in and around the property.

Three days after Reilly had arrived back in Brussels, one hundred and twelve guests checked out of the hotel before noon. One hundred and sixty-one arrived; twenty-one from România Experiența de Dans, including Ionela Soryn.

When she entered an elevator, a CIA agent rode with her. When she visited the ground-floor ladies room, a female agent followed her in. When she hailed a taxi, it was driven by one of the mercenaries.

Operatives switched off at designated intervals on Soryn's travel routes and patrolled Théâtre National before and during the first day of rehearsals.

At midnight, Heath reported back to Langley, "Day 1 Quiet." That meant Day 2 would be all the more intense.

If Soryn was aware of being tracked by NATO forces, America's CIA, private security, or hotel staff, she didn't show it. The dancer went about her business. She had a light breakfast brought up to her room, spent the morning shopping along Avenue Louise, took a taxi to the theatre for a strenuous full dress rehearsal, had dinner at Bistango with the Brussels' art committee chairman, and then a martini at the bar after.

The dogs sniffed, the X-ray machines scanned, the cameras observed and recorded. Nothing.

Directly across the street on the third floor of another art nouveau building, a man peered through binoculars for the second day. He noted everyone entering and leaving, the times they passed through the Diplomat doors, and whether they posed a threat.

He'd rented the empty office the previous day. This would be his full-time post, sleeping only from 2:00 a.m. to 6 a.m. each day and eating out of the three coolers he'd brought.

He was actually surprised the building, let alone the room he was in, hadn't been swept by any one of agencies on duty at the hotel. *Piss poor*, he thought.

* * *

NATO assigned more men the next day. Twenty at the theater for opening night. Ten more at the hotel. This was in response to Ionela Soryn dedicating the performance to her former lover, Janusz Kretsky.

Heath suddenly feared that if Théâtre National was actually the target, they weren't prepared. But the sold-out performance went off without incident.

Back at the hotel after her dancers were retired for the night, Soryn ordered a drink and settled into a couch close to the lobby front window with her business manager. This immediately sent one of Klugo's men watching on the security cameras into an apoplectic fit.

"Jesus!" he complained over their wireless channel. "The fucking waiters were told not to put them there. Get Dancer out!"

Reilly was closest to them, but still on the other side of the lobby. He began to cross the area, pushing past the late night crowd.

Simultaneously, a FedEx truck rounded the near corner and headed toward the Kensington Diplomat. A NATO infantryman from France, briefed on the Tokyo attack, spotted the vehicle. It bore down the avenue quickly. Maybe too quickly. He squawked an emergency code and stepped out in the street, rifle raised. An officer posted at the hotel entrance responded and instantly engaged the bollards. They rose instantly, throwing off a couple standing on the barrier, and breaking the woman's arm.

An alarm connected to the bollards blared. The NATO officer aimed his assault rifle at the driver.

Inside, Reilly yelled for everyone to get down. Even those who didn't understand English got the order.

The truck skidded to a stop. The soldier delayed firing for a tense moment. The driver, wearing a FedEx uniform, raised his hands. Police immediately closed down the streets two blocks in either direction.

NATO troops surrounded the vehicle, pulled out the driver, and dragged him twenty feet from the truck. Twenty feet wouldn't have been far enough if the truck had been carrying explosives. It wasn't. The dogs confirmed it was clean. It was a real FedEx vehicle with an actual driver who had been directed by his app to avoid traffic along Rue des Bouchers, the street parallel to the hotel.

* * *

"My God!" Liam Schorel exclaimed. "One broken bone. A false arrest. Likely lawsuits. A total embarrassment."

"But we learned some important things," Reilly proposed during the postmortem.

"Sure did," Klugo replied. "Including getting your goddamned staff in line. You can't afford another fuckup like this."

"You're right."

"Another thing. Paint the top of those goddamned bollards so people see them," Klugo continued.

"Got it," Reilly said.

"By tomorrow. Bright red."

"Done. Now I have one," Reilly said. "We've got to pull the lobby seating away from the windows. It won't help in an actual bomb blast, but it'll be a reminder to the staff."

The general manager was still muttering.

"Liam!" Reilly barked.

"Okay. I heard. I'll have the house florist fill in the area with potted plants and trees."

Alan Cannon joined them.

"What else can we do with the windows? Any blast resistant glass?"

"As a matter of fact, there is," Cannon offered. "I should have thought of that after Tokyo. The Department of Homeland Security has a Science and Technology Directorate. They've come up with a new bombproof glass that sandwiches glass fibers in the form of a woven cloth soaked with liquid plastic. It's then bonded with adhesive between slim sheets of glass. What's more, it's as strong as the glass in the Beast, the president's limo, but far thinner."

"Sounds good, but how long to order and install?"

"Weeks, probably."

"Damn. And what about the brick and concrete façade?"

"There's another option," Klugo offered. "Quicker, possible better."

"Oh?" Cannon said.

"It's a fabric called Zetix."

"A fabric?" Reilly asked. "How?"

"You'll have to talk to the experts. But it's apparently so strong it can resist multiple car bomb blasts without distress. In principal it absorbs, then disperses the energy. It has pores which open with an impact, allowing blast air to pass through, not solid debris. It could go over your brick and mortar on either side."

"How do we get it?" Schorel wondered, now showing interest in the solution.

"The good news," Klugo explained, "is that it was invented by a UK company. I bet they could send someone in the morning to evaluate and hopefully install. Just Google it. An immediate fix."

When the postmortem concluded, Cannon pulled Reilly aside. "Well buddy, it was a damned good lesson."

"Schorel was right. It was a complete fuckup."

"That too. But we all learned from it and we'll move on. And anyone thinking of taking us down now will see that we're more prepared than expected. They'll rethink going after Soryn."

"You're assuming she's the target," Reilly maintained. "Maybe that's a mistake, too."

* * *

With the exception of the news inquiries, the next morning was quiet. So was the afternoon. The evening dance recital went without incident. There were no problems at night, principally because Ionela Soryn's business manager rudely checked her out of the Kensington Diplomat Hotel and into the Sofitel a block away.

The next morning Reilly flew to Chicago for a quick turnaround.

74

"You don't seemed relieved," Shaw said.

"I'm not. A terrorist needs an audience," Reilly explained. "For all sorts of reasons. Psychological, coercive, recruitment, and political. Radical fundamentalists aim for the first three. They can go anywhere and get the headlines they want. They're willing to kill themselves in the process. But this isn't the case for someone with a true political goal or the people behind the plot. More than anything, they absolutely want to live on. That's who we're dealing with, sir. We may have taken away one opportunity, but we didn't remove their political act."

"You're speculating."

"I'm deadly serious," Reilly sharply countered. "They're still out there."

"Who's out there, Daniel?"

This was the most difficult question of all, but it deserved an answer. A carefully worded answer.

"Russians."

"Now wait!" Shaw saw the immediate political ramifications.

"It's an *idea* based on—"

"One hell of an idea, especially since I've decided to move on the

Moscow management deal."

This was news to Reilly. He didn't hide his surprise.

"We need more time. There are a lot of moving parts," Reilly said, not going into any of them.

"We're not there yet, but we will be in another few weeks," Shaw said. "But this complicates things."

In more ways than you can imagine, Reilly thought.

"You really believe this," Shaw stated more than asked.

"Yes, sir."

"And that *they* will come back?" He was referring to the Russians Reilly suggested were terrorists.

Reilly answered instantly. "I'm afraid *they* never left."

BRUSSELS

Prostitution was a legally sanctioned business in Belgium. Monika, no more her name than the pseudonym Miklos provided, billed out at 500 euros per hour. The night, including all that she would perform plus tip, was 2,000. Miklos paid in cash.

As far as Miklos was concerned, everything was going according to plan. In fact, better than planned. The NATO guard and other assembled security forces had pulled out from the hotel. Something Monika wouldn't let him do. Not for the money she was making.

* * *

The bell at the floral shop door jangled.

"Madame Ketz, as always, you look so beautiful," Liam Schorel said as he kissed the grand dame on both cheeks.

The old woman dressed for another era smiled warmly. "Oh, thank you, Mr. Schorel."

"I trust you're well today."

"Better whenever I get to say hello to you," she said flirtatiously. "Now let me make your day better."

The octogenarian pinned a rose on his suit jacket collar.

"Thank you, madame. You raise my spirits. Now I need your help."

"My pleasure. How may I assist?"

"As only you can do. With a flourish. We need to put a row of large potted plants inside the lobby. You know, to bring some green to the area." Schorel didn't explain the real reason. "What do you have handy?"

CHICAGO

"And if I say it's time for you to move on, that Brussels is safe?" Shaw asked.

"Then I'd have to respond, 'You have the wrong guy in the job,'" Reilly replied.

Shaw laughed. "Well, we both know that's not true."

Reilly grinned.

"There's a lot I don't know about you, Dan," the company chief said. "A bunch I suspect, and a whole lot I admire. So if I put all three together, I have a man on my payroll who I damn well better listen to and let do his job."

"Thank you, sir," Reilly replied.

"Any idea what you're going to do?"

"I'm working on it."

After leaving KR's corporate offices, Reilly stopped at the Midwest Superior Pistol and Gun Range.

"Any experience?" the heavily tattooed owner asked. He couldn't tell by looking at his customer.

"Some. Awhile back," Reilly replied.

"Military?"

"Something like that." Reilly figured that would end the grilling.

The proprietor pursed his lips. "Okay, man. What's your poison?"

Reilly had done homework online and recited what he knew the range had.

"A Gen 2 Glock 19 and a Sig Sauer P229 Elite."

"Okay. You know what you're doing?"

"I do."

"Credit card?"

"Cash."

The owner liked cash.

Reilly took out five $100 bills. "I'll be here for a while."

BRUSSELS

Madame Ketz thought the potted tree in the cooler would work in the lobby, but it was too big for her to move. She called for two house workmen to load it on a dolly. They were just about out the door when Frederik, Johanna Ketz's assistant, returned from a break.

"Stop!" he demanded. "What are you doing?"

"Moving this into the lobby with some others," Ketz explained good-naturedly.

"No, no, no. You can't."

The two men looked to the florist for a decision. Frederik stepped between them.

"This stays in the refrigerator."

"Frederik, I want it in the lobby," she said over his shoulder. "We're getting more delivered and this one—"

"No, Madame Ketz," he continued. "This is a special order for a guest. Remember?"

"No, I don't. And it's been too long," she said. "We'll simply get another."

"No!"

Frederik realized he sounded too harsh. "I'm sorry, Madame Ketz. The man was quite insistent when I took the call. He was specific about the type of plant he wanted in his suite when he arrived and agreed to an extra hold charge."

Frederik took control of the dolly from the workmen and carefully rolled it back to the cooler.

"Who?" she asked.

Ketz's assistant exhaled. "An important NATO delegate. I'll find the receipt. He insisted on a live plant to take in the carbon monoxide.

Can you imagine such a thing?" Frederik added with a laugh.

Ketz lightened. "It's an entitled Englishman, no doubt."

"I think he was. A bit officious. He was uncertain of his exact arrival date. I'm sure you don't want to disappoint him."

"Of course not," she replied. "But we have too little space and it's taken too long. One more week, Frederik. Then it goes out to the lobby where I need it."

Frederik nodded. "Yes, Madame Ketz. One more week."

"Oh, and the temperature is too low in the refrigerator again. Please reset it," the grand dame added before getting back to her own floral arrangements.

"Yes, Madame Ketz." Frederik checked the temperature. It was right where he needed it to be.

75

WASHINGTON, DC

Back at his K Street condo the next day, Dan Reilly dove into more research Spike Boyce had emailed. He printed out twenty-two Excel spreadsheets and arranged them in ascending order on his dining room table—the same table he hadn't eaten at in weeks. He also put State Department advisories for Eastern European nations on the living room floor. The latest warnings from private military contractors were taped to a large mirror. And his own internet searches covered his couch.

After dividing up the content, he began a process of elimination, leaving the bookings to last.

Identify the greatest political hotspots. *Rate* them on an inevitability scale of 1-5, one being highest. Add *subjective analysis*, which was simply his own gut reaction. *Cross reference* against the bookings, looking for any variables that would suggest a credible target.

Reilly remembered the committee discussion about Prussian Army strategist Carl von Clausewitz. The quote that came to mind seemed all the more appropriate. "War is not merely a political act, but a political instrument. The political view is the object, the ultimate truth of the people behind the terrorist."

The political instrument? The political view? The ultimate truth? He thought about all three. The attack was the political instrument. The political view was NATO. The ultimate truth was territory. The terrorist and the people behind the terrorist? Andre Miklos. Behind him? The political stakeholder. The president.

But what territory? Reilly couldn't get the idea out of his head that he was missing something important, something just beyond his reach.

He ran through a mental checklist that spanned his experience. College, military, government, and business. Boston University, Harvard, the US Army, the State Department, and Kensington Royal.

Before he even realized why, Reilly was up and dialing his phone. He remembered.

BRUSSELS

The man kept up his vigil across the street from the Kensington Diplomat. He added a long-lens camera and computer to his tools, taking pictures, printing out headshots, charting delivery schedules, ID'ing security officers, and tracking defensive measures. He even itemized a list of changes that came with the hotel being elevated to Red status.

Wearing sunglasses and a baseball cap and looking every bit like a tourist, he ventured into the target to reassess the active defenses. He casually walked through the lobby, into the restaurant, and back into the public areas. Workmen were installing a fabric of some sort on the windows, both exterior and interior, and a different material on the inside walls. He'd research what it was back in his lair. Large potted plants were in a corner, clearly positioned as a barrier to keep people away from the windows.

All the measures would help contain a blast.

He returned to his perch with dinner. In another few hours he'd sleep.

WASHINGTON, DC

"Colonel, it's Dan Reilly. Sorry to bother you so late. I need your help."

Reilly was using another new cell phone and had called from the roof patio of his building.

Colonel Harrison paused the History Channel documentary he was watching, *The Plot to Overthrow FDR.*

"Not a problem, Mr. Reilly. What can I do for you?"

"Ball's Bluff. Can we talk about the Battle of Ball's Bluff?" Reilly asked.

"I see at least one of my Civil War lectures stuck. The Battle of Leesburg."

"It was considered a humiliating defeat for the Army of the Potomac. For Major General George B. McClellan."

"Quite correct," Harrison confirmed. "Poor intelligence, an inexperienced leader, misunderstood orders, and ill-advised battlefield decisions. It all led up to a disaster."

"Didn't it come down to the Union Army misreading signs? Looking in the wrong place?"

"Precisely. McClellan ordered Brigadier General Charles Pomeroy Stone to identify Confederate troop locations and troop strength near Leesburg, Virginia. Pomeroy sent in a raw officer who reported a line of thirty Confederate tents, but no troops. He assumed the encampment was unprotected. Operating under the limited intelligence, Stone ordered a raid. Three hundred Union forces of the 15th Massachusetts Regiment crossed the Potomac in just two boats, thirty men at a time. At first light they discovered that the trees had obscured the true scene. There was no Confederate camp. So the unit pressed on, but without a clear assessment of the terrain and the danger."

"And the enemy surprised them," Reilly recalled. "From high ground."

"Yes, the North suffered a humiliating defeat. Hundreds killed and captured. For the South, it was a decisive victory early in the war. After the battle, the Union command took to pointing fingers at one another and Congress established a committee that nearly disrupted the war effort."

"The Congressional Joint Committee on the Conduct of War. A Congressional committee made up of politicians," Reilly interjected.

"Radical politicians," Harrison added. "Absent of military training or experience. And what did they do?"

"They put political pressure on Lincoln and challenged his command decisions. They got in the way of prosecuting the war."

"Well, you've proven yourself a good student once again," Harrison said with a full-throated laugh. "So why is this centuries' old battle important to you today?"

Reilly explained that he didn't want to end up like Brigadier General Stone, "looking the wrong way."

"I think you need to tell me more, my boy. What you're really up to."

For the next twenty minutes Reilly explained the through-line from Tokyo to Brussels, his suspicions and his fears. Everything but his work with the agency.

"Well then, if I understand correctly, you've got three objectives to figure out. Exactly when and where the attack will occur, and what the true objective is. Perhaps I can help you with the latter, but the rest is up to you."

"Go ahead," Reilly encouraged.

"If reclaiming territory is Russia's goal, which it most certainly is from a historic standpoint, you must consider the question from a contemporary perspective."

"I am. What country can Gorshkov afford to take?" Reilly asserted.

"No!" Harrison declared. "Go back to your research. Look at your map. Read those reports. But not as Daniel Reilly. Read it through Gorshkov's eyes."

"I'm not sure I . . ."

"Come on," Harrison prompted. "Where's my A student?"

Reilly didn't respond.

"Put it together like a Lincoln, not the Congressional Joint Committee on the Conduct of War. It's not at all what Gorshkov can afford to take—"

Reilly completed the sentence. "It's what can *we* afford to lose."

"And more."

"Without having to go to war."

"Precisely," Harrison told him.

76

WASHINGTON, DC

"Well Dan, you dodged the bullet," CIA agent Bob Heath said, towing the company line. "Time to move on."

They met one another at the Smithsonian American History Museum on Constitution Avenue, walking together for a while, sometimes apart, and constantly scanning to see if they were being followed.

"No," Reilly declared. "We were right and wrong. No victory to celebrate."

"You have something?" Heath countered. "Talk."

"I'm working on it. But I need your help," Reilly responded.

"Look, if you haven't noticed, I don't make all the decisions. They're putting me on something else."

"And when NATO blows up?"

"Wait." Heath noticed someone lingering too close. Not within earshot, but too close for comfort. "Meet me in twenty. Second floor. Political buttons exhibit. Watch your back."

They separated. Heath peeled off to the right. Reilly strolled casually through an exhibit on modern medicine, then World War II Japanese internment. Occasionally he pivoted to see if he was being followed. Only once did he feel concerned. A woman stared just a little too long. He smiled at her, as if to engage. She ignored him and left.

Uncomfortable or burned? Reilly didn't know, but he took extra care until meeting up with Heath again.

"Followed?" the agent asked.

"No. You?"

"Clear."

"Good, then get to it."

"Okay. Stop me when you don't want to hear anymore."

"If it makes you feel better."

"It might."

Reilly talked to Heath quietly while they pretended to examine campaign buttons as far back as Lincoln. Reilly recounted his conversation with Colonel Harrison and the political theory that came out of it. "So, what can we afford to lose without having to go to war?"

Heath didn't stop Reilly.

"I know it's reverse reasoning," Reilly admitted. "Counter to policy, agreements, and treaties. Whatever."

Still no signal to stop.

"So I'm asking you to find out what the Company can't say on the record, but what Nikolai Gorshkov damn well knows is true."

Heath remained quiet.

"It goes right to the core of Gorshkov's beliefs. Nikita Khrushchev built the Berlin Wall in 1961. The US gave up the open city rather than risk war in '61. 1990? A different story. At that point, Mikhail Gorbachev was willing to lose it. Then East Germany. Then the rest of the Eastern Bloc. Now what country or countries have we made a commitment to that we'd be willing to walk away from?"

Reilly fixed his eyes on Heath. The CIA agent thought for a moment and then proposed, "Estonia, Latvia, and Lithuania."

"Damned straight," Reilly replied.

LANGLEY

"Your friend . . . " CIA Director Gerald Watts stated.

"Our associate," Heath replied.

". . . is playing a dangerous political game of chicken."

"Then Reilly's right."

"I hope he's not," Watts stated solemnly.

"He needs help."

Now Watts didn't respond.

Heath rephrased his assertion. "Mr. Director, we *can* help."

Gerald Watts stood behind his desk. "Bob," he began, "tell Reilly to take a breather and stick to his own knitting."

Stick to his own knitting. There was more unsaid than said. In agent-speak it meant "call Reilly off and you dig into the possibilities." Heath heard it perfectly. "Thank you, sir. That'll work for me."

On his way to his office, Heath texted Reilly: "You've got your history professor. I've got mine. Give me a few days."

77

CIA HEADQUARTERS

Heath's expert was a 280-pound PhD from Stanford, as solid in his Baltic history as he was in muscle. This was his tenth year with the agency. Even though he wasn't a field operative, he had trained with them at the Farm. Bob Heath had only met Dr. Ted Policano once, but his reputation preceded him.

"Thank you for coming, Dr. Policano," Heath said with a handshake. The professor had a good four inches on him. He had to look up.

"Ted. Plain and simple. What can I do for you?"

"High-stakes gamble in the Baltic states," Heath said.

Policano smiled. "Somebody finally read my paper."

"No. What paper?"

The PhD was dismayed. "You mean you didn't see what I wrote?"

"No."

"How urgent is your problem?"

"I didn't say it was urgent."

"Yes you did. By calling me," Policano declared. "Sit down. You better take some notes."

REILLY'S OFFICE

It was basic, old-fashioned legwork. The kind that newspaper reporters have done for generations. Detailed, painstaking, exhausting, and mostly unfulfilling. But not unproductive. Crossing names off lists, the process of elimination, no matter how time-consuming, remained the best investigative tool available to him.

Reilly focused on the three possible countries. From north to south, Estonia, Latvia and Lithuania. They all shared borders with Russia. They all had ports on the Baltic Sea. *All strategic . . . like Crimea*, Reilly thought.

Reilly scoured the internet for history on the Baltic states. An hour into the research he began leaning toward Latvia over Estonia and Lithuania. He read about the nation's struggles. German invaders during medieval times, the Polish-Lithuanian rule that followed, the Swedish reign, two hundred years under the Russian Empire, short-lived independence, three governments during World War I, the German march through Latvia, Hitler's order to reduce the population by 50 percent, the postwar Soviet era, which lasted into 1991, and finally the modern era as an EU nation. But, based on what he read, Reilly believed that *finally* might not be so final. He found reports that pointed to a pro-Russian separatist movement that harkened back centuries.

"Jesus," he said aloud. "It's a country with a lit fuse. A damn short lit fuse."

CIA HEADQUARTERS

Policano similarly narrowed his discussion to one country. "The most vulnerable," the CIA historian observed.

"Latvia is really two countries with two distinct populations. The Latvians and *the others*. The *others* are left over from Soviet-era rule. They're virtually second-class citizens who speak Russian and have limited voice in the government. Yet, they represent 40 percent of the population. In Riga, the capital, it's 50 percent. There, Russian is spoken as much as Latvian. For those 200,000 people, their news and entertainment comes from Moscow. Many supported the annexation of Crimea. They're disenfranchised noncitizens. Leftovers from the Cold War. They weren't granted Latvian citizenship after the USSR imploded, and they've been discriminated against ever since."

"They're the perfect scapegoat," Heath concluded.

REILLY'S OFFICE

It gets worse, Reilly concluded as he continued to read. After the Soviet Union broke up, Russia developed a patron relationship over its former states, encouraging partnerships, especially over oil. Latvia's pipelines to Western European markets were absolutely critical. Its ports, essential.

He learned how Latvian ports played a key role in Russia's economic survival and how a new oil terminal in the Gulf of Finland would be a game changer for Russia's economic development.

A report from Stratfor, a leading geopolitical research site, pointed to a political roadblock. Votes. A huge slice of Latvia's population that would support Russian deals couldn't vote simply because as noncitizens, they lacked the right to vote. *It was a disaster waiting to happen.*

CIA HEADQUARTERS

"And that has had a direct impact on the Kremlin's ability to close the deals it wants. But Russia has a poison bullet that's been loaded and ready to fire since 1993," Policano continued.

"What?" asked Heath.

"In 1993 Russia made a declaration not unlike NATO Article 5. It's called the military doctrine. Fundamentally, Russia allowed itself the right to use force if the rights of Russian citizens in other nations were violated or if military blocs that threatened Russian security interests ever expanded."

"Jesus! This has been out there all this time and no one's made hay of it?"

"For years things just moved along, governed by a regard for 'conflict management.' The principal objective? Not to piss off Moscow. But if anyone had read my paper . . ." Policano shook his head. "Hell, I've been talking to a wall for years."

REILLY'S OFFICE

Why? Reilly wondered at the same time. *Exactly why Latvia?* Further research told him. Years ago, Russian President Boris Yeltsin had taken a conciliatory approach, seeking a spirit of friendship with the Baltic states.

He scanned the Stratfor summary further. He discovered a disturbing ticking time bomb. In opposition with Yeltsin, Russian generals and a number of high-ranking ministers wanted the Kremlin to keep its military bases in Latvian territory. Yeltsin disagreed and gave them up. Those generals and ministers were now in control of Russia.

CIA HEADQUARTERS

"We're listening now," Heath said. "The pressure point is Latvia?"

"Yes," Dr. Policano stated. "It goes back to when Russia abandoned its Skrunda early-warning radar sites in Latvia. Those installations had covered Western Europe. But they were disassembled. The facilities become ghost towns. As a result, the Kremlin lost key assets for tracking incoming ICBMs. Big regret."

"Did they get anything in return?" Heath asked.

"Yes. Oil routes. More than half of Latvia's natural gas, oil, and electricity now comes from Russia, with the Latvian ports of Riga, Ventspils, and Liepāja all being vital to the trade. In fact, Latvia traffics more Russian oil than any other Baltic state. On the flip side, Latvia's oil purchases account for one of the largest and most reliable sources of profit for the Russian Federation."

"Then where's the problem?" Heath asked.

"Not where. Who. Gorshkov. He wants more. Actually, everything. A stable transit corridor through Latvia to the ports. New missile installations and the ambitious expansion of Oilvolgo, a massive Russian oil company that could swallow up the lion's share of service stations in Latvia.

"And underscoring those commercial benefits, there's the political issue. The treatment of the Russian-speaking nationals in Latvia. The numbers are down from 500,000 to 200,000 since the end of the Soviet era, but 200,000 disenfranchised, nonvoting, second-class citizens gives Gorshkov some moral high ground in a human rights debate. And when more outspoken Russian-Latvian separatists are arrested—or worse murdered, which happened to one oil magnate very recently—and when Moscow views NATO acting with more bluster, Gorshkov gets ever closer to pulling the trigger with that poison bullet in the barrel."

"Acting in defense of a beleaguered population."

"Exactly. There are two other components that are critical," Policano continued. "One, Russia's Federal Security Services has been recruiting Baltic politicians, members of the business community, Latvia's press, and expats to ascend from the inside. Considering where Gorshkov came from, it's a brilliant strategy. Put sleepers in place and provide the wake up bell they can't miss. Some are awake right now. We know that a number who are negotiators for Russian oil companies were, quote, unquote, 'former agents' who made little effort to hide past affiliations. They routinely ensure the success of big deals in ways that make their business problems and the people who caused them to go away. You don't need a photograph to picture how. These blatant practices reached legendary heights when an ex-KGB officer was brought in as Russia's ambassador to halt the sale of one Baltic oil company to a Western firm in favor of Oilvolgo ownership. As the Russian oil industry grew, profits were siphoned off to the Kremlin, which used the capital to advance its foreign policy ambitions.

"Now, Russia is working on a pipeline that will connect the South China Sea to the Baltic Sea. Gorshkov wants to replace the oil from unstable producer countries such as Saudi Arabia, Indonesia, Nigeria, and Venezuela. He's smartly creating a hedge against ever-increasing US energy domination. At the same time, EU policies are working to increase rather than decrease dependency on Russian oil."

"And the second component?"

"Yes, the most important. The Kremlin houses its Baltic fleet at

Kaliningrad, Russia. Besides being a nuclear base, it's free of ice and perfect to launch from year-round. From there, Gorshkov can project power north toward Latvia, but also to Poland and Germany.

"Shit," Heath fumed. "And this all means?"

"You're asking what poker move Gorshkov will make?" Policano replied.

"Yes," Heath said fully engaged. "Fold, bluff, or double down?"

"In my estimation, one not presently shared by the White House, Gorshkov will not fold. So take that off the table. He's an expert bluffer, or better yet, liar. But that only delays what I consider the inevitable."

"He'll double down," Heath whispered.

REILLY'S OFFICE

Reilly began to conclude that the inevitable was a strike against Latvia. He reasoned that NATO and the United States might bark a little, but in the end, the West would look the other way.

It all came to him. "Crimea two," he whispered. "A second Ukraine."

CIA HEADQUARTERS

"Gorshkov's reckless, but that reckless?" Heath asked.

Policano thought for a moment. "Reckless? I wouldn't say reckless. More brazen. An attitude fueled by the Russian people. They're behind him. They might hate the embargo, the fact that their economy has been tanking, and that their local politics are corrupt. They might hate all of those things. But they love their leader. Like his predecessor, he's provided discipline and order. He exudes confidence and has reestablished Russia's geographic dominance. So far we've done nothing to dissuade them or discourage him. And disenfranchised populations in the Baltic provide Moscow a bully pulpit from which it can preach the gospel according to Nikolai Gorshkov."

REILLY'S OFFICE

Now Reilly wondered why the Baltic states, and Latvia in particular, hadn't asked for more NATO protection. Again, the answer was in the global assessments and talk on the street. It was unlikely that Western allies would have the stomach for a shooting war over the Baltic.

CIA HEADQUARTERS

"And another point not widely discussed," Policano explained. "We have fewer US forces in Europe than there are policemen in New York."

"Christ Almighty!" Heath exclaimed.

"So years after the Cold War when we thought we'd all be safe, Russia actually holds regional conventional superiority over NATO. From my perspective, Russia's land, sea, and air capabilities would wreak havoc on NATO should we mount a defense of the Baltic states."

"But we've got ground forces all through the region."

"Yes," Policano acknowledged. "And we've conducted multiple tabletop war simulations with analysts that envision a surprise Russian ground invasion of Latvia. All of the sims end with the elimination of NATO resistance at the gates of Riga within 36–60 hours from the start of the assault."

"Then we should up our presence," Heath argued. "Move troops further east. Raise noise about Russian long-range bomber flyovers in Canadian airspace and submarines testing our own territorial integrity, and we should make more of the nuclear arms in Kaliningrad."

"Assuming that NATO has a week to consider that an invasion is imminent, we'd deploy up to twelve battalions to the Baltic states, including the 173rd Airborne Brigade Combat Team based in Vicenza, Italy. Also available are some eighteen NATO fighter and bomber squadrons."

"Good." Heath felt he had cracked the code.

"Not good enough. Russia would counter with twenty-two battalions including four or more tank divisions, ready firepower from its Western Military District, and twenty-seven air squadrons to our eighteen. Russia would have air superiority.

"Our consultants at RAND and other agencies estimated that the

NATO M1 Abrams tanks and thirty M2 Bradley fighting vehicles in Grafenwöhr, Germany, would take ten days to deploy. Too late. Our ground troops would be overrun and unable to retreat. The dirty little secret is that geography favors Russia in all the scenarios. And if we act in accord with Article 5, we do so at the peril of plunging ourselves into a nuclear war. What was it that astrophysicist Carl Sagan said?"

"I don't know," Heath replied.

"'Imagine a room awash in gasoline, and there are two implacable enemies in that room. One of them has 9,000 matches. The other has 7,000 matches.' Insightful because no matter who strikes the match, it's the end of the world. The lesson is that while Russia can't challenge us globally, it can do so locally."

"So we fold?" Heath's question hung in the air.

Policano waited a moment to reply. "I don't know," he finally said. "That's a decision for the White House. And of course, that comes down to *who's* in the White House. At this moment, the Joint Chiefs would support engagement. Between us, I don't think this president would."

"So you believe that NATO has no way of successfully repelling a conventional invasion of Latvia by Russia short of nuclear war, which in itself is not an option?" Bob Heath solemnly asked.

"*Successfully*, no way."

REILLY'S OFFICE

Dan Reilly closed his eyes imaging the onslaught. *Troops crossing the border by the thousands, parachuting from transports. Submarines blockading the ports. Then the decision point. To fight Russia or not?*

Not, he concluded.

CIA HEADQUARTERS

"Inevitable?" Heath dared.

REILLY'S OFFICE

More than probable, Reilly thought.

CIA HEADQUARTERS

"And from there?" Heath even feared asking the question.

"The successful reannexation of Latvia would undermine the Baltic people's faith in the EU and NATO," Policano predicted. "The pro-Russian factions linked to Moscow, largely identified as the Harmony Party, are already gaining seats in the local, regional, and national elections, even with so many pro-Russians unable to vote."

"How?"

"Thanks to already nationalized Russians who can vote. All they need to do is scream for help."

"From Gorshkov."

"Yes. Or he acts on his own. Russia crosses the border on whatever pretext it chooses and sweeps in to liberate the country. It wouldn't be a return to Communism, but we'd see a new economic association of nations that begins with an invasion and ends with Russian domination."

Heath repeated his question. "You see this as inevitable?"

"Yes, and imminent."

REILLY'S OFFICE

Dan Reilly had experienced war as a serviceman in Afghanistan and during his term with the State Department. He was also in the line of fire as a Kensington Royal executive; in Egypt at the end of Hosni Mubarak's regime and in Libya for Muammar Gaddafi's last days.

Now he foresaw the fall of a Western ally and feared that he was inextricably linked to it. He needed more than knowledge. He needed a weapon. And he needed his colleague Alan Cannon back in Brussels.

78

BRUSSELS, BELGIUM

The late evening knock on her door surprised Madame Ketz. It was late for a visitor and the foyer doorbell hadn't rung. *Must be another tenant.*

"Coming. Coming. Who is it?"

No one responded.

She looked through a peephole in her heavily bolted door and saw Frederik standing a few feet back. He held up a canvas market bag with French bread and a bottle of wine sticking out.

"Oh dear, it's much too late," she said, loud enough for him to hear.

He knocked again and smiled.

"Oh please, Madame Ketz. I was in the neighborhood and thought—"

"All right. But give me a moment to put myself together."

A moment turned into five minutes. But, true to her word, Ketz, who had been in a bathrobe, returned dressed and made-up nicely. She unlocked the door and welcomed Frederik in, only half scolding him.

"Do you have any idea of the hour?"

Of course he did. Nearly 10:00 p.m.

"I simply wanted to show my gratitude and apologize for the way I acted the other day."

"Well then, I accept. And not to be impolite myself, it really is too late for me to be seen entertaining a gentlemen." The queen of the Kensington Diplomat wasn't just referring to the hour. She joked, "Neighbors will talk."

He began removing items from the tote.

"Allow me one drink with you, Madame Ketz. Then I'll say goodbye."

Goodbye, not goodnight? The word struck her as wrong.

She studied the young man. He hummed a tune and cheerily laid out the contents.

"Here, I'll do that."

She plated the cheese, bread, pâté and knife while Frederik leisurely walked around her flat. He ran his hand along the floral wallpaper just above the wainscoting. He examined his fingers. Not a speck of dust. He admired the handmade quilt spread across an elegant 1920s canapé, and resting in the corner, a sunflower embroidered pillow, soft from years of use.

He continued to tour the flat, living room, kitchen, and dining area all in one. He adjusted a few crooked picture frames. By the looks of them, they were family photos through the years. A few of Ketz, most capturing happy moments as a wife and mother. On the bureau, more photographs with Ketz and a girl Frederik presumed to be her daughter. The oldest appeared to be when Ketz was in her mid-sixties and the young woman around twenty-five, some twenty or twenty-five years earlier.

"Your daughter?" he asked.

"Yes, Adele," she answered quietly.

There were loving letters and postcards from Adele, a photograph of her in front of a house. On the back, a handwritten date, location, and the words, "*La douceur du foyer.*" Home sweet home.

"A beautiful cottage. Her home?"

"Yes."

Frederik continued to hum as he took in other mementos. He examined a baby's handprint in clay, various miniature busts of classical composers given to children for piano recitals, and an open box of letters and post cards. All the things he'd expect to see in an old lady's home.

"Well, I think we're ready. But you must be gone in a few minutes."

"I promise I will, Madame Ketz." It was not a warm reply.

She studied his eyes as she would a patron at her shop. She recognized a heartless look that she'd seen years before as a child. In the eyes of Nazis who marched through Belgium. She'd seen it again and again when Soviet officials stayed at the hotel. It was the look of . . .

Frederik uncorked the bottle.

"Certain to put you to sleep."

An even colder comment.

Madame Ketz put the plate and knife down on the coffee table and instinctively backed away.

"I alarmed you."

Ketz took another step away. She was now aware that he was wearing thin leather gloves. It also occurred to her that he had gotten into her building without ringing the bell.

"Frederik," she said nervously, "I shouldn't have invited you in. I'm very tired."

She took a wide berth around him toward the door. But he grabbed her wrist.

"Madame Ketz. One glass." His grip tightened as he dragged her to the table. "You must."

"Frederik, please! No!"

"Sit!"

"No, no!"

He forced the old woman into a chair. Holding her shoulders down, he felt thin bones that he could easily crack. But that wouldn't be the way. With his free gloved hand he poured the wine.

"A sip." Frederik smiled coldly. *The smile of the Russian thugs*, she thought. *The cruelty of the Nazis.*

Ketz tried to squirm free. She spied her kitchen knife on the platter. Almost within reach. *If only . . .*

"You won't let me drink alone," she said, hoping to give herself time to think.

"Oh, I can't. I have my work—"

"Here, madame." He handed Ketz the glass.

"A toast in your honor," Frederik said. "To a full life well-lived."

She brought the wine to her lips and stopped.

"But you must," he said.

Frederik then forced Ketz to swallow.

It was a good wine, she oddly thought. *Perhaps too much tannin to her taste, but—*

"There," he added. "Wasn't that good?"

She sat transfixed, expecting to quickly die. Frederik assumed the same. He loosened his grip slightly. In that instant, mustering strength and courage, Madame Ketz threw the wine glass in his face. He instinctively released her to wipe his eyes, then stepped on the shattered glass. Again an automatic response. He looked down. That gave her a moment to lunge for the knife.

It was a futile attempt. An old woman against an assassin. Feet for her to cover. Inches for him. He seized Ketz, slammed her back into the chair, and slapped her hard across the face.

"Enough!"

Impatient and furious, he reached for the embroidered pillow and pressed it hard over her mouth and nose.

Through the struggling, Frederik thought he heard the muffled cries of "Adele, Adele." An old woman calling out to her daughter in France. Then, nothing.

79

MOSCOW, RUSSIAN FEDERATION

Gorshkov had his speech on a teleprompter. But if the operator suddenly suffered a heart attack and died, the president wouldn't have missed a beat. This was his own handcrafted speech, precise, pointed, and political. It had three intended audiences with unmistakable messages for each.

He would whip up Russians with patriotic platitudes. Latvians would be reminded that they lived in a dangerous, bifurcated nation split between pro and anti-Moscow loyalties. And finally, NATO would hear a warning. He didn't care about the United States. He was certain his remarks would largely go unreported.

The speech was broadcast live from the Great Hall in the Kremlin. This gave the president his dramatic long walk to the camera. The longer the walk, the more the urgency to his pronouncement. This time he'd take nearly ninety seconds after the news anchor's introduction.

Finally at the podium, he spoke.

"My friends. My compatriots. My fellow Russians, I come to you tonight with a heavy heart."

He didn't smile. Smiling was for pretenders and politicians. Gorshkov cast himself as a leader or an emperor. His philosophy: *Let those who follow smile.*

"Our borders continue to be tested by NATO forces. Our sovereignty is threatened by imperialists that seek to limit us. Our character is meant to submit to the will of nations. Our economy is seen as theirs to exploit. Our will is what they would like to break. This, *we* will not . . . *I* will not allow."

He gave *I* more emphasis than *we*.

"Just days ago, NATO command ran exercises with live ammunition a mere 300 meters from the Russian border in the Latgale region of Latvia, frightening our brothers and sisters, loyal ethnic Russians living under the yoke of tyranny as a belittled second class, devoid of basic freedoms. They're representative of hundreds of thousands of other embittered Russian cousins who have turned to us for help.

"If this were but one example of harassment, we could excuse it as simply an ill-begotten test. Unacceptable on every level, but a test. But NATO's practices are no test. And Latvia's government has banned several Russian state-run television channels, further depriving ethnic Russians of free and unfettered access to information.

"Those are merely a few of many foreboding signs. There are more. Latvia has spent more than 150 million euros on 125 combat vehicles. It's their largest procurement contract ever. The largest ever!" he repeated. "And with their NATO henchmen, they venture ever closer to our homeland. Time and again they fly their planes to test our defenses and our resolve. This is another test they will fail."

The president had barely revved up when he launched into a litany of other offenses.

"NATO troops, including a contingent of six hundred Americans, are rotating through Baltic nations, Poland, Romania, and Ukraine. Recently NATO leaders in Brussels approved rapid deployment forces that could be in Eastern Europe within hours. In preparation, a freight train of American armored vehicles was tracked leaving Dalbe Station in Latvia, heading toward our Western border.

"We have seen other trains transporting at least thirty-eight vehicles including semitrailers loaded with tanks, personnel carriers, petrol tankers,

Humvees, and medical vehicles. Weaponry, ammunition, hi-tech equipment, and medical support? Medical support? Who carries medical support unless they believe there will be the need to treat wounded? I'll tell you who. NATO. The nations of the European Union and the United States of America scheme with their allies to push, prod, and pressure the Russian Federation and loyal ethnic Russians who live beyond the sphere of the Kremlin's protection in countries that share our border.

"These actions are in violation of the 1997 Russia–NATO agreement which expressly forbids NATO nations from having troops permanently stationed in the Baltic states. Let me be perfectly clear. America and its allies may call this an exercise. It is not. I will call it what it is. Subterfuge. Deceit. Lies. Moving troops from one country to another is a NATO shell game. We people of the Russian Federation will not be taken as fools. We know what you are doing, and it is unacceptable. You conduct live-fire exercises in earshot of Russia nationals. You build permanent barracks where tents had stood. You play chicken with our Russian aircrafts.

"What would the American president do if one thousand Russian troops equipped with seven hundred military vehicles, armed assault helicopters, fully loaded tanks, and missile defense arrays parked twenty-five kilometers from New York?"

Next, an unspecific, rhetorical admonition.

"Today, anti-Russian gangsters, supported and directed by the West and its NATO henchmen, have launched attacks against Russian nationals conducting business in Kiev, in Riga, and in Bucharest. They have also campaigned against and attacked pro-Russian nationals exerting the right to speak and protest. All of this will have far-reaching and unfortunate consequences. That's a promise.

"A warning to the United States. You are threatening ethnic Russians. You are threatening the Russian Federation. And you are threatening *me*! In doing so, you and your Western alliance are venturing perilously close to war.

"Take heed. I know your intent. Now know mine. By my word, we will defend ethnic Russians wherever they live. By my word and promise, we will protect Russian ethnic minorities who are discriminated against. By my word, promise, and deed, we will repel any threat to our borders."

Gorshkov continued his tirade for another twenty minutes. He finished abruptly, pivoted 180 degrees on the balls of his feet in a perfectly executed and deliberately commanding military about-face, and paraded away. The camera followed him for all the time it took for his long walk back down the Great Hall.

80

BRUSSELS, BELGIUM

The observer across the street tracked Reilly's return to the hotel through the telephoto lens on his Nikon.

He watched him pull a single suitcase and stop to talk to the doorman and the lone security officer posted at the entrance. Reilly appeared to check the enhanced security measures and the new warning signs at the barriers. The hotel executive took a moment for another conversation with the officer, who pointed inside where couches and chairs had been moved further from the glass.

The observer figured time was growing short. *Reilly was back.*

* * *

Security had also improved enough for Schorel to be alerted that Reilly was on-site. The general manager greeted him at the front desk with his key cards.

A handshake and a hug later, Schorel asked if Reilly wanted to wait to talk until KR security chief Alan Cannon arrived.

"No. He'll be in late. But we can begin."

"Certainly," Schorel said pleasantly.

"You've got everything?"

"Yes."

The IT department had a second computer up and running in the general manager's office. Boyce's hyper-focused search produced upcoming bookings from the Baltic nations, Latvia in particular.

"Here's one," Schorel said. "Out of Riga." The general manager's initial excitement evaporated when he saw that it was a school group. The same thing happened when he found another that was only booked as a stopover on the way to a South African game reserve.

Reilly met similar dead ends. A culinary tour, a senior citizens club, a doctor's group from Liberia that had been mislabeled as Latvian, and a tourist group of twenty-six from St. Petersburg. Then he found sixteen rooms blocked all week and labeled with a VIP code. No names were attached, but the number looked familiar. VIP495.

"Who does this belong to?" Reilly asked.

"Oh, it's my code. We get members of the diplomatic corps all the time. 495 stand for—"

"Russia's telephone code," Reilly interrupted.

"Yes. Right. I code American diplomats similarly. 011. Easy to remember."

"So who are they?" Reilly looked at the spreadsheet again.

"We don't always get the precise names. Mostly mid-level people. They're often in and out for meetings or checking out who's doing what at NATO conferences. They drink us dry in the restaurant."

"Can you get names?"

"Some, not all."

Sixteen rooms, Reilly thought. *Enough to count.*

* * *

After three hours on the computer, Reilly was ready for his room, a quick shower, and a shave. Refreshed, he changed into a light summer sports jacket, blue slacks, and a light blue pullover shirt. Back in the lobby he surveyed the surroundings again.

He admired the architectural touches, the detail, and the style. *Maybe,* he thought, *maybe we should close down. Remove the option.* But he was certain that would only delay the inevitable.

The one thing he did know, security definitely was more visible. Staff had walkie-talkies. Some recognized him and nodded. Those who didn't, heard through their earpieces that a bigwig was on the floor.

One message was getting through, "If you see something, say something."

Reilly slowly scanned the whole expanse, noting the line of potted plants, which created artful space between the windows and the seating area. While the plants themselves wouldn't contain any explosion, the barrier kept people away from the windows.

He also checked the windows to see how the new blast inhibiting Zetix looked from the inside looking out. He could see the difference, but he wasn't sure the typical guest would. The British installer had done a good job.

Most importantly, outside the bollard tops were painted red, the best signal to potential terrorists that the hotel was a harder target. However, bombs placed inside still presented the greatest threat.

To that point, Reilly was surprised only one bomb-sniffing dog and handler walked the property. He'd change that. In addition to the dog at the front of the house there should be another inside, and a third at the loading dock off the back alley.

Reilly looked across the lobby. He saw another vulnerable spot. Bistango had its own street entrance. And once anyone was inside the restaurant, they could walk right into the hotel. The problem was compounded by the fact that no dog and officer covered the exterior restaurant door.

Reilly walked through the lobby toward Bistango, but automatically turned to make a detour into the florist shop to say hello to Madame Ketz.

The bell on the door rang. Ketz's assistant was busy arranging flowers at a work table.

"Pardon," Reilly said in French. *"Où est Madame Ketz?"*

Frederik stepped forward. Recognizing the questioner, he answered in English.

"Ah, Madame has taken some deserved time off to see her daughter in . . ." he paused, "I believe she said Bruges. May I help you?"

"Thank you, no. Wonderful to hear. Do you expect her back soon?"

"Perhaps in two weeks. It's her holiday."

"Well then, I'll probably miss her. Give her my best when she returns."

"Of course, Mr. Reilly," Frederik politely responded.

Reilly did a quick double take, somewhat surprised that the assistant knew his name.

"Thank you. And you are?"

"Frederik. Madame Ketz's assistant." Realizing his faux pas he added, "Madame always insisted I learn names."

Reilly laughed. "That's her for certain."

He scanned the florist shop, noticing the large tree crowded into the cooler.

Frederik followed his eyes. "Ah, your boutonniere. Allow me."

"That's okay. I'm fine. Thank you for your time."

"You're quite welcome."

Reilly left the florist shop and turned left toward the restaurant. He passed through the arch that separated the hotel from Bistango. A short line of patrons preceded him. Once they were seated the maître d' offered, "May I help you?"

"Well, as a matter of fact, yes. I'd love to have dinner in a while, but first a little walk around." Reilly produced a business card and his business was instantly understood.

"Ah, yes. Whenever you're ready, Mr. Reilly."

Reilly walked through the restaurant, into the kitchen, and finally the restrooms. Bistango had an open floor plan except for the private dining room at the back of the house, adjacent to the kitchen.

Finished with his cursory inspection, he returned to the host, who led him to a table. He ordered an old-fashioned with bourbon and studied the people in the room. As he nursed his drink he made up biographies for the patrons. It was a time-honored intelligence practice, but also the tool of writers, artists, and actors. *What's your story?* he rhetorically and silently asked the people he observed.

There was a young American couple on vacation, likely from New York. American because of the shopping bags she had and the classic Brooklyn T-shirt he wore. An easy giveaway.

In the corner were two well-dressed French lawyers being treated to lunch by an older man, possibly a Brussels art dealer. This might even be the meal to seal a deal for their law office art collection, Reilly surmised.

Across the restaurant at a window, a single businesswoman, perhaps in advertising, was waiting for her companion, who was late. Would it be a man or a woman? Reilly thought a girlfriend and they'd trade office war stories.

A waiter interrupted his exercise. Reilly quickly considered the menu and chose the beef carpaccio with truffles and aged Parmesan cheese to start, and snails with garlic butter as his main course.

He returned to his survey and watched as the advertising woman was indeed met by a girlfriend, the lawyers were in fact looking at art on the dealer's iPad, and the Brooklyn accent was impossible to miss when the New York couple walked by his table.

Reilly looked beyond the near patrons to get a better picture of the entire restaurant. Bistango was bright and exciting, in sharp contrast with the hotel decor. He focused on the modern art on the walls that the art dealer had noticed and a new sculpture that could have been influenced by the work of famed Belgium artist Pol Bury. Surreal spiral works and spheres and triangles on pedestals set off quadrants within Bistango. They were distinctive and modern, and added to the open ambiance without blocking any lines of sight. Some reflected the room back into itself, others caught, bent, and filtered the light. *Perfect designs, perfectly placed,* he thought. Even the back private dining room, visible through a glass wall, still had an air of privacy with magnificent cement tree sculptures adorned with bronze leaves that rose five feet and gave the restaurant the feel of the outside coming in. *Relaxing,* was the word that came to mind.

Reilly did relax through his early dinner. He watched people come and go. Tourists, locals, families, and if his assessments were correct, representative of multiple foreign services. Then a troubling thought occurred to him. Something he'd overlooked. Something terribly important.

He signaled for the check, settled up, and returned to the general manager's office.

"Yes, the restaurant's a completely separate operation," Schorel explained. "I'm not sure they'll want to cooperate."

"We won't know until we ask, will we?" Reilly insisted.

"Right. I'll set a meeting for tomorrow."

"Now," Reilly insisted.

"It's their busy time."

He still doesn't get it. Reilly reasoned. Schorel wasn't an obstructionist. He was a nice enough man, dedicated, but he just couldn't recognize the importance, and the danger. *A better manager would have.*

* * *

The restaurateur was off the property, but Claire d'Isle, his general manager, was in the office beyond the kitchen reviewing reservations.

Speaking in French, Schorel introduced Reilly, who presented his business card.

"Thank you," the 28-year-old beauty said, immediately switching to English. "How may I help?"

"The hotel is increasing visible security measures," Reilly replied.

"Is there a problem?" she asked.

"More an ongoing concern. We're examining and evaluating everything."

Reilly didn't want to create undue worry, but he needed the young woman to recognize the gravity of the situation.

"We'll be posting a bomb-sniffing dog at your entrance," he added.

This was even news to Schorel. He stifled his surprise. Claire d'Isle couldn't.

"But this could kill our business!"

"Mademoiselle, rest assured, that's the last thing I want to do."

81

WASHINGTON, DC
THE WHITE HOUSE

"Will someone please translate for me? And I don't mean Russian to English. I have that. Tell me what Gorshkov's really saying."

President Alexander Crowe was dead serious. He tossed the question out to his top foreign intelligence team in the Oval Office. National Security Advisor Pierce Kimball, Central Intelligence Director Gerald Watts, and Chairman of the Joint Chiefs General Jeffrey Jones. Predictably, none of America's news channels had reported deeply on Gorshkov's speech, but it still made the lead in the PDB, the president's daily brief, prepared by the national security advisor.

This was NSA Pierce Kimball's cue.

"He's a revanchist."

"A re-what?" Crowe asked.

"Revanchist. French."

"I said speak English!"

"From revenge," Kimball explained. "Someone who believes that great gain comes from a war. It's an appeal to ethnic nationalism both within and outside a nation's borders. A justification to gain support through patriotism and to regain land once held. It goes back to the period following the Franco-Prussian War when Prussian nationalists wanted to reclaim the lost Alsace-Lorraine territory and avenge the French defeat."

"He wouldn't dare," General Jones bellowed.

"Crimea," CIA Director Watts replied. "Georgia. Damned straight he would."

"Remember the threat. The Kremlin claims it could take any neighboring capital in under a week," Kimball added. "But, on the surface, his speech doesn't have anything new. Sure it was loaded with bellicose threats, but no specific deadlines, no specific warnings—'if you do this, we'll do that,' no ultimatum. What he didn't say and what we know, is that *he's* the one testing the borders. Testing them with his warplanes over the Baltic borders. Royal Air Force jets have scrambled to turn back Russian fighters that speed across Europe to the English Channel. Hell, this year alone 250 Russian planes have been intercepted by NATO aircraft. And as you well know, Gorshkov's subs are probing our own borders. Want some perspective, Mr. President?"

"I have the feeling I'm going to hear it."

"It's the highest number of interceptions since the end of the Cold War. We're responding to his Western Military District's buildup, which he's been increasing every year for the past four years. Of course, he doesn't explain that on TV. Nor does he admit that they've deployed more than 1,500 pieces of new and upgraded military hardware since last winter. Equipment and manpower, which by agreement can stay put while we have to move our troops from country to country."

General Jones picked up the argument. "Gorshkov has ordered 4,000 military drills in the last 12 months compared to our 275. And yet he lies to his own people."

"Back to my question."

"I'll take it," CIA Director Gerald Watts said. "We believe he's either looking for us to provoke him or he's actively working on creating a provocation himself."

"To . . . ?"

"To storm in." He paused.

"Where?" the president asked.

"Actually, we have our suspicions," Director Watts said. "Gorshkov speaks about it, too. Latvia, for one."

"I've heard this before, for years," the president complained.

"Only now we rate the threat higher, Mr. President," the CIA chief added.

Gerald Watts went into an explanation. "No names, sir, but I have an asset who doubles as an international businessman. He concurs. Our man has growing worries that, quite frankly, we didn't value highly until recently. Now, we're considering it credible."

"Why now?" Crowe asked.

"We're building on expanding intel that the Russians have a serious, ongoing, long-standing operation. In its purest form, they're making it look like they're being targeted by anti-Russian nations in Eastern Europe, when in fact, they could be behind the attacks. These attacks have been designed to give them the justification to sweep in and protect their interests, those loyal to Moscow, and their homeland. We have growing concern that it's a sham."

"What kind of attacks?"

"Bombs and assassinations. We're looking into the Tokyo and Kiev hotel bombings, assassinations in Moscow, Kiev, and Riga. All possibly related."

"I haven't seen anything that would link these into a war-worthy response from Moscow."

"No, Mr. President. You haven't, but it's making news in Russia. Gorshkov's hitting it hard and it's the underpinning of Gorshkov's last speech."

"Tell me more about this double agent."

"Not a double agent. An individual. A corporate executive we trust. I'd prefer not to get into more detail. Let's just say he's very busy these days with both jobs."

"So if he's right . . . if the agency is right, how much time do we have?" the president asked solemnly. "A year? A month? A week?"

"Mr. President, we really don't know."

"Well, until you know, we have nothing to work with."

82

BRUSSELS, BELGIUM

The four-man nighttime maintenance crew, three regulars and one substitute, wrapped up their overnight cleaning shift at the hotel by mopping the Bistango floor. As they packed up, the substitute backed into one of the tree sculptures.

"Shit!" he exclaimed as it toppled over.

The impact smashed the piece.

"Jesus Christ. You have any idea how expensive that is?" the crew chief shouted.

"It's just a fucking fake tree," the replacement complained

"Probably more than your yearly salary. Clean that up and when you're finished, find another job!"

The man already had another job. He worked for Andre Miklos.

* * *

Reilly awoke uncharacteristically late at 9:00 a.m. But he awoke refreshed for the first time in days. He checked his phone for emails and texts. Alan Cannon sent him an address. Chris Collins forwarded corporate missives. Nothing terribly urgent. And Brenda Sheldon just wished him a safe day. There were also three new texts from Marnie.

He hadn't called her in days. He realized he had to get over his apprehensions. *Too paranoid. And for no valid reason*, he thought. He'd call her tonight, maybe make new plans.

That was all. It looked to be a quiet day.

* * *

Frederik opened the flower shop for the morning deliveries that would soon be cleared through security. He stepped on a piece of paper that had been slid under the door. It was a handwritten note on hotel stationery: "Problem. Large potted plant needed in Bistango to replace broken statue."

It had no signature, but Frederik knew the author. It was a problem for which he had the actual solution.

* * *

Across the street, the observer pushed aside the curtain of his window. Another day. A rainy day. On a side table: coffee, an almond croissant, binoculars, a notepad, and two other items of his trade—a concealable Glock and an impossible to hide AK47 equipped with a rifle scope and a silencer.

* * *

Reilly opened his curtains to greet the day, a gloomy grey Brussels morning with a light drizzle.

Three floors below, a morning passersby carried umbrellas. Bicycles, mopeds, and motorcycles wove around cars, taxis, and trucks. Across the street, the day was beginning as well for residents of the apartments above the first level businesses.

A rainy Tuesday. Just the kind of day Reilly could use to catch up.

* * *

Frederik rolled the potted tree on a hand trolley. He could have asked for help, but this was a job he'd do on his own. Getting it through the door between the Kensington Royal lobby and Bistango presented a real problem, however. The tree stood too high to easily pass through the entrance. He had to tilt the dolly down to a 70 degree angle, which caused some of the dirt to spill.

"Looks like you need some help," came a voice.

Damn. One of the hired security. "I'll be fine," Frederik replied.

Frederik wouldn't have been concerned if it had been one of the regular hotel staff, but the mercenary was far more savvy—and observant.

"Sure?" Klugo's man asked.

Frederik glanced back. He'd dumped even more dirt on the marble floors since being interrupted. That's when he noticed a loose wire sticking out of the dirt around the base of the tree. He quickly side-stepped and positioned his body to block the guard's view.

"Truly, I'm fine. And I'll sweep up after," he replied calmly, adding a friendly thank-you.

The security officer left. Frederik waited a moment, then nonchalantly knelt to work on the wire. Once finished to his satisfaction, he pushed the pot through the doorway and rolled it toward the back of Bistango's main room.

* * *

By mid-morning Reilly was hungry, but before leaving the hotel, he did what was now part of his normal routine. He scanned the surroundings. Through the front door he saw the single bomb-sniffing dog and handler. Two more teams had been ordered, but it would take another day before they would be on guard. Inside, everything appeared normal. People checking out, families getting ready to tour the city. Nothing suspicious.

Reilly walked past the florist shop. It was open, but empty. He peered inside. The cooler door was ajar and some potting soil was on the floor.

Messy, he thought. *Surely Madame Ketz wouldn't stand for this.*

Reilly closed the cooler door himself. *Worth mentioning to Schorel?* He went to the front desk.

"Sorry, Mr. Reilly," explained the young receptionist. "Mr. Schorel is in a regular morning staff meeting. May I help you?"

"No. I'll catch up with him later."

* * *

"What are you doing?" Claire d'Isle demanded of the florist. He was placing the tree precisely where the statuary had stood and was now repacking the dirt in the pot.

"I'm sorry. I had a note to bring this in." This response immediately gave him power over the restaurant's general manager.

"No one told me," she said. "From who?"

"The hotel. The overnight crew broke one of your tall statues. This will cover the area temporarily. Madame Ketz always had a tree on hand in case."

The general manager frowned.

Frederik anticipated her concern. "This was all worked out with the owner."

"I've never heard of such an arrangement."

"Oh yes. Madame Ketz was quite specific. A long-standing practice."

Claire d'Isle considered phoning the owner, who was vacationing in Cannes. Then thought, *Why bother.*

"Just clean up properly. This room must be spotless." She looked at the tree, which clearly didn't belong. "And turn the damn thing around so the fuller branches face out. Don't you know anything?"

Frederik smiled. Actually he had a learned a little about the florist trade.

"Of course, Mademoiselle. To your liking."

After she turned on her heel and walked away Frederik repositioned the pot and rechecked the wire, which was now tightly woven around the base of the tree.

* * *

From his perch opposite the hotel, the observer focused on Reilly leaving. He didn't appear to be in any rush. The man panned his binoculars back to the hotel entrance. A few minutes later he saw the florist leave. He followed him as he crossed the street and settled under an umbrella at an outside bistro table.

* * *

Reilly walked to Au Pays des Merveilles, or ADPM to the locals. The restaurant was known for the best bagels in Belgium. He took a window seat and ordered the house combination: cheddar, scrambled eggs, watercress, and grilled onions on a multigrain bagel. He had selected ADPM on Avenue Jean Volders because it was close to the next stop he needed to make, a cigar shop on Rue du Fort. That was the address Alan Cannon had texted based on the request he made in DC. With the proper introduction, which he had, he could pick up a Kel-Tec P-3AT pistol.

There was only one problem when he got there. The store, a front for illegal gun sales, was closed for another two hours.

Damn, he thought. *Another day.*

* * *

Reilly bought a small umbrella from a street vender for the walk back. He picked up his pace, eager to talk with Schorel and avoid the rain. He arrived just as the hotel was feeling the checkout crunch and as the lunch crowd was beginning to file into Bistango.

Reilly worked his way to the front desk, maneuvering around groups and their luggage. He glanced one more time at the florist shop. It was closed. A note hung on the door. He went to read it. "Picking up supplies. Back after lunch."

Innocuous, he thought.

* * *

The man who had been going by the name Frederik definitely wasn't on a supply run. His supplies and equipment were already in place. Now he occupied a bistro table diagonally across the street. He casually sipped a latte while holding his cell phone.

* * *

In the lobby, sitting on a high-backed chair facing in was a gentleman traveling on a British passport. He appeared to be reading the *London Guardian*. Except he wasn't. Nor was he British. He was a Russian. An FSB agent. A close friend of his president. And Andre Miklos was happy it was raining. It meant there'd be more people in the hotel.

83

BRUSSELS, BELGIUM

BISTANGO RESTAURANT

KENSINGTON ROYAL

"Welcome to Bistango," Claire d'Isle enthusiastically said, greeting a party of eight. "It's a pleasure to have you joining us today, Herr Müller."

The Bistango general manager oversaw the reservation, made by Horst Müller's Zurich Deutsche Bank office. The request was specific, from lunch in the private dining room to the necessary allowances for the security detail that accompanied the banker's important client.

Müller looked past d'Isle to examine the restaurant layout. "Thank you. Everything is as planned?"

"Yes, to your specifications."

Müller was direct, officious, and humorless. His manner matched his attire. Grey hair, grey glasses, grey suit, grey shirt, grey belt, and black shoes. He appeared to be 55 or 60. Claire d'Isle checked for a wedding ring. Not surprisingly, he had none.

"Good. Show me to the room. My party will be here shortly." He checked his watch. It was 11:55 a.m. "In five minutes."

"Very good. You'll have a dedicated team. Our maître d' will supervise your service and clear the room when you need privacy."

"Good. Service shall begin precisely eight minutes after we are seated."

"Of course, and I assure you everything will be impeccable."

KENSINGTON ROYAL HOTEL LOBBY

"Is he in?" Reilly asked the general manager's assistant.

"Yes, I'll—"

Before she finished, Reilly was at Schorel's door.

"Liam, how are things going?"

"Fine, fine." Schorel was eager to see Reilly leave for good, but he couldn't say so. Instead he politely stood. "Coffee?"

"No thanks."

The general manager decided to test the waters. "So? How are we looking?"

"I don't really know."

There was an awkward silence.

Reilly made it easy for him to understand. "Which I don't like."

"Oh?"

"Liam, let's go over procedures again."

The general manager flipped a page on the yellow pad on his desk and uncapped his sleek Montblanc fountain pen. Reilly explained his newest, still unresolved concerns: reservations at Bistango.

OUTSIDE THE KENSINGTON ROYAL

Frederik checked his watch. He had a perfect view of Bistango and could see people coming and going from both the restaurant entrance and the Kensington Royal front door.

He was already on a refill and had left cash for his waiter so he could just slip away when signaled. The only thing that worried him was the weather. The off-and-on rain. It might delay things, and quite frankly he hated sitting outside.

THE HOTEL LOBBY

Miklos also looked at his watch. In ten minutes he would walk from the hotel lobby, through Bistango, and, if the time was right, he'd nod to his man sitting across the street.

SCHOREL'S OFFICE

"What can you do to coordinate with Bistango?"

"Not a lot. They're a separate entity. We rent to them."

"Not good enough," Reilly said, all the while thinking of the lesson of the Battle of Leesburg. "They rent from you. You're in charge."

"I'll have to check the contract and see what's possible."

Reilly felt that was a dodge. *What was possible* was not acceptable. He pushed the point and made it a requirement. Then he went on to other security issues. "I noticed we're not always checking for room keys as people enter elevators."

"Well, sometimes when staff go on a break—"

"It only takes one, Liam."

BISTANGO RESTAURANT

A sleek black BMW stretch limo pulled up to the restaurant. A second vehicle, a town car, parked directly behind it. Before anyone got out of the limousine, three large bodyguards piled out of the town car. The first, a walking refrigerator of a man, went into the restaurant. The two other guards stood at attention beside the limo and surveyed the street. After a minute, the first man emerged from Bistango. He approached the limo. The back window rolled down only long enough for a short conversation. Then the same man spoke to his two associates. They took up strategic positions: one at the door, another midway along the sidewalk. Only then did the lead guard open the door.

Out stepped a man immaculately dressed in a navy blue three-piece suit manufactured by the same London tailor who used to make his brother's suits. Unlike his dead brother, Sandis Gaiss wore a Kevlar vest under his shirt.

THE LOBBY

Miklos' phone vibrated with an incoming text. He casually lowered the newspaper to his lap and checked the phone. A one-word message from Frederik displayed in French: *Arrivée*.

PSKOV OBLAST, RUSSIA

Three thousand combat-ready paratroopers from the Russian 76th Air Assault Division were amassed at Ostrov, a Russian Navy base, home to the 444th Center for Combat Employment. They were supported by another seven thousand ground troops from Russia's 6th and 20th Guard Armies along with their tanks and missile brigades, and the 1st Air Defense Forces Command from Severomorsk. They flew MiG-29 and Su-25/Su-25SM fighters, and Tu-22M3/MR bombers, which were all battle-ready.

Moscow wanted Riga to be secured within thirty-six hours. General Pavel Makarov, Commander of the Western District, awaited the order.

BRUSSELS

SCHOREL'S OFFICE

"Okay. I'm certain we can fine-tune Bistango," Schorel told Reilly. "I'll meet with the management over the next—"

"Immediately," Reilly affirmed. "Too vulnerable."

"Okay."

At best, it was a dismissive *okay*.

"Look Liam, I'm sorry, but as long as a credible threat exists, and trust me, it still exists, this hotel will stand at Red. That includes all the businesses associated with it."

"I understand."

"Good," Reilly said. He stood, walked to the door, but stopped before leaving.

"Oh, one more thing," he said. "Actually a question."

"Yes?"

"Madame Ketz's shop?"

Schorel shook his head. "What about it?"

"It's closed. Seemed unusual."

"Lunchtime I suppose."

"And earlier?" Reilly asked. "It was open, but empty."

"Probably on a delivery."

"Really?"

Schorel hesitated. "Maybe Frederik hasn't been the best of hires."

"Especially with Madame Ketz away visiting her daughter."

The general manager shot him a confused look. "Her daughter?"

"Yes. She took a holiday to visit her in Bruges."

"Who told you this?" Schorel asked.

Reilly read real concern on his face.

"Frederik," he replied. "The other day. You hadn't heard?"

"Daniel," Liam Schorel said very slowly. "Madame Ketz's daughter was hit by a car in Paris. She's been dead for six years."

84

Miklos closed and folded his newspaper. Slowly. Nonchalantly. Just as anyone ready to move on would. He stood, straightened his jacket, and took in a full breath. Again, slowly. Nothing he did for the next few minutes could seem out of the ordinary or draw attention.

He tucked the day's London *Guardian* under his arm, dropped his head to avoid direct contact with the hotel's CCTV cameras, and walked through the lobby, but not to the front door. He strolled toward Bistango.

One last look.

The assassin entered the restaurant. He stopped at the hotel-side reception desk. The maître d' was busy leading a young couple to a table. *Good,* he thought. *No explanations.* Miklos studied the surroundings and the patrons: romantic couples holding hands, executives conducting business, families with their children. All fifteen mid-house tables filled. Likewise the ten along the street-side window and the private dining room in the rear of the restaurant where a meeting was taking place. Not just a meeting. *The* meeting.

He brushed past the two remaining statues and a single large potted tree that provided a barrier between the public and private dining areas. Three beefy men stood guard outside that room.

Time, he thought. *Time to leave. Time for people to die.*

* * *

Reilly ran out of Schorel's office. The general manager followed.

"What's going on?" Schorel asked as he caught up with Reilly in front of Madame Ketz's shop.

"Call security!"

"Why?" Schorel insisted.

"To evacuate!"

Reilly looked at guests in the lobby. He read their faces, their manner, and mannerisms. He saw nothing that signified trouble. Smiles, light midday conversations. People staying out of the rain.

He peered inside the flower shop again. He spotted a trail of dirt on the floor leading to the door. It didn't mean anything to him until he saw a patch of dirt a few steps away that a housekeeper was sweeping up. Reilly ran to the woman.

"Where did that come from?" he demanded.

The woman didn't understand English. Confused, she turned to Schorel.

"Ask her! Now!"

Schorel translated. She pointed to Bistango and explained in Flemish.

"Dirt from the restaurant. Some workers must have—"

"No," Reilly shouted. "Not from there. From here!" He pointed to the florist shop. "To there!" Reilly ran into the restaurant.

"M. Reilly," the maître d' said. "Are you looking for a table, I may be able to—"

"No," he said abruptly. Reilly continued a few steps further.

What the hell am I looking for?

He filtered out the questions from Schorel, the restaurant host, the cacophony of lunchtime chatter. Reilly concentrated. He divided the restaurant into quadrants. Near, front, back, sides. The windows. The kitchen. The private dining room. The art pieces. The entrance off the street.

At that moment Reilly saw a man about to leave. He had no

umbrella, no raincoat. As he pushed the door open, he looked over his shoulder and smiled at no one in particular. It was a sly smile.

Reilly's heart raced faster. Instinct and experience alerted him.

"Mr. Reilly, will you be joining us?" the maître d' asked again.

The question broke Reilly's concentration. He turned.

"What? No."

Reilly shifted his gaze back to the man at the door. The man with the smile. *Not sly. Satisfied. Satisfied and cruel.* He seemed . . . Reilly searched for the word. It came to him. *Smug!*

They were twenty feet apart.

A waiter came between them. Reilly sidestepped to get a better view, but the man was gone.

Damn!

He maneuvered around another server. This put him in direct eye contact with the bodyguards posted outside the private dining room— and one thing out of place. The potted tree in line with the expensive statues.

The dirt.

The maître d' was on him again. "Mr. Reilly, may I?"

"What happened to the other statue?"

"One of the maintenance crew broke it early this morning. The florist brought in the—"

Reilly didn't wait for the end of the sentence. He ran toward the tree. This drew eyes in the restaurant, the guards automatically stiffening. A hush spread through Bistango.

The three guards stepped forward. Reilly continued to the tree. He knelt down, touched the ceramic pot. It was cold. Very cold. So was the dirt. Then he spotted a wire wrapped around the tree trunk up to about six inches above the potting soil.

Facts, figures, and intelligence flooded his consciousness. *Madame Ketz. Her regular assistant left. The replacement who lied about where she was. The tree that had been in the cooler. Cold temperatures that can throw off bomb-sniffing dogs.* All of this in a second. *And the man at the door. The man with the smile.* Reilly looked over his shoulder. He knew who he was.

"Everybody!" Reilly declared. "Listen to me!"

One of the guards grabbed Reilly's arm. Reilly brushed him away. A second guard came forward.

"We have an emergency. You must leave. Now!"

But which way? he thought.

"Through the hotel. Turn right at the exit. Right, not left!"

"Translate!" Reilly shouted to the host.

The maître d' repeated the order in French, but by now people were getting the idea. Everyone but the guards.

"What the fuck?" the lead guard asked in guttural English.

"Do it! Get your people out! Now! Through the lobby." Then he added, "Walk!"

"Why?"

Reilly pointed to the wire sticking out from the bottom of the tree trunk.

"Shit!" The guard exclaimed in Russian. He signaled to his associates and they all but picked Gaiss up and hustled him out. They left the bankers to fend for themselves.

* * *

Miklos crossed the street and established brief eye contact with Frederik, still sitting under an umbrella at the bistro. One nod. Frederik returned the signal and rose. At the corner, without a word, Frederik slipped Miklos an iPhone. The phone had only one number preloaded. Miklos slipped it in his pocket.

* * *

Reilly rushed into the kitchen to warn the staff. Getting people out through the hotel was a risk, but anyone with the remote detonator would be quicker on the finger if he saw a panicked rush from Bistango. There also might be another device planted at the restaurant exterior, so to Reilly's mind, the hotel exit offered the safest route—if they went calmly.

"Walk. *Marche. Ne pas courir.* Don't run!"

Reilly decided to leave through Bistango, but not as calmly.

* * *

The man posted at the window on the other side of the street saw Reilly exit, then, oblivious to the rain, look up and down the avenue. He dropped his binoculars and ran down three flights of stairs in under twenty seconds.

* * *

Miklos angled away from Frederik and proceeded along the sidewalk up Avenue Louise. Frederik passed him at double the speed and took up a position fifty yards ahead. Miklos slowed. Another few steps and he'd have enough distance between himself and the restaurant. A safe distance. Neither man saw Reilly leave Bistango.

* * *

The rain fell harder. Reilly looked to his right. People were filing out of the hotel. Liam Schorel and the paid security detail directing them away from the restaurant. The bollards had been extended. He heard shouts, though muffled by the traffic and rain. Orders to evacuate. Fast.

Reilly tried to guess how much time had passed. *A little over a minute since he entered the restaurant?* Now another question. *How much time did he have?* He figured less than a minute.

To his left, people were unaware of what was going on. But two members of the security detail immediately in front of the hotel were hustling cars away. Other officers began holding traffic, setting up a perimeter, and getting drivers and passengers out of their cars.

Reilly had automatically gone away from the hotel. Instinct told him that was the direction his quarry went. The best place to observe the explosion. *Something Smug liked to do.*

* * *

Miklos ignored the rain. He was solely focused on his mission. The assassin had a clear view of the corner from where he stood, but the obtuse angle prevented him from seeing the hotel's main entrance and the mass exodus. He also failed to notice that traffic was backing up. Not that any of this would have stopped him at this point.

He removed the iPhone from his sports jacket pocket. *Time.*

The assassin began to dial the number of the Samsung phone which was buried in the pot: the cell phone with the thin wire antenna extending out from the chassis and wrapped around the tree. The receiving cell's mechanism contained a motor with an asymmetrical wheel. The wheel would vibrate with the incoming call. The shaking would trigger a relay wired to twenty-five pounds of gelatinous dynamite buried five inches down.

The charge was appropriate for the job. It would kill everyone within an eighteen-meter radius. Sixty feet. More as fire spread. There was the Russian delegation staying in the hotel, many of them eating lunch now. There were business executives and tourists, and most importantly, the pro-Russian oilman, whose death, on the heels of his brother's, would become a dramatic flashpoint, an emotional trigger that would give Russia its reason to invade Latvia.

Miklos slowly punched in the memorized ten-digit phone number. He preferred the drama of entering one number at a time rather than just hitting the speed-dial button that Frederik had preprogrammed.

* * *

Reilly ran across the street and up the sidewalk. He knew who he was looking for. He completely pictured him now. With a moustache, without a moustache. Short hair or long. Blond, black, or grey. Beard or clean-shaven. Younger or older.

Through all the identities there was that cruel smile.

Yes, he knew who he was looking for. He just hadn't thought through what he'd do if he found him. And he didn't have the gun he had wanted.

Then . . . there! No more than thirty feet ahead of him.

"Miklos!"

* * *

The shout startled the Russian. He automatically turned to the voice.

Miklos focused on the direction. He focused on the source.

"Reilly," he barely whispered.

Miklos' finger moved over the touch screen. He looked down and touched the last number.

Reilly raced toward Miklos at full speed. He saw what Miklos had in his hand and how he looked up when he finished dialing and smiled that same smile. But he didn't move.

Without warning, another man half the distance to Miklos stepped into his path and raised a pistol. He hardly needed to aim. Reilly was that close.

Reilly's conflicting thoughts were: *The gun. The bomb.*

A shot rang out.

85

The explosion would have drowned out the gunshot, except there was no explosion. Miklos looked at the cell phone. The number was still ringing. The wrong number. He'd lost his place and misdialed when Reilly shouted.

Reilly stood waiting for the pain, the bleeding, the weakness in his legs, the end. None of it came. Instead Frederik dropped to the ground with a last look of shock that rivaled Reilly's awareness that he was alive.

"Go!" demanded a deep, measured voice from behind. A voice that caught up with him and said, "Take this!" The voice belonged to the man who had killed Miklos' partner. The voice that gave Reilly his Sig Sauer P238 pistol with six rounds left.

"Lenczycki!"

"Damned straight," said the yacht owner from the Caribbean, the ex-CIA agent, the observer who believed that Reilly had been right. He removed another Sig from a holster belted to his side and commanded, "Go!"

They ignored the dead man on the sidewalk and the screams on the street. Lenczycki yelled for people to clear out of the way. The order from a man brandishing a gun didn't go unheeded.

Miklos began redialing. He had four more numbers to punch in, and while cell phone range wasn't a problem, survival was. So he ran.

The stalled traffic gave him a maze to traverse, and protection.

Cars parked along the Avenue Louise sidewalk also helped. Reilly and Lenczycki separated. Reilly's trajectory took him across the street in hopes of overrunning Miklos, turning, and cutting him off. Lenczycki followed Miklos' exact route.

As Miklos darted around the stalled traffic, a car door suddenly opened and slammed him hard in the chest. He dropped the phone. Miklos swore and shut the door on the driver so hard it broke the man's arm. He reached down, picked up the cell, but it was dead. He swore again.

Seconds. He had lost precious seconds and a working phone.

Miklos glanced back. One of his stalkers was closing in. The other wasn't in sight. That could mean he was trying to cut him off. Miklos sprinted right, back to the previous direction to buy more time. He reached for the Makarov pistol tucked in his jacket, stopped, turned, aimed, and fired.

The only thing that saved Lenczycki's life was the sudden pivot he made around a Passat. He lost his balance and fell to the left. Miklos' bullet missed him, but pierced a man's shoulder in a car behind him.

With no time to take a second shot, Miklos sped ahead, adding another twenty meters—about half a block.

But there were two chasing. As Miklos suspected, the second charted a sharp angle toward him from the opposite side.

Reilly!

Miklos didn't just run. He skillfully maneuvered with a sense of familiarity. He knew the avenue and had the stamina to outpace his immediate pursuer.

Lenczycki, back on his feet, rejoined the chase, yelling at pedestrians to move and banging car hoods to stop them from inching forward.

Reilly kept Miklos in sight. He began to think that Miklos' flight had purpose. Despite the twists and turns he took, Miklos seemed as if he kept returning to the same route, hugging the north side of the street.

The foot chase took them by the prestigious shops along Avenue Louise—all busy with people gazing in store windows and international shoppers going in and coming out with name-brand bags.

The avenue was crowded with bicyclists daring to weave around the bottleneck. The traffic, the horns, and the complaining made it easier for Miklos and harder for Lenczycki and Reilly.

They ran past Chanel, Hermes, Louis Vuitton, Versace, and Christian Dior. Then back into the street, crossing the trolley tracks, and scooting around cars.

Miklos caught Reilly in his peripheral vision running parallel to him between the light-rail tracks and stopped vehicles. The Russian faked a turn into a Bose Store, knocking down a businessman. Then he sprinted further up Avenue Louise to Apostrophe and around a group of young women. More lead time. He used the passersby as cover and hit a woman hard going into the fashionable designer shop, Liu Jo.

Lenczycki kept his quarry in sight, but he couldn't catch up. He also couldn't risk taking another shot. Not with so many people. Not with the potential of getting shot himself by Federale Politie, which so far had not shown up despite Brussel's constant state of alert.

He began to slow, searching for Reilly. But by taking his eyes off his quarry, he lost him.

Reilly didn't. He saw Miklos run toward Serneels Jeux & Jouets, a world famous toy and games store.

Miklos used a couple exiting to his advantage. He knocked them down. People gathered to help them. Another obstacle.

Serneels? Reilly thought. *Hostages?* He quickly dismissed the notion. *Escape.*

Reilly helped the man and woman to their feet. A winded Lenczycki caught up.

"He's inside. Go through. All the way to the back!"

"Okay. You?"

Reilly pointed as he began to run further down the avenue.

Lenczycki pushed the glass door open and was assaulted by a surreal contrast. Somewhere inside the most opulent toy store he'd ever seen was a killer. But to get to him, he had to navigate through plush toys, porcelain and plastic dolls, a ceiling-high giraffe, classic replicas of cast-iron soldiers right out of his childhood, and high-tech playthings for today. In the room ahead were steam engines, remote control cars, handcrafted music boxes, and traditional parlor games. Row after row. Room after room. A child's dream come true and a murderer he'd dreamt of capturing or killing for decades.

But where?

He kept his pistol tucked into his holster. His fingers on the grip.

Through. All the way to the back, Reilly had told him.

He cut in and around kids, new fathers, pregnant mothers, and salespeople. Children sat on the floor conjuring up fantastic adventures while others balanced on huge stuffed animals.

And suddenly, he saw a door close ahead and to his left.

Lenczycki nearly tripped twice over kids. Miklos had a good twenty seconds on him. It expanded to thirty because the former CIA agent had to wait for a family with a stroller to enter just as he was trying to exit.

Once out, he got his bearings. He was in a luxurious, open hallway leading into a hotel. But not just any hotel. A magnificent, historical hotel. Posh, opulent, magnificent. Marble and inlaid parquet floors. Dark wood walls that framed shops filled with things he could never afford. Bronze statues and period paintings and further ahead, curved stairs to an expansive lobby adorned with more statues, fresh flowers, classic artwork, and crystal chandeliers.

Had Lenczycki entered from the expansive courtyard off Avenue Louise, he would have seen the marquee for Steigenberger Wiltcher's, arguably the most beautiful hotel in Brussels. Its nineteenth-century façade shouted high-class comfort. But the retired operative was only focused on finding his prey again.

* * *

Miklos slowed to appear as if he belonged. The last thing he wanted was to alert hotel security. He walked through the lobby, avoided looking into CCTV cameras, picked up a newspaper to cover his face, and followed another hallway.

* * *

A half minute later, Lenczycki stood under the center chandelier searching for Miklos. He spotted his target ahead. The Russian bumped into a group of businessmen, disappeared in the mass, then reemerged.

Lenczycki picked up the pursuit across the lobby, down a hall, and into a stairwell. The door was still closing when he reached it. Footsteps echoed from below.

Lenczycki had his pistol ready. He raced down the stairs, taking each corner sideways to offer the narrowest profile if Miklos shot at him.

The sound of another door opening.

The former CIA agent felt he was catching up.

He cautiously opened the door, his gun at the ready. It was clear left and right.

Ahead more running. The sound of shoes landing harder on the lower level cement floors.

Lenczycki, tucked his gun under his jacket as he passed house-keeping staff, an electrician, and the kitchen. Employees made way. The hall dead-ended. Two ways to go, and now no sound coming from either way.

Lenczycki stopped. He couldn't believe he had gotten this close only to lose Miklos. And then a crash from behind. Dishes in the kitchen and swearing in French.

Lenczycki pivoted and ran back to the kitchen. The rubble on the floor, the screaming chef, and the hands pointing to a door told him what had happened and which way to go. He skirted the broken pieces, between stove tops and food prep tables. He pushed aside see-through plastic strip curtains and emerged in another basement hall that opened up to a loading dock. Beyond that, a driveway.

* * *

Reilly hugged the sidewalk adjacent to the traffic circle at Avenue Louise and Chaussée de Charleroi. He made a tight left around a travel office and raced at full speed along a line of high-end stores and a garage, barely avoiding a car exiting.

"*Clair! Clair!* Out of the way," he shouted.

Now in sight, two escape routes that he fully expected to be there: the Chaussée de Charleroi passageway to Steigenberger Wiltcher's. Ahead, forty feet down the street, the back service entrance to the hotel.

If Lenczycki didn't get Miklos inside, Reilly counted on him coming out one of these two ways. Or at least he hoped so. He took the middle ground, caught his breath, and faced the buildings.

* * *

Lenczycki jumped off the loading dock. The Russian was just twenty feet ahead. "Stop!" he shouted.

Miklos ignored the warning. Lenczycki raised his gun, but he had a low percentage shot and faced a big chance of hitting a car or pedestrian. He yelled, "Stop!" again.

Reilly turned to the sound of the voice, which he recognized. It came from the service entrance to his right.

* * *

A young couple, oblivious to what was going on, sauntered along the other side of the street. The woman was on the arm of her lover and talking on her cell.

The Russian needed a diversion. He'd create one. And he needed a phone.

Using a passing trolley for cover, he charged across the street.

Lenczycki emerged from the driveway. The Russian ran up to the couple, wacked the man with the butt of his gun, and grabbed the woman. She shrieked.

"No!" Lenczycki shouted. He'd seen this before. In Potsdam, all those years ago. A woman and a man dead because of Andre Miklos. Dead because he hadn't prevented it.

Lenczycki planted his feet and aimed. He still didn't have a good shot, but he needed to try.

Where the hell's Reilly? he wondered as he squeezed the trigger.

His shot went slightly wide, through a bank window.

Suddenly, another shot rang out. This one found its mark. Reilly's aim was true.

For a moment, the Russian wobbled, then staggered with the woman still in his grip. He dropped his gun and held out his hand for her phone. The woman, in shock, gave it to him.

"*Merci,*" he said uncharacteristically.

Reilly sped up as Miklos slowed. But the assassin concentrated on his mission. He ended the call she was on and desperately entered the numbers he'd memorized. With one digit left, he looked down. A pool of blood was forming at his feet.

Miklos took in a deep breath.

"No!" Reilly cried out. *Time to end this.*

Reilly couldn't have missed at this distance, even without his recent training at the range. He fired just as the killer touched the last number in the sequence. A nine.

The FSB agent rotated 180-degrees from the force of the shot and pitched forward. His skull cracked on the pavement. An ATM outfacing camera recorded his last expression. It wasn't a smile.

86

ONE HOUR LATER

Brussels Politie took control of the crime scene. A search of Andre Miklos' pocket produced a Latvian passport under the name Mihails Kajinsh and a phone number that linked him to a fiercely anti-Russian, pro-Riga nationalist group. The other man, Frederik LaPorta, had the same number in his wallet. Both were false identities.

The first officers to arrive held Reilly and Lenczycki and confiscated their weapons. But a call from Washington to NATO Command, which passed over to the chief of Politie, and on to the commander of the 1st Division, got them released. Washington also put a gag on talking about the identities of those killed.

Reilly and Lenczycki walked the half mile back to the hotel. All traffic had been diverted off the major avenues to make room for SWAT teams, city and NATO bomb squads, and oncoming fire trucks, ambulances, and other emergency vehicles. Two blocks short of the hotel they were stopped by four enlisted men from the Belgian Armed Forces brandishing FN FNC M3 standard issue assault rifles. Yellow police tape cordoned off the sidewalk and street.

"Entrée interdite! Vous ne pouvez pas aller plus loin," ordered the Belgian Armed Forces soldier closest to them.

Reilly got the gist. He produced his hotel ID. It took a conversation with a lieutenant, then a captain, before they were allowed through.

Past the military barrier, Reilly and Lenczycki broke into a run. Reilly feared the worst as more emergency vehicles, sirens blaring, passed them.

They darted around abandoned cars and people who had evacuated the area. Three more blocks and they rounded a corner and finally saw the Kensington Diplomat Hotel. It was completely cordoned off, but it stood tall.

* * *

Liam Schorel intercepted Reilly.

"The bomb? How—?" Reilly was baffled.

Schorel gestured with his thumb, pointing over his shoulder. A man emerged from the crowd.

"Hello there, Dan! Whatcha been up to?"

Reilly shook his head. Alan Cannon. "You didn't . . . ?"

"Hey, it's not like I disarmed the damn thing. I'm not that crazy. But it's amazing what a whole roll of aluminum foil from the kitchen wrapped around a potted tree can do to block cell signals. A Faraday cage. My son Jake taught it to me! The pros took over from there."

* * *

The next morning CNN International carried two stories. The anchor reported that overnight, NATO mobilized an unprecedented 12,500 troops into the Baltic nations, Estonia, Lithuania, and Latvia, with the largest contingent already on Latvian soil. A release from NATO command explained that the rapid deployment exercise was a routine test of NATO's capabilities and was not intended as a provocation.

There was no news report about another intervening event. President Alexander Crowe's phone call to Nikolai Gorshkov. It was short and definitely not sweet. A warning: "Do not test America and NATO resolve over the Balkans. Do not test me."

It was the latest hand in a dangerous game of political poker. Crowe realized the win might only be temporary. War didn't break out, but the war of words was not over.

The Kremlin issued a statement of its own. The text rolled across the screen.

The Western Military District of the Russian Federation condemns NATO's military exercise and its operation within five kilometers of the Russian border. The maneuvers threaten the peace of the region.

Another paragraph followed with surprisingly uncharacteristic contrition.

However, in the interest of good will and to avoid any misinterpretation, troops from the 76th Air Assault Division and the 6th and 20th Guard Armies, currently conducting their own exercises near the NATO operation, though fully within the legal border of the Russian Federation, will be airlifted back to their home bases in the Russian Federation.

Moving to a roundtable discussion, the CNN anchor speculated that NATO's exercise was designed to dissuade Gorshkov from pursuing any action against Latvia. He also advanced unconfirmed reports that the Latvian president was about to issue executive actions to ease the barriers to citizenship for ethnic Russians. Seen together, the anchor posited that Russia's withdrawal was a measure of its desire to create peace in the area.

Meanwhile, further up the channel choices, the Fox News anchor concluded his telecast with a commentary.

"To Russia, its Kremlin ministers and President Nikolai Gorshkov, tonight this commentator offers you congratulations. You have responsibly chosen to de-escalate a potentially volatile situation. For that, all fair-minded Americans will take you at your word. You saw risks ahead and you stopped short of a line that history has so often called the Rubicon. Rather than crossing it, you pulled back. Bravo.

"Without a doubt, there comes a point in any conflict, potential or developing, where serious rational thinking becomes a powerful tool in the hands of enlightened leaders. Your awareness of this essential geopolitical fact is abundantly evident. Though you termed it merely an 'exercise,' we commend you for recalling your air assault divisions and ground armies from your Baltic borders. So without further questioning your motives or expounding on eminently consequential historical foot-notes, we simply say, with a spirit of good will, 'Mr. President, damn smart move.'

"Now a warning to our own president. A show of force is good. But let's not force a show."

WASHINGTON, DC

CAPITOL HILL

KENNEDY CAUCUS ROOM

SIX WEEKS LATER

"Mr. Reilly, we've called you back in consideration of the thwarted attack on your corporation's hotel in Brussels."

Senator Moakley Davidson peered at Reilly over his reading glasses. Then he paused to take in the packed hearing room. The mood was definitely different than during the previous sessions. So were the members in attendance.

Flanking Reilly to his left were Alan Cannon and Chris Collins, and Lou Tiano was to his right. Behind Reilly, just over his left shoulder and visible to the C-SPAN camera covering him was an even more formidable member of the Kensington Royal team—Edward Jefferson Shaw.

Beside Shaw were the CEOs and presidents of three other major American hotel corporations. Collectively, they represented more than 225 billion dollars, which, through their own profits and the salaries of their employees, annually contributed to a significant portion of the US tax coffers. That point wasn't lost on most of the committee members. Neither was the political clout these titans of business could wield.

Yet, despite the turnout, Senator Davidson couldn't resist

grandstanding, especially with a larger television audience. Ever arrogant, ever the bully, he went where instinct directed.

"According to the report I've read, there was only one explosive device found at your hotel. One, Mr. Reilly, not two or three or four or five. One was found in a restaurant within the Kensington Diplomat Hotel."

"That's correct, Senator," Reilly replied.

"And it caused no damage. No one was harmed."

"Two terrorists were killed, sir."

"Yes, yes. I know that. But not part of any known group. And not in your building."

Reilly didn't respond.

"Oh, and this one bomb was found and defused by hotel security."

"To be accurate, it was discovered by a member of the hotel staff, but bravely defused by the Brussels bomb squad."

Davidson ignored Reilly's response. Waving a half-inch file, he continued.

"Other than the death of the two suspected terrorists and descriptions of the bomb, there's little detail in the intelligence briefing. This committee is not working with much."

"Quite to the point of my past testimony, Mr. Chairman. Information."

Davidson glowered at Reilly. "It does include the fact that you were on the scene."

"Yes, sir. I was."

"I would like to understand how you were there, Mr. Reilly."

"Mr. Senator, we had suspected the hotel was surveilled weeks prior. As a result, our team worked with the mayor, Brussels police, and NATO command. Again, for the record, I am vice president of International for Kensington Royal. I spend most of my time on the road and not behind a desk. It was my job to be there. We got lucky this time."

"And were you, at any time, acting outside of your duties? There is cell phone video. You were seen running in possible pursuit of a suspect. It could be construed that you were armed and chasing one of the men that was subsequently killed."

"I ran after one man until the police took over."

In so far as to what Reilly testified, he did not lie. No footage had publicly surfaced of him shooting Miklos. He certainly wouldn't volunteer his involvement now. CCTV footage had been withheld at the request of the Central Intelligence Agency and NATO. The Latvian passports, viewed as a cover, simply disappeared. As they often do, eyewitness reports presented conflicting versions of the event.

"Is that typical of your duties?"

"No it's not, Senator. May I ask what your point is?"

Davidson didn't really have a point to make other than to taunt Reilly and look good to his constituents.

"Mr. Reilly, it's my job to ask the questions. Yours to answer. But returning to the testimony from your last appearances, you seemed to do very well without the help you requested from this committee. Isn't that true?"

Low murmuring spread throughout the hearing room.

For Reilly, under oath, this was something he had to answer very carefully.

Was he fishing or did he know? Reilly wondered. *A leak somewhere?*

"As I said, we got lucky this time. We had the full cooperation of Belgium and NATO authorities and the city government. All foreign nationals. Allies of the United States. All who expect us to effectively and safely run our businesses."

The chairman realized he wasn't getting anywhere and his time was nearly up. He leaned into the microphone, but Reilly continued.

"Sir, you are quite correct, this is my third appearance before this committee," Reilly said, raising his voice for impact. He sensed the camera zooming in. "The third, Mr. Senator, to request this committee's support. Support that will provide open help from *our* intelligence services to fight terrorism."

Open was the operative word.

"Mr. Reilly—"

Reilly spoke right over the arrogant senator.

"There were Americans in the hotel and the restaurant, Mr. Davidson. Americans who could have been killed. The American public is watching this hearing, perhaps many on a computer booking a trip right now. We, the members of the industry represented here today . . ." The cameras panned the room. Each of the key CEOs and presidents were identified on screen. "We request that you fund the apparatus for America's intelligence services to work with us. Without it, you, sir, are very clearly telling Americans citizens that you don't care whether they're safe when they travel. Is that your intention, Senator Davidson? You don't care if they're safe abroad or safe here at home where the threat against our industry is equally real? Is that your intention, Senator Davidson? Because if it is, it is the most shameful lack of judgment I have ever seen."

The audience erupted in applause. Davidson tried to gavel down the gallery. He couldn't. Even members of Davidson's committee nodded approval. Republican and Democrat. The bully's objections were drowned out until the bully gaveled the hearing to a close and left with his papers.

LONDON

Marnie Babbitt switched off the TV in her London office. She contemplated calling Reilly to congratulate him on his appearance, but reconsidered.

He's still got doubts, she thought.

She'd made a mistake coming on too fast. Of course it appeared more than coincidental. She'd have to go slower. Take more care. Give him a little encouragement, but not push too hard.

A simple text would suffice. She typed, "You were magnificent," and hit send.

Reilly's phone beeped instantly. He read Marnie's message. It didn't require an answer, but he had one. "Restaurant or room service?"

Now the bigger question. Whether to send it?

WASHINGTON, DC

TWO WEEKS LATER

Little in terms of hard facts got out, but reporters pushed for critical answers. In the course of discussing Russia's pullback from the Baltic nations with National Security Advisor Pierce Kimball, the morning MSNBC anchor turned to the issue of NATO's future and with it a pointed question.

"Sir, right or wrong, NATO nations should fear dissolution? Or at the very least, fracturing?"

Kimball appeared via a satellite hookup from Washington. He gave his response in a measured tone and the fewest possible words.

"The United States remains firmly dedicated to our commitments. The president of the United States remains dedicated to our commitments."

"Yes, but isolationist voices in the US and in numerous countries in Europe are becoming louder, more brazen," said the network anchor. "Especially in those countries that see no upside to defending the Baltic nations should Russia attack, as was rumored this summer."

"Those voices are a small chorus and have no political standing."

"Neither did those who were in favor of Great Britain's withdrawal from the EU until they did it," the host countered.

"We're working with our allies to strengthen NATO," said Kimball. "That is what Europe requires. That is our avowed mission in Europe. It doesn't take high-level intelligence to figure that out. Look at the recent exercises near the Russian border. We, and our NATO allies, have added troops and equipment. The Russians have pulled back."

"But Russia's nationalistic goal is to have those former Eastern Bloc countries returned to their rule, or at least their dominion," the host added.

"And that will not happen on this president's watch."

"But there will be other presidents," the MSNBC anchor said, putting a button on the reply. "But while we're on the subject of intelligence—"

"I'm afraid I really can't comment if you go down that road," Kimball replied.

"Fair enough. No secrets. Just a comment. American corporations with holdings abroad, particularly in the hotel industry, have testified before the Senate Appropriations Subcommittee on State, Foreign Operations, and Related Programs. Chairman Moakley Davidson has insisted that corporate America shouldn't be given access to warnings."

The host called for video of the heated exchange between Reilly and Davidson.

The sound bite ended with Reilly asking, "Is that your intention, Senator Davidson? Because if it is, it is the most shameful lack of judgment I have ever seen."

"Sir," the anchor continued, "in the face of hotel bombings, Davidson's stand looks patently ridiculous, particularly when he walked out on the last hearing and hasn't called for a committee vote. So tell me, what is the White House's position in this debate?"

Kimball didn't hesitate. "The intelligence community now provides up-to-date briefings to American hotel corporations in the manner we advise the airline industry. We are looking at expanding that relationship through Homeland Security, the FBI, and other agencies."

"Without the Appropriations Subcommittee vote for approval?"

"We've studied the situation and determined there is no need for additional appropriations. Therefore the process is free of the subcommittee's purview."

"It's already begun?"

"Yes."

"When?"

"An hour after Senator Moakley Davidson walked out."

The news anchor showed uncharacteristic surprise. "And Davidson's reaction?"

"Senator Davidson has been informed," Kimball plainly stated.

"He must have been livid."

"You'll have to ask him," the White House national security advisor said, showing some delight.

* * *

True to Kimball's on-air revelation, Bob Heath had told Dan Reilly that the pipeline was officially open. His work in Brussels and his testimony on Capitol Hill had been the deciding factors.

In the two weeks since, reports began to flow openly. Reilly elevated a hotel in Morocco to Red status. He hired Donald Klugo to supervise the upgrades and bolster the security team.

As the MSNBC anchor thanked Pierce Kimball and teased the next segment, Reilly read a new intelligence report in his Chicago office. It was a chilling intercept from the NSA, via Syria. Immediate and frightening. He printed out the advisory and ran down the hall, first to inform his domestic counterpart, then to call an emergency crisis meeting. It was all too familiar to Reilly. He'd written a report for the State Department on the very subject. Some of it word for word.

ACKNOWLEDGMENTS

RED Hotel is a thriller about the global hotel industry in a challenging and dangerous world. Gary and I used many fictional characters and incidents which occurred in the forty years I worked with Marriott and the twenty-two years I was President and Managing Director of the International Lodging Marriott. During that time I founded and led the Marriott International crisis committee.

I am grateful to the individuals listed below who made our successes possible, who influenced, mentored, guided me, and played key roles in making this novel possible. Several of them might find themselves in this creative work.

Linda Bartlett, Yvonne Bean, Katie Bianchi, Harry Bosschaart, Stan Bruns, Nuala Cashman, Paul Cerula, Weili Cheng, Don Cleary, Mark Conklin, JoAnn Corday, Henry Davies, Victoria Dolan, Roger Dow, Brenda Durham, Ron Eastman, Joel Eisemann, June Farrell, Franz Ferschke, Jim Fisher, Fern Fitzgerald, Paul Foskey, Geoff Garside, Robert Gaymer-Jones, Jurgen Giesbert, Marc Gulliver, Tracy Halphide, Debbie Harrison, Pat Henderson, Jeff Holdaway, Andrew Houghton, Ed Hubennette, Gary Hurst, Beth Irons, Andrea Jones, Pam Jones, Simon Jongert, Nihad Kattan, Kevin Kearney, Chuck Kelley, Karl Kilburg, Kevin Kimball, Tuni Kyi, Buck Laird, Henry Lee, Mike Mackie, Kathleen Matthews, Alastair McPhail, Scott Melby, Raj Menon, Anton Najjar, JP Nel, Scott Neumayer, John Northen, Jim O'Hern, Alan Orlob, Manuel Oview, Jim Pilarski, Belinda Pote, Barbara Powell, Reiner Sachau, Mark Satterfield, Bill Shaw, Brenda Shelton, Craig Smith, Brad Snyder, Arne Sorenson, Alex Stadlin, Jim Stamas, Peter Steger, Pat Stocker, Susan Thronson, Chip Stuckmeyer, Myron Walker,

Bob Watts, Hank Weigle, Steve Weisz, Carl Wilson, and Glenn Wilson.

And finally, there are simply no words to describe my enduring thanks to J. W. Marriott.

Several people encouraged me to take a leap from my business book, *You Can't Lead with Your Feet on the Desk,* to writing a novel. These people include my coauthor, Gary Grossman, Bruce Feirstein, June Farrell, Pam Jones, Pam Policano, Andy Policano, and my wife, Michela Fuller. Thank you all very much.

ED FULLER

First and foremost, thanks to my wonderful collaborator, Ed Fuller. We've had an amazing time working together, with *RED Hotel* the first in a new international thriller series.

Special thanks to author, screenwriter, columnist Bruce Feirstein for introducing us. Additional thanks to our agent, Carol Mann, the Carol Mann Agency; our publicist, Meryl Moss and her team at Meryl Moss Media; my wife, Helene Seifer for her ongoing support and understanding; Sasha, Zach, and Jake Grossman, and friends and associates including my technical advisor, Army veteran Bruce Coons; Vin DiBona, Michael O'Rourke, Nat Segaloff, Sandi Goldfarb, Jeff Greenhawt, RJ Haynes, and Jeffrey Davis.

My additional heartfelt thanks to the members of the International Thriller Writers Association for so strongly supporting the genre and writers, with particular thanks to ThrillerFest Executive Director and author Kimberley Howe, and authors Steve Berry, Daniel Palmer, John Land, and my TV partner in our television series *Renegade Writer*, master storyteller, best-selling writer, and adventurer W.G. Griffiths.

Finally, thanks to my readers who have supported me through the years with my other thriller series and nonfiction books right through *RED Hotel.* What a great ride we're all having together!

GARY GROSSMAN

ABOUT THE AUTHORS

GARY GROSSMAN'S first novel, *Executive Actions*, propelled him into the world of high-intensity geopolitical thrillers. *Executive Treason*, *Executive Command* and *Executive Force* further tapped Grossman's experience as a journalist, newspaper columnist, documentary television producer, reporter, media historian, and playwright. In addition to the best-selling series, Grossman delivered again with *Old Earth*, a geological thriller that spans all of time. The novel has garnered international praise, taking top book honors at festivals in the US and Europe.

Grossman has written for the *New York Times*, *Boston Globe*, and *Boston Herald American*. He covered presidential campaigns for WBZ-TV in Boston, and has produced more than ten thousand television series, specials and documentaries for networks including NBC, CNN, ABC, CBS, FOX, PBS, USA, National Geographic, Food, HGTV, CNBC, Fox News, Discovery, and Discovery Military.

He is a multiple Emmy Award-winning producer. He served as chair of the Government Affairs Committee for the Caucus for Television, Producers, Writers and Directors, and is a member of the International Thriller Writers Association and Military Writers Society of America. He is a trustee at Emerson College and serves on the Boston University Metropolitan College Advisory Board. Grossman has taught at Emerson College, Boston University, USC, and currently teaches at Loyola Marymount University. He is a contributing editor to *Media Ethics Magazine*.

ED FULLER is a hospitality industry leader, educator, and bestselling author. He is president of Irvine, California-based Laguna Strategic Advisors, a global consortium that provides business consulting services to corporations and governments. Fuller is also director of the Federal Bureau of Investigation National Academy Associates Foundation(FBINAA).

Fuller's forty-year career in the industry was capped by his role as President and Managing Director of Marriott International for twenty-two years. As worldwide chief, he directed and administered corporate expansion with 555 hotels in 73 countries, the creation of 80,000 jobs, $8 billion in annual sales, and the implementation of multiple environmental, philanthropic, and educational initiatives. During that time he oversaw the creation of Marriott International's Global Security Strategy. His role put him in world hot spots at crucial times, from Tripoli to Cairo, Jakarta to Mumbai, with close contact with domestic and foreign intelligence operations.

Ed Fuller has served on numerous industry, educational, and charity boards. He is President and Chief Executive Officer of the Orange County (California) Visitor's Association and a Commissioner for Travel and Tourism for the State of California. He was Trustee of The Prince of Wales International Business Leaders Forum, a Boston University trustee, president of the Alumni Association, and Vice Chairman of Boston University's Board of Overseers. Fuller serves on the Advisory Board for California State University at Fullerton and has been an adjunct professor of Leadership at the University's College of Hospitality in Pomona and San Diego State University. Other board service includes Mind Research in Irvine, CA, Concord Hotels, Merage Investment Group, Safe Kids, and United Way International.

Ed Fuller served as a captain in the US Army and was awarded the Bronze Star and Army Commendation Medal for service during missions in Vietnam and Germany.

His colorful and real-world experiences are recounted in his Top-20 bestselling business book, *You Can't Lead with Your Feet on the Desk*, published globally in English, Chinese, and Japanese.

Ed Fuller continues to consult on security issues around the world.